THE HOUSEKEEPER

James R. Vance

First Printing

Author's Note:

Some events depicted in the novel are based loosely on accounts and stories uncovered during my research.

This book is a work of fiction, though some of the characters and locations are real, and existed as portrayed in the story.

The main characters are fictional, and any resemblance to persons, living or dead is purely coincidental.

ISBN: 978-1-84961-213-5
Published by RealTime Publishing
Limerick, Ireland

Liberté Egalité Fraternité

Living in France, discovering memorials to the martyrs of WWII and meeting survivors of that dark period in the country's recent history inspired me to write novels about life under Nazi dominance. I dedicate this novel to all who gave their lives fighting for the freedom denied by the often brutal and terrifying occupation.

James R. Vance

Also by James R. Vance

Animal Instinct
Crime Thriller: Trilogy #1
*Rape & murder mystery with unexpected outcomes
for the investigation team.*

Killer Butterfly
Crime Thriller: Trilogy #2
*A serial killer on the loose in Greater Manchester, England
with links to the 2006 Tsunami in Thailand.*

The Courier
Crime Thriller: Trilogy #3
*A bio-terrorism threat in London is traced
to Northern France with time running out.*

Eight
Mystery & Suspense
*A new recruit in SIS is assigned to France
to uncover the threat of suicide bombers in the UK.*

Les Ruines
Historical Fiction
*Two women holidaying in France discover shocking
evidence of resistance atrocities during WWII.*

Risk
Historical Fiction
*Recruited by the Special Operations Executive, a British soldier
returns to occupied France to organise escape lines across the Pyrenees.*

Something Old, Something New
Historical Fiction
*Two young sisters discover war memorabilia in an attic and set
out to trace their family history with devastating consequences.*

Without Yesterday: Mona's War
Historical Fiction
*Two women from different backgrounds meet under terrifying
circumstances in occupied France and engage in a pact to outwit
the enemy.*

**Memorial to five F.T.P.F resisters, who gave their
lives for France 11th June 1944, Bellac, Haute Vienne.**

Location Maps

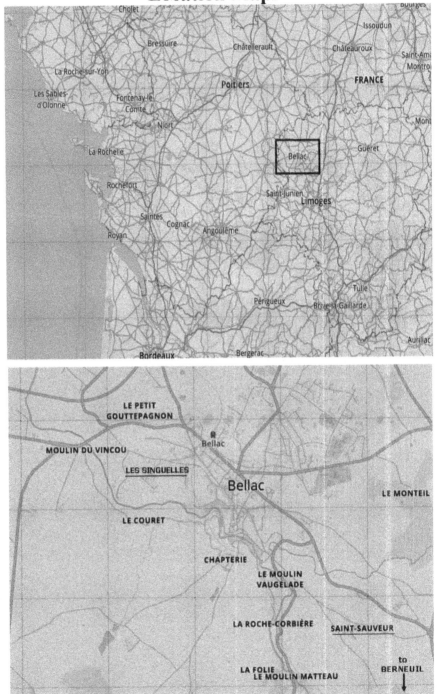

Prologue

Bellac, Haute Vienne, France
1944

It would be a day to remember; a night to forget. Clouds parted briefly; spasmodic shafts of moonlight revealed the hunched figures of two men, each wielding a spade. One grunted, exasperated as the metal blade hit a lump of granite beneath the rough terrain. His accomplice cursed the darkness. Alongside them, a sniffling young woman scraped away more earth with a rake. Moistened by the damp air, lank strands of auburn hair cascaded over her pretty but troubled features.

"It'll take ages to excavate a hole deep enough," she whispered, wiping her nose with the cuff of her coat sleeve.

"We've at least three hours of darkness, plenty of time to clear up this predicament," the older man snapped. "Just keep digging."

Apart from the occasional blasphemy from the younger man, for the next twenty minutes, they continued in silence. At one point, he apologised, not for the expletives but for his work rate. "I'm sorry it's slow progress…shovelling's not my favourite pastime at this moment in my life."

Trembling partly from the cold night air but mostly from fear, the woman continued raking earth, ignoring his gripe. "How will we know when it's deep enough?"

The younger man clambered into the shallow excavation they had created. "The sooner, the better." He discovered heavy clay had now replaced the initial layer of loose soil. "The deeper we dig, the more solid the earth." He stopped to wipe perspiration from his face.

"We'll stop when your shoulders are at ground level," the older man said, dismissing his remark. "It's not ideal, but it'll be sufficient for our purpose."

Another half hour passed until he estimated they had dug to a suitable depth. After the younger man had clambered back to ground level, the three exhausted individuals silently surveyed the result of their labours. Spots of cool rain provided a welcome antidote to their hot sweaty bodies.

The older man quietly cast aside his spade. "Time to finish the job; let's get it over with."

They dragged a large bundle across the rough ground before tipping it into the narrow pit they had dug. They stood in silence for several moments before the woman spoke, wiping tears from her eyes and visibly shaking.

"What have we done? I'm so scared."

The younger man turned towards her. "What have *you* done? We're just helping to cover up your stupidity."

The older man picked up a spade. "This isn't the time to start apportioning blame. In any case, it wasn't entirely her fault," he retorted, whilst looking skywards. "Look, the rain clouds are beginning to clear; we'll be exposed to the moonlight and soon it'll be dawn. Grab the other spade. We need to press on."

After filling the pit with the previously extracted earth, they set about blending the patch with the remainder of the rough ground. In time, weeds would grow to conceal their activity.

The older man leaned on his spade and mopped his brow with a piece of cloth from a trouser pocket. His voice trembled as he spoke. "Remember, tonight never happened. We must promise to wipe it from our minds. Go home. I'll deal with any other issues."

As they walked away, the distressed woman turned to look back. The clouds had parted, revealing the new moon; it hovered like a beacon above the freshly dug earth. She shivered but no longer felt the cold. Subconsciously attempting to block out the world at large, she wrapped her jacket tightly around her slender body. Reluctantly, she entered the house; a sensation of loss and betrayal caught her breath.

Unwilling to climb the stairs, she lay trembling on a sofa. Still wide-awake, her sad, tearful eyes stared towards the ceiling. Behind closed shutters, the darkness enveloped her; outside, the moon taunted her. There would be no peace; the truth could not lie buried forever. The nightmare had begun.

Part One

Les Singuelles, Bellac

Chapter 1

Bellac, Haute Vienne
1942

A fine dusting of frost covered the surface of the road as a young woman cycled briskly towards her parents' house. Wrapped in a cloth, a side of home-cured ham protruded from the cycle's wicker basket. Acquired earlier from a black market contact, she would exchange it for butter and cheese from a neighbouring farm. Such practices were commonplace, employed by many to bypass the stringent rationing and requisitioning imposed by the Nazis' recent occupation of France's free zone. Rosy-cheeked and breathing heavily, she reached Chez Dutheil in record time. Beneath a cloudless blue sky, the early morning chilly air had sharpened all her senses. She was in a buoyant mood; a friend had offered to look after her young daughter until late afternoon. Today was a rare opportunity to enjoy a leisurely bike ride, visit her parents and spend some time catching up on local gossip.

Concerned to find a car shrouded in frost standing on the road in front of the house, she braked involuntarily, skidding to a crisp halt by the wrought iron gate. It must have been there throughout the night, she thought. It certainly wasn't her father's car; who could the owner be? Since the occupation, the lack of fuel ensured fewer vehicles on the road, apart from those used by the Germans or occasionally, the Gendarmerie and others in key positions.

With some trepidation, she pushed her bicycle and its illicit bounty behind a clump of bushes in the driveway. Nervously, she walked towards the front door, knocked before entering and, despite her concern, tried to appear at ease whilst calmly shouting, "Maman, papa...it's only me...everything alright?"

Her mother appeared, looking anxious as she embraced her only daughter. "Eliane, we have a guest," she whispered.

As she spoke, a German officer appeared in the doorway of the salon. Eliane recoiled at the sight of the grey-green uniform, bedecked with military insignia.

"Bonjour, Mademoiselle." Clicking his heels and politely inclining his head, SS-Standartenführer Rausch introduced himself.

"It's 'Madame' not 'Mademoiselle', sir," she replied, nervously.

Smiling, the handsome young officer stepped forwards, offering his hand. "I apologise. It is inconceivable that such a young vision of beauty would not be married. Your husband is indeed a fortunate man."

My God, he speaks French. Embarrassed, Eliane felt her cheeks glowing even more. "You're very kind...thank you." She glanced at her mother, her expression seeking an answer as to why he was there, and so early in the morning. Instantly, the frost-covered car sprang to mind. *Had he stayed overnight? If that was the case...why? What terrible thing had happened to warrant his presence?*

Her father walked into the entrance hall from the kitchen to greet her with less affection than normal, seeking instead to resolve her concerns. "SS-Standartenführer Rausch is staying with us...he is billeted here for the foreseeable future. Apparently, several large houses have been requisitioned locally to accommodate high-ranking officers."

She sensed anger in his tone whilst his words sought to offer her an excuse for the situation.

"We were about to eat. Would you like to join us for breakfast, my dear?" Without waiting for a reply, he ushered everyone into the salon. "Is Sylvie not with you?"

Momentarily lost for words, Eliane shook her head before following her mother into the salon, where a table was set for breakfast.

"Sylvie?" asked Rausch. He held up a hand. "Let me guess...you must have a baby daughter."

Eliane nodded, unsure of his motives. Aware that he was the enemy, doubts flooded her mind. *Was there a more sinister reason for staying here? What had her mother told him about her? Would he know about her husband and her brother? Where was David? Why was a Nazi behaving so courteously?*

She sat at the table, whilst her mother set another place. Eliane tried to relax and, gaining strength from her parents' presence, turned to face the soldier. "She's not a baby...she's two years old. A friend has taken her out for the day."

Rausch either failed to notice the chill in her reply or chose to ignore the tone of her voice. He sat opposite. "And your husband...is he working?"

His intrusive questions were beginning to annoy her. "The war is supposed to be over. There was an armistice but you're still holding my husband captive. Perhaps you can explain why he is still a prisoner of war when he should be at home with his family."

Unruffled, Rausch shrugged his shoulders. "A consequence of war. Such matters will be resolved in good time. Would you pass me the jar of conserves, please?"

Her father, usually placid in nature, sensed undertones of a tense atmosphere. "Would you like coffee, colonel?"

Eliane's jaw dropped. *My God, he's a colonel...he's too young to be a colonel.* She stared at his face. With his cropped fair hair, steely blue eyes and pink unblemished skin, he could have been still at college. *Why must such a smart, handsome young officer be so attractive but so arrogant with his smug air of superiority? Damn the attitude of the Boche. They take our men folk, harass our women, plunder our land, treat everyone like lesser beings, and yet see themselves as heroes deserving of our gratitude.*

She had experienced their obnoxious behaviour in the town where, fully aware of the scarcity of local Frenchmen, they regularly attempted to charm all the young women. Because so many men had died in the Great War and many of those captured in 1940 remained in captivity, the French population was predominately female. Consequently, some misguided women had succumbed to their charms, seduced no doubt by the uniform and their posturing as victors; others, seeing them as a threat, stubbornly and sometimes rudely rejected their advances, regardless of the consequences.

She shuddered, contemplating the gossip that breakfasting with the Boche would encourage. *Their intrusion has now invaded our*

11

personal lives, demanding accommodation in our homes. What next…mixed marriages? Is this the future for my beloved France?

"Coffee, dear?" Papa interrupted her thoughts before joining them at the table. "The colonel has been billeted with us because the *Mairie* had a list of the town's more substantial properties with spare rooms. He has moved into your brother's room; it has a commanding view of the valley, and the colonel finds Gérard's desk extremely useful." Forcing a smile, he poured the coffee. "We are fortunate to have been allocated such a distinguished guest."

My God, already papa is fawning over him. How can this arrogant man sit there, a guest in the luxury of my parents' house, whilst their son and their son-in-law are both languishing in some dreadful German prison camp? It's disgusting.

Eliane glared at the German. "No doubt you will treat my brother's room with respect until he too is released. When he returns, you'll have to move into what used to be my little room, though I'm afraid you won't find a desk in there."

Her father glowered at her, fearful of her attitude upsetting their guest, despite feeling some inner pride over his daughter's stance. The officer seemed oblivious to the tone of her comments.

Knowing she would be unable to tolerate another minute in the soldier's presence, Eliane decided to invent an excuse to leave. "I can't stay. I'm on my way to see a friend in Berneuil." She sipped her coffee.

Rausch spooned another portion of conserve onto his plate. "It must be bitterly cold out there. Share some breakfast and allow me to give you a lift. You'll find my car far more comfortable than battling the elements on your bicycle."

He must have watched me arriving, and now he's using his position to placate me. Anne-Marie would be horrified to see me stepping from a Boche car. "That's very kind of you but I'll still need my bike to return home later."

"No problem. We can take your bicycle with us in the car. Stay and enjoy some breakfast with me." He leaned across the table to whisper. "It will be a pleasure to chat with someone of a similar age." He winked whilst nodding towards her parents.

Damn him…how can I refuse? "Thank you," she muttered, feeling trapped. *Surely, Anne-Marie will understand when I explain.* She glanced up at her mother as though imploring her intervention.

Madame Dutheil remained silent whilst shaking her head behind the soldier's back, implying some kind of disapproval. She placed her forefinger across her lips, her eyes pleading with her daughter to limit her conversation.

Confused, Eliane sensed fear in her mother's expression. *What's going on? Maman's trying to warn me…but why? Have I said too much already?*

Her father interceded. "If you're going to see Anne-Marie, perhaps you could take a book I promised her a few weeks ago."

Still perplexed, Eliane shrugged. "I suppose so."

"She is interested in Guy de Maupassant's short stories but I have several such books. Just come with me to my study to choose one. You can finish your breakfast afterwards whilst I wrap it and write a short note for her."

About to protest about the interruption to her meal, she caught sight of her mother's eyes motioning her to accompany her father. Excusing herself from the table, she followed him into his study. "What's going on?" she asked, closing the door behind her. "Why is maman acting so strangely, and since when has Anne-Marie been an avid reader of Maupassant?"

Her father ignored her cynicism. "We have a problem…your cousin."

"Where is he? I thought David was perhaps still in bed asleep."

"We had to take drastic action after hearing the news about Rausch. A neighbour's looking after him…temporarily."

"Why all the fuss?"

"Eliane, your cousin is an Austrian Jew. You know Uncle Johann sent him here to shield him from Hitler's violence against the Jewish community. He and Aunt Thérèse entrusted him to us for safekeeping. Your aunt and uncle would never forgive us if we failed to protect him." He sighed deeply. "We can hardly send him back home, and with the colonel lodging here for the foreseeable future, it's not possible for the youngster to stay. Apart from the difficulty of explaining his presence, he has no official papers…and, if he had, they would class him as a Jew."

"But he's only half Jewish. Aunt Thérèse isn't a Jew."

"The fact that she is married to a Jew doesn't bode well for the youngster. Anyone with Jewish ancestry is at risk"

Eliane slumped into a chair, her earlier petty concern rapidly fading as the severity of the situation became clear. "So what do you propose to do with him?"

Her father hesitated before sitting in a chair behind his desk. "Your mother and I wondered if you could take care of him...treat him as your own son...until this damn war has been resolved. I'll make enquiries to see if we can acquire false papers to prove he is your son...just in case."

"Why can't he have documents showing he's my cousin? Surely, that's the obvious solution."

"We would have to invent a story about why he is with us ...or you...without his parents. They might ask questions about them, which could place them in a difficult situation. It would be safer and simpler to show him as part of your immediate family."

"And what happens if that's not possible?"

"We can't disown the poor child. We'll just have to take that chance and hope no one delves into his background."

Eliane stood and paced the room. "You're asking me to put Sylvie at risk."

"From what I have witnessed since the Germans arrived in the *zone libre*, I believe all our lives are in danger."

His daughter remained silent. Life had become so complicated since the occupation of the free zone. Somehow, she had to face reality whilst finding strength to resolve the dilemma facing her family.

Her father pleaded with her. "I could bring him over later when I'm certain Rausch is unlikely to be around."

"But for how long is this situation going to continue? He's almost three; by the end of next year, I'll need to register him at the school in the village. I can hardly declare I have suddenly given birth to a four-year old son."

Monsieur Dutheil leaned back in his chair. "Alright, how about staying with a modicum of truth...explain he is your cousin whose parents were killed in a bombing raid in northern France? Maybe that's a better option...perhaps we could acquire papers to that effect."

"Papa, he speaks German...Austrian...whatever the damn language is...but little or no French."

"We can say he's from Alsace."

Shaking her head in disbelief, Eliane forced a smile. "You never cease to amaze me, papa. You always have an answer." She stood and walked towards the door. "Oh, whilst we're bending the truth, what book are you going to give me for Anne-Marie...not that she will care? Your house guest is bound to ask."

Monsieur Dutheil stood and reached towards a bookcase. "I have a copy of *Boule de Suif* or *Mademoiselle Fifi*...or *La Maison Tellier*, which is a collection of Maupassant's short stories."

"It really doesn't matter. Whatever I take, she'll think I'm losing my mind. Give me *Mademoiselle Fifi*...the title may distract him from asking more awkward questions."

"I'm sure you'll find a suitable explanation for the gift...and don't forget to tell her to return the book after she's read it."

His daughter opened the door. "Like I said, you never cease...." She lowered her voice. "By the way...just a thought...whilst you're in a devious mood, you might slip out to recover some food items from my bicycle before he retrieves it from the shrubbery in the front garden. I'll collect any payment in kind on my next visit...or you can maybe add some extra items to my cousin's suitcase when you bring him over. I'll have another mouth to feed."

Her father smiled, playfully shaking his head in mock disdain. "Not only me with an answer for everything."

She walked back to her father's desk after gently closing the door again. "I've just thought. We need to decide whether David remains my cousin or becomes my son. Your guest is bound to ask me about my family. I have the impression he's a natural interrogator."

"Good point." Her father stroked his chin. "Let's stick with the status quo but hope he doesn't ask." He chuckled. "Less complicated for maman."

*****

Anne-Marie was not at home.

Rausch switched off the car engine and lit a cigarette. "That's inconvenient. Did she know you were coming?"

Partly relieved that her friend had not seen her consorting with the enemy, but feeling guilty for having lied about the visit, Eliane decided to go on the offensive. "Do you constantly ask questions?" She turned to confront him. "Is that your way of making polite conversation or is it part of the Nazi interrogation technique to terrorise the population?"

"You had no intention to come here, did you?"

"There you go again," she snapped. "Another damn question."

15

He wound down the window to exhale a cloud of cigarette smoke, letting in a blast of frosty air. "Can we start again? We seem to have set off on the wrong foot."

Eliane said nothing.

"I didn't ask to come here," he continued. "I'm only in this part of France because it is my duty to obey orders. I'm a soldier of the German Reich where discipline is paramount. Our presence is merely to help the French authorities to maintain law and order until we have achieved the Führer's aim to create a New Europe. If we had met under different circumstances, perhaps we could have been friends."

"I'm married. I love my husband, whom you are illegally holding prisoner, and I'm not looking for male companionship…and furthermore, I couldn't care less about your Führer's schemes for a New Europe."

Ignoring her jibe, Rausch drew nonchalantly on his cigarette. "Obviously, you must miss your husband."

"Of course I miss him…and it's your damn German Reich that is keeping us apart."

"I wish I could help."

"Why? You don't know me or him, so why say that?"

He glanced at his watch before restarting the car. "I'll drive you home or wherever else you decide. I would prefer to continue this conversation but I have to report to headquarters at Limoges. You must realise that we Germans are not monsters. Like you, we are normal people doing the job we have been ordered to do. We also have families; we laugh, we sing, we have dreams. Because I'm a soldier, I happen to wear a uniform but beneath this outfit, I'm a human being just like you."

"So why is my husband still a prisoner? He was only doing his job but that's all over now. He should be here looking after his family, laughing and singing with us. We also had dreams but your aggressive Nazi war machine shattered them…invading our country for no reason." She glowered at him. "Just take me home…to my empty house."

"I thought you wanted to deliver the book your father gave you. Can you not leave it for your friend?"

The book lay on her lap. Eliane blushed, sensing she had been found out, like a naughty child. "Oh yes, my concern over my husband made me forget. I'll leave it in the outbuilding…it's always open."

16

She walked across the frost-covered grass to the adjacent barn, placed the Maupassant novel on a wooden crate inside the doorway and returned to the vehicle, feeling embarrassed by the absurdity of the situation.

She directed him towards Saint Sauveur, a small hamlet outside the main town. Eliane glanced through her side window, watching the empty fields and hedgerows sail past as they headed back in silence along the Bellac road. They stopped outside her house where he unloaded her bicycle. Before returning to the car, Rausch placed his hand on her shoulder.

Eliane flinched, firmly gripping the handlebars as she attempted to push it towards the front door. Previously, she had only observed German soldiers from a distance; the proximity of a uniformed officer made her uncomfortable but his touch nauseated her.

"I'll see what I can do."

Though desperate to distance herself, she stopped abruptly. "About what?"

"Your husband. There are discussions taking place regarding the exchange of prisoners for workers. I'll make enquiries. What's your husband's full name?"

With some hesitance, she gave him the information, even though fearful of the officer's motives. Was he genuinely offering to help? Could she be placing her husband in danger? He's a Boche soldier, so why should she trust him?

Watching Rausch drive away, she could feel her heart thumping. She rushed inside the house and vomited into the kitchen sink before sagging to her knees in despair. Even with her eyes closed, she was unable to obliterate the intimidating image of the SS insignia on the officer's uniform.

What have I done? Please forgive me, my darling husband. I miss you so much. Please be safe.

Chapter 2

Wiebelsheim, Germany
1940-41

Jean-Claude Tricot stepped gingerly from the truck; severe pain from his wounded leg seared like a sliver of hot metal through his body. Weary from a journey in cramped conditions, he ached in every limb, adding to his discomfort. When the last prisoner had descended, the vehicle pulled away to reveal an endless sea of disconsolate French soldiers. Few words passed between them as, pushed and goaded by their German captors, they trudged towards a processing area hemmed in by rows of wooden barracks. Low pressure cast voluminous clouds overhead like an ominous shroud, the grey damp weather compounding the bleak images that confronted them. Topped with barbed wire and interspersed by watchtowers, formidable perimeter fences only served to underscore their desperate plight.

Rumours had been circulating that an assessment of wounded prisoners could lead to immediate repatriation for those needing long-term treatment. Though founded only on hearsay, the possibility brought some relief to Jean-Claude. Unfortunately, he would discover his captors deemed the wound to his leg insufficiently serious to warrant his release. He soon began to realise the duration of his confinement in a Stalag would depend on discussions between the victorious German Reich and the vanquished French government, which, they had learned from their captors, had fled to Bordeaux. In the coming months it would re-establish itself at Vichy, where his uncertain future would be decided by the complex schemes that were about to evolve from settlements between Pétain's provisional government and the Nazi occupiers.

Despite regulations laid down by the Geneva Convention with regard to the treatment of prisoners of war, the Germans seemed intent on harnessing this mass of redundant manpower as an additional resource for the envisaged expansion of the Reich. Unlike the Oflags—camps designated for officers—the Stalags would provide the Kommando workforces for armament factories, mines, steelworks and farmland spread across various parts of Germany and its conquered territories. As one of those prisoners initially declared unfit for such a demanding role, Jean-Claude remained a prisoner, restricted to the confines of the camp at Wiebelsheim.

18

For the first months of captivity, life in the camp was chaotic with most prisoners still believing they would be released under terms agreed following the armistice in June. The rumours persisted until the following spring when some order became established, leading to the more organised formation of Kommando work groups and specific routines for those who remained behind in the camp. Eventually, letters and parcels from France began to arrive, followed swiftly by aid and advice from the Red Cross about their rights as prisoners.

By the summer of 1941, Jean-Claude's wounds had healed, leaving him with an annoying limp and the occasional bout of pain in his injured leg. He had finally accepted that hopes of repatriation were fading as quickly as the war was escalating. Determined to remain positive about his predicament he, along with other like-minded inmates, assumed a modicum of authority over fellow prisoners as *un homme de confiance*, a dependable individual who acted as a liaison officer with their captors.

Finding himself in a tentative position of trust, his thoughts turned to the possibility of escape and the inevitable threat of punishment if apprehended. Looking ahead to the coming winter, he and three other inmates began to plan their subterfuge for that time of the year when dark nights and bad weather might help their venture. Even if their attempt were to fail, they believed the activity would restore some pride and dignity to their lives, values they had forfeited following France's ignominious defeat.

*****

"I've discovered a few more details about the exact location of this camp." Jean-Claude sat with his co-conspirators on the wooden steps leading to their barracks. He grinned. "I merely bribed a guard with chocolate and cigarettes. It was that easy."

"So where is this bloody Wiebelsheim place?" A sour-faced prisoner paced back and forth, creating a mini dust cloud from the dry earth and gravel surrounding the huts. He had yet to be convinced about the proposed escape plan.

A searing hot sun bore down on them. In contrast to the earlier spring when melting snow had turned the earth to slush and mud, the compound had become an arid dust bowl. With little shade from the afternoon heat, tempers were inevitably frayed.

"According to the guard, we're about one hundred and fifty kilometres from the border."

"The border with France?" The youngest of the group, Emile, a slender youth with dark hair and a pasty complexion sat alone on the steps above Jean-Claude. His eyes constantly darted from side to side as though wary of any invasion of his personal space. He seldom smiled; he had little about which to smile. His face and neck still showed the burn scars from the ferocious tank battle that had almost taken his life. Many units of the Second French army had not survived the Panzer onslaughts that had broken through the lines at Sedan on the Meuse.

The doubter in the group kicked up more dust. "That's a bloody long walk home...even if we manage to get out of this damn place."

Ignoring the remark, Jean-Claude took a stick and drew a rough outline of Germany and France in the dust. He pointed to a spot in the centre. "We're approximately here, just north of the Saarland." Scraping a line to where he had drawn the borders, he prodded another point beyond the groove that divided the two countries. "The town of Metz; it's probably a German garrison by now." He pointed at other areas in the dirt at his feet. "I was captured not far from there on the Maginot line...and over here stands the Chateau de Malbrouck." He leaned back, a grim expression on his face. "That will be our destination. If we have to split up, we will rendezvous there. I know people in that area who will help."

"And how do you propose to escape before embarking on this epic journey?" Louis, the doubter climbed the steps, before leaning with folded arms against the wooden wall of the barracks.

A fourth individual, Jacques, another *homme de confiance* walked over to him. "We've worked that out already. It's simple; even you could have reached the same conclusion if you had spent more time watching instead of whingeing." Smirking, he relit his pipe. "We walk out with one of the Kommando groups and disappear on the way to the factory."

Blind to the earlier derisive comment, the doubter grinned. "Very amusing. Now tell me what you really intend to do."

"I've told you. We attach ourselves to a Kommando group."

"But there's a roll call...before they leave and when they return. If you're part of the initial head count, there'll be a discrepancy when they return. That'll raise an alarm even before it's dark. The area will

20

be swarming with bloody Boche before you set foot out of the town. Is that the best you can offer?"

Jean-Claude stood and, climbing the steps, leaned nonchalantly against the wall alongside the argumentative Louis. "We'll join them after the Kommando assembly roll call. If they don't count us in, they'll not miss us until evening roll call. By that time, we'll be well on our way."

"What if you're stopped out there? You'll have no papers."

"It's mostly a forested region. We'll travel by night and lie low during daylight hours. We think crossing the border will be the main problem, but it might be achievable under cover of darkness. That's why it's important to postpone our attempt until later in the year when the days are shorter and the cover of night will give us more time to distance ourselves."

"You're all mad."

Jean-Claude slowly returned to the steps. "So, I assume you're not joining us?"

"I didn't say that." Louis shrugged. "I suppose you can include me. Even if we get caught, it seems better than languishing in this shit-hole." He wandered down the steps onto terra firma, disturbing more dust as he paced back and forth. "One more question. How do you intend joining the Kommando without being counted in the departure roll call?"

Jacques dragged him away from the barracks before turning him to face the entrance to the camp. "The Boche counts the Kommando numbers in the parade ground before marching them towards the main gate, where escort guards join them. En route to the gate, the group passes very close to the gap between two rows of barracks...F and G. That's where we'll slip unnoticed into the Kommando."

"But they'll be four short when they return."

"You're not listening, are you? We won't be in the original count."

A sly grin spread across the doubter's face. "Oh yes...I see now. I suppose it might work but I still think it's a long way on foot. If we had papers, we could take a train." He brushed the dust off his trousers.

His flippant attitude worried them. Jacques broke the ensuing silence after re-joining Jean-Claude on the steps. "Apparently, only two guards accompany the work party: one at the front and one at the rear. Over the next few weeks, we're going to check out the route to

21

the factory to determine the best point to slip away unnoticed...mainly out of sight of the rear guard. We have already asked one member of the work detail to establish a suitable location. His only demand for this service is to join us in our bid for freedom."

He looked up at the doubter. "Don't worry about the shortfall in the roll-call following the Kommando's return. We will arrange for him to be declared ill and unfit to work the night prior to our escape. He'll join us and the work party between the barracks the following morning."

"What if others workers also try to slip away when they realise we're making a run for it?"

Jacques sighed. "That is the only flaw in our plan. If it becomes a mass rout, I'm afraid it's every man for himself." He drew on his pipe before commenting further. "Don't forget, there are many who still believe repatriation is imminent. They won't risk the opportunity of a legitimate release for a breakout that could result in recapture...or worse."

Somewhat concerned, young Emile rejoined the conversation. "I have a question. What will happen if they do catch us?"

Jean-Claude shrugged his shoulders. "I suppose there'll be some kind of punishment...probably a period of solitary confinement."

"They're more likely to bloody shoot us," Louis added.

Emile looked across at the surrounding pine forests, shimmering dark green against a clear blue sky. Like the Sirens of Greek mythology, the evergreens were luring him with false promises. "I refuse to be captured again. They'll have to shoot me...preferably out there in the tranquillity of the forests. That's where I belong...not here, cooped up behind barbed wire fences like a caged animal. I'd rather be free and dead than alive in captivity."

Jacques put his arm around the youth. "Don't worry lad, you'll be home well before Christmas."

Guessing that the British would neither surrender nor sue for peace, he wisely refrained from specifying which Christmas. Aware of the news about the Dunquerke evacuation, he guessed this war of attrition would endure for some considerable time.

Emile moved to one side, apprehensive but encouraged by the prospect of freedom. He yearned to be home in the peace and tranquillity of France's Ardèche region. Gentle by nature, fighting and killing other human beings were anathemas to him. If repatriation were to be delayed or withheld, he was willing to take the risk and suffer any consequences if their attempt were to fail.

At this point in the war, there was little indication of the barbaric might of the Nazi war machine. No one could have imagined the horrific reprisals the Nazis would inflict towards non-compliance or resistance. Like his fellow prisoners, Emile was about to confront the reality of Adolf Hitler's total subjugation of humanity across Europe…and beyond. The fanaticism embodied by the SS would bring terror, death and destruction to millions during the years ahead. These young French prisoners of war were unaware of the deadly step they were about to undertake; in their eyes, it was merely their patriotic duty.

Chapter 3

Bellac, Haute Vienne
1942

Bernard Dutheil earned a modest salary as a solicitor in Bellac. A veteran of the Great War, he had started his working life as a clerk, and within ten years, he had progressed to a junior partnership in the firm, a career that had provided a reasonable lifestyle for him and his family. He had married his childhood sweetheart, Jeanne Matthieu following his demobilisation in 1919. Twelve months later, Jeanne gave birth to twins: Gérard and Eliane.

Gérard developed into a handsome but reserved individual, studious and somewhat introverted. At university, he studied history and economics before pursuing a career in local government until his recruitment into the army in 1940. After his capture during the withdrawal of the French IXth Corps from Dieppe towards Le Havre on 9th June, he became a prisoner of war.

Eliane paid scant attention to furthering her education, relying on her wit and *joie de vivre* throughout her formative years. She married in 1939, giving birth to Sylvie the following year. The Germans captured her husband, Jean-Claude on 15th June 1940 when they penetrated the French lines before Saarbrücken.

What had seemed to be a perfect family, disintegrated with the outbreak of the Second World War; their lives would never achieve the potential future they had envisaged. The impact of the occupation would even change the ideology, society and politics of their country. France would discover life under the Nazis to be an intrusion; the enemy would impose their will on every aspect of their lives, and in many instances, with catastrophic consequences. Eliane's family was no exception to this brutal destruction of society's framework.

Since that first encounter with SS-Standartenführer Rausch at her parents' house, Eliane's existence had become increasingly stressful. His offer to free her husband via the prisoner exchange programme had become his excuse to visit her on a regular basis with updates on progress, even though he seldom had any relevant news. Though wary at first, with each visit she began to welcome his attention, naively believing his intentions were honourable.

However, her friend, Anne-Marie, widowed following the loss of her husband during the first months of the conflict, doubted the

24

colonel's sincerity. Still bitter and antagonistic towards the enemy, she constantly warned Eliane to remain alert to possible alternative motives behind his generosity.

"He has charmed his way into your life by promising your husband's release and showering you with gifts but remember, he's still a Nazi at heart. No wonder he spends so much time round here...you make him too welcome."

"You'd have done the same for Antoine...if he had survived." Eliane lowered her gaze, wishing she had not mentioned her husband. Though two years had passed, both women found it difficult to accept that those enjoyable times the two couples used to spend together were now distant memories. Their country's defeat and subsequent occupation had consigned that era to the scrapbook of yesteryear.

"People are beginning to talk."

"They're just jealous."

"You might see it as idle gossip...but in the town, they're linking your name with 'collaboration'. Some are even suggesting that your association with him is an intimate affair."

"Is that what you believe?"

"Can't you see I'm concerned for you, Eliane? If his efforts deliver your husband as he has promised...fine...but he's a man, away from home, probably feeling lonely, and missing female company. It's obvious to everyone that he's a smart, handsome soldier and you're an attractive young woman. He's bound to fancy you. Just be careful."

"Do you really think I'm going to jump into bed with him? I love my husband. I'm desperate to have him home again and, if tolerating Franz brings him back, my efforts will not have been in vain."

Anne-Marie almost sneered. "Franz, eh?" She turned away, emphasising her disgust. "First name terms now?"

"I can hardly keep calling him 'colonel', can I?" Eliane snapped, growing increasingly impatient with her friend.

Anne-Marie, realising she was wasting her breath, decided to change the subject. "What about the boy? What have you told him about David?"

"As of now, he's not seen him. I intend to tell him the same as I've told everyone else...that he's my cousin who lost his parents in a bombing raid. I had to satisfy the neighbours' curiosity but, since my explanation, their sympathy towards the child has embarrassed me a little. I must admit I don't find lying easy." She smiled. "However, in the colonel's case, I'm hoping it'll work out well...they both speak a similar language."

"Surely, Rausch will be able to notice the difference between Austrian and Alsace German?"

"David's merely a child with odd words, barely capable of holding a conversation." Though trying to appear relaxed about the situation, Eliane's face conveyed a deeper more noticeable concern.

"I sense there's a problem."

"I'm still waiting for false documents to support his fictitious Alsace background. Papa has contacted a friend who knows someone who can help with a birth certificate but it's taking too long. I'm afraid people may ask me questions about him that I cannot answer."

"Such as?"

Eliane was almost in tears. "I don't even know his birthday. I know so little about his past life...even though he's only two years old."

"Just choose a date...any date and stick with it."

"How can I, when his false birth certificate may say something else? I'm desperate to have some confirmation of who he is...or who he has become."

"Surely, he must have arrived here with some details of his background."

She shook her head. "My aunt and uncle witnessed how Hitler was persecuting the Jews in Germany, Czechoslovakia and Austria before the war, and decided to send him to a safer place. They smuggled the child out through Switzerland. Papa knew someone in the diplomatic service who arranged David's passage with a nun. His Austrian background had to be erased but nothing has replaced it."

"So, what's happened to his parents?"

Eliane shrugged. "That's the problem; we don't know. We've heard nothing from them since last year."

"Aren't you concerned that Rausch might ask you awkward questions if he encounters him?"

"He's never given me the impression he's interested in that sort of thing. Anyway, he's probably too important for trivial details. It's out there in the town where they're always checking people's papers. That's what frightens me."

"You're too trusting of him, Eliane. Boche soldiers are always the Boche...arrogant, devious creatures. The youngster's a Jew for goodness sake! There was a census of all Jews here in the free zone

26

last July; according to the Jewish Statute, he should have been registered whether here or in Alsace. Look what happened in Paris this summer; thousands were deported...and it's beginning to happen here. We all believed Nexon near Limoges just to be an internment camp for foreign nationals but, since the Boche occupied this region, rumours about deportations are rife. It's become a transit camp. Everyone knows Vichy is collaborating with the Nazis to round them up and punish anyone protecting them. If Rausch discovers the truth, they will arrest not only you but also your parents...and what will happen to the children? Think about young Sylvie; why should she suffer?"

"If anyone were to ask, papa advised me to say the bombing raid destroyed his family's documents, and we're still waiting for replacements. I'm sure Franz...the colonel...would understand. Everyone knows the difficulties we face when dealing with administrative processes."

Anne-Marie shook her head in despair. Realising that arguing would not resolve the situation, she left Eliane's house that day, more worried than angry over her friend's indifferent attitude. In spite of the officer's promises, it seemed reckless to welcome the German into her home. Since the occupation of the free zone, tighter security and constant checks had replaced the reasonable measure of liberty they had previously enjoyed. With the SS taking over policing from the army, and Gestapo agents spreading like a virus across southern France, a more intensive level of repression had descended on the population. In such an unpredictable environment, Anne-Marie feared Eliane and her family were heading towards an inevitable tragedy.

Inwardly, Eliane understood her friend's concern but, if Rausch could influence her husband's repatriation, perhaps the risk was worth considering. She knew it was vital to resolve her cousin's situation; she just needed paperwork to corroborate the story of his Alsace background.

She glanced across at the calendar hanging on the kitchen wall; in less than a week it would be Christmas. No longer the joyous occasion of her younger days, the event had become an unwelcome addition to the insufferable austerity caused by the occupation. Besides the dearth of quality food and the general lack of goods in the shops, for many, poverty prevented any over-indulgence during the festive season. In many families, the former breadwinners were either dead or prisoners of war. Of course, the black market existed, but favoured those privileged few who still had steady incomes. Since her husband's captivity, Eliane had relied on the generosity of her parents, the inadequate military benefit paid to prisoners' wives, and contacts in the village for the occasional bargain.

A few months prior to December, she had scraped together sufficient provisions to send a parcel to her husband via the Red Cross, hoping he would receive it in time for Christmas, if at all. There had been no mail from him since a short censored letter in the summer of the previous year. According to her father, no news was good news, but she continued to miss him more as each day passed. The lack of information haunted her, especially alone in her bed. To compensate herself for such solitude, she often allowed her young daughter to share her pillow.

In desperation, Eliane visited her parents that same afternoon to discuss Christmas and to ask about David's long-awaited paperwork. With some relief, she discovered that Rausch would be returning to Germany to spend the festive season with his own family. Her father suggested that Eliane and the children should stay over at Les Singuelles, pool resources and enjoy what they could salvage from the disjointed situation that faced them without their loved ones.

"Your chickens will be fine for a few days, providing you leave extra food for them."

Eliane shrugged. "No need; the foxes had them a few weeks ago. It's a pity because Sylvie loved feeding them. However, Sebastien showed no interest whatsoever; in fact, he seemed scared of them."

Bernard Dutheil grinned. "That's why you no longer bring eggs. Maman thought she must have upset you. She'll be pleased to hear a fox was the culprit!"

Her father always had the knack to make light of difficulties; he was a safe haven in her eyes. Having been assured that the documentation would arrive within days, she returned home in a less stressful mood.

*****

The following morning Anne-Marie called to return the Guy de Maupassant book and, because the weather had brightened, offered to take David into Bellac to give Eliane time with her daughter who seemed out of sorts. Since waking, Sylvie had been restless, crying for no reason, pouting and refusing to eat her breakfast. Eliane decided the child was either sickening for something or was bored. To create some

28

distraction, she persuaded Sylvie to help make decorations for grand'maman's house. They both sat at the kitchen table creating paper chains from coloured paper. With their hands covered in glue and sticky strips, neither mother nor whinging daughter heard the vehicle draw up outside. A knock at the door interrupted their efforts.

Lifting the latch and opening the door, Eliane felt a shiver run down her spine. The smiling face of SS-Standartenführer Rausch confronted her.

He bowed slightly whilst holding out his hand to greet her. "Bonjour, Madame Tricot. May I impose on you? At last, I have some news."

Awkwardly, she wiped her hand down her apron before proffering it towards his outstretched hand. "I apologise. It's a little sticky…we're making Christmas decorations."

Rausch peered past her. "I see your daughter is already entering into the festive spirit. I was hoping to bring her a most memorable Christmas present. Unfortunately, there is good news…and not so good news."

Confused by his words, Eliane stepped back, allowing him to enter. "Be careful near the table. I'm afraid Sylvie is rather generous with the glue." She glanced at the clock. Anne-Marie had not long since headed into town. Knowing her friend's propensity for gossiping, she would not be back for at least a couple of hours. With luck, Rausch would be gone before she returned with young David.

Curious to hear what he had to say, she decided she could afford to indulge her visitor. "Would you like a coffee…I'm afraid it's ersatz…the real coffee seems to have disappeared from the shops, and I cannot afford black market prices…even if I knew where to look," she added quickly.

"I could bring you some good quality coffee, if you wish."

Blushing, she turned away. "I'm afraid I couldn't possibly afford it."

"Oh, there'd be no charge."

"I don't think I should. People might question how I acquired it or even report me for dealing with black marketeers."

"Well, if you have second thoughts…in the meantime, ersatz will be fine." He turned to the child. "May I help you with your decorations?"

Looking up at the soldier, Sylvie seemed fascinated by his immaculate uniform with its shiny buttons, coloured ribbons and distinctive badges. She pushed some strips of paper towards him. To her, he was not the enemy; she had merely gained another playmate.

Whilst making coffee, Eliane found it ironic that her beloved France could witness displays of Nazi power and grandeur everywhere, yet here she stood, secretly discussing the procurement of an everyday item like coffee. The Germans were constantly proclaiming that future prosperity lay in their New Europe but, behind their flamboyant spectacles, they were slowly despatching their defeated nations to the dark ages.

The water boiled; she made the coffee and poured some juice for her daughter. Rausch continued to entertain the toddler as he pressed the paper into rings, extending the chain started by her mother.

"You've done this before," Eliane said, serving the drinks. "Do you have any children at home?"

Rausch shook his head. "I'm still waiting to meet the woman of my dreams…maybe one day…" He looked at her wistfully, with the hint of a smile.

Eliane hung her head, embarrassed by his stare. "You said you had some news."

"As you know, I have called in a few favours from some very important people regarding your husband. When I eventually traced his whereabouts, I thought it may be possible to have your husband back early in the New Year... if the paperwork were to be completed on time and provided his name can be added to the list."

Eliane gulped and, with trembling hands, placed her cup unsteadily on the table. Moisture glistened in her eyes; she turned to Sylvie. "Did you hear that, my precious? Papa's coming home." Smiling, she leaned across towards Rausch. "What did you mean about a list?"

"The exchange of prisoners for workers is principally about expanding the workforce for the various projects commissioned by the Reich. Obviously, prisoners who are incapable of work because of some incapacity or illness would have been the first to be selected for any proposed exchanges."

"Does that mean my husband must be ill or injured to stand a chance of coming home?"

"I have contacts who can add his name to a list, irrespective of his state of health."

"I can't believe it. Where is he a prisoner?"

Rausch sipped his coffee. "I'm afraid that's the 'not-so-good' news."

A shiver ran down her back.

"He's not where he's supposed to be. He escaped from the internment camp."

Eliane recoiled into her chair, unsure how to react. What would be the consequences for an escapee? "Oh, my God," she uttered. "When did he go missing?"

"From my enquiries, I have ascertained he disappeared some time ago...last year, in fact." Rausch stared at her intently. "You wouldn't be hiding anything from me...would you?"

For a moment, Eliane was speechless until she grasped the veiled accusation. "You think he's here! How could you believe I would be imploring you to release him if he had already come home?"

"I'm sorry, Eliane. I had to ask." He leaned across the table to gently touch her hand. "You see, we don't know where he is...most of the escapees were recaptured shortly afterwards but your husband was not amongst them. It will require making further enquiries to determine if he is still at large or perhaps held in some other facility."

Eliane slid her hand away, instinctively reacting to Anne-Marie's warning about over-familiarity. *How could Jean-Claude have been so stupid? I hope he's safe...and is still free...if only for the time being.* She looked imploringly at the German. "What will happen to him if you have recaptured him?"

Rausch shrugged. "That's up to the individual camp commandant; it depends on where he is. I imagine the authorities will mete out some form of punishment...perhaps a period of hard labour or solitary confinement...I really don't know."

"Please don't let them hurt him," she pleaded, before her fears for his safety swiftly turned to anger. "He should have been repatriated anyway."

"I'll be leaving in a few days. If I have further news, I'll call before I depart. Don't worry; I'll do what I can to help. As I explained to you when we met for that first time, we are not monsters. I understand your feelings, and I only wish to help you and your family. At home, I have a sister. If our situation were to be reversed, I would hope the occupiers of my country would treat my family with the same respect and courtesy they would deserve."

Eliane remained silent for a moment. "And what do you expect in return?"

31

"I'm your friend, Eliane. I hope you too can be my friend."

She nodded slightly, believing she had no other option. *How can I outwardly return his friendship? Everyone would perceive me as a collaborator. At the same time, he's still promising to bring home Jean-Claude, so how can I refuse?* "I can only thank you, Franz…and I'm sure my husband will be eternally grateful for your kindness and timely intervention."

Though warming towards the officer, she feared his involvement and felt uncomfortable by the favour he had promised. She felt confused and, casting aside any irresponsible thoughts, offered him more coffee to conceal her embarrassment. As she refilled his cup, she glanced at the clock on the mantelpiece, inwardly praying that Anne-Marie would not return too soon with David.

"You must know some very important people if you can arrange the return of one individual prisoner, especially one who has escaped. I would have thought that, as a soldier, you would be more involved in military matters." Eliane hesitated, conscious she may appear to be prying. "I'm sorry…I shouldn't ask, should I?" She laughed nervously. "And to think, I complained about you asking me so many questions when we first met."

Rausch sipped his coffee before replying. "I trust you are not a spy, sent to entrap me…distracting me with paper chains." He winked at Sylvie. "What do you think, Sylvie? Is your maman a communist spy?"

The youngster looked at her mother, said nothing, and continued glueing strips of coloured paper into odd shapes.

Rausch turned towards Eliane. "You're correct in assuming I'm well-connected. I liaise with the Minister of the Interior whose responsibility is to gather information about public opinion. I file and evaluate reports on the data collected by Vichy from the prefects in the various areas they administer. Consequently, though attached to the SS Kommandantur based in the Limousin region, I supply the administration in Paris with all data gathered southwest of what used to be the demarcation line. Eventually, my findings will reach Doctor Goebbel's Reich Ministry of Enlightenment and Propaganda."

"I don't understand why you need such information."

"It's important we know how the population is reacting to our involvement in the governance of your country."

"But how do you know what people think? Take me, for example. What do I think about German rule?"

Rausch laughed. "Not a lot, I imagine. But of course, your main grievance is about your husband's captivity."

"There's also rationing, restrictions on fuel, food shortages, high prices for poor quality...like this awful coffee...and lack of other everyday items in the shops...like shoes because you requisition everything for Germany and leave us with little else."

"I'll note your comments in my next report."

"Yes...and I suppose I'll then be arrested." She crossed to the sink to busy herself with washing dishes, fearing she had said too much. "Anyway, you cannot possibly know how everyone else feels. It would be impossible to interview every inhabitant in southwest France."

"Oh, you'd be surprised how much information we receive."

She turned to face him. "Is it true you open people's letters and listen to telephone conversations?"

"It's not really representative of the general public. Most people do not have a telephone and few in this region are sufficiently literate to write letters on a regular basis."

"So, it is true, then?"

"Surely, it's in all our interests to monitor the occasional communication if only for reasons of security, but that activity can also throw up topics that reflect public opinion."

Eliane returned to the table, wondering if Rausch was being truthful. Could it be possible that he passed any information he gathered to the Gestapo? In reality, were these innocent conversations a disguised interrogation? She would have to choose her words carefully. "I still don't see how your work will help in releasing my husband."

"I meet many individuals in Limoges, Vichy and Paris...people whose aim is to facilitate initiatives like the prisoner exchange programme. Such schemes can help in creating mutual trust and good public relations. Releasing prisoners can only bring about approval, even from those not directly concerned."

"So why don't you release all the prisoners of war."

"Many are content to remain in Germany where they can earn wages working in our factories instead of returning to seek limited opportunities here in France. They can send money home...even take leave to visit their families. Perhaps your husband may wish to choose that option. There are many young men in France who were too young to be mobilised; sadly, most are unemployed, especially in this part of

33

France. The Reich...with the approval of ministers at Vichy...is offering good opportunities in exchange for the repatriation of prisoners. You and your family will become beneficiaries of that scheme...if we can locate your husband. Surely, you must welcome that."

Eliane remained unconvinced. He seemed to believe the Nazi dogma that poured from his own lips. Should she trust him?

He glanced at his watch. "I'm sorry, I must leave. I'll contact you as soon as I have some news. I'm afraid it may be after the festive season."

He stood, gently patted Sylvie's head and turned towards the door. "I hope you enjoy Christmas as much as I have enjoyed our chat this morning. I look forward to seeing you in the New Year."

Eliane watched him drive off, wishing she could hate the enigmatic man who had charmed his way into her affection. As the car disappeared from view, she wondered how long she would have to wait for his next visit. A small part of her wished her husband might have found employment in Germany. Vexed with such selfish thoughts, she closed the door, leaned against it and closed her eyes, intent on extinguishing any further fantasies.

Chapter 4

The Kommandos, Germany
1941

The conspirators within the Wiebelsheim escape committee had spent the remaining summer months planning for an escape later in the year, still convinced longer nights would aid their trek south. Since those first days of capture, the camp had settled into a more relaxed atmosphere with only a moderate level of security. Some inmates seemed to think their repatriation was imminent. However, others believed the authorities would delay their release because Germany was short of manpower, having conscripted most of its male population into the armed services. Through conversations with the Red Cross, they had learned the Reich was applying various criteria to determine how any repatriation might benefit the rapidly expanding war. In some cases, prisoners who were in poor health, thus being a liability or having no labour potential, gained early release; some who had worked in key industries before the war also made the journey home, where they could return to their jobs to support the war effort. Others with skills in trades specific to the war effort found themselves assigned to camps near factories where they could employ their expertise. Remarkably, veterans of the First World War became eligible for immediate repatriation.

It soon became evident that release was becoming a lottery; some able-bodied men considered more useful remained as workers in factories, mines and agriculture, whereas repatriation became automatic for others with no apparent reason behind their selection. It was this uncertainty that had bolstered the desire to take a chance on escaping to the border. One of the workers, having established a close friendship with an elderly German employee in a local factory, had made tentative enquiries about acquiring false documentation to enable the escapees to travel less covertly. The negotiations depended on finance and the necessity of photographs for their identity cards. Sympathising with their plight, the contact had promised a camera but so far it had failed to materialise.

One Sunday towards the end of June, Jean-Claude was sorting items of clothing sent by the Red Cross for distribution amongst the neediest prisoners. It was hot and humid; distant clouds threatened thunderstorms. Jacques appeared, somewhat excited and breathless.

"Have you heard the news?"

"News about what?" Unresponsive to meaningless banter, Jean-Claude continued working.

"The Boche invaded Russia this morning."

"Never! Hitler had only recently signed a non-aggression pact with Stalin." Jean-Claude stopped sorting clothing. The unexpected news made an instant impression.

"Well, we all know about Hitler's inability to keep promises. It seems the Soviets must have thought otherwise. Apparently, the Nazis have been massing troops along the Polish and Rumanian borders for some weeks. It seems the rumours of an invasion of England must have been a smokescreen."

Immediately, Jean-Claude's mind considered the possible effect of this new development on their plans. "We need to bring forward our escape. If the Nazis intend to continue holding off the British in the west and prosecute a second front against the Russians in the east, I don't fancy spending this war stuck in the middle. They'll either conscript us into their army or force us to work in the armament factories where you are most likely to die from British bombs. I'm going home."

"We're still awaiting a camera."

"Sod the documentation. Let's go with the original plan."

"It's the height of summer...long days...short nights."

Jean-Claude had a stubborn streak; his resolve was firm. "It'll just take longer than we planned. Are you with me?"

Jacques nodded. "I'll speak with the others before making the necessary arrangements with our friend in the Kommando."

He left the hut, slightly nervous about reacting too hastily but understood his compatriot's concern. His most formidable task lay in convincing the others that to bring forward their escape was the right decision. Two weeks later, more unexpected news convinced them that there was no other option.

Each day that summer had brought news of yet another Nazi victory: in April, Greece and Yugoslavia overwhelmed after only three weeks, further advances in North Africa, the fall of Crete to airborne troops, success in Ukraine. The relentless flood of fascism seemed to be engulfing the globe. Despite the stubborn resistance of Russian troops, the Wehrmacht armies advanced rapidly on the eastern front, their lines of attack stretching from the Baltic States towards Leningrad; through the Baranovitch gap with Smolensk and Moscow as their objective; from Poland towards Kiev; from Rumania into the Southern Ukraine and Odessa. Berlin radio broadcasted regular reports of the Blitzkrieg's superiority over the enemy's counter-attacks, exaggerating the enemy's losses and minimising their own. Receiving daily updates via the work Kommandos, the prisoners in the camp quickly realised the process of repatriation would no longer be high on the authority's agenda; the war in the east had become their new priority.

As the campaign in Russia reached its seventh week, Jean-Claude and Jacques were ready to implement their escape plan. Their decision was further justified by a passing comment from one of the guards, indicating the authorities would be closing the camp in November with all existing prisoners expected to transfer to factory camps in the east. It seemed likely that the Nazis were increasing armament production to support the Russian front.

As the news spread, the insecurity of the prisoners' detention gave rise to new anxieties. One could sense panic spreading like a virulent disease. In some, their faces became windows to their inner fears; in others, desperation lurked behind their vacant stares. For the first time, suicides were no longer isolated circumstances.

*****

On a damp, misty morning during the last week of August, six 'inmates' slipped unnoticed from between blocks F and G to join the Kommando group before plodding towards the factory on the edge of town. At a pre-determined moment, they stole into a narrow alley as the main group turned into the road leading to the workplace. As agreed earlier, they split into pairs, each veering off in a different but generally southern direction. With extra garments and food items hoarded during previous weeks beneath their work clothes, they walked inconspicuously into the surrounding countryside.

Suffering badly from poor nutrition and lack of regular exercise during his confinement of over twelve months, Jean-Claude struggled to imagine how he would survive the long trek towards the French border. He bolstered his determination to succeed by reminding himself that each stride would take him further down the road to a family anxiously awaiting news of his release. In contrast to his debilitated body, his mental attitude remained positive; the journey would become a trial of endurance and survival. Though the injury to his leg had healed, he worried whether it would withstand the rigours confronting them.

Emile, six years younger, was his companion; his fitness was in no doubt, an attribute that compensated his lack of worldly experience. Jacques had suggested they should pair off; each could rely on the other's strengths whilst supporting their weaknesses. Jean-Claude had concerns about slowing down the younger man's progress but conceded Emile's bravado needed a degree of restraint.

By mid-day, the two men had walked almost twenty-five kilometres, passing through an agricultural area where women seemed to be the principal workers on the land. A couple of times they murmured a brief '*Guten Tag*' as they plodded along dusty roads leading towards a distant forested region beyond the town of Argenthal. Finding a stream flowing invitingly beneath a canopy of dense foliage, they refreshed themselves before crouching in the undergrowth to nibble the bread and sausage they had liberated from the camp kitchens.

Emile took a deep breath. "Just breathe in the fragrance from this pine forest. This is what I miss."

"Where did you work before being conscripted?"

"For as long as I can remember, I always loved the outdoors. After leaving school, I only wanted to work on the land...though not in farming...I was more interested in woodland, rivers and mountains. They fascinated me so much that I would have worked willingly in a sawmill or even as a charcoal-burner in the forests. However, my parents, especially my father, were adamant that I should choose a more mundane profession. Unbelievably, I became a trainee accountant."

Jean-Claude smiled at the youth's attitude towards his previous employment. "Whereabouts in France were you living?"

"In the Ardèche...not far from the Pont d'Arc."

"Little wonder you were entranced by the beauty of the area. I hear that region is spectacular."

"It's ironic that if I had been employed in the timber industry, I would probably have escaped conscription, and avoided this." He indicated the scars on his neck.

"The rout at Sedan."

"I saw the full horror of war in that hell-hole...tanks destroyed, dead and wounded everywhere, many of my compatriots totally unrecognisable. I was one of the lucky ones." He shook his head as though trying to rid himself of the memory. "I can handle killing wild boar and deer in the forests; slaughtering other humans is unnatural."

"Did you mean what you said about preferring to die if escape was not possible?"

"What's the point of rotting in a prison when there's the opportunity to do this…to be free to tramp through pine forests?"

"Perhaps with your good fortune and my determination, we might reach the border and freedom."

"How far do think we've walked so far?" Emile asked.

Jean-Claude shrugged. "Maybe twenty kilometres…it's hard to tell. All I know is there's a long journey ahead. We'll work our way through this forest but lie low when we hit open ground. We'll need some rest before continuing during the night."

"How do you know if we're heading in the right direction?"

"If we follow the setting sun as it sinks in the west, we must eventually reach the border…if not with France, with Luxembourg."

Emile looked down at the cloth bag he had pulled from his jacket pocket. "This food's not going to last long."

Jean-Claude smiled. "We've two options; we either steal or beg."

"I reckon steal. If we beg, they'll hand us over once they realise we're escaped prisoners."

"We could say we're refugees…made homeless by British bombing raids on Frankfurt…so we're heading for relatives in Saarbrücken."

"Why choose Frankfurt?"

"When I asked one of the guards whereabouts in Germany the camp was situated, the idiot showed me a map. Not only did I notice the location of Wiebelsheim, but I also took in the general view of the rest of this part of the country."

"But what if there's been no air raid on Frankfurt?"

Jean-Claude laughed. "It wasn't difficult to work out that those British aircraft flying east over the camp were destined for Frankfurt, the closest major town worth bombing." He carefully wrapped the remainder of his sausage in some paper before returning it to his bag. "In any case, my friendly guard inadvertently confirmed what I had guessed."

"It might be an acceptable story about why we're making this journey but we don't speak German."

"Leave the talking to me. I've picked up enough words over the past twelve months to hold a limited conversation, and if they question my ability or accent, I'll say I'm originally from Alsace where I spoke mostly French because it was the main language at school."

"How d'you know all this?" The young man stared at him with a hint of admiration; he seemed impressed.

"I've worked with a few Alsaciens as a telephone engineer, so I learned a few German phrases before the war. I'm afraid that region's identity and heritage swings to and fro like a pendulum on a clock, depending on who last conquered the territory."

Emile grinned. "I suppose they'll all be speaking German again now." The youngster leaned against a tree. "Do you think Germany will win this war?"

Jean-Claude stretched as he levered himself upright. "Not if I have my way." He turned a full circle to check the area. "C'mon, let's pick our way through the remainder of this forest."

They had walked only a few metres when Jean-Claude pushed his companion to the ground.

"What's that for?" Emile cried, rolling into deep clumps of bracken.

"Sssh! Keep your head down and listen;"

The ground beneath them vibrated; they felt a succession of tremors like the rumblings of an earthquake. What began as a distant buzz became a roar. The deafening noise drew closer. The whole forest seemed to shake.

Jean Claude restrained the young man from peering above the undergrowth. "Heavy armour...probably tanks," he whispered. "Keep your head down."

A convoy of armoured vehicles trundled along a dirt road less than a hundred metres in front of them; fully laden personnel carriers, medium and heavy tanks, armoured cars, motorised anti-tank guns and other military vehicles crossed from west to east through the forest. Several minutes elapsed before the thunderous noise rumbled into the distance and the dust finally settled.

"Stay down for a while." Jean-Claude waited for a short period in case any stragglers were following on behind the convoy. Now alert, they carefully approached the road, checking in both directions before scurrying across the rutted tracks into the thick forest beyond. Two and a half hours later, they reached a small clearing; here, the forest became less dense until it yielded its cloak of foliage to open fields and the possible threats posed by a scattering of habitation. A number of dwellings dotted the otherwise agricultural landscape.

Jean-Claude knelt down in a hollow close to a wooden fence marking the boundary of the forest. "We'll rest here until the sun goes down." He shaded his eyes from the sun's glare as he peered into the distance. "We'll avoid going in that direction," he said, spotting the beckoning spire of a church above the hedgerows. "Churches signify towns or villages, which in turn, denote an abundance of dwelling places. I reckon its location is due south of here, so when we move off, we'll take a more westerly route." He turned to face his companion. "Try and get a couple of hours sleep. I'll keep watch before we swap roles."

Emile gratefully accepted his suggestion, wondering whether Jean-Claude's stamina would hold out because of the rumoured weakness in one of his legs. Within minutes, he fell asleep.

A cacophony of sound woke the sleeping youth. A squadron of Messerschmitt 109 fighter aircraft soared high above the treetops in an easterly direction.

Jean-Claude looked skywards. "More reinforcements for the front."

"How long have I slept?"

"Not long…go back to sleep. There are several hours before the light fades."

"What about you?"

"Don't worry. I'll wake you when it's my turn." He watched the youngster turn on his side, trying to shut out the daylight with a coat that had seen better days before it had become a Red Cross donation. Though he himself was only in his mid-twenties, he thought it sad that so many youths would never reach maturity because of this damn war. He hoped their sacrifice would not be in vain. Sadly, many more young French patriots would join Maquis groups, only to die in horrific circumstances fighting to regain France's liberty.

Having shared the rest period, and now refreshed from their break, the two fugitives headed off towards the setting sun on the next stage of their journey. The roads were quiet; Emil found the silence eerie, joking that it was like 'the quiet before a storm'. Ahead, dark clouds had gathered from the south, heralding the prospect of rain. As dusk enveloped them, the temperature plummeted, bringing some relief to the unwelcome heat their bodies had endured in the earlier sunshine.

Jean-Claude looked into the distance as the light faded. "We may have to find some shelter later if those clouds veer in our direction. Rain during the day is bearable but it can make travelling on foot at night pretty miserable."

"Why can't we walk during daylight hours? The roads we've used so far seem quiet with little or no traffic."

"At night, one can hear vehicles approaching in the distance, allowing time to find a hiding place. During daylight hours, the enemy could spot us from afar before we would know they're even drawing close. It's safer this way but unfortunately, more inconvenient. We'll keep our options open, depending on the terrain and the environment. Trust me; I learned a lot about outdoor life during my work in the field as a telephone engineer."

"If that was your job before the war, will you go back to it when the war is over?"

Jean-Claude nodded. "Maybe...but I've stopped thinking about the future. Since being captured, I live for the present...how to survive another day...one day at a time."

For the next few hours, mostly walking in silence, they followed an undulating road until dusk descended. They reached the outskirts of a small village. Nearby, a dog barked. The few houses that lined the main street were in darkness. Not a soul in sight.

Emile looked at his companion. "What now?"

"We'll walk through. If anyone approaches, let me do the talking."

It was the hour when daylight collides with darkness, when images are vague but still discernable. A blackout must have been in force; the only light they observed emanated like a fine thread of liquid gold from a chink in a damaged shutter.

In silence they walked briskly through the village, their presence attracting nothing more than the curiosity of a weary dog that came alongside to sniff, before ambling back to its spot in the shadows. Apart from the odd scurrying cat, the main road and side streets were deserted. Relieved not to have encountered anyone, they quickened their pace, leaving the inhabitants of the village to enjoy an uneventful night in the comfort of their beds.

As they passed the last house, Emile stopped abruptly, before tugging Jean-Claude's sleeve. "Look over there," he whispered.

His companion peered through the gloom. Leaning against a wooden fence that fronted the house was a bicycle.

Emile grinned. "It'll save our legs and speed our journey."

"You're proposing to steal it?"

"Why not? They've stolen our country."

Minutes later, they pedalled off, hunched together. With Jean-Claude in the saddle and Emile perched behind on an uncomfortable rack, they wobbled at speed down the road, their ragged jackets flapping in the breeze. They disappeared into the night like two witches on an erratic broomstick.

Aching in every limb, they regretfully discarded the bicycle after a couple of hours. The anticipated rain had forced them off the road to seek shelter in the ruins of an abandoned farm building. They decided to continue their epic journey at first light if the weather improved. After devouring what remained of their food, they both slept, too exhausted to take turns on guard duty.

Dawn had broken when Emile felt something rough and wet on his face. He opened his eyes to find a dog licking his cheek. Startled, he pulled himself into a sitting position. Behind the dog, an elderly man with short-cropped hair and a grey moustache stood glaring at him.

"*Was machen sie?*"

Without replying, Emile leaned over and nudged Jean-Claude. He sat upright before smiling at the intruder.

"*Guten Tag. Wir schlafen…müde von unsere Reise.*"

The stranger grunted, seemingly satisfied they had been sleeping because they were tired, but still demanded to know why they had chosen to spend the night on his property.

Jean-Claude patted the dog reassuringly before standing to confront the old man. Having practised en route a version in broken German, he attempted to explain the unfortunate circumstances that had befallen them in Frankfurt as related earlier to Emile. He ended by asking if he could provide them with some water before they continued their journey.

The man listened intently, his eyes darting back and forth from Jean-Claude to Emile in an effort to establish the validity of his explanation. When he asked to see their papers, Jean-Claude shook his head in mock sorrow, whilst briefly describing how they had lost everything, including his wife and father in the bombing raid.

Emile looked on in admiration, mesmerised by his new hero's credible performance. With tears in his eyes, Jean-Claude first played

43

on the man's sympathy before angrily berating the British airforce that had criminally destroyed his family.

At first, the man said nothing. He seemed to be peering closely at Emile, particularly the burn scars on his neck and face.

"*Schwer gebrannt*," said Jean-Claude before explaining how, following the bombing, the young man had been lucky to escape the collapsed building with major burns. He added that the shock had left him unable to speak, traumatised by the bombing.

The fugitives glanced at each other, wondering how the stranger would react. Emile looked down at the dog; a German shepherd. It would certainly attack them if Jean-Claude decided he must silence the man. He could feel the tension in the stillness of the moment.

The man moved towards Jean-Claude before grasping his hand in a demonstration of solidarity. Having introduced himself as a local farmer, he invited them to share some food and drink with him before continuing their journey.

Unable to fully understand the conversation, Emile watched the stranger's expressions. With relief, he assumed Jean-Claude's story must have been convincing.

Grateful for the offer of sustenance but still wary, they followed their 'Good Samaritan' along a track to a farmhouse where the man's wife offered them home-produced ham, sausage and bread with generous mugs of coffee. Greedily, they cleared their plates, too engrossed in replenishing their hungry bodies to notice the farmer had disappeared. The woman explained her husband had gone to attach a trailer to his tractor; he would transport them to Baumholder, the next town where there was a railway station.

The minutes ticked by. Jean-Claude found himself glancing at an ornately carved clock on the wall opposite. The woman poured more coffee. Fifteen minutes passed; a long time to attach a trailer. Alarm bells began to ring in Jean-Claude's head; too late. They heard the screech of tyres as vehicles drew up outside the property. The door burst open. Gestapo and armed local police had descended on the farmhouse. There was no escape, no point in resisting arrest; the benevolent farmer had betrayed them.

Jean-Claude looked across at Emile. Mindful of the youngster's assertion that he preferred death to imprisonment, he hoped the young man would not throw away his life by committing some reckless act. "Next time," he whispered. "We'll make it next time. Keep calm."

Cuffed and bundled into separate vehicles, they headed to police headquarters at Felsenkirche where Gestapo agents interrogated them. Both fugitives had agreed, if captured, they would tell the truth. They would rely on explaining their desire to escape merely being indicative of their impatience with the promised but slow repatriation of prisoners to France. In fact, as Jean-Claude pointed out to his captors, they were doing the Germans a favour; two less individuals requiring processing and transportation subject to their camp's predicted closure. The Gestapo officer was not impressed.

Chapter 5

Hinzert-Pölert, Germany
1941-42

After two days of isolation in separate cells at the police station in Felsenkirche, soldiers arrived to drive the two captives twenty kilometres to Hinzert-Pölert concentration camp on the Hochwald plateau, a camp used initially for prisoners from the occupied countries of France and Luxembourg. Pleased to find they were closer to the border, Jean-Claude and Emile were unaware that early in 1942, Hinzert would become a death camp under the jurisdiction of the SS, aided and abetted by the Gestapo of the Trier and Luxembourg region. The majority of inmates would become slave labourers who would form a number of Kommando groups, some of which would work in various SS sub-camps in the surrounding area. The future looked grim for the two Frenchmen.

In contrast to their experience at Wiebelsheim, the regime at this new camp was harsh; lives were threatened daily by brutal beatings, torture and executions. Located on an elevated plateau, conditions were further exacerbated by inclement weather with strong winds, heavy rainfall and freezing temperatures during the winter. Unlike Wiebelsheim, some of the Kommando groups here were engaged in the maintenance and development of the camp by working in the surrounding forests, quarries and other locations producing useful materials. Within days of their arrival, it had become obvious that discipline at this camp would be tighter and more severe.

Despite being aware of his leg wound, the SS assigned Jean-Claude to the 'coal' Kommando, requiring him to work in a group transporting carts loaded with coal from the local railway station. To avoid the prospect of execution for displaying any frailty arising from his incapacity, he endured intense pain throughout that first winter. Emile was more fortunate; attached to the 'forest' Kommando, he achieved his pre-war ambition of chopping down trees to provide lumber and logs for the camp.

Naturally, at times when they could communicate in safety, the conversation focussed mostly on escaping, now more urgent because of the harsh conditions of their incarceration. Set in the midst of pine forests, enclosed by barbed wire fencing with watchtowers, and regularly patrolled, the chances of breaking out were slim. Determined

46

to abscond, Emile regarded working in the forests beyond the perimeter presented the ideal opportunity to slip away undetected. He had noticed on several occasions that the guards, especially towards the end of the day when they were tired, were less vigilant.

"But there must be a head count?" Jean-Claude asked.

"Only back at the main gate."

"That hardly gives you sufficient time to distance yourself."

Emile pondered for a few seconds. "How far d'you reckon we are from the border?"

Jean-Claude shrugged. "Not sure...maybe twenty-five, thirty kilometres to the border with Luxembourg...but that country's also occupied by the Germans...and you would have to cross the Moselle."

"It's no different than France...surely, locals will help."

"I wouldn't count on it in Luxembourg. When we escaped, I knew I had friends near Metz who would have hidden us until it was safe to continue our separate journeys. What you're proposing is too risky. With so little time advantage, you'll be easy prey, and they'll increase surveillance along the border before you even reach it. Why not wait until we can acquire false papers, a new identity and a change of clothing."

"But we've been trying to acquire those for ages...and still we wait."

Jean-Claude shook his head. "Spur of the moment never works. As you know, even precise planning has no guarantee of success but the odds are better."

Respectful of his friend's advice and concern for his safety, Emile dropped the subject. However, deep inside, the yearning for a return to France gnawed away, especially when working in the forest beyond the confines of the barbed wire. Desperate to maintain the young man's morale, Jean-Claude spent the remainder of their time together trying to convince him that an opportunity would eventually present itself. As winter turned to spring, such hopes began to fade as quickly as the snow turned to slush. Jean-Claude knew he was losing the struggle to keep the young man; any day, he expected Emile to grasp the first opportunity now the weather was improving.

They were still debating the issue when, on 30th May, news filtered through about an intensive bombing operation, involving 1000 Allied bombers, on the city of Köln, almost 200 kilometres north of the camp. Naturally, the destruction of such a large city and the consequent loss of many lives became the focus of the guards' conversations, distracting them from their duties. In Emil's misconstrued logic, the heavy bombardment should work in his favour, its impact on morale creating the perfect opportunity to slip quietly into the forest undetected. Convinced his moment had arrived, possible repercussions against those deemed responsible for the attack were not on his mind. Insensitive to the population's anger and desire for revenge on anyone perceived as their enemy, he saw his chance and decided to take it.

The following day, he made his move, tearing through the wild undergrowth like a rampaging boar, initially avoiding the numerous tracks that criss-crossed the dense forests. Determined to distance himself from any pursuers, eventually he turned to using the more open paths, hoping it would speed his flight to freedom.

Though the forest provided reasonable cover, steep inclines leading to a higher plateau hampered his rate of progress. After toiling for a couple of energy-sapping hours, he followed the river Ruwer until he reached the outskirts of Kell am See, a town silhouetted against the fading light as daytime melted into the western skyline. After a brief respite, he continued in a south-westerly direction towards Mandern.

With a thumping heart, he silently descended towards his first major obstacle. Crouching exhausted behind a stone wall, he deliberated how to pass through unnoticed. Not wishing to put himself at risk, he decided to skirt the town, using the river as a guide to continue in a southerly direction. Eventually, he realised that by following the river he was heading towards the faint glow in the sky where the sun had set, a westerly direction; he would have to cross the river to head south. An hour had passed when he spotted a bridge spanning the Ruwer near the small town of Zerf, but observing a few people going about their daily lives was enough to rule it out. How he wished Jean-Claude was present if only to discuss the options: bridge, swim, or preferably find a boat to steal.

As dusk began to enshroud him, he crossed several fields keeping close to the hedgerows. The grass and foliage, still wet from an earlier shower, had soaked his clothes so much that a dip in the river was no longer an issue; there seemed scant alternative to the cold, damp night that lay ahead. Settling down on the riverbank, he remembered what Jean-Claude had said about sensing the presence of the enemy before discovery. He looked through the gloom at the flowing water, wondering if the enemy could be employing the same tactics. The river hardly looked inviting; the bridge spelled danger, and there was no sign of abandoned boats. It was decision time for Emile.

He lay full-length on the riverbank before plunging his arm into the water. As expected, the current felt strong, and the icy water numbed his flesh. He reckoned the opposite bank to be at least ten metres distant; the depth of the river was impossible to gauge. The strength of the current could extend time in the water, causing more discomfort in precarious conditions. Withdrawing his arm, he glanced again at the nearby bridge as an alternative. Neither option appealed to him; both offered only a slim chance of success. He decided instant death by a bullet to be preferable to the prolonged process of drowning. Stealthily, he set off towards the bridge, praying it would be unguarded.

*****

The twice-daily roll-calls at Hinzert-Pölert were often grim affairs conducted in all kinds of inhospitable weather, and lasting far longer than was necessary. Prisoners would line up in their Kommando groups for the early morning count on the central parade ground. They would assemble for the evening one in groups determined by their individual barracks. Inadequately clothed and often in poor health, many prisoners collapsed from their inability to endure such savage conditions. Often, those who collapsed or were too ill to attend found themselves dragged to the 'hospital block', never to be seen again.

Such prisoner assemblies were also opportunities for the camp commandant to issue new directives or to instil more fear into the captives by publicly administering various forms of punishment to those who had 'stepped out of line'. One such event took place on a mild evening in early June; the effect on Jean-Claude would determine his future resolve towards the enemy. Earlier in the day, a work party of prisoners had erected a stout wooden pole in the centre of the parade ground. Following the evening roll-call, a group of SS soldiers appeared, dragging a dishevelled individual across the gravel before lashing him upright to the pole. Despite his wretched state, it was not difficult to determine his identity.

Standing in line with the other inmates, Jean-Claude grimaced to see his young friend, Emile at the mercy of his barbaric captors. The loudspeakers reminded them of the severity of retribution that would always follow escape attempts. The dire warnings reverberated across the camp as the inmates watched the drama unfold. Forcibly watching SS brutes mete out the punishment left them in no doubt that escaping and recapture would result in unbearable consequences. The soldiers used iron rods to beat the poor young man about the legs until the bones cracked; he would never walk again. A tearful Jean-Claude prayed they would shoot him to release the youngster from his torture. Mindful of their past conversations, it's what he would have wanted.

Averting his eyes to the merciless spectacle on the parade ground, Jean-Claude clenched his fists in anger. He vowed that, once he was free again, he would avenge Emile's horrific treatment by killing any Boche soldiers he might encounter. Several minutes passed before the barbarity finished, leaving Emile's shattered body hanging limply from the wooden stake. A final warning blared from the loudspeakers prior to dismissing the inmates to their respective barracks. Shocked by what they had been compelled to witness, the barracks were quieter than usual that night. Jean-Claude lay on his bunk, wondering what circumstances had prevented his friend from avoiding capture. He would never discover that the young man had stumbled by chance into an unexpected area of high security only twenty kilometres from the border.

*****

Spanning the river Ruwer, the bridge near Zerf had seemed deserted from Emile's position on the riverbank. He had lain in the damp grass for about ten minutes, peering through the gloom, watching, waiting and contemplating how or if he should use the bridge. For some time, nothing had stirred, no sound apart from the occasional hoot of a distant owl. Gradually, he had edged closer to the road that led into the town. Again he waited, watched and listened before racing to safety on the far side. With great relief, he encountered no one. Leaping from the road, he scrambled through a hedgerow into an adjacent field before running towards a wooded area; he had avoided the town.

He disappeared into the dense green abyss of the forest, intoxicated by the heady cocktail of fresh pine and the enhanced prospect of freedom. Unfortunately, the darkness concealed a small airstrip, hidden between the forest and the town. Though surrounded by perimeter fences, the area's security was bolstered by regular patrols. Any movement in the immediate vicinity would be noticed and investigated. Despite the cover of darkness, the logic imparted by Jean-Claude had failed the test; the Germans played the same game.

Unobserved, two guards tracked Emile as he wove his way through the forest. After ascertaining they were not hunting down a wild animal, they ambushed him. Astonished to confront two armed soldiers barring his path, Emile readily surrendered. Despite his bravado with Jean-Claude about preferring death to capture, he quietly sank to his knees with arms raised. His bid for freedom had failed under the most unexpected circumstances and in a less than dramatic fashion. Within twenty-four hours SS soldiers from Hinzert-Pölert had escorted him back to the camp.

*****

As dawn broke following the night of his torture, two guards dragged Emile's almost lifeless body from the parade ground to the hospital. Jean-Claude awoke to find only the bloodstained pole as a reminder of the previous evening's horrific atrocity. He would never see Emile again; from that moment, hatred and thirst for revenge towards every Nazi would dominate his life. Though weakened by the conditions in the camp, his anger and bitterness sustained him, keeping him alive for his 'day of reckoning'. He longed for repatriation or for the war to end, aware the Nazis were losing ground. General Zhukov's counter-offensive had halted further advances in Russia, and Rommel's armies were in retreat in North Africa.
He had a score to settle that strengthened his determination to live, despite the constant pain from his leg wound. He occasionally entertained the idea of a second escape attempt but conceded the chance of survival to achieve his aims would be minimal. Though the back-breaking forced labour in unbearable weather conditions drained him physically, mentally he remained strong, ensuring the prospect of freedom remained a reality. He decided to wait for events to unfold. Unfortunately, time was running out for Jean-Claude but his luck was about to change.

Chapter 6

Saint Sauveur, Bellac
1943

Eliane tore December from the redundant calendar hanging on her kitchen wall before throwing the remnants into the wood burner. She had spent the previous evening alone, watching the clock tick away the final minutes of 1942 whilst the children slept. Friday, the first of January had heralded a cold grey day interspersed with a light drizzle.

Dreading the thought of another year without her husband, she exhaled the deep sigh of someone who perceived her life as an impasse. Clearing the remains of breakfast from the oilcloth-covered table was no antidote for self-pity. For her, this latest festive season had been another ordeal of restrained sadness. Under such demoralising circumstances, there had seemed no point in decorating the house with garlands or even bothering with a tree. It had irritated her that, to provide some sense of normality for Sylvie and her cousin, circumstances beyond her control had forced them to spend Christmas at Les Singuelles where her parents would take turns making a fuss of them. She scolded herself for treating her children as an irritation, a further imposition on her melancholia. Fortunately, Rausch had taken the opportunity to pass Christmas visiting his own family in Germany, resolving one dilemma that had plagued her when her parents had suggested the arrangements.

She had returned home with the children on the last day of 1942. Consequently, New Year's Eve had been a lonely experience but *le Réveillon de la Saint-Sylvestre* would bring dramatic changes to Eliane's life.

She had barely unpacked her suitcase when Anne-Marie called to exchange pleasantries and to share her personal sadness of another festive season without her husband. Her father lived alone in Oradour-sur-Glane, his wife having passed away before the war. His only daughter had felt duty bound to spend time with him in an effort to minimise the grief that touched them both during those special periods when families socialise and celebrate together.

"How is your father?" Eliane asked with genuine concern. "I hope you passed on my wishes for the festive season." Having met him on several occasions, she understood his loneliness and dependence on his daughter since the death of his wife.

"Like me, he still misses maman but immerses himself in his carpentry...and the neighbours keep an eye on him when I'm not around. To be honest, I think he copes better than I."

"At least, she died from natural causes, not from Nazi bullets like so many other innocent people."

Anne-Marie smiled. "That's why I love that little town; it's so peaceful. During the whole time there, it was so easy to forget the brutal controls inflicted on the rest of the country by the Boche. I felt I had stumbled into another world...the world we used to enjoy with friends and family." She glanced dreamily towards the dresser; a selection of framed photographs rekindled memories of happier times. "By the way, where are the children?"

"They're playing with a neighbour's youngsters...two doors down; Madame Ferrer offered to keep an eye on them. I thought it would give me time to sort out the house following our stay at Les Singuelles."

"Oh, whilst I was at Oradour, I told papa about your German officer; he was not impressed by what he called 'hollow promises' regarding their new initiative to exchange prisoners for workers. He still has bitter memories from the Great War, and was most adamant that you should never trust the Boche."

Eliane had made coffee. "He's probably right; there's still no news. D'you think he'd like me to take the children to see him one day. He came to Sylvie's christening but he's never seen the latest addition." She poured two cups of hot ersatz. "It won't be for a while...I'm still wary of taking the youngster anywhere until I have some paperwork verifying David's fictitious origin."

"You worry unnecessarily; no one is interested in a toddler like David. Even if they stopped you and asked to see your papers, they wouldn't query the child. He doesn't even look Jewish if that's your main concern." She sipped her coffee. "However, it does seem ages since you asked for documents. What's the hold up?"

"I'm not sure. Papa maintains he continues to ask his contact but even he doesn't know who's actually responsible...apart from the fact he thinks it's someone in the Résistance." She shrugged. "It's one of those situations where someone knows a man who knows a man who can, and one must not ask questions. Papa says I should be patient...but they've had David's information for nearly two months

53

now. If resisters are that slow in producing false documentation, I doubt they'll be much of a threat to the Boche."

Anne-Marie sipped her coffee but said nothing, creating an awkward silence.

"What's the matter? Have I said something to upset you?"

Her friend leaned across the table before lowering her voice. "Can you keep a secret?"

Eliane nodded, her furrowed brow registering her concern.

"I met some people at papa's...old friends from Blond and one from Bellac. Aware of my circumstances, living alone in a remote area, they asked me if I would be prepared to run a 'safe house' at Berneuil."

"What's a 'safe house'?"

"A place where people can hide temporarily or stay over en route to another 'safe house'."

"I don't understand." Eliane's puzzled expression betrayed her innocence.

"There's a demand for such places so the Résistance can hide fugitives from the Germans."

"You mean Jews?"

"Well, I suppose so, but there are Allied airmen who have survived being shot down who are passing through to reach the Spanish border. They need somewhere to lie low before moving on. Apparently, there are also British agents who parachute into France needing places to stay, places where they can transmit and receive radio messages with London."

Eliane's jaw dropped. "You've been asked to join the Résistance?"

"Ssh! Not so loud!"

"But if the Germans discover what you're doing..."

"I suppose it's a risk but I've never seen any Boche in Berneuil...apart from when they pass through to Limoges or to Bellac and beyond. Who would know?"

"Your neighbours, for a start."

Anne-Marie laughed. "I have no neighbours; the nearest house must be at least a kilometre from mine."

"You never know who might be passing. What if someone mentions you have visitors coming and going and the Gestapo overhear? It could be just an innocent remark...or even worse, it could be an informer, out to betray you. They would interrogate you, ask about your contacts. Oh, my God, they might even think I'm involved with you. It doesn't bear thinking about!"

"At least I'm not playing 'happy families' with a German officer."

Indignantly, Eliane rose from the table. "I'll ignore that remark. I need a drink." She crossed to the dresser. "Papa gave me a small bottle of Cognac." She withdrew two glasses and a bottle, before rejoining her friend at the table.

Anne-Marie thought it wise to close the subject. "It's not like you to drink Cognac…especially during the day."

"It's not often I'm consorting with the local Résistance."

*****

The following day, whilst still worrying about Anne-Marie's proposed involvement with the Maquis, a knock on her door interrupted Eliane's thoughts. To her surprise, the local priest, Father Milani was the visitor.

"Good morning, Madame Tricot." He glanced nervously over his shoulder before lowering his voice whilst offering his hand to greet her. "May I come in? I have something rather confidential to discuss."

She attended mass regularly at the nearby church but this was only the second time he had visited her at home. Apart from services at the church, there had been no contact with him since his brief pastoral care visit following her husband's capture. A shiver ran down her spine as she stepped to one side, allowing him to pass. Her immediate thoughts turned to her husband; the priest must have bad news. Closing the door, she could think of no other reason for a priest to call on her.

"Are the children not here?"

Eliane nodded in the direction of the garden at the rear of the house. "They're playing outside…well wrapped up against the cold but enjoying the sudden spell of sunshine."

Father Milani withdrew a large envelope from beneath his cassock. "I believe you have been patiently awaiting this." He passed it into her trembling hands. "I can only apologise for the delay. We had difficulty acquiring the correct paper and blank documents. I'm afraid the authorities regularly change the format to hinder authentic duplication."

Suddenly, Eliane realised the reason for his visit. "David's Alsace documents?"

The priest nodded. "May I sit?"

Flustered, Eliane showed him to a chair at the table. "I didn't realise you were involved."

He settled into his chair. "You could say I'm an intermediary, a messenger with an important delivery."

Flustered but excited by his news, she felt obliged to offer a modicum of hospitality. "Can I offer you a drink, Father?"

He smiled. "Provided it's not that awful coffee substitute."

"If you prefer, I have a small amount of Cognac that papa gave me at Christmas."

"Cognac will be perfect, my dear."

Eliane poured a generous measure into two glasses before joining him at the table. "I was under the impression that someone connected to a member of the Résistance would be handing this to papa." She picked up the envelope.

Father Milani shifted uneasily in his seat. "We've taken the liberty to make some changes..." He cleared his throat. "...mainly for security reasons."

Eliane opened the envelope and withdrew the contents before studying them closely. "They've made a mistake with the name on the birth certificate."

"I'm afraid his real name, Steinberg sounded too Jewish. Using your family name seemed more appropriate, and it would fit with him being here...with you."

"But David's mother...my aunt's maiden name was Matthieu, the same as maman's maiden name...not in the least Jewish. Why not use that? Tricot is my husband's surname; why choose his name? I only carry that name through marriage."

"The Alsace story was somewhat loose...no proper address, no family records there, no background of education or employment with regard to his parents. Don't forget, the German presence in that region is and always has been extremely strong. An investigation would have discovered it to be a fabrication very easily."

Eliane threw the documents onto the table. "So, who is the child supposed to be?"

"Your son."

"My son!" she cried. "Everyone knows he's my cousin; I've told all the neighbours...and my friends."

56

"But not the Germans," Father Milani added quickly. "Anyway, I doubt they will ever ask about the children. Personal identification papers are not required until they are sixteen years old. That's when he'll need this supporting documentation. If there is ever any question regarding evidence of the child's birth, they will accept what is on the documents. You can tell those close to you that you are adopting him; just treat him normally as your son. In the future, no one will know any different."

Eliane scanned the documents that she held in her trembling hands. "Do you believe the Germans will still be here fourteen years from now?"

The priest smiled. "Whether they remain here or not, the youngster deserves to have a family. It'll be up to you to decide if and when you tell him the truth. You will know when the time comes."

She stared at the papers spread across the table. "The date of his birth is the same as Sylvie's. How can that be?"

"In reality, he's a similar age. As far as the Germans are concerned, they will perceive them as twins, in accordance with their papers." He sipped his brandy. "It's easier that way. It would not be possible for him to have been born after Sylvie because your husband was in a prisoner of war camp during that period. To have been born before, there would have to be a noticeable difference in the two children, both physically and mentally, and more importantly, he would have been conceived out of wedlock. Your parents are adamant that David and Sylvie have similar attributes, so portraying them as twins would be quite acceptable. I also understand that you and your brother are twins, so it seems natural that the gene runs in the family."

"But what about his real parents? They'll want him back after the war when this stupid charade will be terminated."

He coughed rather nervously before sipping more Cognac. "Apparently, following extensive enquiries...that's another reason why it has taken so long to produce the documents...it has been established that David's parents were transported with other Jews from the same area of Austria to one of the concentration camps in Dachau, Buchenwald, Lodz or Mauthausen. It's highly unlikely they will ever return."

"How can you be so sure?"

"Various sources are beginning to confirm that certain camps are death camps. We have testimonies and other evidence to that effect. You alone have David's life in your hands."

57

Eliane's shoulders dropped as she slumped backwards into her chair. "So, all the Jews that were deported from Paris last year, and all those taken from the camp at Nexon near Limoges are heading for..."

"Liquidation...I'm afraid. In August and September last year, transports took over four hundred Jews from Nexon to Drancy in Paris prior to deportation to the death camps. It is reckoned that more than four thousand Jews have been deported from internment camps in the free zone alone."

"How do you know all this?"

"Amongst the authorities in Vichy, there are contacts opposed to those traitorous collaborators, Pétain and Laval, and we also have witnesses who can support these findings in the internment camps. One only has to read the Jewish Statutes, issued by Vichy almost eighteen months ago, to guess what would happen."

Eliane grasped the documents again. "How will I explain all this to Rausch?"

"Rausch?"

"The German officer who is billeted with my parents...and who keeps visiting me."

"Ah, the one who is supposed to be expediting your husband's release? Is that his name...Rausch? " He frowned. "Rausch...are you sure?"

She nodded. "SS-Standartenführer Rausch to be exact. He only knows about Sylvie. How will I explain why I haven't mentioned I have a son...in fact, her twin? He'll find it strange that I never mentioned him...and he'll wonder why he's only seen Sylvie during his visits here."

"Yes, your mother did mention that the German officer had seen only Sylvie. I suggested you should tell the colonel that your son has been convalescing at a convent in the Creuse following the removal of his tonsils. I'll vouch for that, and if necessary, provide supportive documentation."

Eliane sighed. "I can't do this; it's too complicated...and why change his name to...to Sebastien? Of all the names you could have chosen...why Sebastien?"

Father Milani smiled. "Sebastian spelled with an 'a' is my name."

"Oh, I'm sorry, Father. I didn't mean to..."

The priest held up his hand. "You have every right to protest." He smiled. "I doubt I would have chosen it for myself, but my parents must have thought it appropriate at the time. However, we thought it would be easier if you were able to provide additional evidence if, at some time in the future, the authorities were to query its authenticity. These items might help to support the deceit in the event of an official visit."

He reached into a deep pocket and withdrew a small leather-bound prayer book that he pushed towards her. The name 'Sebastian' was embossed in gold on the dark brown cover. Another delve into his pocket produced a tiny gilt-framed photograph.

"I'm afraid the quality is not good but this is a photograph of me as a baby with my name penned below."

Again he reached into another pocket to extract a small silver goblet, inscribed with the same name. "A christening gift, I believe."

Lost for words, Eliane stared at the objects spread out on the table before her.

"Your parents and I discussed the situation concerning the German officer. If he returns and stays with them, it is highly likely...given his promise to secure your husband's release...that he will visit you again. These few artefacts placed discretely around your living room will add credibility and support the story about Sebastien's existence and your earlier reticence regarding his convalescence. As a military man, he perhaps won't understand your maternal feelings about the child's illness, but he will accept any corroborating evidence on show."

"How will I explain the different spelling on these objects when compared to the spelling of his name on the documents?"

"I doubt anyone will notice, but you can always blame the engravers."

Tears began to trickle down Eliane's cheeks. "He'll still think it strange I haven't spoken about him. How can you be so sure it will work?"

"It is God's will that we have an opportunity to save the life of this child. Just think, Eliane; no more hiding him away. It is in your hands to grant him a future alongside your daughter."

"Oh dear, how will I explain all this to Sylvie?"

"She's very young. I'm sure she will accept the simple explanation that David is going to be your son, her brother, and now you will call him Sebastien. Initially for her, it will be perhaps an amusing diversion. Gradually, it will become reality; children are very adaptable."

Eliane continued to weep. "I'm sorry to question every detail; I'm finding it difficult to grasp how to deal with such unexpected changes. You are so kind. I will never be able to repay you."

"Just give young Sebastien the life he deserves. God expects no more than that."

Eliane stroked her forehead; the subterfuge seemed to weigh heavily. "The world's gone mad."

"One of many reasons why we must rid the earth of those Nazis who threaten our lives." He emptied his glass. "Don't worry, Eliane. You're a strong woman; you can carry this off. If you need any help...no matter when...I'll be there for you...until our struggle against the occupiers is over."

She stared at the priest. "You're with the Résistance."

"I'm with France to liberate her from the tyranny of Fascism. It's my duty to protect my flock in every way possible."

"Thank you for helping me."

Father Milani stood and faced her. "May the good Lord protect you."

She watched him walk across the road towards the church, convinced he was involved with the Résistance more than he was prepared to admit. Snippets of conversation in the town inferred that the local Maquis was gaining in strength and numbers since the Germans had occupied the free zone. There had been several incidents in the area of Limoges but locally, nothing of consequence had yet happened to enrage the German presence in and around Bellac. The soldiers who occupied the town behaved more like tourists, purchasing goods and souvenirs in the shops, frequenting the bars and distributing chocolate to children.

Beneath this semblance of calm, however, there lurked an undercurrent of unease and distrust amongst the resident population. The sudden presence of enemy troops two months earlier had initially stirred an air of curiosity, followed by passive acceptance. The mood in the town was beginning to change towards resentment, a sentiment that members of the Résistance were ready to exploit.

Chapter 7

Haute Vienne
1943

Eliane spent the next two weeks, sowing the seeds of her proposed adoption. Only her parents, Anne-Marie and Father Milani were acquainted with the truth. She wondered how her husband would greet the news that he had acquired a son during his captivity.

"I hope he doesn't think I've had an affair during his absence," she joked with Anne-Marie. Her friend thought it would be more prudent to ask the priest to explain the detail; after all, it was his idea.

In a more relaxed mood, having received Sebastien's documents, the two young women had taken the children to Oradour-sur-Glane to spend the day with Anne-Marie's father. It was a chilly but sunny Saturday, always a busy market day in the town. They had lunch at Hôtel Milord on the main street before passing time walking along the banks of the river Glane. Later, outside the post office, they caught a tram that rattled down rue Emile Désourteaux towards Limoges, where, after a stroll through the Jardins de l'Evèche, they boarded the train to Bellac, arriving home with two very sleepy children. Carrying the weary toddlers, they walked the short distance to Saint Sauveur. Because of the curfew, Anne-Marie decided to stay overnight, preferring to cycle home the following morning.

Despite her original discomfort in implementing Father Milani's outrageous suggestions, Eliane began to discover more freedom and relaxation since 'inheriting a son'. There were the usual squabbles between the youngsters but generally, they were well-behaved under difficult circumstances. Although food was in short supply in many areas, especially since the Germans had entered the free zone, inhabitants of rural areas found adequate supplies of fruit and vegetables, together with the occasional chicken or pork fillet. Sometimes when demand outstripped supply, commodities depended on the *marché noir* or the barter system. However, under Eliane's careful management, the children were well-nourished. Life for Eliane Tricot seemed to have improved since the turn of the year.

*****

Now known to others in the resistance network as Zeta—her *nom de guerre* in her role of safe house provider—Anne-Marie had received her first 'lodger'. The young man was an American navigator, whose aircraft had been shot down on a bombing mission over St. Nazaire on 3rd January. Shepherded through enemy-occupied territory by members of various resistance groups, he was en route to the border with Spain where a *passeur* would guide him and other evaders or escapers to safety across the Pyrénées. Though Anne-Marie had become part of a network, she had no knowledge of others who were involved. Guides, who brought and collected people needing temporary accommodation, used *noms de guerre* and communicated very little. Proud to be involved, she viewed her commitment as a form of retaliation against the Boche for the death of her husband. The only person in whom she confided was Eliane, who would have loved to have been in a similar situation but for the continued presence of Rausch.

On the day the British 8th Army regained Tripoli from General Erwin Rommel's retreating Afrika Corps, a car swept into the tranquil village of Saint Sauveur. Driven by SS-Standartenführer Rausch, it drew to a halt outside Eliane Tricot's house. This German officer was not retreating; on the contrary, he was about to advance further into her life.

Hearing the vehicle, Eliane peered through an upstairs window. Her heart skipped a beat, an instinctive reaction to the moment she had dreaded since Father Milani's visit. Without thinking, she checked her appearance in the mirror on the wardrobe door before descending to answer his knock on the door.

She trembled slightly as their eyes met. He smiled confidently; she blushed nervously. Without any invitation, he stepped inside, whilst offering greetings for the year ahead.

"I have news. As expected, your husband is once again a guest in one of our prisoner of war camps. He is currently working for the Reich. I have requested his release on the condition that, following his return to France, he will continue working for Germany in his capacity as a telephone engineer. I anticipate his repatriation will take place within the next two months."

Eliane felt relieved but at the same time agitated. A lot could happen during two months. Would Jean-Claude survive imprisonment long enough to see his family again? Would the officer keep his word?

"Thank you for all your help," she uttered, concerned by the colonel's obvious position of complete control over her emotional state.

"You should celebrate your good fortune," he replied, striding across the room towards the wood-burning stove. He removed his leather gloves before warming his hands.

She realised the officer intended to prolong his visit. "Yes, yes...of course. Can I offer you a drink?" She turned away from the intense stare that seemed to follow her every movement. "I'm afraid it's either coffee or Cognac."

"Cognac sounds perfect."

Drawing a chair towards him, Rausch sprawled by the table, stretching his black leather boots across the tiled floor. At that moment, Sylvie and Sebastien appeared. Trying to appear relaxed, Eliane took two glasses and an almost empty bottle of Cognac from the dresser.

"Good morning, Sylvie," Rausch bent forward to gently stroke the youngster's fair hair before turning his attention to Sebastien. "And who is your new friend?"

Sylvie ran to her mother, shyly wrapping her arms around Eliane's legs, whilst continuing to stare at their visitor. Sebastien stood still, his eyes glued on the uniformed soldier.

"This is my son, Sebastien," Eliane said, nonchalantly passing a glass of Cognac to Rausch.

"You never said you had a son."

"You never asked."

Rausch sipped his brandy. "So where have you been hiding him?"

Eliane felt a sudden shiver...*he knows*...but tried to remain calm. "He was in hospital and later, convalescing but was discharged in time for Christmas."

"I'm surprised your parents never mentioned his illness. What was the problem?"

"Oh, nothing serious. It was a small operation to remove his tonsils and adenoids, following an infection."

"Who is the elder?" He laughed.

"The boy," she replied without thinking.

"They could be twins."

For a split second, her mind went blank. "They are twins...but the boy was the first by several minutes," she added apprehensively.

"How very interesting. Well, they'll soon be reunited with their father, provided he doesn't attempt another escape."

"He hasn't seen them. They were born after his mobilisation."

"Is he aware that he has become a father in his absence?"

"I've written several letters but received only one reply shortly after his capture almost three years ago."

Rausch finished his Cognac, stood and walked towards the door. With an expression of smug satisfaction, he turned to face her. "Well, these two little ones should put a smile on your husband's face. My good deed for the day; you can thank me on my next visit."

He clicked his heels, bowed slightly and strode confidently towards his car.

With a pounding heart, Eliane stood in the doorway, gripping the children's hands as they watched him drive away. Dreading the prospect of his promised return, she emptied her glass before sinking with mixed emotions into an armchair. He seemed to have accepted the story of David's false identity, but still hinted at some form of recompense. Was it merely bravado, she wondered…or a more sinister threat? Her earlier euphoria about life returning to some kind of normality had rapidly subsided since the reappearance of SS-Standartenführer Rausch.

The children clambered onto her lap; she drew comfort from their innocence and unconditional love. Whatever the future held, they must be protected at all costs.

*****

Like many people, Eliane preferred the summer months with warm sunshine, longer daylight hours and a more convivial lifestyle. In contrast, the harsh winters with extended darkness, boredom from evenings spent in isolation and extra measures to keep warm created frustration and occasional periods of depression. After bathing and putting the children to bed, she craved company to while away the long dark nights, made even gloomier by the blackout restrictions. With radios forbidden, there was little else in the way of entertainment. To occupy her mind, she would read, often wrapping herself in blankets by the wood burner, before retiring to an icy bedroom, a cold bed and the loneliness of a temporary 'war widow'.

In some ways, she envied Anne-Marie with her 'safe-house', a risky situation but one that brought periods of companionship until her 'guest' moved on. Despite its associated dangers, she viewed her friend's role as an exciting diversion from the constant drudgery of occupation. It was in this despondent atmosphere that Rausch's visits gradually became a welcome antidote to the tedium of her life. Over the unfolding weeks, even though news of her husband's release date had not yet arrived, she began looking forward to the engaging young officer's company.

Flattered by his charm, the young woman found it hard to resist his amorous advances. On each occasion that he tried to seduce her with gifts and compliments, she had to summon all her will-power to prevent the relationship developing into something she would forever regret. For the handsome colonel, Eliane had become a challenge. SS soldiers were proud of their successes; failure was not acceptable in taking up such gauntlets, especially those concerning their manhood. Rausch could no longer hold back his affectionate desires.

Eliane's resolution was in vain; she succumbed, allowing him to desecrate her body and numb her mind. She offered no resistance. The following night, she never slept; nausea and guilt tormented her. When dawn broke, she craved for the darkness to return, to engulf the trauma of her compliance to his self-gratification.

Rausch felt no shame; he believed their intimacy had evolved from love, not lust. Perhaps under different circumstances, it may have been time to move on. However, there was unfinished business at Saint Sauveur with regard to her husband's repatriation. Despite the warning from Anne-Marie's father about hollow promises, Eliane would discover this German intended to fulfil his pledge.

Almost two weeks passed before his next visit. He informed her that Jean-Claude's repatriation was imminent but as at that moment he was unable to give the exact date of his return. Expecting to provide him with a further instalment on her debt, she was surprised at his coolness towards her. She convinced herself that one night of lust had satisfied his male desire for dominance; she believed and hoped he would not trouble her again.

The next weekend, an unexpected event interrupted this strange period of indifference between them. The atmosphere seemed edgy, as though the cannons on both sides, primed ready for firing, only required someone or something to light the fuse, to rouse the latent passion. Rausch brought the news she had craved for almost three years: the authorities had scheduled Jean-Claude's return for Thursday, 11th March.

She restrained herself from kissing him, perhaps distracted by her two children running naked around the living room; for them it was their normal playful prelude to bath-time. At first Rausch seemed amused but, as Eliane tried to thank him profusely for her husband's release, his previously relaxed demeanour changed.

He gripped her shoulder, spinning her round to face him. His steely blue eyes glared at her so intensely that she recoiled away from him. Her mouth became dry. His grip tightened. She felt pain, sensual pain not physical pain.

The children seemed responsive towards the mood change; having stopped running, they stood innocently staring at their mother. A wave of panic swept over her.

Rausch pointed at Sebastien's naked body. "Why has the boy been circumcised?" he demanded, shaking her violently.

Eliane understood his sudden anger but not the sadness in his eyes.

Chapter 8

Berneuil, Haute Vienne
1943

Dark rain clouds appeared in the distance. Eliane felt the first biting droplets on her face as she alternately free-wheeled and pedalled down the hill into the village. Turning by the church, she followed the road past the cemetery back into open countryside. By the time she reached Anne-Marie's house, the rain was falling heavily. Leaning the bicycle against the wall of the outbuilding, she dashed through the downpour to the main house.

A loud thumping on the door startled her friend, sending shivers down her spine. Since receiving spurious guests, Anne-Marie had feared every unexpected visitor. She withdrew the bolts to find a tearful, bedraggled Eliane; breathless and seemingly extremely agitated, her distressed friend tumbled past her. Anne-Marie locked and bolted the door before hugging her, overcome by a mixture of relief and anxiety.

"Eliane, what's happened?"

Exhausted, her visitor slumped into an armchair, burying her head in her hands. "He knows...he knows everything," she exclaimed, trying to catch her breath and sobbing at the same time.

"Knows what...who knows?" Anne-Marie knelt beside her, stroking her shoulder.

"Rausch," she whispered. "He knows about David...I mean Sebastien. He knows he's a Jew."

"Oh, my God." Anne-Marie stepped away, looking towards the door as though she expected Rausch to burst in at any moment. "Who told him?"

Eliane shook her head. "He saw him running around naked playing with Sylvie; it was bath-time. Immediately, he noticed that he had been circumcised."

"The sly bastard!" She flopped distraught into an adjacent chair. "You'll be arrested...and your family...and your friends...shit!" Her own position suddenly seemed vulnerable. "What are we going to do?" She stood up again, a puzzled expression on her face. "But you're here...and where are the children? What about your parents?" She knelt by Eliane again. "What did he say? What's he going to do about it?"

Eliane wiped the tears from her face; her eyes were bloodshot from crying so much. "The children are safe for the time being; they're with maman and papa." She took a deep breath before burying her head in her hands. "I think Rausch is implying that having regular sex with me would guarantee his silence," she mumbled.

"Typical Boche! That's what they do...they manipulate and intimidate people just to satisfy their evil demands...no respect whatsoever...arrogant bastards." She patted Eliane's hand to console her. "You should never have entertained him in the first place." Gradually, the hint of a smile appeared. "Mind you, it would be better than being arrested, interrogated and shot." She stood and crossed to a cupboard, removed a bottle of wine and two glasses. Her warm smile barely concealed her relief. "You never know...you may enjoy it."

"I have already."

"Oh my God!" She poured the wine, handing a glass to Eliane.

"It happened before he knew about David."

"Tell me more."

"He took advantage of me a couple of weeks ago when he came with the date of Jean-Claude's repatriation. I suppose I was so grateful, my defences were down. I tried to resist but he forced himself upon me. Looking back, I suppose I did little to discourage him. I felt terrible afterwards but consoled myself with the thought that Jean-Claude would be home soon, and I'd be able to put the nightmare behind me. Now this has changed everything."

"But when your husband returns..."

"Rausch promised he would say nothing." She sipped some wine. "They're forbidden to cohabit with French women but, if I were to report him, I'd be signing my own death warrant, and placing everyone else in jeopardy...probably you too."

"My God, you make him seem like a really evil bastard." She topped up her glass. "What if I asked my resistance contacts to arrange his disappearance?"

"You mean kill him?"

"Why not? I'm sure they could organise something that wouldn't reflect on you or your family."

"There would be terrible retribution...I've heard they shoot ten hostages in retaliation for the death of one Boche soldier...probably more for an SS officer." Eliane shook her head. "I couldn't have that on my conscience."

Anne-Marie leaned back in her chair. "It's ironic, isn't it? A few years ago before we were both married, if your colonel Rausch is as handsome as you say, we'd have been fighting each other for the offer of unlimited sex with him."

Eliane sighed deeply. "What a mess. There are so many people's lives at stake that I can't refuse. Let's hope he gets transferred."

"And, in the meantime, enjoy the pleasure!"

Eliane glared at her friend. "You're incorrigible."

"Surely, he'll back off when Jean-Claude returns. If he discovers what's going on, he won't think twice about killing him. How are you going to keep it secret?"

"Apparently, according to Rausch, Jean-Claude must return to his previous job but this time working for the Germans. I assume he'll ensure my husband will be fully occupied…probably able to check the times when he can take advantage of me."

"I thought I was taking a risk accommodating fugitives but your situation…shit! That's far more precarious. What if he changes his mind or you can't satisfy him any more?"

Eliane sniggered, albeit nervously. "I've had no complaints so far in my brief promiscuous life." Tears welled again. "But you're right. He could abandon the idea at any time and denounce us. I'm worried I may not have the stamina to satisfy him with that threat hanging over me. He keeps asking what else I am hiding. It's as though he's become more inquisitive…no, not inquisitive…more possessive…like a jealous lover." She shivered before sipping more wine. "I'm sorry to burst in like this…is there anyone staying?"

"Shit! I told him to hide in the orchard when I heard you coming up the path."

"He'll be soaked out there." She glanced through the window. "It's still pouring down."

Anne-Marie grinned and drained her glass. "So engrossed with your catastrophe that I've forgotten the poor sod."

"Whoever he is, you'd better fetch him in."

Anne-Marie disappeared, returning with a rain-soaked man in a navy sweater and grey trousers. She threw him a towel. "Sorry, false alarm…it was just my friend."

The man acknowledged Eliane with a curt nod before wiping the excess water from his balding head and dripping face. He turned towards the staircase.

69

Anne-Marie poured another glass of wine before inviting him to sit near the wood burner. "Join us for a drink whilst you dry off by the fire. My friend was just cycling by and dropped in to say hello."

"On a bicycle...in this weather?" He looked across at Eliane. "You must be mad."

He spoke French but with a strange accent. Eliane guessed he was one of the evaders on his way south. Thinking it prudent not to ask questions, she just smiled, creating an awkward silence.

Anne-Marie relieved the situation. "It's alright; we can be open with each other. My friend can be trusted." She turned to Eliane. "This gentleman has literally dropped in to support the Résistance. He'll be staying with us for some time...not here with me...but in the area."

Eliane looked him over. He could have passed for a Frenchman; well-tanned features, dark moustache, slim build. She guessed he was in his late thirties.

Anne-Marie interrupted her assessment of the stranger. "At last, we have a connection with London; events are moving in our favour. According to all the news reports we're receiving, the Germans are losing ground everywhere. Many are already suggesting the war could be over before next Christmas."

"Hmm. They said that in the Great War...and that dragged on for almost five years."

"Don't worry, Eliane. Something will turn up. Boche soldiers are not invincible. I'm sure you'll have your day of reckoning."

"Am I missing something?" the agent enquired, concerned his host was saying too much. He continued to warm his hands over the stove.

Anne-Marie grinned. "You don't want to know. My friend's in deep trouble but, knowing her as I do, I have great confidence she'll find a way to resolve the problem." She reached for the wine bottle; it was empty. "Let's open another bottle and drink to a Boche-free France."

The agent seemed ill at ease. He studied Eliane whilst his host crossed to a cabinet beneath the window. "Are you also with the Résistance?"

Before she could answer, Anne-Marie brought over another bottle of wine. "Not at all...just the opposite. Eliane entertains German soldiers." She smiled as an expression of incredulity appeared on her guest's face.

Eliane glared at her. "That's not fair." She faced the stranger. "A German officer is billeted with my parents. He occasionally visits me because he's arranging the release of my husband, a prisoner of war."

"I know it's none of my business," the man said, "but isn't your involvement with an enemy soldier rather risky...given your association with a member of the Résistance?"

Anne-Marie laughed. "He's not just any old soldier; he's a colonel in the SS."

The agent looked concerned. "The Schutzstaffeln? Hitler's security? That's even more dangerous."

Eliane tried to soothe the situation. "He's attached to some department in this area's Kommandantur; it collects data on public opinion for Vichy. He's not with the Gestapo or anything like that."

Anne-Marie was enjoying the repartee. "She fancies him really. Mind you, I don't blame her. From her description, he seems quite tasty. Having said that, the American airman that stayed here recently was quite handsome, and far less intimidating than an SS officer."

Take no notice of her." Eliane hesitated. "I'm sorry; I don't know your name."

"Just call me Hector." The man began to feel somewhat perplexed, not expecting such an open conversation. As an S.O.E. agent, he would have been trained to be discreet at all times. During any training at Beaulieu, there would have been major emphasis on the importance of tight security, whereas here were two young women openly sharing confidential information that could incriminate others if they were caught and interrogated. Anne-Marie only knew that the Allies had sent him over to prepare the circuit for the impending invasion. Another agent, a wireless operator would be joining him to provide telegraphy links with London.

"Well, Hector. I apologise for my friend's flippant remarks. I am only tolerating the officer to bring about my husband's release."

The agent leaned forwards from his chair by the wood burner. "I only arrived here yesterday. For all you know, I could be a German spy. During the past fifteen minutes, I have learned you are involved with an SS officer who, working for the local Kommandantur, is trying to get your husband released...perhaps unofficially...I don't know. I am also aware that an American airman recently passed through this safe house, presumably on his way to Spain."

He stood and walked towards the stairs. "I hope neither of you chat with friends or family about these issues, and specifically about my presence here. If the Gestapo or the S.S. gets a whiff of your involvement, you will be cruelly tortured to give up every detail of information that might be useful to them. They will interrogate not just you, but also your friends, relatives and everyone else with whom you have contact. In such circumstances, death would be a welcome release. I tell you this because I know about their barbaric methods."

He opened the door to the staircase. "Think about what I have said. You are both involved with a movement that is vital to defeat the enemy. Be extra wary of putting yourselves and others at risk." He faced Anne-Marie. "Someone will be picking me up at mid-day. In the meantime, talk about the weather or something trivial."

He disappeared upstairs to a room furnished with a double bed surmounted by an enormous oak headboard, a heavy oak wardrobe and a dresser adorned by a porcelain jug and washbowl. Closed wooden shutters guaranteed gloomy privacy with basic facilities.

Eliane turned to her friend; she was not impressed. "What a rude man, telling us how to behave in our country. Who does he think he is?"

Anne-Marie sat in the chair by the wood burner. "I suppose he has a point. We should be more careful about what we say...and to whom we say it. It appears he must have been here before...probably with another circuit."

"Do you think he's been interrogated by the Gestapo?"

"What makes you ask that?"

"He seemed to know how brutal they can be...unless..."

"Unless what?"

"Could he be a German spy, an infiltrator, a Gestapo agent? He did say that he could be a spy...perhaps, just to confuse us."

Anne-Marie looked thoughtful. "Do you think we should warn whoever is coming to pick him up?"

Eliane shrugged. "We have no proof. Surely your resistance friends will check him out."

"I'll make some coffee. Returning to what we were discussing earlier, what do you intend to do about Rausch?"

"It's an impossible situation. The only solutions are his transfer, an Allied victory or the man's death. None are on the immediate horizon, so it seems like an impasse, unless you have any ideas."

"I'd kill the bastard but, as you pointed out earlier, the consequences would be horrific." She put a pan of water on the hob. "You could stay here with me. He wouldn't dare to try it on with me as a witness. You could make the excuse that I'm unwell, and you have offered to care for me."

"I suppose that would work until Jean-Claude returns."

"At least, when your husband's back at home, his opportunities will be limited. You never know, he might lose interest."

Eliane smiled. "Are you sure about my moving in here with two children?"

"Why not? Once Hector's on his way this afternoon, what's to stop you?"

"Rausch will be suspicious."

"Tell him it'll be for just a short time until I'm feeling better. Surely, he can keep it in his pants for a day or two."

Eliane giggled. "No matter how serious the situation, you always see the funny side. What shall I say is ailing you?"

"It can't be anything contagious because of the children. What about a broken arm or a leg, something that prevents me from looking after myself?"

"Knowing Rausch, he would come here to check if I was being truthful. You would need to be hobbling around with your leg in plaster."

"So, I borrow a crutch from Doctor Jerome or ask him to make a sling for my arm. You can tell Rausch I fell off a ladder in the barn."

"I doubt Doctor Jerome will agree to provide you with a crutch or a sling for no reason. Anyway, how do know my doctor?"

"No problem; he's one of us."

"My God, is everyone in the Résistance?"

"The circuit needs a doctor for wounded fighters. Apparently, he was extremely pleased to volunteer. He has a makeshift hospital in the forest." She poured the coffee. "By the way, I take a long time to heal...an excuse to extend your stay."

"What if you receive an escaper or another agent like our friend upstairs?"

"No problem. They'll have to use the barn; there's plenty of straw and the odd rat to keep them warm. It's a better proposition than languishing in Limoges prison or Gestapo headquarters."

"You're like papa...an answer for everything."

"That's settled, then. I'll get the necessary from Doctor Jerome, and you can break the good news to Rausch."

"I'll tell my parents; they can explain to the colonel. That way, it'll be less confrontational, and I won't have to answer any intrusive questions that he's bound to ask if we're face to face."

"There you go...problem solved."

"I just hope Rausch believes it."

"Your papa can be very convincing. I hope he's not averse to telling lies."

Eliane smiled. "I'll be telling the lies. It's a case of maman and papa believing my story about your incapacity."

"Since the occupation, it seems everyone has rejected the truth in order to survive. You and I are already living a lie, and all my other acquaintances are compulsive liars, leading double lives. Surely, it was never like this before the Boche arrived."

"I'm afraid trust disappeared when Adolf Hitler came to power. Hopefully, an Allied victory will restore our faith in humanity."

Anne-Marie scoffed. "And I'll guarantee all who collaborated, including traitors like Pétain and Laval will swear they were not working alongside the Nazis."

Eliane finished her coffee. "I am so angry we have to live like criminals. I never lied until the Boche took control of our country. Before all this, we were just ordinary people living ordinary lives. Look at us now...involved in these awful secret activities. I shall be forever trapped in dark memories of deceit and lies. Our lives weren't meant to be like this. Even Father Milani, the local priest seems to be involved. He brought David's false documents. What's the world coming to when you can't trust the church?"

"I thought you had faith in your priest."

"He did say he would be there for me if I ever needed help...but everyone says that, don't they? Yet, when you're in desperate need of assistance, they let you down. I don't suppose he's any different." She glanced through the window. "The rain's stopped. I should go. Thanks to you, there's a lot to arrange. I'll ask Papa to drive us here with our luggage; I hope he has sufficient coupons."

Anne-Marie hugged her friend. "My guest is leaving today, so come as soon as you can make arrangements. I fancy your colonel has finally met his match. We'll just have to be more devious than he is."

Part Two

Gare Bénédictins, Limoges

Chapter 9

Haute Vienne
1943

Despite the usual menacing presence of German soldiers and the accompanying groups of Sicherheitsdienst officers, the Gare Bénédictins at Limoges seemed more crowded than normal. To a stranger, it must have appeared to be just like another busy day at a major railway station. However, for a few families gathered on the concourse, this day in early March 1943 held a special significance. As smoke belched from an approaching locomotive, an air of expectation bubbled beneath the perceptible tense surface. The general buzz of activity increased as people flocked towards the platform where the incoming train had slithered to a grinding, steaming halt. Necks craned to glimpse the alighting passengers. The military presence stiffened its resolve in anticipation of any over-reaction.

Emerging from clouds of steam, passengers began to appear, some with baggage, some with children, some wearing the grey-green uniforms of the Wehrmacht. In the midst of this mass exodus, a small group of emaciated, wearisome men walked nervously towards the barrier, accompanied by three soldiers. Four haggard individuals, each carrying a brown paper parcel, their ill-fitting clothes draped over their skeletal bodies, passed unchecked onto the concourse where photographers rushed forwards to capture the moment for the Nazi propaganda machine. Waiting families fought through the ensuing scrum to greet their loved ones; in floods of tears, they welcomed home the ex-prisoners of war. German officials looked on with expressions of smug satisfaction as this latest batch added credibility to Vichy's perceived success of the *relève*, the system introduced by Sauckel in his role as Reich Minister to exchange prisoners for the much-needed labour force to aid the war effort.

Several months earlier, 3,000 inhabitants of Limoges had thronged the town centre in silent protest against the principles of the *relève*. This contrived method of repatriation, though welcomed by the few recipient families, held little comfort for the majority, despite the German authorities using the publicity generated by this homecoming event as an opportunity to dispel that antagonism.

A young woman, desperately clutching the hands of two tiny children, recognised her husband despite his changed appearance after more than two years in captivity. With tears streaming down her flushed cheeks, Eliane jostled through the crowd to embrace his brittle body. Jean-Claude Tricot's vacant expression of relief concealed the deep resentment that had strengthened his will to survive. Sparing him the confusing details, she introduced him to the children he had never seen; this was not the moment to explain the complex deception. Several emotion-charged moments passed before she was able to usher him towards the domed exit where the mayor of Bellac—not wishing to miss an opportunity for promoting his public image—waited patiently beside his car. Petrol having become restricted even to some in officialdom, he had still offered to drive them home in his gazogene-converted Peugeot motor vehicle. A local photographer stood nearby to capture the moment for the local press.

Looking on from the main entrance, SS-Standartenführer Rausch lit another cigarette. Exhaling smoke from the first draw, a smile spread across his face; the gift he had promised had finally arrived. Eliane Tricot would be returning to Saint Sauveur, and eventually, after a short period of rehabilitation, her husband would find himself working again. The power over inconsequential lives relaxed him. He was in a position to manipulate people, so why not use it to his advantage. Besides, it was all part of his plan. His annoyance at Eliane's decision to relocate to Berneuil had subsided several weeks earlier after successfully arranging a work contract for her husband. Now he could spend some time recouping the reward for his efforts in the community.

Almost six weeks would pass before Jean-Claude regained his former strength, and could cope mentally not only with the horror he had endured in the prisoner of war camps, but also with the strange world to which he had returned. Bouts of depression and a recurrence of severe pain from his original leg wound had delayed his recovery longer than expected. He rarely ventured from the house during his recuperation, relying on the occasional visit from Father Milani to administer his version of pastoral care: sharing cigarettes and a small flask of brandy. Of course, Doctor Jerome stopped by on a regular basis to provide appropriate medical treatment and black market nourishment. Apart from what he considered unnecessary calls by the German officer whose intervention had apparently secured his release, they became his only contacts with the world beyond the protective shutters.

The convoluted tale regarding David's covert metamorphosis to Sebastien shocked him; he was unaware of the depth of anti-Semitism across France. Coming to terms with having a two-year-old daughter was difficult; accepting a distant relative as his son was even more painful to accept. However, having witnessed SS atrocities first hand, he understood the family's concern for the child's welfare.

Although relieved by her husband's return, Eliane sensed an invasion of her routine, as though she had lost the liberty experienced during his long absence. Whatever the cause of her confusion, she cast her thoughts to one side to focus on her role of caring spouse. Nursing her husband back to health became her priority. However, in occasional moments of reflection, that underlying resentment towards his presence was never far from her subconscious.

After weeks confined to the house with few visitors, he sensed an atmosphere of isolation from the neighbourhood in contrast to the close community he had left behind, following his mobilisation. The presence of the Germans seemed to have destroyed the social spirit that existed prior to hostilities. Those random calls by colonel Rausch also appeared to aggravate the situation at a personal level. When Jean-Claude questioned his wife about the frequency of the soldier's visits, her explanation about his intervention helping to secure his release seemed a lame excuse. Nor was she able to offer any reason why he had chosen to facilitate this specific case. Her only defence was to suggest his visits were to determine when he would be fit enough to recommence work for the Germans as part of the agreement.

She explained how she had met the soldier after the Wehrmacht had entered the free zone during the previous November, adding that some higher-ranking officers had been billeted amongst families with spare rooms because of insufficient accommodation in the area. Consequently, the grandiose *maison de campagne* belonging to her parents near Les Singuelles had been commandeered to provide temporary lodging for SS-Standartenführer Rausch. With reluctance, Jean-Claude accepted how the young man had infiltrated their lives but remained steadfast in his deep-rooted hatred for the Boche.

She emphasised their first, rather unfriendly encounter but admitted that, after realising he could assist in securing his release, she decided to tolerate his intrusion into her life. Indeed, his polite manners, together with the interest afforded towards the children, were not what she had expected from a member of the occupying forces. However, she thought it prudent not to admit that on the few occasions she had encountered the colonel, he had been quite attentive towards her.

After hearing how his wife's determined efforts had secured his release, he accepted, albeit reluctantly, the reason for the awkward situation created by the German officer's familiarity with his family. Deep down, however, he sensed there were other issues lurking beneath the simple account of what must have been a complicated negotiation. He had learned that at every level, from Pétain downwards, there appeared to have been compliance and collaboration regarding the prisoner exchange policy. How far it extended at this level and to what degree would plague his mind for the immediate future.

Unwilling to undermine his wife's perseverance in befriending the SS officer to secure his release, he decided not to reveal the brutal atrocities he had witnessed. Although his determination to kill Nazis had not diminished, SS-Standartenführer Rausch would not fall victim to his vow of retribution for Emile. He convinced himself there would be other opportunities, once he had recovered sufficiently from his injuries.

*****

A light but cool drizzle greeted Jean-Claude as he took his first steps from the house into a town still striving to maintain some vestige of normality since the previous year's occupation. As he walked towards the church, it became obvious that people either made an effort to ignore him or regarded him with a look of disdain. The woman at the bakery acknowledged him briefly before turning away. The butcher, the normally verbose Monsieur Joliot, nodded curtly as he passed by the open doorway of his shop. Though still walking with a slight limp, he quickened his pace, eager to ask Father Milani why those he had known before the war seemed intent on avoiding him as though he was carrying some infectious disease.

The priest welcomed the ex-soldier before drawing him into a quiet corner of the chancel.

"You seem preoccupied, Jean-Claude. Are you sure you're ready to venture out alone?"

"What's going on, Father? The whole town seems to be opposed to my returning home. It's as though they're resentful that I am one of the lucky recipients of Pétain's deal with the Germans."

"Sit down, my friend. You need to catch up with events since your capture and imprisonment." He guided him to a nearby pew before sitting alongside. "Initially, the concept of the free zone resulting from the terms of the armistice seemed a reasonable outcome for two-thirds of France. However, I'm afraid Adolf Hitler outwitted our beloved Maréchal and his Vichy colleagues. With each passing month, it's becoming more apparent that our self-elected ministers are collaborating with the Nazis, just as Pétain demonstrated following his meeting with the Führer at Montoire, where he accepted the principles of collaboration."

"But what has that to do with me?"

"Sadly, your wife's zeal to secure your release involved the services of a German officer. Many in the town perceive your release as a product of her collaboration with the enemy, and naturally, that sentiment tars you with the same brush."

"Eliane loves me, Father. She merely grasped the unexpected opportunity that confronted her. As you know, she has spent the past few weeks convincing me that the arrangement with Rausch was purely to gain my release."

"I fear you are both paying the price."

Jean-Claude leaned forwards, burying his head in his hands. "I owe my freedom to my wife. How can I put things right?"

The priest placed his arm across the shoulders of his friend. "There is a way to resolve the issue. Unfortunately, it involves an activity that you must keep secret, but you will be able to satisfy your own conscience and prove to a select few where your allegiances lie. In time, others will learn about your total rejection of collaboration. It's a chance to salvage your reputation."

"What about my wife?"

"I'm sure that, in time, people will forgive her."

Jean-Claude's eyes were moist; he turned to face the priest, seeking reassurance. "Forgive her, Father? She rescued me from hell...forgive her for what?"

"For inviting the Boche into your house."

"I am led to believe he was billeted with her parents."

The priest shrugged. "Everyone is aware of the circumstances, and can understand any fervent pleas she might have made for your release...but...you know how people gossip in a small community like this."

"So, why would they consider what she had done to be collaboration? Surely, she had committed an act of compassion."

Father Milani chose his words carefully. "Some speculated on what he had received in return for his intervention in your release." He clutched Jean-Claude's arm. "Just unfounded rumours by petty people. You should ignore them...try to forgive them...focus on rebuilding your lives together as a family."

Jean-Claude sat silently with his hands on his knees; he could not feel the pain as his finger nails dug into the flesh beneath his cloth trousers.

"I'm sorry. I know your wife would never err from the path of righteousness. Eliane is a good woman. You should be proud of her."

Despite the latter comments, the priest's words hurt. He felt nauseous, his chest tightened, his heart beat fiercely, moisture filled his eyes. He turned away from the priest, his head filled with an image of the German officer embracing his wife...or worse.

Father Milani broke the silence. "It's just idle gossip, Jean-Claude. Remember, there are men from Bellac and the surrounding villages still in captivity. There is bound to be some jealousy and resentment over what your wife has achieved on your behalf."

Distraught, Jean-Claude was not listening. He turned to face the priest. "You said earlier there was a way to counter the smears...you know...all this nonsense of collaboration."

The priest nodded, pleased that his friend had omitted any reference to his wife's perceived infidelity. "How aware are you of the activities of the Résistance in this area?"

"I've been away a long time, Father. What do you think?" He smiled. "Don't tell me you're involved."

He ignored the comment. "Would you be interested?"

"I suppose my participation may quell the rumours but how can I contact them?"

"I can organise a meeting but you cannot discuss it with anyone...including Eliane. Trust is vital for survival and, the less she knows, the better for her. Leave it with me. I'll speak to someone who can help."

"But won't they reject me if everyone believes my wife is a collaborator?"

"Not after I have stated your case." The priest stood. "You were a telephone engineer before the war, weren't you? Those skills will be most welcome."

"Apparently, part of the deal involving my repatriation is that I return to my previous occupation...for the Boche, of course. Rausch has been making regular visits to check on my progress. I think he knows I am fit enough to start work again."

"Excellent. You'll be able to keep up-to-date with the latest developments...inside knowledge is always useful."

The two men shook hands, one pleased to have recruited a useful asset to his local Maquis group, the other with mixed emotions about confronting his wife.

*****

Gathering speed whilst grimacing with every turn of the pedals, Jean-Claude sped down the hill towards the river Vincou. Earlier, Eliane had complained about his leaving at such a late hour; it would be dark soon. He had insisted. It was about returning to work with the telephone company.

"But I thought the Germans were organising that as part of the deal. Why must you return to your old job?" she demanded.

81

"The Germans could send me anywhere to carry out telephone maintenance and repair work...even back to Germany. I need to prove I have honoured their demands by already being employed...locally."

In fact, Father Milani, aware of the situation, had swiftly arranged employment for him with the telephone company, principally to outsmart Rausch who seemed to be determined Jean-Claude should be absent from the house as often as possible. The arrangement would suit both parties but for very different reasons.

Her protests had continued. "But why is it so vital to go now in such inclement weather?"

"I must act before they do," he lied. "I'm meeting a supervisor to complete the necessary paperwork."

In her heart, Eliane needed him to work locally, based at home rather than in some distant part of the country; in her eyes it would create fewer opportunities for Rausch to call on her. She took care to omit that crucial factor in her attempts to reason with him. Ironically, the conflicting desires of everyone provided a harmonious cover for their individual deceitful motives. The prolonged argument finally ceased when he walked out, collected his bicycle and rode off beneath a grey cloud-laden sky that reflected his current mood.

A blustery wind caught his breath as he started the climb from the river to the town centre. Bellac sat on a promontory overlooking the valley, the church of Notre Dame rising like a guardian angel from the hilltop sprawl nestling around its towering ramparts. The head wind drove rain into his face, stinging his flesh as he battled the elements.

His anger propelled him through the adverse conditions, such was his determination to prove his commitment to the cause; the time to show solidarity was within his grasp. Following the conversation with Father Milani, he could almost taste the bitter feelings of hatred and suspicion that had invaded his thoughts. Deep down, a burning sensation festered like a germ, threatening to destroy his faltering love and affection for Eliane. What if it were true? What if his wife had returned favours to the German officer? Perhaps she preferred him to work away from home.

The thoughts that rattled around his head disgusted him. Would his faith in her be sufficient if his job were to take him away from home for long periods? Staying locally was the only option. The combination of working for the telephone company and joining the Résistance would provide opportunities to achieve both aims:

discovering the truth about Eliane's relationship with Rausch and the opportunity to kill Germans, whilst keeping alive his vow to avenge Emile.

He seemed destined to carry the pain forever. The more he thought about it, the more likely it seemed to be so. Since the initial welcome home, there had been an atmosphere, a coolness, a distraction as though his wife's thoughts were elsewhere. He could confront her, demand to know the truth, but she could be innocent. His accusation would devastate her, would destroy any trust, and that would hurt him even more, especially knowing she had devoted herself to securing his release without forfeiting her integrity. With each turn of the pedals, he agonised over the dilemma that confronted him.

Angry and tormented, he reached the grey exterior of the Hôtel Central. Inside, bluish layers of cigarette smoke hovered in the damp but warm atmosphere of the bar's interior, where he quickly spotted the gendarme with whom Father Milani had arranged a meeting. In deep conversation with another man, the police officer seemed not to notice him. In the far corner of the salon, a group of German soldiers sprawled laughing and drinking heavily around a table littered with empty glasses. They paid him no attention as he crossed to the bar where he ordered a beer. He joined the gendarme and his companion. They shook hands before he drew up a chair and sat down.

The gendarme turned to face him. "You will always address and know me as Martial. My friend here is Laroche. I know your identity but other strangers in the group will know you only by your *nom de guerre*. Do you understand?"

Jean-Claude nodded. They remained silent until the waiter who came over to serve him with his beer had returned to the bar.

Martial continued. "Have you considered a name?"

"I thought Lacloche...given my background and proposed involvement."

Martial smiled. "The connotation is evident to me but you must understand that Boche investigators are clever bastards and will make the same connection. You may think it clever but it's an open invitation to a sentence of death if the Gestapo were to pick you up."

"Father Mi...er...I mean Danté...suggested Claudius."

"That's fine; at least you should remember it easily." He lit a cigarette. "I believe you're on friendly terms with an SS officer."

"I'd hardly call it friendly. For my part, I merely tolerate him. He visits the house occasionally…too often, in fact."

"You seem uncomfortable with the situation."

"Would you be content finding your home and especially your wife constantly frequented by the enemy?"

"I'm just interested to know what aspect of the relationship concerns you. Are you worried that others might perceive you and your wife as collaborators or are you troubled by his attentiveness towards your wife?"

Jean-Claude shifted uneasily in his seat, embarrassed by the gendarme's bluntness. "I understand and accept why he is billeted with my wife's parents but resent his persistent harassment at our house."

Martial smiled. "But I hear he was instrumental in securing your release. Surely, you owe him some leeway…some gratitude."

"He's the bloody enemy. Why should I be grateful to the Boche when they took me prisoner in the first place?" Jean-Claude's annoyance was beginning to show. He lowered his voice. "See that lot over there. They may seem like normal soldiers on a night out; not at all…they're barbaric murdering bastards. I saw things in those camps that would make you want to kill every Nazi you encounter."

Laroche looked on impassively.

Leaning back in his chair, the gendarme calmly lit a cigarette. "Fortunately, I am able to detach myself from what frustrates you. You must not allow it to boil over, to obstruct the clarity of your role. You see, there is also a positive angle to your situation. Think of the advantages." He drew on his cigarette before exhaling a plume of smoke. "Let's face it. Your Boche visitor could be a source of vital information…and your wife could be the key to open the 'flood gates'. Would she be capable of exploring such possibilities?"

Jean-Claude frowned. "You want her to spy on him?"

"You can describe it as spying, I suppose. Besides, you also could play a part. Even small snippets or any loose talk could be useful to us." He sipped his beer. "What d'you reckon?"

"I have my doubts…he rarely talks about himself."

"Well, try to control the conversation. Ask him if he enjoys life over here; ask him if he misses his family or knows when he might expect to return home. Focus on mundane topics. Drop them casually into your conversations with him…make it look like 'small talk'. Such questions would appear more natural coming from your wife. It's not unusual for lonely soldiers to bare their souls to a woman…especially if they already have a soft spot for her."

"That's what I'm afraid of. Where might it lead?"

"No need. Most women have a knack of handling such situations." He sipped more beer. "Think about it. I'm sure your SS officer could be quite a useful asset to our cause."

Jean-Claude leaned across the table before lowering his voice. "There's only one problem. I haven't told Eliane about my involvement with the Résistance. Father…I mean Danté told me not to involve her."

Martial's brow furrowed. "That's good advice but where will she think you are when you go missing for several hours…especially late at night?"

"Because the Germans have taken full control of the telephone network systems, she'll believe I'm working for them; apparently, it's a condition of my release. Consequently, knowing I'm returning to my former job with the telephone company, she's aware it often involves urgent repairs and maintenance, hence the abnormal hours."

After being a silent observer throughout the conversation, Laroche finally spoke. "With regard to spying on your SS officer, tell your wife that de Gaulle has stated specifically that it is her duty to spy on him."

Jean-Claude glared at him in astonishment. "She won't believe that."

Laroche grinned. "Everyone knows that London is sending over agents, arms and finance to support the various Maquis groups. Why should she not accept spying as part of their plans?" He lowered his voice. "Whisper your proposition to her as though it's a closely guarded secret that you are disclosing. She'll be fascinated. You'll be her hero."

Martial smiled. "It's his version of silent psychology. Tell her not to ask you any questions because you are sworn to secrecy. I'll guarantee she'll buy into it."

Jean-Claude said no more. *You don't know Eliane.*

Martial stubbed out his cigarette in a tin ashtray. "Enough about the SS officer. Let's move onto other more tangible matters, starting with your assignments."

"My assignments?"

"Let me finish...I'll explain what we will expect from you, and you can give me a list of any additional materials and equipment you might need."

"You want me to write a list?"

A cynical smile spread across Laroche's face.

The gendarme grasped Jean-Claude's arm and nodded in the direction of the Germans in the far corner. "Like you indicated earlier, they're just ordinary foot soldiers on a night out but, if one entered here on duty to check everyone's identity papers, he might be accompanied by a member of the *milice*, a gendarme or even someone from the Sicherheitsdienst."

He sipped some beer. "Any one of those could ask you not only to show I.D. but also to empty your pockets. It's vital to never carry anything with you that could incriminate you or make them suspicious. If you need to carry something that might be a problem, ensure you have a watertight cover story for having it on your person. The S.D. is well-drilled in identifying and interrogating suspects, even over insignificant scraps of paper containing a list of innocent items."

He sipped more beer. "You'll soon realise how difficult these bastards have made our lives now you are back in circulation. They even stop people on the street for no reason."

Jean-Claude said nothing, already aware of the problems the German occupation had created in his own life. Listening to Martial only reinforced his perception of the fragility of the step he was about to take.

"When will you be prepared and ready to start?"

"I intend to re-apply for my job tomorrow. That shouldn't be a problem; I've heard they're desperate for qualified technicians. If I can tell Rausch...our SS officer...that I am employed locally, there's less chance of him sending me to Limoges or farther afield. As soon as I'm in situ, I'll check what equipment I've received, and contact you with a list of any additions I may require...depending on what you expect from me. This may sound stupid but how will I communicate with you in future to ask for help or receive an additional item securely without raising any suspicion?"

"We use several dead-letter-boxes...drops where you can leave or find messages, hide or collect materials and equipment, et cetera. For example, in the cemetery near you, there's a grave with an old iron casket next to the headstone; it serves such a purpose. Danté will acquaint you with it and other drops that you may find useful."

Jean-Claude looked across at Laroche who had remained silent for most of the short exchanges between himself and the gendarme. Apart from his one interruption about de Gaulle, the man had spent the time studying him. He finished his beer and, rising from the table, reached across to shake their hands. He seemed to nod to confirm his accord with Jean-Claude's involvement before leaving. Hesitating at the doorway, he turned up the collar on his jacket, stepped out into the pouring rain and headed towards the railway station.

Having waited until after Laroche had left, Martial commented on the man's behaviour. "Don't worry about Laroche. A man of few words; he lets the explosives do the talking."

Jean-Claude forced a smile. He was more bothered about his relationship with Eliane than with Laroche. He began to wonder why he had allowed himself to become involved in such a clandestine way of life just to restore his wife's reputation. Nevertheless, the additional opportunity to kill Germans more than compensated.

"Another beer?" Martial interrupted his thoughts as he beckoned the waiter.

"Why not?"

The conversation changed to general chit-chat about the recent invasion of Sicily by the Allies and the continued advance of Soviet troops westwards with the prospect of hostilities possibly ending by the following spring.

The hotel bar was empty when he left. Despite the imminent curfew, he set off to cycle home in the gathering dusk; the rain and light wind had abated. He felt more at ease with the path he had chosen. Joining the Résistance seemed to be the optimum choice, not only to tolerate the Nazi occupation, but also to resolve the issue of perceived collaboration. Still agonising over the latter issue, he approached his house. The pain and heartache returned.

Chapter 10

Bellac, Haute Vienne
1943-44

Eliane's life was falling apart. The threat of Jean-Claude discovering her shameful dalliance with Rausch hung over her like the heavy oak beams that supported her ceilings. Whenever he visited, the handsome German still seemed capable of charming her despite her fear of exposure. Sleepless nights, loss of appetite and constant regret drained her. Usually placid and tolerant towards the children, her moods had become irritable and unforgiving.

Anne-Marie, though sympathetic to her situation, often berated her over neglecting the children. On one of her visits, she was shocked to see Eliane so distraught and unable to cope. She needed help, but revealing the cause of her misery would endanger too many lives.

"I cannot carry on like this," she whispered between tearful outbursts. "I feel sick every time I see a Boche soldier, I no longer have any patience with Sylvie, and though I feel sorry for Sebastien, there's a part of me that hates him for being a Jew. Never knowing when Jean-Claude will be home terrifies me every time Rausch turns up in case he discovers the truth."

"Surely, he would understand if you explained."

Eliane put her head in her hands. "He's changed. Since his repatriation, he seems filled with hate. Something terrible must have happened in that prison camp but, whenever I raise the subject, he refuses to talk about it. He's obsessed with killing the Boche. I dread to think what might happen if he were to discover my secret. Any reaction would have unbearable consequences."

"Look, it's becoming more and more obvious the Nazis are losing the war. The Allies are already on European soil in Italy; soon, they'll be in France and the Boche will be in full retreat to Germany. I know it's difficult but you must hold on. Sylvie and Sebastien need you."

"I'm still fearful that Rausch will not keep his word. He's changed too. Before the episode with young David, he was charming, courteous and quite captivating in a fanciable way, but since he discovered I was hiding a Jew, his Nazi aggression surfaces on the odd occasion. It's as though he no longer trusts me."

Anne-Marie sneered. "They're the ones who can't be trusted."

88

Eliane's desperation showed in her anguished expression. "Why are they so hostile towards the Jews?"

"It stems from Hitler. If you remember, the persecution started long before the war, and let's face it, France has never made them particularly welcome. According to some, Laval is not only condoning and supporting their policies but also assisting in mass deportations. There are traitors around every corner. Be wary, Eliane; there are many of our own people in this town who would betray you without a second thought if they knew about the boy's background. Can you not stay with your parents for a while…just to have some breathing space? You could tell Rausch you're unwell and need some help with the children. Before Jean-Claude returned, you stayed with me at Berneuil without any problem."

"I don't think Rausch was convinced; I'm sure he suspected we were deceiving him."

Anne-Marie laughed. "Especially that day he called to see you when he passed me cycling into town, despite my fake broken arm."

"I swore to him that Doctor Jerome had been amazed at your rapid recovery!"

"You see, he's young and gullible. He'll accept your being ill, especially if your parents corroborate your story."

"But Rausch is still living there."

"Yes, but he wouldn't dare touch you under your parents' roof."

"Jean-Claude wouldn't be pleased if I stayed there, especially after being apart for over two years."

"Tell him the same story. From what you've been saying, your health is really suffering. Just look in the mirror. You look awful; your hair has lost its lustre, you often neglect your make-up and your eyes no longer sparkle. You need some space from all this anxiety. He'll have to accept it; he's rarely at home anyway."

At that moment, the children rushed in from the garden. Anne-Marie swept them up in her arms. "You owe it to these two darlings."

"I've no energy. I just want to close my eyes, fall asleep and wake up, hoping to discover that all this torment has gone away."

"All the more reason why you should seek some help."

Sylvie climbed onto her knee. Sebastien ran to Eliane; she stroked his head.

"Take them to Les Singuelles. Your maman will spoil them, and don't forget, your parents are aware of the situation regarding Sebastien. You'll be safe there. I would offer again but I doubt Jean-

89

Claude would be pleased, and I don't need Rausch sniffing around when I might have temporary residents passing through."

"Thanks, Anne-Marie. You're probably right. I'll speak with my parents first before I broach it with Jean-Claude."

"Why does he work such long and erratic hours?"

"Besides working during the day, he often goes out at night on calls. Sometimes, he's needed to finish off a job; sometimes, one of the engineers comes for him because of an emergency."

Anne-Marie looked unconvinced. "I'll have a word next time I see him. He needs to spend more time at home. At least his presence will curtail Rausch's activities if you decide to stay here." She stood to leave.

Eliane sent the children out to play again before joining her by the door. "Tell me to mind my own business if you wish...but are you looking after anyone at the moment?"

Anne-Marie smiled. "Let's just say I have a steady flow; none have stayed longer than a couple of nights."

"Aren't you frightened of prying eyes or someone giving you away?"

"I rarely see anyone...and anyway, my lodgers are well hidden and fully drilled in evasive action." She smiled. "I see my involvement as a game to outwit the enemy. I like to think I'm always one step ahead. Without having to take up arms, it's my chance to avenge the death of my husband. I think Antoine would be quite proud of me."

"I don't know how you can be so cavalier. If the Boche knew what you were doing..."

Anne-Marie shrugged. "At the end of the day, I can always shoot a few of the bastards before they shoot me."

"You would need a gun first."

"Not a problem. Allied agents are supplying them from the armament drops, and the Résistance have managed to provide me with a revolver."

Eliane looked shocked. "You know how to use it?"

"You point it at the Boche...like this." Raising her arm, she shaped her hand like a small pistol. "Pull the trigger...and bang, the Nazi pig is dead."

Eliane stood open-mouthed. "My God, what has this occupation done to everyone? They're turning us into gangsters."

"Would you prefer a lifetime of tyranny and humiliation like you're experiencing with Rausch?" She grinned. "Or would you like me to come over here and shoot the bastard?" She walked a short distance down the path before turning. "That's one solution but sadly, we know there would be recriminations and many innocent hostages would suffer unnecessarily."

She strutted over to where she had left her bicycle. "Worth thinking about, though!"

Eliane watched her friend cycle up the hill towards Berneuil. She envied Anne-Marie's independence and carefree attitude. Her thoughts turned to the children; she longed for a normal family life. It vexed her that the invasion of her country had affected their lives with such detrimental consequences. She prayed that it would end soon. Her hopes would materialise but not how she would have expected.

Chapter 11

Bellac, Haute Vienne
1943-44

Rain from earlier in the day dripped annoyingly from the foliage above and around them. The small group of resisters had arranged to meet in an often-used clearing in the Bois du Roi, close to Bellac. Darkness was closing in rapidly. Sitting on a damp, mossy bank beneath a beech tree, Laroche silently checked the equipment he had emptied from a canvas bag.

"I don't know why I'm here," Jean-Claude protested. "If Laroche is going to blow up the switchboards at the telephone exchange, why ask me along? My turn comes later when they ask me to repair the damage."

Laroche grunted and continued to lay out various items on a waterproof sheet, stopping occasionally to wipe raindrops from the back of his neck. Martial, the gendarme looked on, whilst two other young men with unkempt hair leaned against a nearby tree, smoking cigarettes.

"You're going with him," Martial said, stepping down the bank to sit alongside his new recruit. "I know little about telephone exchanges, and I imagine Laroche knows even less. You're the expert, so it's obvious that you'll be able to indicate where he can do the most damage." He drew on his cigarette. "Preferably, causing damage that takes longer to repair...yes?"

Jean-Claude nodded, aware that temporary repairs could ensure continuous functioning of the exchange within hours. The only serious way to interrupt communications severely would be to blow up the whole building but he doubted they had devices that powerful or the relevant expertise. In his mind, the Résistance was a bunch of untrained amateurs occasionally scratching or denting the impregnable armour of the German war machine. Those thoughts would fade before the night was over.

"You do realise that the Germans will call in engineers...maybe even me...to repair any damage, and it'll probably be functioning again within hours."

Martial smiled. "If you're the repair man, perhaps you could ensure the job will take longer or require some part that might take days to arrive."

"I don't think they're that stupid."

"Well, if called upon, just make sure you do a shoddy repair job."

Reflecting on the demands made on the Kommando groups at the camps, Jean-Claude shuddered. Martial and his small group of resisters had no idea how ruthless the Nazis could be. Sabotaging a repair under their noses could have repercussions not only for him but also for other workers and even his family. He was beginning to believe the only way to combat the Boche was to kill as many as possible as often as possible, irrespective of the consequences. If innocent people were to suffer because of their actions, dead Germans would be a higher price for the enemy to pay, than a few damaged telephone exchanges.

Interrupting his thoughts, Laroche walked over, carrying his canvas bag. "Ready?"

Jean-Claude nodded, picked up his own bag and followed him through the trees. The two younger men went on ahead to check the route was clear. The journey to and from the target was the most dangerous part of the mission. Martial had earlier assured Jean-Claude the young vanguard were reliable, having often performed similar duties.

They cycled into a town shrouded in darkness and, because of the curfew, lacking in visible occupants. On reaching the brick and concrete building, the two outriders signalled that the coast was clear. Laroche forced open a rear window to gain access, and the two saboteurs clambered inside. They were in a dark corridor; Laroche shone his torch in both directions.

"Which way?" he asked.

Jean-Claude tried to remember the layout of a building he had not entered for over four years. "The door at the end; I think it should lead into the generator room. The switchboards are located in a room on the other side."

"How about also blowing up the generator?" he whispered.

"You're the explosives expert; take your pick. They can easily replace the generator. The ideal would be to destroy that and the switchboards." He prodded him, urging him forwards. "Why are you whispering? There's no one here…it's not manned at night."

"How does the Boche communicate then?"

"Urgent calls are re-routed via Saint-Junien."

"It hardly seems worth the trouble," he muttered.

"I suppose it's one way of letting the bastards know we have the capability. In any case, it'll cause a few days' inconvenience for them...and the town in general."

Jean-Claude watched his accomplice setting the charges where he reckoned they would create the most damage, whilst listening intently for any warning whistles from their sentinels outside. Surprisingly, he had no fear, not because of the protection offered by the Sten gun he carried, but because the thought of killing a few Germans in a shoot-out surpassed any other emotions. The image of Emile in the camp at Hinzert-Pölert remained fixed in his mind.

"Done," Laroche muttered. "Let's get out of here."

"How long?" Jean-Claude was already running down the corridor.

They scrambled through the broken window and, dropping to the ground, urged their companions to follow. Within a minute they were cycling furiously through the darkened streets towards the outskirts of town.

"You didn't say how long the fuses were," Jean-Claude shouted as he tried to keep up with the other three, despite the pain in his leg.

"You'll know when you hear the explosion."

They had scarcely left the road for the track leading to the forest when a muffled roar echoed from behind them.

"I'd say they must have been three minute fuses," Laroche shouted.

"You mean you didn't know," Jean-Claude yelled, pedalling faster.

"Forgot to check!"

"Bloody amateur."

Fifteen minutes later, they reported to Martial who, accompanied by Father Milani and three more resisters, was waiting at the usual rendezvous in the forest.

"Claudius, how did it go?" the priest asked, adopting his role as Danté and addressing Jean-Claude by his *nom de guerre*.

They shook hands before the saboteurs recounted the details of their attack on the exchange. Martial introduced the newcomers whom he had escorted to the clearing. He explained they were seeking help with plans to blow up the tramway bridge over the river Semme near La Passerelle.

"A waste of bloody explosives," Laroche whispered to Jean-Claude.

The gendarme overheard his remark. "With the fuel shortage, both soldiers and admin personnel rely on the system for their transportation needs. It's vital to cause disruption wherever we see the opportunity. The newly formed resistance group, Forces Françaises de l'Intérieur in Le Dorat wants to prioritise such actions as opposed to direct combat against the enemy."

Laroche spat dismissively into the ground. "Gutless cowards. What do they bloody know?"

"What about the inconvenience to local people who use it on a regular basis?" Jean-Claude asked.

"They'll understand."

"It would be more disruptive to blow up the railway viaduct across the Vincou." Laroche glared at the F.F.I. resisters. He was not alone in his contempt for this new body that General Koenig had formed in an effort to unite all armed Résistance into one military force. He argued that his group, the Francs-Tireurs et Partisans already had structure. The F.T.P., a mainly Communist movement, had commanders responsible for key areas: military, recruitment, liaison and provisions. The chain of command was devolved further with regional and departmental leaders, Martial being one in the Bellac area. Though abrasive in attitude and always outspoken, Laroche enjoyed organisation and discipline at every level.

Martial stood his ground. "I'm not prepared to destroy the main lifeline to our town. In any case, we have insufficient material for such a massive undertaking."

One of the young men, who had been a lookout on the telephone exchange raid, nudged Laroche. "The older man over there...I know him. He's a travelling salesman who lives in Rue Thiers in Bellac. What's he doing in the Résistance? He's a Gestapo agent!"

Laroche spun round. "How d'you know...are you sure?"

"Everyone knows. He uses the post office in Bellac on a regular basis. The postmistress said he always presents a card, '*Priorité Gestapo*', when conducting any business via La Poste. He's known to make regular trips to Limoges, tells everyone it's business but he's been seen meeting Meier from the Gestapo headquarters situated near the railway station."

Laroche drew Martial to one side. "An agent of the Gestapo has infiltrated us." He repeated what he had heard.

"That's impossible. They've assured me they're all with the F.F.I."

"Obviously, they're not aware of his background in Le Dorat. Bloody unprofessional, if you ask me."

Martial asked Father Milani to join them, before taking them to one side where they could discuss the situation. It soon became apparent they had no option but to follow strict but unpleasant procedures. If he was a spy for the Gestapo, all their lives were in danger. There was doubt but they were faced with no opportunity to seek verification. In all such cases, insufficient resources, time and operating without a fixed base prevented the Résistance from taking prisoners. Though often difficult to accept, those were the rules.

Father Milani urged caution. "You must also consider his companions. Are they aware of his secret...or are they innocent? What do you intend to do about them?"

Martial glanced at his watch. "I'll interview them...separately. Keep an eye on the other one."

Jean-Claude quickly realised a problem had arisen but was not prepared for what would follow. After brief conversations with the two other suspects, the gendarme summoned Laroche who, in turn, ordered the salesman from Bellac to kneel at the foot of a tree. Holding him down with the heel of his boot, in one swift movement, he withdrew his revolver and shot him through the back of the head.

Jean-Claude looked on in shock.

Father Milani stood over the man's lifeless body, and mumbled a short prayer before turning to the man's companions. "Not a word or you will suffer the same end to your miserable lives. Now go."

They departed swiftly and silently into the forest, relieved they had not suffered a similar fate.

The gendarme acted as though nothing untoward had happened. "We'll cover the body with foliage and bracken." He checked his watch again before turning to the two lookouts. "Too late now but I want you here at first light with spades to bury the traitor. What happened here tonight stays here...understand?"

The youths nodded their heads but remained silent. After only two months as resisters, they were learning a Maquis code that sponsored extreme violence to ensure survival.

Martial was a firm but intuitive leader. He shook hands with the young men. "Thanks for a good job at the exchange. I'll be in touch. Take care going home."

Home for Gilbert and Marcel was a hayloft above a cow shed on a farm belonging to Laroche's brother-in-law. Originally from Peyrat de Bellac, they had become S.T.O. fugitives, the new directive Vichy had introduced to provide conscripted labour for Nazi Germany. *Service du Travail Obligatoire* had forced many young men into hiding, often finding refuge in the Maquis to avoid transportation to the Fatherland.

Martial walked off, followed by Father Milani who beckoned Jean-Claude to join him. "I'm sorry you had to witness that but now you can see the fine line between patriotism and collaboration. One cannot afford to display any sign of allegiance or empathy towards the enemy."

"I hope you're not including my wife in your assumptions."

"The fact that you are supporting the Résistance deflects attention from that situation. The Nazis are in retreat; soon they will have vacated our country. When the war is over, people will forget the bad times but will remember all those who contributed to our glorious victory. Eliane will live in your shadow but you and those close to you will know what she had to endure."

He placed his arm around Jean-Claude's shoulder. "Put what happened tonight behind you. There's a long hard road ahead with many twists and turns but we will overcome Hitler's fascist barbarians. Trust me. We have some dedicated individuals who risk their lives for us."

The three resisters went their separate ways, leaving Jean-Claude with much to digest following his first assignment. Foremost in his mind was the instant execution of a potential informer. He hoped the Maquis were not descending to the brutal levels of cruelty he had witnessed in the camps. Had he exchanged one barbaric adversary for an organisation with a similar disregard for any morality? He feared for Eliane and the damaging reputation she had earned by securing his release. It was time to repay the debt he owed her; despite the possible consequences, he knew what he must do.

Chapter 12

Haute Vienne
1944

August Meier paced the room; the head of the Gestapo in Limoges was not in a pleasant mood. Passing his desk for the umpteenth time, he stubbed out another cigarette.

SS-Standartenführer Rausch remained calmly seated in his chair, waiting for further comment. He had brought bad news at a time when the Gestapo chief had expected him to be the bearer of vital information. He enjoyed upsetting Meier; he had no time for the Gestapo and their indiscriminate thuggery.

August Meier slumped into the comfortable chair behind his desk. "Surely, someone must know what's happened to him. What about his wife? When did she see him last?"

"According to the report compiled by the local gendarmerie, he left the house a couple of hours before curfew two nights ago. He said he was meeting some friends for a drink. She waited for him all evening and went to bed, thinking he had lost track of the time. She guessed he had stayed the night with his friends, rather than risk breaking the curfew. When he failed to surface by the following morning, she reported him missing to the gendarmerie. Subsequently, they took this statement from her."

"Does she not know the names of these so-called friends who had arranged to meet him?"

"According to her version of events, he didn't say who they were or why and where he had arranged to meet them. She presumed he would be heading to one of the bars in the town. One of my officers, who was present during her interview, noticed that the gendarmes seemed more concerned with some incident at the telephone exchange. It seems someone had planted an explosive device in the switchboard room."

"Much damage?"

Rausch shrugged. "Nothing that cannot be fixed. I've got my engineer working on it."

"Is that the ex-prisoner?"

The SS officer nodded. His thoughts turned to Eliane; this was a missed opportunity to be in Saint Sauveur rather than reporting to August Meier in the Villa Tivoli. For several days, he had been toying with the idea of contacting trusted associates in the Wehrmacht to damage a telephone installation south of Limoges, a repair job that would keep Jean-Claude absent for at least several days. Naturally, the Résistance would be held responsible. He was quite proud of his scheme; devious and guaranteed to be effective.

August Meier interrupted his fantasy. "Has my salesman from Bellac previously mentioned the names of any potential suspects to you?"

"Not to me. The last time I contacted him, he said he had arranged a meeting through a contact in Le Dorat, but refused to divulge the contact's name because he assumed the man could also be useful in identifying resisters in the area of Magnac Laval. He hoped that, following the meeting, he would have a detailed terrorist list for you. I trusted him. I was told he's never let you down before...that you trusted him implicitly." Rausch was enjoying apportioning blame to the pompous Gestapo chief.

"Yet, he's now disappeared...strangely opportune, don't you think?" An angry August Meier lit another cigarette. "What about your lady friend? Do you reckon she could be a source of information?"

"Personally, I think almost everyone knows someone who's involved with the Résistance, but it's a subject they tend to avoid."

Meier leaned back in his chair, a smug expression replacing his furrowed brow. "We never have any trouble getting them to talk here...after a certain amount of persuasion, of course. The main problem is finding the bastards in these damned hills and forests. There's been a steady increase in ambushes, and covert Allied arms drops have become more frequent since the turn of the year. The terrorists seem to be better armed and organised...even our armoured patrols are less confident in confronting them these days."

"You should use the *milice* for search and arrest operations; they're French traitors and expendable. Why put our own troops in danger when there's a volunteer armed militia readily available?" Rausch looked at his watch. "I have a meeting at the Préfecture in twenty minutes. I'll make more enquiries in Bellac about your missing salesman. If I gather any information, I'll be in touch."

The two shook hands, saluted and parted company. Rausch decided to drive straight to Saint Sauveur. The Préfecture could wait.

*****

The house on Chemin de Geroux seemed unusually quiet; closed shutters prevented Rausch from looking through the windows. In frustration, he tried the door again; definitely locked. He thought about driving to Berneuil but, spotting a neighbour peering from a nearby upstairs window, he crossed the road and thumped on the door.

A timid looking woman answered, seemingly petrified to find an SS officer on her doorstep.

Rausch bowed courteously before wishing her *bonjour*. "I wonder if you can help me. I need to speak with Madame Tricot who lives opposite but the house seems abandoned. Have you any idea how I may contact her?"

The woman shook her head.

"Did you see her leave? Has she taken the children out for the day?"

The woman shrugged before shaking her head again.

"What about Monsieur Tricot?"

A vacant stare was the response.

Exasperated, Rausch turned on his heels, crossed to his car and drove off, leaving a cloud of dust and exhaust fumes in his wake. The woman watched the vehicle disappear before spitting into the road. "Filthy Boche," she muttered, closing her front door.

Rausch drove to the gendarmerie in Bellac to check if there was any fresh news about the missing salesman. An apologetic gendarme reported that, despite extensive enquiries, they had been unable to gather any further information on the man's whereabouts. The gendarme was Martial.

"What about his friends. Have they been questioned?" Rausch demanded, impatiently. He considered helping Meier with local enquiries to be a waste of his valuable time; he had more important issues to resolve. A missing Eliane was far more important then a missing salesman.

"Apparently, he was a loner...spent a lot of time away from home on business. Is there any reason why you are concerned about his disappearance?" Martial knew the answer but wanted to see his reaction.

"He was a commercial traveller who regularly supplied office equipment to the Kommandatur in Limoges. He had an important appointment there yesterday. It was unusual for him to miss meetings."

Martial was enjoying this unexpected opportunity to put the SS officer on the spot. "Perhaps recent events have frightened him off; maybe he thought it was time to disappear."

"What d'you mean?"

"He was Jewish...and the current treatment of Jews might have been the reason for his sudden departure."

Rausch was irritated. "He didn't look Jewish. How d'you know he was a Jew?"

"He was born to Jewish parents; Albert Albrecht and Lilie Goldstein in the 13th arrondissement at Paris on March 12th 1915. I've been examining his residence records." Martial studied the officer's face wondering if the Germans were aware of their spy's background, if they had checked his papers. The SS officer's expression told a different story.

Rausch remained silent, not wishing to comment. If it were true, Meier's Sicherheitsdienst had really blundered. Perhaps the Jew had decided to deceive the Gestapo. It began to make sense; the man must have intended to disappear intentionally at some point. But why had he offered to spy for them in the first place? Of course, he had official papers, extra petrol coupons, and special passes to allow him free, unrestricted access to help him infiltrate the Résistance. Unwittingly, they had supplied a Jew with the means to abscond. Rausch found the revelations rather amusing; August Meier's reaction to the news would be priceless.

Martial realised he had possibly deflected any suspicion of involvement by the Résistance, despite the fact the Boche must have known about the salesman's proposed meeting to identify its members. Thanks to Gilbert's keen eye, they'd had a lucky escape, and thanks to his forethought to check the man's residency papers, culpability for his absence was firmly pointing towards the Jew himself.

Rausch thought he should re-establish his authority. "His wife must know where he is. Have you questioned her?"

Martial glared at him. "Of course, we questioned her when she reported him missing. One of your men was present; he has a copy of the report. We are confident she knows nothing. Her husband's disappearance has come as a great shock. The woman is distraught."

Rausch turned towards the door. "I will interrogate her myself."

"I'm surprised you're showing so much interest. Was he a friend of yours?"

Rausch ignored him and quickly left the building, intending to abandon any further involvement in the case. It was time for the Gestapo to put its own house in order.

The gendarme watched him drive off. He found it strange that the SS officer seemed unmoved by the fact that Albrecht was a Jew. He must have known, otherwise he would have reacted differently; he seemed interested only in how he, Martial knew. After a few moments, it suddenly became clearer. The Jew must have offered to spy in return for his freedom from internment or deportation; the Gestapo must have made a deal. Maybe, Rausch was unaware.

"Obviously, they'll guess he's double-crossed them," he uttered quietly. Nevertheless, it continued to baffle him why Rausch seemed so interested in the case as opposed to the Gestapo. He wondered if some conflict existed between SS-Standartenführer Rausch and the Sicherheitsdienst. On the other hand, could there be another reason?

Deep in thought, he walked back into the gendarmerie.

The following day, the Gestapo arrested Albrecht's wife and took her to Limoges. She never returned.

*****

As summer approached, resistance activity increased; Nazi reprisals spread across the region as the probability of an Allied invasion became the main topic of conversation. The occupiers seemed to be dealing regularly with insurrections and skirmishes across a wide area, taking up valuable resources, time and effort. Power was passing into the hands of the people; the Germans were finding it difficult to exert their normal authority and controls. To overcome these difficulties, arrests were commonplace, many leading to execution or deportation.

To provide additional support for D-Day, parachute drops increased in frequency but often caused problems with ammunition not matching armaments. In some cases, resisters required training in the use of different weapons the Allies were sending, and consequently, new recruits were ill prepared for combat. Despite the general mood to mobilise and engage with the enemy, based on the expectancy of a second landing on the south coast of France, local rural Maquis groups limited their involvement to sabotage and similar disruptive attacks.

In this atmosphere of anticipation, Anne-Marie found herself drawn further into resistance activities. Instead of accommodating escapers or downed airmen, she had become a courier, carrying messages to and from various factions allied to the main F.T.P. groups in the area. The structure of each group ensured that contact with other individuals remained minimal. This would ensure that, if the Germans apprehended any resister, he or she would be able to disclose only a few names, thereby protecting the group as a whole.

The agent, Hector had opted for a safe house in Bellac; apart from couriers, his main contacts were Martial and Laroche. The wireless operator, who had now joined him, used different locations to reduce the chance of German detection patrols picking up her signals from one specific spot. Security had become a key issue, especially since the exposure of the treacherous salesman.

In her new role, Anne-Marie occasionally met people she never imagined to be involved in the Résistance. One such meeting occurred when she was despatched to Saint Sauveur to deliver a note to the dead-letter-box in the cemetery. Because it was her first visit there, she had memorised a plan of the graveyard showing the location of the grave with the iron casket. She took the precaution of rolling the note into a tubular shape; which she could insert into the hollow handlebars of her cycle. As she approached the crossroads linking Saint Sauveur with Saint-Junien-les-Combes, she saw that the Germans had installed a new checkpoint. Too late to turn back, she slowed as a soldier stepped out demanding to see her papers.

Trying to look disinterested and bored with the interruption to her trip, she waited patiently whilst he checked her identity card.

"Where are you going," he asked.

"Visiting a friend."

"Why?"

"Because I want to. That's what friends do, unless of course, you have none." She glared at him.

"Who?"

"Madame Tricot, not that it's any of your business."

Still holding her papers, the soldier turned to a senior officer. "Do we know a Madame Tricot?"

Smiling, the officer stepped forward and, with a firm grip, placed both his hands on the handlebars, jutting his face centimetres from Anne-Marie's. Despite feeling his hot, stale breath on her cool skin, she remained unmoved; defiantly, she stared back at him. There was an uncomfortable silence until the officer straightened his posture.

"She can go. Madame Tricot is a close friend of Standartenführer Rausch." He sneered at her before walking away.

Anne-Marie collected her papers and, relieved but angry, pedalled quickly towards Saint Sauveur before they changed their minds.

At the cemetery, she slid the curled note from its hiding place, leaned her bicycle against the wall and from memory, picked her path through the tombstones that littered the graveyard. Spotting the one with the casket, she checked no one was watching before leaving the note. As she returned to collect her cycle, Father Milani appeared at the main entrance. She recognised him as the priest who had visited Jean-Claude after his release from captivity.

"Are you visiting a loved one?" he asked.

Unsure how to reply, she quickly straddled her cycle to make a swift departure.

"You're Anne-Marie, a friend of Madame Tricot, aren't you?"

My God, Eliane's name again, but how does he know my name? "Yes, that's right," she replied with some hesitation.

"Leave your bicycle. Come with me to the church for a moment."

She looked at him, wondering whether she should pedal off or acquiesce to his demand.

"Don't worry about the note. I'll collect it later." He turned and walked back towards the church.

Anne-Marie meekly obeyed, wondering why he seemed so insistant. *He mentioned the note; he must have watched me!* Intrigued, she followed him. He disappeared into the dark interior where she hesitated before deciding to enter. The echo of her footsteps seemed to reverberate in tandem with every thumping heartbeat. Adjusting her eyes to the gloomy interior of the stone edifice, she became aware of another figure standing in the shadows.

Chapter 13

Haute Vienne
1944

"Are you sure it's not too much trouble?" Eliane dragged a bulky suitcase into the salon.

Her mother helped the children to remove their coats. "It's fine, Eliane. It'll be lovely having Sylvie and David…sorry, I mean Sebastien staying here." She wrung her hands. "I'm finding it difficult getting used to his new name. Perhaps staying here for a while will help. I fail to grasp why they had to change both his names."

"I understand your concern, maman, but please be careful when colonel Rausch is here."

Showing her displeasure about having to tolerate the soldier's unwelcome presence, Madame Dutheil changed the topic. "Papa's borrowed two small mattresses for the children, and I've rooted out some extra bedding. We've managed to find room for everything by removing your old trunk and the bedside table. It's a tight squeeze but you should all be comfortable in there." Inviting the children to join her on the sofa, she smiled at her daughter. "It'll be quite nostalgic to find yourself back in your old room. Leave the suitcase; papa will take it up later. We don't want you overdoing it; you're here to rest, my dear."

Despite her concern over Rausch's reaction to her move, Eliane sighed with relief at being back in the comparative safety of Les Singuelles. She was counting on the fact that he would have little or no opportunity to confront her in her parents' house. It would be inconvenient but consoled herself by knowing Jean-Claude had agreed she needed a short break, if only for a few weeks. She would miss her husband but the temporary separation was incomparable to the distress she had suffered during his incarceration in the prisoner of war camp. Besides, he would be able to visit and enjoy the occasional meal with the family when work commitments allowed.

Jean-Claude, though regretting that demands of his job and his involvement with the Maquis left him little time for family life, worried mostly about leaving his wife at the mercy of Rausch's attentions. Having taken an instant dislike to the man, he trusted him even less as each month passed. He considered she would be more content and far safer under the watchful eye of her parents. The temporary arrangement suited both of them, even though they had not shared their true feelings. The simple logic of her decision to leave Saint Sauveur lay buried in the complexity of the situation.

*****

The ancient church smelled damp and musty. As the shadowy figure moved towards her, Anne-Marie was surprised to see the uniform of a gendarme emerging from the gloom. She trembled with a mixture of fear and excitement; instinctively, she took a few steps backwards towards the entrance.

The gendarme held out his hand. "I'm Martial..." He turned towards the priest. "...and this is Danté." He beckoned her to follow him. The two men walked towards a vestry.

"Come and join us." Father Milani waved towards the vestry door. "I'm sure you would welcome a reviving drink after cycling from Berneuil."

Hesitantly, Anne-Marie followed them into the room where, in alcoves, candles in brass holders cast shadows that danced across the vestry walls. After she entered, Father Milani closed the door. The slight draught fanned the flames; the waltzing images became a fleeting foxtrot. After crossing to a small oak table, he poured red wine from a decanter into three cut glass goblets.

"Vive la France." The priest raised his glass before sipping. He addressed Anne-Marie. "Forgive me for getting you here on a pretext. The note in the casket is of no importance. However, I wish to thank you for your services. We also have a proposition for you, an assignment...not without danger, I must add...but one we believe might suit you."

The surreal nature of this encounter left Anne-Marie speechless. Her eyes darted around the room. A floor-to-ceiling cupboard, featuring beautifully carved doors, covered one wall. The other stone walls were bare, apart from a large wooden crucifix at one and, on the opposite wall, a gilt-framed picture of Christ. Above head height, two tiny arched windows of leaded glass admitted shafts of rainbow daylight. As the priest's words sunk in, her gaze settled on the gendarme. She picked up one of the glasses and sipped some wine; her mouth had become unusually dry.

Martial pulled out a chair from under the table. "Take a seat. We have lots to discuss."

In such a daunting atmosphere, Anne-Marie struggled to stay calm. Nervously, she sat down, placed her glass on the table and looked up at the priest.

He pulled out a chair and sat beside her. Martial sat opposite. Gradually, her initial fears subsided, replaced by curiosity. She leaned back, prepared to listen, gaining the impression that Martial seemed to be the one in charge. Through Eliane, she knew the priest to be Father Milani, but here the gendarme had called him Danté. Obviously, they were both with the Maquis.

"You accommodated an agent called Hector," the gendarme said.

Anne-Marie hesitated, suddenly unsure whether they were with the Résistance, especially as a gendarme was facing her. Her thoughts turned to the note, the casket, their *noms de guerre*, the presence of Father Milani. *They must be Maquis.*

She nodded. "I was told he would be staying with me for a few days, that he had parachuted in, and a wireless operator would follow but I believe he has not arrived yet."

"The wireless operator has arrived. She's working with Hector. What were your impressions of the agent?"

Why is he asking? What has happened? "The man was quite rude. We didn't like him at all."

"What d'you mean by 'we'? Who else met him?"

"My friend, Eliane was there." She looked at the priest. "You know…Madame Tricot."

The priest leaned over to Martial and whispered in his ear. "The wife of Claudius."

Martial leaned back in his chair. "The one who enlisted an SS officer to assist in her husband's release?"

"That's her."

"Shit!" He rose from his chair to pace the room before turning his attention to Anne-Marie. "Did you introduce your friend to this Hector chap?"

"Well, yes…it was only natural to do so…and courteous, of course."

"Anything else?"

She shrugged. "Such as?"

Martial was becoming agitated. "Well…anything. What did you discuss? I must know everything that was said. It's important. Lives could be at stake." He returned to his chair and, leaning across the table, stared at her.

Anne-Marie looked up at Father Milani, fearing she had committed a grave error.

He nodded. "He's right. We need to know every word that was spoken."

"You're frightening me. What have I done?"

"Just calm down," Martial added. "We believe Hector is possibly an imposter, a German spy, a double agent, or similar; we're not sure but it's vital we find out quickly." He lit a cigarette before passing the packet to the priest. "Now, tell me everything that you discussed with him."

Anne-Marie related their conversation, including what they had told him about her friend's connection to SS-Standartenführer Rausch.

Martial looked at the priest. "If he is Boche, the problem's bigger than I imagined. We need to act quickly."

"But he had parachuted in and he said the Maquis had been there to meet him. He also warned us about loose talk, saying he could be a German spy. Why would he reproach us if he was an infiltrator?"

"A double bluff. You see, we suspect him because the British agent should have landed near Messières-sur-Issoire but there were strong winds that night; he drifted into the Monts de Blond area. Two days passed before he turned up. According to this Hector, because there was no reception committee where he landed, he hid in a barn. Finally, he decided to trust the farmer who contacted a local gendarme. Fortunately, the gendarme was sympathetic to our cause, and he contacted me. The farmer was instructed to deliver him to your safe house…being the nearest one…until we were able to pick him up."

Anne-Marie looked at them both in turn. "So why is that suspicious?"

"Why was he missing for two days? He said he was unsure whether it was safe to make contact…but why wait two days? We think it's possible that the real agent was picked up by a patrol, interrogated and instead of trying to trace a handful of resisters, the Gestapo probably thought they could use the opportunity to infiltrate a complete network with a bogus agent."

There was a silence as the possible outcomes flooded her thoughts. Anne-Marie turned to the priest.

"If he is Boche, would Rausch, the SS officer know about this?"

108

"Possibly. However, I would imagine that few would be aware of the insertion of a spy into our Maquis; that would be a closely guarded secret. It depends who is running the operation. Rausch isn't Gestapo, so what's your concern about him being aware of the situation?"

Anne-Marie shot a glance at Martial before turning back to Father Milani. "The youngster, Sebastien."

Martial turned to the priest. "What's this? Who is Sebastien?"

Father Milani related how he had been involved in procuring false papers and a new identity for Eliane's Jewish cousin.

Martial shrugged. "Well, if you're certain the documentation is good...I suppose, so long as this SS officer doesn't discover the truth, it's not an issue."

Anne-Marie stared at the gendarme. "It's too late. He already knows."

Father Milani looked aghast. "How...how on earth did he find out?"

"Apparently, he called at the house one night when the children were running around naked before bath time. He spotted that the boy had been circumcised."

"Shit!" Martial rose angrily from his chair before rounding on the priest. "We are talking about Claudius's wife, aren't we?"

Ignoring Martial's outburst, Father Milani turned to Anne-Marie. "Are you sure? If that's the case, why haven't they been arrested?"

"Eliane did a deal with Rausch."

"What kind of deal?"

"I think you should talk to her about that."

Martial paced the room before facing Anne-Marie. "I hope she hasn't betrayed her husband."

"I take it that Claudius is Jean-Claude. How could she? Eliane is unaware he's in the Résistance. Is that why he spends so much time away from home?"

Father Milani tried to calm the situation. "His knowledge of the telephone network is a useful asset. Not telling his wife is merely to protect her."

"You just don't realise, do you?" Anne-Marie looked up at Martial. "That poor woman is being harassed by Rausch, neglected by her husband, and terrified about the consequences if Sebastien's false identity is revealed...and you only care about how you can exploit her husband. No wonder, she's distraught."

109

Martial returned to the table. "We're at war; sacrifices must be made. Look, I appreciate what you are doing; many others support our cause in many different ways but, sadly, there will be victims along the way. We're close to an Allied invasion. It's important we hold our nerve and, more importantly, maintain a high level of security to stay one step ahead of the bastards."

He looked sternly at Anne-Marie. "Are you prepared to help our investigation concerning Hector?"

She nodded. "What do you want me to do?"

*****

After putting the children to bed on their first night in her old room at Les Singuelles, Eliane finally relaxed, eventually finding time to sit with her parents, undisturbed by the distraction of two lively youngsters.

"Is the colonel not here tonight?" she asked.

Her father lit his pipe. "I think he said he would be working away for a day or two."

Eliane wondered if she had thwarted his plans. She knew Jean-Claude was also working on a job south of Limoges and would not be home until late. If Rausch had designs on visiting her, he would have been sorely disappointed.

"How is Jean-Claude reacting to your staying here?" her mother asked whilst clearing the table following the evening meal. "I hope he will be eating sensibly in your absence."

"He had no objections to my staying here; in fact, he seemed in favour of the idea because he spends so much time away at the moment. I told him he would be welcome here for meals if necessary."

"Time away…at work?" her father asked.

"Yes, he occasionally works in other areas and is often called out at night for emergency repairs. We spend so little time together."

"Really? I would have thought younger, single engineers would be more suitable for such undertakings. Does the company not realise he has a family and furthermore, has been a prisoner of war?"

"I really don't know. I suppose it would make more sense, but he seems quite content to offer his time when asked."

"After what he has endured, together with his leg injury, I'm surprised they are making such unreasonable demands of him. You should complain. How often is he called to one of these emergencies?"

"I suppose the number of times has increased more recently. I think most of the work is the result of resistance activity. I hear they're also blowing up railway lines, besides bringing down telephone lines."

Her mother sighed. "I'll be glad to see the back of the Boche. Our lives have been a nightmare since they removed the demarcation line."

"Maman, you shouldn't talk like that. You never know who might be listening."

"It's what I feel. Can one not speak one's mind anymore? I'll be glad when De Gaulle arrives with the Allied armies to send them back to where they belong. Animals...that's what they are...animals."

Eliane turned to her father and smiled. "I hope she doesn't make comments like that in front of the colonel."

"Your maman is only expressing what everyone is thinking. Every day, there are rumours of an invasion. Let's hope it's soon. The Résistance can only do so much. Without some form of military support, they can only commit acts of sabotage. To fight the Germans effectively, they need more armaments."

"Well, at least some are getting through along with British agents to instruct the resisters in how to use them."

"What makes you say that?" her father asked in astonishment. "Who has told you about British agents?"

Eliane blushed. "Oh, it's just another rumour."

"You seemed very sure. Who is spreading the rumour?"

"I can't remember, papa." Eliane rose from her chair. "Maman, let me help you clear the table."

Her father raised his voice slightly. "Eliane, sit down. I want you to tell me how you acquired that information."

She looked at his stern expression, one he always used when she and her brother were naughty as children. She knew he would not relent until she told the truth. "Anne-Marie mentioned it to me." She sat down again.

"And how does she know?"

Eliane leant forwards, allowing her hair to cover her face. "She's involved," she whispered.

Her mother dropped some cutlery onto the table before kneeling alongside her daughter. "You mean with the Résistance?"

Eliane nodded but remained silent.

"I hope you're not involved...are you?" Her mother held her hand. "Tell me you're not involved."

Eliane shook her head, but tears ran down her cheeks. "I met one at her house."

"A resister?"

"No. A British agent was staying with her. That's what she does. She runs what they call a 'safe house'.

Gasping, her mother half-covered her mouth with her hand. "Oh, my God. The poor girl. Why is she taking such a risk?"

Eliane shrugged. "She sees it as a way of repaying the Boche for Antoine's death. She also accommodates escapers...like downed airman or anyone trying to evade capture by the Boche."

Her father shook his head slowly, before puffing on his pipe. "She's a brave young woman. I thought we were taking a risk with David's false papers. God help us if they ever discover we're harbouring a Jew."

Eliane burst into a flood of tears. She wanted desperately to tell them that Rausch already knew but could not bring herself to confess the price she was paying for his silence.

Her father leaned across to her. "Don't upset yourself, my dear. Those papers were first class and would pass any scrutiny."

Eliane wiped the tears from her face. "I think I'll have an early night. I'm quite exhausted." She stood and walked towards the door. "Thank you for letting me stay here. I promise it won't be for too long." With her mind in turmoil, she left the room.

Her mother glared at her husband. "You should choose your words more carefully, Bernard. You've upset her."

Monsieur Dutheil continued to puff on his pipe whilst watching his wife finish clearing the table. "I wonder which Maquis group Anne-Marie has joined," he muttered to himself.

Chapter 14

Haute Vienne
1944

Clouds drifted intermittently across an indigo sky. From her bedroom window, Anne-Marie looked up at the full moon. It was the 8th May. Hector was downstairs ensuring his bicycle was in good working order.

He had returned to Berneuil on the advice of Martial who had suggested Anne-Marie's house was in a perfect location to supervise the imminent parachute drop of armaments, scheduled for later that night. Two days earlier, Anne-Marie had cycled with him to check a flat expanse of pastureland near Le Mas d'Or, the spot designated to receive the containers. Her brief had been to tumble from her bicycle on the return journey to fake a twisted ankle, preventing her from partaking in the clandestine activity. So far, everything had gone to plan. Hector, having spent the previous day finding a pharmacy that could supply appropriate strapping for her injury, was now preparing to meet the reception committee of *maquisards* alone.

Along one side of the drop zone, a narrow strip of woodland gave ideal cover for an approach from the main Bellac to Limoges road. On the other side, a thickly wooded copse afforded similar cover, but could only be accessed with difficulty from the nearby village of Saint-Junien-les-Combes. The closest and most trusted members of Martial's Maquis had chosen the perfect spot for their trap.

Before leaving the church at Saint Sauveur, the gendarme had explained to Anne-Marie a scheme he had devised to determine whether Hector was a bona-fide British agent. At first, the young woman had seemed sceptical.

"What if he is working for the Germans, surely they will not only apprehend the resisters but also take delivery of our much-needed weapons."

Martial had smiled. "Firstly, there will not be an arms drop; it is a hoax. We will inform Hector that it is a combined operation organised by another group to supply shared supplies. If he tips off the Germans, without doubt, they will approach the drop zone from the main road; the access is easier and the woodland offers extensive cover for their soldiers. We will conceal just two observers in the copse on the far side. When Hector arrives there, he will head for the copse. If our two sentinels have seen that there are Germans in position, he's finished. If the enemy is not present, our observers will receive word that the drop has been cancelled."

Anne-Marie still had doubts. "What if he is a spy but just fails to inform the Boche?"

Father Milani had stepped in. "That's a risk we must take. However, I doubt he would pass up such a great opportunity to betray us, knowing that they would be able to make quite a killing."

Despite not relishing the idea of having Hector back as a 'lodger', Anne-Marie agreed to play her part in the deception. In fact, by the time she arrived back at Berneuil, she had become quite thrilled to be involved in what she perceived as 'real action'.

From her bedroom window, she watched Hector disappear into the darkness, his path illuminated solely by the moon whenever it emerged from behind passing clouds. At last, she thought, I no longer have to hobble around...whatever the outcome. If he returns unscathed, I will merely thank him for acquiring the strapping to aid a rapid recovery. She settled down to wait in the living room with a glass of wine, hoping everything would go to plan.

A gentle tap on the door interrupted her reverie. Her heart skipped a beat, despite knowing a loud thumping knock would be more likely to herald the arrival of enemy soldiers or the *milice*. Without thinking, she limped to answer. Another heavily built man, a stranger to her, accompanied Martial.

"Any news yet?" the gendarme asked.

Opening the door wider, Anne-Marie shook her head, invited them inside and offered them a glass of wine.

"If there are Germans hiding in the woods, what will happen to Hector? Will he come back here?"

"Our two observers will attend to that problem. They have been in position for several hours on lookout duty. They will have known before Hector arrives if the enemy is present. I instructed him to meet them in the copse, where they will decide his fate."

The other man, Laroche intervened. "No Boche, he'll be cycling back here, probably pissed off with the cancellation. Boche in the woods..." He drew his hand across his throat. "...goodbye Hector...swift and silent."

Anne-Marie shuddered. This was her first hint of the brutality that involvement with the Résistance could generate. She looked across at Martial; he was too young, too handsome to be a killer. She could never imagine him being ruthless but obviously, he equated truth and lies to life and death. She glanced at Laroche; if anyone could kill, it would be him. His resolute expression, his piercing eyes were enough to suggest he would fight to the end. She felt she had entered another world, tainted with the desperation of survival. She thought of the revolver hidden beneath a loose floorboard upstairs. Would she have the courage to use it to defend herself?

With a slight shiver, she rose from her chair. "It's quite chilly. I'll make a pot of coffee for when they arrive." She walked to the stove, wondering if Hector would be back. Though she disliked the man, she hoped he was genuine. The thought of him lying in that copse with his throat slit open revolted her.

Her two visitors were talking but she was unable to hear the conversation. Martial crossed the room towards her, pointing at a rear door. "What's beyond?"

"A passage, another door and the garden."

"What's in the small barn opposite?"

Anne-Marie shrugged nonchalantly, wondering where his questions were leading. "Straw, some agricultural equipment and logs for the wood burner. There's a hayloft where some of my 'guests' have occasionally hidden before moving on."

Martial turned to Laroche. "The loft seems a likely spot."

Anne-Marie squared up to him. "What are you plotting now?"

"We have a wireless operator needing a new location in preparation for our involvement when the invasion takes place."

She smiled. "Are you saying it's imminent?"

"We're just waiting to hear the coded message. It could be this month, next month…even next year, but we think it will happen soon. Every resistance group throughout France will have a part to play. It's vital to be prepared."

Martial checked his watch before addressing Laroche. "We'll give them another hour. If they or Hector haven't returned by then, we'll have to walk to the drop zone to check." He turned to Anne-Marie. "How far is it?"

"Just short of two kilometres. It won't be easy in the dark. The track is narrow, overgrown in places and there is a large field to cross."

"The full moon will help. I need to know if there's Boche about. I don't like being caught with my pants down."

She smiled. "I take it you intend to stay here for the rest of the night."

"I hope you serve a decent breakfast," Laroche added. "I'm famished."

"I'm sure I'll be able to satisfy you both."

Martial laughed. "I don't doubt it."

*****

After three days in Les Singuelles, Eliane realised that, in her haste to distance herself from Rausch's attentions, she had committed an error. Although she appreciated how her parents had made an effort to look after her and the children, she missed not only Jean-Claude but also the comfort and familiarity of her own house. Somehow, being a guest even in her former home was not as easy as she had thought. She found even normal conversations somewhat guarded in order to hide uncomfortable truths; she also worried that her parents might be forcing themselves to tolerate two boisterous youngsters.

Strangely, Rausch must have been working away; he had failed to appear during her short stay. Perhaps, he had other issues to concern him, especially as the news of an impending invasion gained more credibility with each passing day. Anticipating that the situation caused by the colonel's obsession with her would soon be resolved, she decided to return to Saint Sauveur.

In a similar way, Jean-Claude had also found his wife's absence difficult to accept. An empty house immediately lost its appeal; coming home to the hollow silence of loneliness hardly compensated for his long period of captivity, its boredom and isolation from his loved ones. After work on the day following Eliane's departure, he decided to seek company with friends in one of Bellac's many bars. At that time, local hostelries were hubs of speculation and rumour, places where he could draw comfort from the prospect of liberation.

Returning home two days later after another drinking session, he discovered Eliane and the children waiting patiently in expectation of renewing normal family life. Still unaware of his wife's main reason for leaving, he apologised for his inebriated state whilst promising to spend more time with his family. Tearfully, Eliane hugged him, hoping their lives would now settle down into a pattern comparable to her pre-marital dreams.

Suddenly, that bubble burst.

116

Sinking into an armchair, he lit a cigarette. "I suppose that Boche officer was pleased to see you."

Eliane turned away, fearful her eyes might betray her. "He wasn't there. He must have been working in Limoges or Vichy or wherever else he visits." She shepherded the children towards the stairs. "I'll put them to bed; it's late." His comment irritated her, left her wondering if he suspected something.

She had imagined that her simple vision of a new life, uninhibited by German oppression and bathing in the glory of liberation, would give her strength to endure the current privations of occupation. With those few words, Jean-Claude had extinguished the beckoning light at the end of the country's dark years.

Her husband was more pragmatic. His short time with the Résistance had alerted him to the difficult journey towards final victory. He had no illusions about the sacrifices that he and many of his fellow countrymen would have to make. On the domestic front, if it were true Eliane had strayed, he would blame the German officer. He would be justifiably entitled to kill the man.

Neither shared their true beliefs with each other. Closely bonded only by their mutual love, the dreamer and the realist could not have foreseen what lay ahead.

*****

Escorted by two resisters, Hector staggered through Anne-Marie's front door. Ignoring his host, he glared at Martial, red-faced and eyes bulging. His companions' expressions communicated that there had been no German presence.

"Which bloody group organised tonight's fiasco?" he snarled. "I reckon they gave you false co-ordinates so they could keep the whole damn consignment for themselves."

"You know I cannot give you that information," Martial replied. "The message I received said it had been cancelled. I must accept that. I'm sorry I was unable to inform you before you left." He pushed a chair towards the agent. "Take a seat; join us in a drink." He smiled. "Anyway, the exercise will have been good for you."

Anne-Marie wanted to laugh, partly at the contrasting attitudes of the two men and partly with relief at seeing Hector had 'passed the test'.

117

Begrudgingly, Hector accepted Martial's invitation, joining the others seated around the table. Anne-Marie brought out a baguette, a platter of cheese and slices of cured ham. Another bottle of wine added to the impromptu meal.

"So, when are they going to deliver armaments?" Hector demanded. "From what I've seen, we're pretty desperate."

"I'm waiting for your wireless operator to contact me," the gendarme replied. "I'm suggesting she transmits to London from here next time…she can use the barn."

"Why didn't she inform me the drop was cancelled?"

"The message came via another group's courier direct to me." Martial shrugged. "That's life, I'm afraid."

The feasting, the drinking and the conversation lasted well into the early hours. Eventually, Ann-Marie went to bed, leaving them to sort out their own sleeping arrangements; they all seemed determined to stay until dawn. The night was warm for the second week of May; sleeping rough in the barn was not an issue, especially after having consumed a considerable amount of red wine. Hector retired to his former room, still smarting from a wasted bike ride yet ignorant about how close he had been to losing his life.

Chapter 15

Haute Vienne
1944

Over the next few weeks, the mood of the population underwent a noticeable change; an air of expectation began to replace the previous atmosphere of hopeless resignation. Even the behaviour of the Wehrmacht soldiers seemed abnormally apprehensive in contrast to their usual arrogant manner. No longer on the streets to shop or socialise, they patrolled in pairs, ever watchful but visibly edgy. The *milice* had become more active, rounding up suspects and raiding premises in their frantic search for weapons. In contrast to this oppressive activity, perceived collaborators looked over their shoulders, their hopes of a bright future in the Nazis' New Europe suddenly in jeopardy. For the citizens of France, D-day was on the horizon; preparations for operation Overlord were almost complete. It all depended on the weather.

In the Terminus bar, Martial, Laroche, Jean-Claude and Marcel were drinking and playing belote. On an adjacent table, Hector and his wireless operator shared a carafe of wine with Doctor Jerome. The underlying topic of conversation amongst this apparent social gathering of friends was the strategy of disruption during the days leading to and following the invasion. With armaments and explosives secreted in various locations, the discussion also covered distribution, targets, procedures and the responsibilities of individual group leaders.

Martial, supported by Hector, remained adamant that training in the use of weapons should be stepped up for the new recruits whose numbers had increased dramatically during the previous months. Fuel dumps, railway marshalling yards and all lines of communication were legitimate targets to support the invasion's impact. Hector stressed that taking on the German army with its firepower would be unproductive and would cause needless casualties. Jean-Claude and Laroche were content to supervise all attempts to create mayhem and destruction of the Nazi's capacity to move freely in the region.

On June 1st, London transmitted a series of *messages personels* to wireless operators across France to signify that within days they could expect a Second Front. The stage was set for a period of concentrated sabotage and revolt against the occupying forces. At this point, however, they were unaware that, following the Normandy

119

landings, some 15,000 troops and an armoured column of 1,400 vehicles of the Das Reich 2nd SS Panzer Division would be relocating from Montauban in the south to reinforce the German defences in northern France. To achieve that objective, they would be passing through the Limousin region.

*****

A teacher from the *lycée* at Bellac was the first to arrive at Berneuil; he had cycled from Saint-Junien-les-Combes. Doctor Jerome, authorised to use a petrol-driven car because of his profession, rolled up outside the house shortly afterwards. Father Milani and Jean-Claude accompanied him. Anne-Marie ushered them quickly into the barn where Hector sat on a bench chatting to the teenage daughter of the local baker in Berneuil; she had been one of the group's couriers since the turn of the year. The pop, pop of a moped signalled the arrival of Laroche. Several other resisters who lived nearby wandered in to swell the numbers. Ten minutes later, Martial's car drew to a halt outside; his passengers were Céleste, the recently arrived wireless operator, Gilbert and Marcel. As they entered the barn, a hush descended on those already gathered inside.

Martial stood before the group, a smug smile of imminent redress replacing his usual serious expression. "By now, you will all know that Maquis groups across France have received their *messages personels* to signify that the Allies have commenced the invasion. The time has come to liberate our beloved country from these Fascist barbarians."

He sat on one of the steps leading up to the hayloft before looking resolutely at each individual standing before him. "It's important to remember that we are not here to confront the military might of the enemy but to disrupt their movement and especially their communications. The more we can occupy their manpower across the country, the less chance they have of supporting their troops in the north. Whatever we achieve in this region will, in turn, benefit the troops engaged in the Normandy landings. Under no circumstances will we take on their firepower unless we come under attack, forcing us to defend ourselves. Our role is to strike swiftly where it will hurt them, and retreat into the shadows. We will focus on destroying fuel dumps, sabotaging telephone communications and, with help from the *cheminots*, blowing up rail tracks, especially in complex areas such as

120

marshalling areas, junctions, points and signalling systems. The railway workers will help with identifying appropriate targets."

He lit a cigarette before continuing. "Following this meeting, you will return to your groups and arrange the issue of armaments, ammunition, explosives and other materials necessary for your assignments. There has been a steady influx of young men escaping the compulsory labour scheme. It is vital to train these recruits in the handling of weapons before letting them loose with any firearms."

He turned towards the British agent. "Hector has assured me that there will be more *parachutages* over the next months with additional supplies: sten guns, gammon bombs, et cetera. London will contact Céleste with dates and will co-ordinate drop zones. The couriers will communicate any new information as and when it happens." He looked at Anne-Marie and Lili, the baker's daughter as if to confirm their acceptance of that role.

Laroche leaned against an oak pillar. "What if we see any Boche soldiers on their own or in pairs...like easy targets? Can I shoot the bastards?"

A wry smile spread across Martial's face. "Though I'd like to say yes, we must refrain...unless of course they are attacking us. If we spend our time haphazardly shooting Boche, there will be heavy reprisals. Already, you will have seen posters declaring that they will hang or shoot ten innocent hostages in retaliation for each assassination. We're relying on the support of the local population for food, extra ration cards, tobacco and of course, their collaboration. Boche reprisals will have a negative effect on that vital co-operation."

He moved across the straw covered earth floor towards a table where Anne-Marie had earlier placed a number of cups and glasses. Father Milani lifted a cardboard box onto the table from which he extracted four bottles of wine.

"Help yourselves," he announced, cheerily. "With the blood of Christ on your lips, the good Lord will protect us." It seemed like an impromptu communion in preparation for their offensive against the enemy. Their enthusiasm and joy would be short lived.

*****

Within days, the Das Reich, 2nd SS Panzer Division would arrive in the Limousin region, frustrated and enraged by constant skirmishes with the Résistance en route from Montauban. It was paramount that

121

tracked heavy armour including the Panzers should be transported north by rail; travelling on tarmac roads would be detrimental to the caterpillars. However, they were unable to conduct the essential entrainment; most railway flatcars were unavailable and destructive actions by the Résistance had rendered the remainder immovable. Consequently, the armoured formations were forced to rumble over surfaces that would cause major breakdowns and delays. Some, requiring spare parts, remained at the roadside, abandoned by their crews.

As the Division pushed on, small groups of resisters blocked roads with felled trees, barricaded bridges and ambushed the convoy, resulting in many diverse skirmishes with losses on both sides. By the time they reached the Limousin region, the Das Reich found themselves fatigued, exasperated and vexed by the problems they had endured. As local resisters prepared to restrict their progress further, it came as no surprise to witness some brutal reactions.

Following an insurrection at Tulle, south of Limoges, the SS soldiers of a reconnaissance battalion hung ninety-nine hostages from lampposts and balconies as a reprisal against the failed liberation attempt. Arriving at Limoges, the main Das Reich Division split into three battalions to contain and defeat the various pockets of resistance activity in and around the city. One headed out to Guéret, one to Argenton-sur-Creuse and the other to Saint Junien. The following day, the battalion from Saint Junien entered the small market town of Oradour-sur-Glane where, after rounding up every inhabitant, they massacred 642 men, women and children, burning the dead and the dying before plundering and setting fire to every building.

*****

Against this terrible backdrop of barbaric carnage and wanton destruction, the Maquis stepped up their activities. Martial's advice about not engaging with the enemy became difficult to sustain. After several mini battles, the various battalions recommenced their journey towards Normandy. One such group, heading towards Poitiers, passed through Bellac before climbing from the town into the open countryside beyond its northern boundary.

Returning from a mission involving explosives and railway tracks, Laroche, Jean-Claude and Gilbert encountered other members of their group who had been erecting a barricade at Bel-Air earlier that day. Believing the Das Reich Division would have already left the area, they decided to take the opportunity to head homewards. Before splitting up to go their separate ways, they headed along a narrow country lane that would join the *route nationale* linking Bellac with Poitiers.

Approaching the junction, Laroche brought them to a halt. "Boche," he whispered. Through a gap in the trees that lined the main road, they spotted an army truck, seemingly stationary and surrounded by a small group of soldiers. They quickly crouched into the ditches along both sides of the lane.

Despite orders not to engage with enemy troops, they decided the opportunity was too good to ignore; besides killing a few soldiers, the truck might contain armaments, useful booty. The element of surprise together with their shared firepower convinced them to mount an assault. Stealthily, they edged forwards along the ditches beneath the cover of the prickly hedgerows of wild hawthorn that rose above their shoulders like protective ramparts. As they drew near, they could see a group of SS soldiers standing on the roadway, chatting and smoking and two more leaning against the tailboard of the vehicle; one other stood by a tree, relieving himself.

Unfortunately, they were unaware the rest of the column had also parked up along the main road. Several metres farther down the hill leading up from the Pont du Vincou, the main part of the convoy remained hidden by the trees lining the route. Still ignorant of the danger that confronted them, at a signal from Laroche, they scrambled from the ditches, firing their Sten guns. Gilbert tossed a Gammon grenade that struck a tree, missing his principal target, the group of soldiers. Drawing close to the junction, they realised with horror that they had stumbled upon an armoured battalion. Within seconds, extra troops raced up the hill, firing at the fleeing resisters. The onslaught threatened to engulf their world in a hail of bullets.

Gilbert and four other resisters lay dead, their bodies scattered across the lane and the ditches. Severe wounds to both legs prevented one youngster from escaping. The soldiers took him prisoner. Later, after the convoy had moved on, the SS hung him at Bussière-Poitevine. On the way, they destroyed the barricade at Bel-Air, killing two more resisters. Laroche, Jean-Claude and three others had fled across the fields into the woods where they remained until they were sure it was safe to descend into Bellac. Leaving their weapons at a safe house, they split up to return to their individual homes.

123

Jean-Claude stopped at the gendarmerie where he broke the news to Martial. The gendarme expressed his rage at their stupidity but agreed to summon other members of the group to collect the bodies after informing the families of the tragic news. There had been losses before in the area but not on this scale, and few from this Maquis. By the end of the following month, many more would die before the Limousin region tasted the sweetness of its long-awaited liberation.

*****

The sun had almost dipped beyond the Monts de Blond by the time Jean-Claude reached Saint Sauveur. He stopped pedalling to freewheel the final few metres to his house, trying to calm his frustration before confronting Eliane. Somehow he had to clear the sadness and anger that tormented his soul. Out there in the sunshine, ordinary youngsters, some of whom he had known for several years, had died needlessly. He found it deeply upsetting that he and others in the group had been incapable of saving them. Martial had been justified to feel incensed by their recklessness.

He found his wife upstairs, busy putting the children to bed. Hearing him closing the door, she stepped onto the landing. "I'll be down in a minute. Do you want to say goodnight to Sylvie and Sebastian before I tuck them in?"

Taking a deep breath to clear his head, he climbed the staircase. She smiled before kissing him lightly on both cheeks as he entered the dim interior of the bedroom. She turned to the children. "There you are; I told you papa would be home soon."

Relieved by the warmth of her reception and the children's smiling faces, Jean-Claude kissed the delighted youngsters before wishing them sweet dreams. As he turned to leave the bedroom, the fading light from a window fell upon him.

Eliane recoiled, shocked by his appearance. "Oh, my God!" she exclaimed, pointing at his shoulder. "What have you done?"

Puzzled, her husband looked down at his jacket; splatters of blood covered the lapels and the collar of his shirt. He stared vacantly at his wife. "I'll get cleaned up."

Despite a tirade of questions from his wife, Jean-Claude merely changed into clean clothes before joining her in the living room. In silence, they sat facing each other whilst eating their evening meal.

"Are you going to tell me what happened?"

He chewed on a stringy piece of *rouelle*; the pork fillet was courtesy of a local farmer who supplied most of the village with black market meat. "It was just an accident at work; one of the engineers slipped off a ladder and gashed his leg."

Eliane glared at him. "I assume he fell onto you, wrapping his injured leg around your neck."

Jean-Claude continued eating.

"To cause so much impact on your clothes, that blood must have spurted with some force. How about telling me the truth? I know when you're lying to me."

"It's not important."

She pushed her plate to one side before leaning towards him. "Jean-Claude, what are you hiding from me?"

He swallowed hard as the image of his fellow resister's shattered face choked his mind; tears welled in his eyes. A few centimetres to his left, he could have been the victim instead of the unfortunate youngster. He leaned back in his chair. "Sorry, I can't eat any more of this."

Eliane stretched her hand across the table. "Please...please tell me what really happened."

"The Boche shot Gilbert...sorry, you know him as Bertrand Menot."

"Why? He doesn't work on telephones; he's an optician. What had he done...and why were you involved?"

Jean-Claude looked up; his sad eyes seemed to be appealing for understanding and forgiveness. "We were with the Maquis."

His wife withdrew her hand. "The Maquis? What in the name of God were you doing...or no...don't tell me you've joined the Résistance."

He nodded and turned away.

Eliane rose from her chair before pacing the room. "How long?"

"Since the first day I walked to the church to see Father Milani. It was necessary to prove my release was not the result of your collaboration. Father Milani suggested I should join the Résistance to clear your name. It would give out the right signal."

"Don't tell me he's involved."

Jean-Claude nodded.

"Oh my God!" she shouted. "...and under Franz's nose. How could you be so stupid?"

"Who the hell is Franz?"

"Colonel Rausch…that's his first name."

He stood and turned round to confront her. "And how long have you been using first names?"

"I can't keep calling him 'Colonel Rausch' all the time, can I?"

"What d'you mean by 'all the time'?" he snarled. "How often is he round here? How often have you been entertaining the enemy in our house?" He glanced towards the staircase. "In front of the children?"

Eliane's anger spilled over. "Since I asked him to facilitate your release. How else do you think you are standing here…freed from your prisoner-of-war camp?"

After a few moments of silence, Jean-Claude returned to his seat. "He's SS…a dangerous individual." His fingers drummed the table. We need to find a way to stop him from coming here."

Eliane folded her arms. "It's a bit late for that."

"I don't understand…I mean there's no reason for him to continue to come here. Why? Just tell me why he visits so often."

She joined him at the table. "He's young, away from his family. He finds it difficult to be alone. Perhaps he sees me as some kind of replacement for his mother…or his sister."

"Or his wife."

"He's not married."

"So, you've obviously talked about his family in Germany. Why don't you ask him about the families the SS massacred at Oradour? Ask him why they murdered babies and all those children from the schools. He's an animal, a brute…savages, all of them."

"Look, I don't want him here. I'm hoping the occupation will soon end and he'll go back to Germany. Please, Jean-Claude, don't do anything rash. The repercussions would be awful; think of the children." She leaned over and touched his arm again. "The Allies are making progress. Everyone believes liberation is within touching distance. You must stay safe. Once this nightmare is over, we will have our lives back again."

In his mind, he knew she was right but his original vow to avenge Emile's agonising death at Hinzert-Pölert had become even more deep-rooted. The sight of that poor young man's terrible death still haunted him, and the more recent atrocities committed by the Das Reich had only served to compound his hatred towards everything German. Even if liberation was in sight, nothing had changed; he needed to execute one final act of retribution.

Chapter 16

Bellac, Haute Vienne
1944

For the maquisards who lived permanently beneath a canopy of parachute silk deep in the forest of Rochechouart, the struggle against the occupiers would continue. They yearned for the day when they would be free to march through the streets of Bellac in a victory parade. For Jean-Claude, work had become secondary to his resistance activities. Despite losses, small groups across Haute Vienne continued to harass German troops whenever they appeared vulnerable. Enemy patrols, especially those including the *milice*, became prime targets as Maquis numbers swelled, encouraged by intensified Allied airdrops of munitions.

Hector lost control of the group as the scent of victory infected them like an unstoppable epidemic. Like many of his compatriots, Jean-Claude took every opportunity to engage the enemy, attaching himself to various F.T.P. groups within the Maquis de la Vienne. In one such group, he found eleven gendarmes from the area who had been involved with the Résistance for almost two years. On another occasion, he suffered a severe puncture in his cycle tyre, causing a visit to the local cycle shop. Recognising him from a previous action against a patrol near Rancon, the owner explained he was about to leave to collect a consignment of arms in his van. Jean-Claude offered to join him provided he would replace the split tyre on their return.

Having completed their mission without incident, Monsieur Fournier, the shopkeeper repaired the bicycle in his shop. As dusk descended, Jean-Claude set off home in good spirits, satisfied with his evening's adventure. His euphoria was short-lived. As he cycled into Saint-Sauveur, he stopped abruptly; a black Citroen sat menacingly outside his house. Immediately, his buoyant mood turned to anger. *Rausch! While I've been fighting Boche, one is here consorting with my wife.* He needed to control his emotions to prevent him from reaching into the bag that contained his work tools; beneath his equipment, an oily cloth concealed a loaded revolver.

Tormented by the image of an unfaithful wife, he dismounted and stood staring firstly at the vehicle and then at the house, fearful of what might be happening inside. The situation he had dreaded since his return from captivity was beginning to unfold; now he must confront those inevitable demons. Perhaps, it was just a casual visit; perhaps he was over-reacting, but why did Rausch still need to visit? Over twelve months had passed since his release. Despite his wife's attempt to make light of the question, it still bothered him. He glanced down at his tool bag; the risk was too great. Any action resulting in the death of an SS colonel would have repercussions, not just for him but for his family, his friends and any others associated with him; the cost would be horrendous. The German could be innocent, resulting in needless tragic consequences, but if he was guilty?

His pent up anger penetrated every limb; his heart raced. Still no sign of the German leaving the house. What was going on in there? Once again, his eyes fell upon the bag; he could feel the revolver in his hand; he imagined pulling the trigger; a dead SS officer, the enemy, one less to oppress him and his family. He sighed deeply and pictured the retribution, the scale of barbarism the Boche inflicted on the inhabitants of Oradour. No one lived there anymore. Could that happen to Saint Sauveur, or even to Bellac? With blankness in his eyes, he became aware of the silence. The light had begun to fade as night closed in. *I must go home. I must stay calm.*

In the distance, two figures were approaching, walking but with hasty, purposeful strides. There was something familiar about them. He strained his eyes to see their faces. As they drew near, he gasped, immediately recognising the odd couple. They were heading towards his house. More questions suddenly flooded his mind, as though he had slipped from reality into some bizarre dream. Confused, he relaxed his grip on the bicycle. It clattered to the ground, breaking the silence. The approaching figures stopped and stared. Their lives would never be the same again.

Part Three

Villa Tivoli, Limoges

Chapter 17

Saint Sauveur, Bellac
1944

Two weeks had passed since the D-day landings. Despite fierce resistance on and beyond the beaches, the Allied armies had forced the Wehrmacht to retreat. Aided by superior air power, the establishment of several bridgeheads allowed a gradual increase of troops and armaments. Across France, the Nazi's regional military commands were preparing to scale down their operations locally, despatching troops to support their beleaguered colleagues in the north. Already, some Kreiskommandanturen were closing down local offices whilst still attempting to maintain control through the *conseils départmentals*. Though Vichy was in turmoil, the Feldkommandantur at Limoges remained operational, determined to inflict severe damage on those who continued to resist.

SS-Standartenführer Rausch was on a personal mission. Hitting the accelerator pedal, he swept up the hill to Saint Sauveur before braking hard outside the house of the Tricot family. In one swift movement he leapt from the vehicle. The front door was ajar. He entered the living room. Upstairs, Eliane had just put the children to bed. Hearing the door below creaking open, she assumed her husband had returned from work.

She stood at the top of the stairs. "Allo!" No response; usually, he would greet her. She shouted again, this time louder.

Rausch appeared at the foot of the stairs. Her heart skipped a beat. In the fading light, she could not discern the look on his face but his stance frightened her. Resplendent in his SS uniform, he stood with legs apart, gloved hands on his hips and head tilted upwards, a dramatic posture that exhibited dominance.

"Where is he?" he demanded. "Where's your terrorist husband?"

"I...I don't understand."

"Jean-Claude...where is he?"

"He's at work...why, what's happened?"

Rausch bounded up the stairs, placed one of his gloved hands firmly around Eliane's neck and pushed her against the landing wall. "First, you defy me with your Jew, and now you lie about your husband. Why didn't you tell me he was with the Résistance?"

"I...I didn't know. Truthfully, I didn't know. Please, you must be mistaken. He works for the telephone company." She was finding it difficult to speak; his grip around her throat had not relaxed.

"A Wehrmacht soldier was shot dead at the railway station a short while ago. Gestapo agents have arrested a witness, a station employee, whose description of the assassin accurately matches your husband. I've known about his resistance activities for weeks...I kept him safe, but now...now I am angry. Why has he killed one of our soldiers? It was so needless at this moment; it's obvious we'll be moving out soon."

For the first time, his expression frightened her; a shiver ran down her spine. "It must be a mistake," she gasped, trying to calm him. "Ask him yourself. He'll be home soon."

His hand slowly and deliberately slid from her neck to caress her breast. He pressed his whole body against her; she could feel his erection against her inner thigh.

"I will. Why do you people create so much unnecessary rebellion against authority?" He pressed his face closer. "You know how I feel about you. Why do you betray me?"

She could feel his hot breath; a cocktail of nicotine and alcohol entered her nostrils.

"I need you, Eliane; you must entertain me whilst we wait." His smile seemed unnatural, as though it had lost its sincerity. "You can start by pouring me a drink."

"I think you've drunk enough already."

He reeked like an inebriate; his speech was slurred, his blue eyes, normally bright and controlled, were glazed.

He fumbled to pull up her skirt with his free hand. She felt his fingers feeling their way up between her legs.

"I've been celebrating, Eliane. I forgot to tell you it's my birthday. It's time to open my present." He thrust a knee between her legs, forcing them apart.

Gasping, she tried to slip from his grip. He pressed harder, pinning her to the wall, his hand sliding beneath her silk knickers.

At that moment, a female voice cried out below. "Eliane...are you there?" Anne-Marie had seen Rausch's car outside. Not wishing to interrupt what might have been an embarrassing situation, she had entered the house and decided to make her presence known.

Rausch spun around, pushing Eliane back against the wall with one hand whilst withdrawing his revolver with the other. He pushed the barrel against Eliane's neck. "Not a word," he whispered. Dragging her towards the top of the stairs, with his free hand he pressed her against the wall again. "Now, tell her to come up."

Shaking with fear, Eliane managed a loud whimper. "I'm upstairs, Anne-Marie."

Unaware of the drama above her head, Anne-Marie smiled. "I understand. I'll call back later."

"Tell her to come to the bottom of the stairs," Rausch growled.

"It's alright...you can come up."

Intrigued, Anne-Marie appeared below. On seeing Rausch, she froze.

Drunk and angry, Rausch swung the revolver round and levelled it at the young woman. "Another one from my list! How many escapees are you hiding today? Yes, I know what you do. Why risk your life? You will be caught, tortured and shot. You cannot win; you and your terrorist friends will be annihilated. You must stop; it's over." He was so drunk that his speech was slurred, his movement erratic, and all reason had forsaken him.

Without any thought of the consequences, Eliane panicked. Sweeping aside the arm still gripping her, she pushed him away. Unbalanced, his leather boots lost their grip on the polished wood floor. He toppled headlong down the solid chestnut staircase.

Anne-Marie screamed as the SS officer tumbled onto her, pinning her in a corner.

Eliane yelled, "Oh, my God!"

131

At the foot of the stairs, Anne-Marie disentangled herself before stepping back in horror at the crumpled heap slumped in the well of the stairs. Rausch lay motionless at her feet.

Horrified, both women stared in silence as the enormity of what Eliane had done sunk in. Anne-Marie bent down to touch him.

"What have I done?" Eliane whimpered. "Is he alright?"

"Maman!" The pleading cry of a child's voice reawakened them to reality. Sylvie appeared in the doorway of the bedroom, disturbed by the commotion. Eliane quickly ushered her back to bed.

Downstairs, Anne-Marie leaned unsteadily against the wall. In the dim light, her face looked ashen. Trembling, she looked down at the lifeless body. "He's dead, Eliane. Oh, shit! You've killed him...a soldier...an SS officer. Oh, my God!"

Shaking and sobbing, Eliane stood unsteadily on the staircase above Rausch's corpse. "He was drunk; I've never seen him like that before. I thought he was going to kill us. He said he knew Jean-Claude was in the Résistance...and he must have known about you and your safe house."

Anne-Marie remained silent for a brief moment as she reflected on the terrifying consequences. "I don't think he did intend to kill us...at least not immediately."

"What makes you think that?"

"If he had intended to arrest us, he would have arrived with troops, the *milice* or gendarmes. It would have led to an interrogation and imprisonment...probably torture...but he came alone. You know what he's like. He probably intended to blackmail us...forcing us to betray those involved in the local Maquis. He already had you in his pocket with David's Jewish heritage...sexual favours or the boy's life. I bet he intended to use Jean-Claude and me in a similar way; collaboration and betrayal or torture and death. That's how the bastards operate...before they shoot you."

For a second time, Sylvie wandered onto the landing in her nightgown, whimpering and rubbing her eyes. Eliane ran upstairs, gathered her up and tucked her into bed. After soothing the child, she checked that Sebastien was asleep before returning to the landing, still trembling.

"What are we going to do?"

"Stay here with the children. I'll fetch Father Milani."

"This is hardly the time for a priest...and what will he think when he sees what's happened?" Eliane wrung her hands in despair.

132

"Please don't leave me here...not with him like that. Look at him! I've killed him! What can Father Milani do to help me? You mustn't bring him. He'll be outraged."

Anne-Marie forced a smile. "Don't worry about that...he's also with the Résistance. He'll know what to do."

Eliane endured the longest ten minutes of her life waiting for their return. Trying to make sense of the chaos, she sat alone in the living room as far away as possible from the staircase; every few minutes she glanced towards the doorway. The image of Rausch's lifeless corpse would haunt her forever.

Anne-Marie ran to the priest's house, her head full of horrific scenarios that might follow if they were unable to cover-up this tragic episode. Breathless, she hammered on his door; no answer. She ran to the church and found him pinning a leaflet to a notice board. Her urgency and the expression on her face immediately signalled that there was a grave problem.

Father Milani listened patiently to Anne-Marie's desperate tale, occasionally tutting and shaking his head in disbelief. "This is most unexpected and unfortunate. Are you sure it is the SS officer, Rausch?"

She nodded.

The priest wrung his hands. "What a stupid thing to do. What possessed the woman?"

"She thought he was going to kill us."

He shook his head, seemingly exasperated with the situation. "Surely not."

"He had a gun!"

"You mean he threatened you with his gun?"

"He pointed it at me."

Deep in thought and with head bowed, he walked towards the nave. Even without knowing the exact details of what had transpired, he realised the situation required swift action. After several more moments of contemplation, he turned to face his visitor. "You said his car's outside the house; that must disappear. It seems that we'll also have to bury the poor man's body."

"Could we not put Rausch inside his car, drive it into the countryside and set it alight?"

"They'd blame the Résistance and use that as an excuse to shoot innocent hostages. We need both to disappear without trace to prevent any prospect of reprisals. I believe he travels about a lot. It could take days before the authorities miss him. As far as they're concerned, he could be anywhere in the southwest."

"I could take the car back to Berneuil and hide it in the barn."

"What if there's a Boche raid?"

She shrugged. "I'll chance that. If necessary, I know people who could dismantle it and bury the parts."

"You'll have to remove it tonight."

"No problem. There are few patrols since the invasion and none at night. They've scaled down their operations...too busy preparing to leave."

"How can you be so certain that this SS officer hasn't shared his information with anyone else...the Gestapo for example?"

"I told you. He thrives on power over his victims; he would use the knowledge to control us. He's already blackmailing Eliane."

"Really...blackmail?"

"He knew about Sebastien...that he was a Jew. He held the boy's life in his hands."

"If that's the case, why did he not report it?"

"He made a bargain with Eliane."

"If so, what did he demand in return for keeping quiet? She has no money or..." He hesitated, a look of anguish on his face. "Oh no, surely not that? I cannot believe he would behave in such a way. Who told you all this?"

"Eliane spoke to me in confidence. I promised not to say anything...but it's over now. You must never to speak with Jean-Claude about it."

The priest hung his head, wondering why Rausch had tried to manipulate one of his closest neighbours. "I'll treat whatever you say as though it were a confession."

"He demanded sexual favours from her...on a regular basis."

He sighed before sitting on a nearby pew. "I find it hard to believe." Dismayed by her account, he shook his head in disgust. "I shouldn't say it but, if he has sinned, he deserved to be punished. I trust the good Lord will forgive him." Wiping a tear from one eye, he looked up at Anne-Marie, almost pleadingly. "I hope she didn't lead him on and yield to his desires."

"I wouldn't know," she lied, and quickly changed the direction of the discussion. "More importantly, what are we going to do about the body?"

The priest frowned before easing himself to stand beside her. "I have an idea. C'mon, let's get the job done. Eliane needs our help; she's now our priority. We'll use his car to transport the body before you drive it away." His eyes lifted upwards as though seeking divine intervention. "Let's hope all the inhabitants of Saint Sauveur are sound asleep in their beds."

It was almost dark as they cautiously walked down the lane together. Approaching the house, they spotted the figure of a man wearily wheeling a bicycle towards them. Jean-Claude was on his way home. Suddenly, the bicycle clattered to the ground, shattering the silence.

*****

Eliane sat hunched on the sofa whilst Jean-Claude and Father Milani stood over Rausch's corpse. Anne-Marie leaned against the doorframe of the children's bedroom; they were sound asleep.

"Can you find an old sheet or something similar to wrap around the body?" The priest had removed the SS officer's revolver before examining his pockets for any documents that might have some use. He announced that his thorough search revealed nothing important.

Having recovered from the shock of finding a dead German officer in his house, Jean-Claude instinctively reacted to the situation. He bent down to straighten the corpse. "What about his leather belt and his boots? They could be useful."

"Take nothing that cannot be immediately destroyed or that might link us to him. There must be no evidence that could place him here tonight...his iron cross, his insignia...everything that he is wearing. We will bury him intact. As a soldier, he deserves nothing less."

Anne-Marie stepped down from the landing. "What about the neighbours when we leave?"

"It's a chance we'll have to take," Father Milani replied. He smiled. "They miss nothing during daylight hours when they can peep through the slats in their shutters but at night, they use those same shutters to barricade themselves against the world at large."

Having forced herself to vacate the sofa, Eliane commented as she watched from the doorway. "You're right, Father. They hide behind their closed shutters and never admit to witnessing anything. They only see what they want to see. Nowadays, it's normal to be

135

unaware of events beyond one's four walls, especially when it's the Boche asking questions. Ignorance is a virtue since the occupation."

Still wondering what had happened to cause this situation, Jean-Claude put his arm around his wife. "Leave this to us. We'll sort it all out." His relief at finding Rausch dead was evident in his changed demeanour; tenderness had returned.

Eliane's thoughts were elsewhere. "I'll help. After all, it's my mess; I should clear it up."

"There's no need." Father Milani gently dragged Rausch's corpse into the living room. "Anne-Marie will conceal his car. Jean-Claude and I will dispose of the soldier's body."

"I'm responsible so I'll help. Don't try to stop me." She wiped her tear-stained face with the cuff of her sleeve before staring down at the dead officer. "Where are you taking him?"

The priest held her hand. "I'm going to give him a Christian burial; it's my job; it's my duty."

"What...now...in the cemetery?"

"Generations of local families lie in peace in that place. You and the community would be appalled if I were to openly desecrate their resting place with the corpse of an enemy soldier, especially a Nazi SS colonel. Besides, imagine the furore if our secret activity ever leaked out. We can bury him on that patch of wasteland adjacent to my garden. The good Lord will decide the fate of his soul thereafter. At least he will be at rest on land that belongs to the church. As Christians, we owe him nothing less than that."

Jean-Claude had found an old linen sheet. "Let's wrap him and get this over." He brought up a length of rope from the cellar to tie the sheet tightly around the soldier's uniformed corpse.

Father Milani discovered the officer's cap by the door; he placed it on the man's chest before folding his limp arms across it. He looked at the others. "I know what you think of him, but he was a soldier carrying out what he believed in. Despite what we feel, he deserves our respect as fellow Christians."

Still shedding tears, Eliane nodded a silent approval; the others began wrapping the body. They carried Rausch to the car. Anne-Marie drove it up the lane to the priest's house, where they dragged the bundle onto the wasteland. As the car jerked away in the direction of Anne-Marie's barn at Berneuil, Father Milani disappeared to find forks and spades from his garden shed.

Eliane clung to her husband whilst tearfully explaining how Rausch had threatened them, resulting in his accidental fall down the staircase. Increasing cloud cover obscured the moon; the darkness suited their purpose. In the midst of tangled undergrowth, three shadows set about their sombre task. The cover-up would soon be complete.

Clouds parted briefly; spasmodic shafts of moonlight revealed the two men wielding their spades. Father Milani grunted, exasperated as the metal blade hit a lump of granite beneath the rough terrain. Jean-Claude cursed the darkness. Scraping away more earth with a rake, Eliane sniffled. Moistened by the damp air, lank strands of auburn hair cascaded over her pretty but troubled features.

"It'll take ages to excavate a hole deep enough," she whispered, wiping her nose with the cuff of her coat sleeve.

"We've at least three hours of darkness, plenty of time to clear up this predicament," the priest snapped. "Just keep digging."

Apart from the occasional blasphemy from Jean-Claude, for the next twenty minutes, they continued in silence. At one point, he apologised, not for the expletives but for his work rate. "I'm sorry it's slow progress…shovelling's not my favourite pastime at this moment in my life."

Trembling partly from the cold night air but mostly from fear, Eliane continued raking earth, ignoring his gripe. "How will we know when it's deep enough?"

Her husband clambered into the excavation they had created. "The sooner, the better." He discovered heavy clay had now replaced the initial layer of loose soil. "The deeper we dig, the more solid the earth." He stopped to wipe perspiration from his face.

"We'll stop when your shoulders are at ground level," the priest said, dismissing his remark. "It's not ideal, but it'll be sufficient for our purpose."

Another half hour passed until they estimated they had dug to a suitable depth. After Jean-Claude had climbed back to ground level, the three exhausted individuals silently surveyed the result of their labours. Spots of cool rain provided a welcome antidote to their hot sweaty bodies.

Father Milani quietly cast aside his spade. "Time to finish the job; let's get it over with."

They dragged Rausch's corpse across the rough ground before tipping it into the narrow pit they had dug. After standing in silence for several moments, Eliane spoke, wiping tears from her eyes and visibly shaking.

"What have we done? I'm so scared."

Jean-Claude turned towards her. "What have *you* done? We are just trying to cover up your stupidity."

Father Milani picked up a spade. "This isn't the time to start apportioning blame. In any case, it wasn't entirely her fault," he retorted, whilst looking skywards. "Look, the rain clouds are beginning to clear; we'll be exposed to the moonlight and soon it'll be dawn. Grab the other spade. We need to press on."

After filling the pit with the previously extracted earth, they set about blending the patch with the remainder of the rough ground. In time, weeds would grow to conceal their activity.

The priest leaned on his spade and mopped his brow with a piece of cloth from a trouser pocket. His voice trembled as he spoke. "Remember, tonight never happened. We must promise to wipe it from our minds. Go home. I'll deal with any other issues." He made the sign of the cross whilst muttering a few words of prayer.

As they walked away, Eliane turned to look back. The clouds had parted, revealing the new moon; it hovered like a beacon above the freshly dug earth. She shivered but no longer felt the cold. Subconsciously attempting to block out the world at large, she wrapped her jacket tightly around her slender body. With fearful reluctance, she entered her house; a sensation of loss and betrayal caught her breath.

Unwilling to climb the stairs, she lay on a sofa; still wide-awake, she stared towards the ceiling. Behind closed shutters, the darkness enveloped her; outside, the moon taunted her.

Jean-Claude wearily walked upstairs to check on the children. The stairs creaked, a revealing creak; a sound accentuated by the uneven steps of a limping man. Digging a grave on rough terrain and shovelling aside mounds of earth had not helped; his wounded leg was suffering. Memories of Hinzert-Pölert had flooded back. Several minutes passed before he descended to reappear in the doorway.

"Come to bed."

Huddled in the corner of the sofa, Eliane briefly looked up at her husband's drained expression before turning away.

He lit a cigarette. "I realise you're upset."

"Of course I'm upset…just look at what's happened."

"I thought you might be relieved to see the last of him."

"Relieved?" she shouted. "Relieved? I'm devastated. He would have been gone within weeks; the Germans are retreating in panic. It's because of you and your resistance activities that we're in this mess!"

"I don't understand."

"He came to arrest you...and Anne-Marie."

"Is that what he said?"

"No, not exactly...but why else would he have asked about you and accosted Anne-Marie when she arrived?"

"It's over. Put it behind you," he insisted.

She spun round to face him. "A young man died here tonight."

He sneered. "A Boche soldier! Just another Nazi brute."

"You're right. You don't understand. You're missing the point. He arranged your release and the end was in sight. How can you be so spiteful towards him...and so stupid?"

"What is there to understand? He was the enemy. They stole our liberty. Look at Oradour...premeditated slaughter of the town's inhabitants. Why set him apart from the rest?" Former doubts and suspicions returned, reducing his voice to a whisper. "Unless there is something else I need to know."

Her eyes smarting and moist from her tears, Eliane looked up at him angrily. "What d'you mean by that?" She suddenly felt vulnerable, fearful that any further prying might force her to lie.

"Nothing," he replied, similarly concerned about what he might discover if he pursued the topic.

Her eyes turned towards the staircase. "His lifeless eyes stared at me; blood trickled from his mouth." She glared at her husband. "He only came here tonight because of you...and Anne-Marie...and probably Father Milani...and all your other friends in the Résistance. He didn't deserve to die like that."

"You wouldn't say that if you had witnessed their brutality in the camps." He stepped closer to her. "Come to bed. Put it behind you." He reached out his hand. "We shouldn't let it drive a wedge between us."

Eliane recoiled. "I can't," she sobbed. "I cannot pass those stairs after what happened there."

"Eliane, you cannot spend the rest of your life downstairs. You must blot out what happened here. The end of the war is close; no more Germans, no more atrocities, no more pain to endure."

In defiance of her husband's entreaties, she withdrew into the corner of the sofa. "I'm not moving from here tonight. Go back to bed.

139

The children need their father. Perhaps tomorrow I may feel differently."

Accepting her stubborn attitude to be the result of the night's events, Jean-Claude decided there was no point in continuing the discussion. He returned to the bedroom as the first streaks of dawn spilled through the slats in the shutters. Perhaps a new day would soften or even dispel the shocking outcome of the earlier drama.

Despite the passing of many more dawns, Eliane would remain trapped forever in her memories.

*****

Jean-Claude slept fitfully for a couple of hours, the night's traumatic events preventing any possibility of a sound sleep. Reluctantly, he dressed and came downstairs to find his wife still hunched up on the sofa, staring vacantly at a blank wall.

Without turning her head, she spoke to him as though she were thinking aloud. "He said he had a list."

Her husband walked across the room to sit beside her. Gently, he held her hands until she turned to face him. "Who had a list?"

"Rausch. He threatened Anne-Marie, saying she was another one on his list...besides you."

"So, we were on a list." Jean-Claude shrugged his shoulders. "It doesn't matter now, does it? He's gone."

"He said it was a list...not just a scrap of paper with your two names on it. A list of suspects could mean many names, begging the question as to who else was on this list."

Her husband remained silent whilst considering the implications of her remark. "Did he show it to you?"

"Of course not!" She looked at him in despair. "He was hardly going to flaunt it in public! He ranted about it when he was threatening us. We need to find it."

"Well, it wasn't on his person. Father Milani searched his uniform and found nothing."

Eliane shook her head. "No, he said that he found nothing important. What if he missed it, perhaps believing it was just an innocent piece of paper?"

"If that's the case, the list is now beneath two metres of earth; problem solved."

"There could be a copy in his office at the Kommandantur in Limoges."

"What about searching his room at your parents' house?"

"You've forgotten already that what happened last night did not happen. How can I justify searching his room without explaining why. As far as maman and papa are concerned, Rausch is away on one of his business trips. They must never know the truth. Gestapo agents are bound to interview them when they discover he has disappeared. Imagine if they find his room ransacked; it would be their death warrant. For my parents' sake, I must act as though Rausch is still alive." She leaned forwards, her head in her hands. "It wasn't meant to happen like this."

Jean-Claude rose from the sofa and crossed to the window. He opened the shutters; daylight flooded into the darkened room. "If there is a copy of his list in Limoges, Anne-Marie is still in danger," he commented as he ran his fingers through his thick dark hair.

"So are you...and all the others on his list. I wish I knew why he had made a list...and who's on it."

"It's obvious. He's making a list of resisters for the Gestapo and the *milice*."

"If that's the case, you'll have to disappear. You do realise that going to work is off the agenda. We need to inform Anne-Marie."

"I can melt away into the Maquis and I suppose she could do the same. I'm more worried about you and the children. If the Gestapo or the *milice* come looking for me, they'll arrest you in the hope that you'll give me up. In fact, they'll torture you until you do." He leaned back against the wall. "The bastards have cruel methods to make people talk. All of us must disappear."

"The children cannot spend months hiding in the forests...nor can I." She looked at the clock on the mantelpiece before walking towards the stairs. "They'll be awake any moment. I'll dress them and we can decide what to do." She hesitated at the spot where Rausch had fallen.

"Are you alright?" he asked, seeing her troubled expression.

She took a deep breath and nodded. "This new situation puts everything in perspective. It's now about survival, isn't it?"

Jean-Claude smiled to himself. *She's over it.* "I'll boil some water. I need a coffee."

Chapter 18

Berneuil, Haute Vienne
1944

Anne-Marie arrived home unscathed. With no evaders at the house who might have assisted her, she drove Rausch's car deep into the barn beneath the hayloft. Concealing the vehicle completely would have to wait until daybreak when she would have more time and more energy to bury it beneath a mountain of straw.

After checking she had secured the barn door, she strolled across to her house, deep in thought. Mulling over what had occurred earlier, she concluded that Rausch must have gathered some intelligence about their involvement with the Résistance, but from where, or from whom?

She reflected on some of the more recent interventions by the *milice* and Boche soldiers in the Bellac area. There had been the alarming incident in the forest that had resulted in the shooting of a salesman who had been trying to entrap them. The following week, three resisters had deployed to a spot near Peyrat-de-Bellac to blow up a stretch of railway track but by chance, they spotted a vehicle nearby that belonged to a member of the *milice*. They immediately took the decision to abort the operation. Several resisters had also died in gun battles in situations where the *milice* appeared to have received forewarning. There was still a question mark over Hector, another issue that they had not resolved with any conviction.

Eliane had also mentioned an informer had told the Gestapo that he had recognised Jean-Claude as the resister who had shot the soldier at the railway station. Everything seemed illogical; several incidents but no arrests, including the night's earlier episode. If Jean-Claude was a suspect in the shooting at the station, why had the Gestapo not arrived to arrest him?

She fell into bed believing that Rausch and his contacts at Limoges must have infiltrated their network. Someone was feeding them with information. Like Eliane, she concluded that he must have compiled a list of suspects…but once again, why no arrests? She lay awake for some time, her thought processes resulting in no credible conclusion. Having consumed several glasses of wine after arriving home, she slept soundly until the noise of a motor vehicle woke her. In a panic, she threw on some clothes, lifted the loose floorboard beneath her bed, withdrew her revolver and raced downstairs.

Before she reached the door, she heard the squeals of young children. She tucked the gun into the waistband of her skirt and, smiling with relief, opened up to find Eliane standing there with her father. Sebastien and Sylvie were chasing each other around the extensive patch of land she called her garden. After apologising for her unkempt state, Anne-Marie invited them inside.

Monsieur Dutheil declined her invitation. "Eliane asked if I could drop her off with the children. I'm on my way to the cathedral in Limoges; it's the Requiem Mass for the victims of Oradour."

"Oh, my God. I'd forgotten about that. I expect my father will be there to pay his respects."

"I'll be back about mid-day if that's alright with you."

"Fine," Anne-Marie replied. "I'm just delighted to see the children again."

The two young women watched him drive off, as though it were just another ordinary day. After hugging each other, they sat at the kitchen table, sharing their thoughts about the current situation.

Though they had drawn similar conclusions regarding the existence of Rausch's list, Eliane expressed surprise at her friend's suggestion there might be a spy in Martial's Maquis. If that were the case, with or without the list, all their lives were in danger.

Anne-Marie shrugged. "I suppose that's the risk I took when I volunteered my services." She forced a smile. "However, I doubt you feel the same. You're just an innocent bystander in all this."

"I was until I killed the colonel. Now, I'm implicated as much as the rest of you...probably more. That's why I'm here...to ask a favour...more for the children than for me...if it's feasible."

"How can I help?"

"You mentioned your father earlier. I remember you saying that, having survived the atrocity at Oradour, he was lodging elsewhere."

Goose-pimples invaded the skin of Anne-Marie's neck and arms. "It was a miracle. The first time he had visited his brother in Limoges for months...and he chose that day, that one day when he could have become another statistic of the Nazi's barbarous brutality. God, he was so lucky. Mind you, they destroyed his house and its contents."

"You said he was now in a house at Blond."

"That's right. He lost everything when the Boche destroyed the village. There's a rumour that the department will provide temporary accommodation for those who lost their homes but survived. 'When' is anyone's guess!"

143

Eliane wiped tears from her eyes. "I wondered if he would take care of the children until I can find something more permanent for them...just in case there's a knock on my door. I can't use my parents because they'll be under suspicion as soon as the Kommandantur realise Rausch has disappeared."

"What about you...and what's Jean-Claude going to do?"

"He reckons he can disappear into the Maquis." She shrugged. "I suppose I can do the same without the children." She burst into tears. "I'm frantic with worry...I don't know what to do."

"Leave it with me. You can all go there. In fact, it's not a bad idea. I could do the same...at least for a short time. The atrocity at Oradour will have destroyed my father's family connections so, as his daughter, I would be untraceable at Blond. Yes, I'll organise that today."

"Are you sure? How big is this house at Blond?"

"Not a clue...but it doesn't matter. If it's tiny, we'll just be a little cosier! In any case, there's no immediate rush; it could be days or even weeks before the authorities miss Rausch. With luck, the Boche will be gone soon anyway. It'll just be a temporary measure." She stood and crossed towards the door. "Now, you owe me a favour...and the children can join in too."

Puzzled, Eliane rose from the table and followed her friend outside. The children raced towards them.

"C'mon little ones...we're going to play a game." She turned to Eliane. "I didn't have time last night to conceal the car with straw. We can all have fun emptying the hay loft."

As she unlocked the barn door, Eliane grasped her arm. "Before we start, how about checking inside the vehicle...unless you've already done so?"

"I was in too great a rush to conceal the bloody car than to spend time inspecting its interior."

"The list?"

Anne-Marie grinned. "It's worth a try." She turned to the children. "Inside the car, everyone; let's see what we can find!"

Sylvie found something; a leather document case beneath the driver's seat. Unable to read German, most of the official papers inside seemed to have no relevance to their search. They shuffled through each document two or three times, trying to decipher the general content.

"Just look for French names," Eliane kept repeating, as they became more exasperated.

"I give up," Anne-Marie muttered, stashing the papers back into the document case. "Stand clear, everyone. I'm going to start the motor." She turned to Eliane. "I'll drive it up against the far wall beneath the opening to the hay loft. It'll be easier to drop the straw straight down onto the car, and it'll look more natural to have a huge pile in one corner rather than in the middle of the barn."

Eliane held the children by the hand whilst Anne-Marie manoeuvred the car into position. After several attempts, she managed to position the vehicle where it would suit their purpose.

"What about the *coffre?*" Eliane shouted as Anne-Marie slammed shut the driver's door.

"I thought you had checked the trunk before we inspected inside," she replied.

Eagerly, Eliane twisted the handle to lift the lid of the *coffre*. Inside they found a small suitcase; it was locked.

"Take the children outside," Anne-Marie ushered them towards the door. "I've been looking forward to doing this." She placed the suitcase on the floor of the barn.

Eliane looked puzzled until she saw the revolver. "Oh my God! Be careful!" She quickly ran towards the house, dragging the children with her.

The first shot missed but made two holes as the bullet entered and left the suitcase before burying itself in the earth floor of the barn. The second shot shattered the lock and a large part of the suitcase's front panel as it ripped away both the lock and the handle.

"It's open," she shouted, as she rooted amongst several items of clothing and splintered toiletries.

She found no documents or papers.

Eliane stood alongside, still clutching the children. "You're crazy! Did I ever tell you before?"

"Damn…it's not here!"

"There's a pocket in the lining at the back."

Anne-Marie slid her hand inside the silk-lined pouch. "Nothing…it's empty."

Sebastien, having found a wooden box of tools in the *coffre*, was busy relieving it of the contents: spanners, screwdrivers, pliers, what looked like a manual, probably a handbook for the car, and a Michelin map of France.

Eliane took them from him whilst scolding him for soiling his hands with oil. She began returning the tools to the box when she noticed another small item beneath the map.

It looked like a diary; it was a notebook. Inside, there was a list of names...French names. Her heart thumped with excitement as she held the notebook aloft.

*****

The children were in the barn, frolicking beneath their mini mountains of straw. The car had earlier disappeared under a gigantic heap that, accompanied by lots of laughter, had cascaded from the hayloft. Eliane and Anne-Marie were inside the house drinking coffee.

Both had studied the notebook several times, each time expressing their astonishment at the numbers of local people involved with the Résistance.

Eliane pointed at one of the names in the list. "Look at this. Who would have guessed that Fournier, the owner of the bicycle shop was a resister? I only spoke with him a few weeks ago when he fixed the chain on my bike. Surely, he's too old to run around fighting the Boche."

Anne-Marie grinned. "I believe he provides a delivery service with his van. He carries cycle parts to prove he is en route to carry out repairs. Apparently, hidden compartments in his van contain weapons."

"He's a bit doddery...maybe that's why he gets away with it." She sipped her coffee. "There are so many names of people I know but I would never have guessed they were involved. I wonder which one of these might be spying for the Boche?"

"There are numbers and letters after the names. What d'you imagine that's all about?"

Eliane ran her fingers down the list where she discovered her husband's name. "Look at Jean-Claude's name. After 'Tricot', he has written 'MTF1EZ'. Many of the others just have the letters 'MNV' or simply 'MT', some with and some without a number." She turned the page. "Your name only has 'F2' written after it. It's obviously some kind of code...but for what?"

Anne-Marie took the notebook from her and closed it before placing it between them on the kitchen table. Folding her arms, she leaned back on her chair. "Have you noticed anything else unusual about the list of names?"

"Not really, apart from discovering some important people seem to be involved. What about you…what have you noticed?"

"It's more about what I've *not* noticed."

"Now you're talking in riddles!"

"Ask yourself whose name is missing."

Eliane reached for the notebook.

Anne-Marie checked her. "I'll tell you. My name is there, so is your husband's name and many others with whom I have had contact, but nowhere is the name of Father Milani."

Eliane withdrew her hand. "What are you suggesting?"

"Don't you find it strange that he's not on the list? If you were handing a list of suspects to the Boche, you would hardly include yourself…would you?"

Eliane felt sick. "I can't believe he would do such a thing. He's been so helpful." She pushed the notebook to one side. "No, you're wrong. He helped us to bury Rausch…on his land!"

"I asked him for assistance. He could hardly refuse…and, by helping us, he was the only other witness to what had happened."

"Oh, my God. He's probably already reported us."

"I doubt that. Think about it, Eliane. The only people who know about Rausch's death are you, Jean-Claude, him and me. It would be too obvious if the Gestapo suddenly paid us a visit about the SS officer's disappearance. If the townsfolk discovered he had betrayed us, he would end up like your despicable colonel."

She fetched a bottle of wine and two glasses. "I think we need a proper drink." She poured a large measure into their glasses. "In any case, we are only guessing. He might not be the Boche spy. He recruited Jean-Claude and more recently, me. Why would he turn, unless Rausch had some power over him…like he had over you?"

Feeling calmer, Eliane sipped her wine. "But there's still the mystery why his name is not on the list."

"Perhaps, whoever provided the list was unaware that the priest was involved."

"What are we going to do?"

"I'll pass the notebook to Martial, the leader of our Maquis group before heading to Blond. He's one of the gendarmes whose names are on that list." Picking up the notebook again, she flicked through its pages. "His name is followed by letters and a number,

'M1NVT'. It doesn't make sense." She took a large gulp of wine. "Do you realise that by killing Rausch, you've unwittingly become a resister…" She sneered. "…or in the eyes of the Boche…a terrorist."

Eliane shuddered. "I never thought of it like that. What will my parents say if they discover I'm in the Résistance?"

"Your father made the arrangements to acquire false papers for your cousin. Whom d'you think he contacted? He's a solicitor, Eliane. He knows the right people…no matter on which side of the fence they conduct their affairs." She returned to the notebook. "See, even he's in there. 'Bernard Dutheil', followed by 'M1NV'. He probably offers legal advice to the Maquis."

Eliane grinned. "I doubt that. The Résistance have little regard for the rule of law."

"You know what I mean. He can check false documents to see if they will pass scrutiny…like the papers you acquired for Sebastien."

Eliane remained silent for a short while, seemingly shocked by the reality of her situation. "Look at us, Anne-Marie. Four years ago we were normal people leading ordinary lives. Now we're all terrorists and criminals."

Anne-Marie continued to scan through the notebook. "There are also a couple of pages of writing…in German, of course. I wonder if Martial can translate them?"

Deep in thought, Eliane remained silent and sipped her wine. Part of her wished they had not discovered the notebook. In her world, inadequate knowledge can evoke a sense of insecurity; on the other hand, total ignorance can often prolong feelings of happiness. She reflected on the carefree life they had enjoyed before the war, praying that such blissful times would return.

Anne-Marie sensed her friend's inner turmoil. "Cheer up; the occupation could be over in a couple of weeks. Provided the Allies continue the much needed arms drops, we'll be free again to pursue our dreams." She emptied her glass. "Anyway, we have more pressing matters needing our attention. We'll pursue our original plan regarding Blond; it's a risk but we have no other option."

Chapter 19

Bellac, Haute Vienne
1944

The Terminus bar seemed unusually busy for mid-afternoon. Though two weeks had passed since the Normandy landings, the general conversation still revolved around the possibility of another invasion in the south, despite the intensive battles in the north. The Wehrmacht soldiers who frequented the premises looked more uneasy as each day passed. Several young soldiers in their grey-green uniforms sat drinking near the doorway. Gone was their usual bawdy behaviour, replaced by a more subdued, apprehensive demeanour.

Martial sat on a corner seat on the far side of the bar; he was reading a copy of *Le Courrier du Centre*—soon to be openly replaced by the clandestine newspaper, *Le Populaire*. From his vantage point, he could see the whole of the public area. Anne-Marie entered and quickly scanned the room before joining him. As she took her seat, she passed him the notebook. Concealing it beneath the surface of the table, the gendarme flicked through its pages.

"How did you acquire it?"

Anne-Marie faced him, arms folded as she scrutinised the expression on his face. She had agreed with Eliane not to make any mention about what had happened nor their discussion over the omission of Father Milani's name from the list. "I can't say."

Martial raised his eyebrows. "Can't or won't?"

"It was discovered by chance in the trunk of an SS officer's car. That's all I can tell you," she whispered.

"Would I be acquainted with this particular officer?"

She shrugged dismissively. "I have no idea with whom you consort in your private or professional life."

He smiled. "I'll take that as a 'yes'. Any thoughts on what seems to be some kind of code after the names?"

She shook her head. "It's possible that the letter 'T' could stand for 'terrorist', because that's how they describe us. As for the other letters, I've not a clue. I only brought it because I thought you should be aware that the SS appears to have a list of our Maquis members."

"Considering this information must have been in their possession for some time, they don't appear to have acted on it."

"How do you know they've had it a long time?"

149

"Some of these people are dead, killed in action earlier this year or have moved elsewhere." His took a sip of his beer before beckoning the barman.

"Surely it proves that someone in the group is providing them with information about us."

Martial closed the notebook. "They could have acquired this information under interrogation and torture of a captive. Since the Boche arrived south of the demarcation line, the *milice* have often assisted in the arrest of hostages and suspects, many of whom have disappeared. I wouldn't worry too much about this list."

"But my name is on there."

"Mine too and many others. What are they going to do…arrest everyone on the list?" He lit a cigarette. "What would you like to drink?"

Wondering how he could remain so calm and almost indifferent, she turned to the barman. "A glass of red."

"You'd be amazed how many people contact us anonymously at the gendarmerie to betray someone; most likely, some individual with whom they have a score to settle. We ignore such information…as I'm sure the authorities do."

"But this was in the possession of an SS officer."

"Are there other copies?"

Anne-Marie shrugged. "I don't know."

"Well, if this is the only list, you have nothing to worry about. It's now in our possession."

"Aren't you going to warn the others?"

"What's the point? Every resister is on high alert constantly…or should be. Look, I have contacts in high places who would warn me if there was the slightest suggestion of any potential round-ups in the Bellac area. Anyway, the Boche will be gone soon."

The barman returned with her drink.

Anne-Marie waited until he was out of earshot. "That's what everyone keeps saying but they're still hunting down the Maquis. The father of one of my friends told us that, ten days ago, the Kommandantur at Limoges attached posters everywhere advising the population that the authorities had taken over executive powers in the Limousin region. This has given them total control to summarily execute anyone considered a threat, especially resisters. Young men are especially vulnerable."

"It's always been the case. They stick up posters just to reinforce the message and frighten people...often hoping collaborators will come forward to betray offenders to save their own skin or to gain some financial reward. Lingering grudges tend to re-surface occasionally, even between neighbours or so-called friends. This occupation has brought out the best but sometimes the worst in human nature. We had one individual trying to infiltrate our group not long ago. We dealt with it."

"Yes, I heard." She took a large gulp of wine. "Oh, despite your assurances, I'm moving to live somewhere else, so the safe house at Berneuil will be closed down. If you want me to stay involved as a courier, I'll need a different letterbox."

"Where will you be?"

"I'm not prepared to say. It would put other innocent people at risk."

"So, how can you be contacted?"

"A box in the area of Lassalle or Panissac?"

"So, you're not moving too far away, then?"

"I don't want to use the box at Saint Sauveur any longer."

"What's caused this sudden change of circumstance?"

"I have my reasons."

"Is your decision connected to the discovery of the notebook?"

Anne-Marie sighed. "To some degree, but I can't say any more."

"Alright...you win. I'll let Danté know the new arrangements and he can contact you regarding the location of a letterbox you can use."

"Danté? Why the priest?" He was the last person she wanted to know about her movements.

"You use his box in the cemetery; he'll need to know you have moved elsewhere." He slipped the notebook into a pocket. "I'll keep this for now."

"I have no use for it. There's some writing on other pages that I don't understand...I don't speak German."

"I know a language teacher at the *lycée*; he should be able to translate it for me...and he's discreet. At the same time, I'll see if he can shed any light on those codes."

Not pleased she would have to rely on Father Milani for future information, yet desperate to avoid further questions, she quickly finished her drink, leaving Martial to finish his beer alone. Her next trip would take her to her father's temporary accommodation at Blond, where she had a huge favour to ask.

*****

"*Bonjour, ma petite.* I wondered how long it would take before you visited me in my new abode." Albert Fauvet stepped to one side, allowing his daughter to enter the house.

"I thought I'd give you time to settle in," Anne-Marie replied, kissing him on both cheeks. "How are you after your ordeal?"

He ushered her into the living room, sparsely furnished with a table, three wooden chairs, a plain oak dresser and a well-worn armchair. A musty smell lingered, a reminder of its previous lack of residents. Across the ceiling, aged cobwebs draped like gossamer hammocks between the oak beams. Faded floral wallpaper merely added to the general air of neglect.

"I'm afraid my mood vacillates between anger, grief and gratitude. God must have been looking after me that day but, unlike a true Christian, I will never forgive the Nazi bastards whose ferocious bestiality destroyed such a peace-loving community."

"How are you coping with it?"

"I'm finding it difficult." He dabbed a tear from his eye. "I re-live the memory even when I sleep. It was a beautiful summer's day; a slight haze over the Glane promised a scorcher. As I walked through the market place to catch the tram to Limoges, small children were playing their games, mothers were busy with their individual chores; everyone was looking forward to the weekend. I chatted and joked with friends...everything was normal, just like any other Saturday morning. I can still see their faces, hear their laughter." He wiped his eyes again. "After collecting my tobacco ration, I watched the tram rattling down the main street. It stopped outside Hôtel Milord."

He slumped into the worn armchair. "After spending the day with your uncle Baptiste, I returned on a late tram that arrived just after seven in the evening. German soldiers stopped it on the Saint-Victurnien road intersection. Sometime later, they ordered us out of the tram and marched us towards Les Bordes. After separating the men from the women and checking our papers, many heated discussions amongst the SS officers took place before they eventually released us."

"You must have been terrified."

"We all expected to be executed. I ran to a friend's house in Les Bordes. I can't find words to describe what Giles and I found on the Sunday; my house like many others had been almost burned to the ground. I found it difficult to believe it had actually happened. When German soldiers reappeared, presumably to plunder more valuables...I don't really know...we quickly left the smouldering ruins and the stench of burned flesh. Sickened by what we had witnessed, we returned to his house at Les Bordes."

He sniffed, took a deep breath and crossed to a cooker where a kettle was boiling. "You're just in time for coffee unless you'd prefer something stronger."

"Coffee will be fine, papa."

"Giles put me in touch with Pascal; he offered me this place for the immediate future. It's not perfect but it serves a purpose...and he's not charging me rent. I owe him a great favour."

"I'm here to also ask a favour if it's possible."

"I hope you're not in trouble."

"In a way...but not what you might think." She sat on one of the chairs by the table. "How big is this place?"

"Why...are you thinking of moving in?"

"You always could read my mind."

"You're welcome here anytime. You know you don't even need to ask."

"I know...but I'm not here just for me. Seriously, how many rooms are there? It looks quite large from the outside."

"It used to belong to the post office next door until Pascal bought it before the war; he intended to redecorate it and either sell it at a profit or rent it out, the wily old bird! I have this room, a small kitchen, two bedrooms and a bathroom. There's also a hangar with an asbestos corrugated roof and metal doors...but it has no electricity and only an earth floor. What d'you need?"

"Not sure yet. I definitely need space for two young children; you've met them...Eliane's little ones, Sylvie and Sebastien. There's also me and possibly two more adults."

"Hiding from the Boche?" He served the coffees.

Anne-Marie nodded.

"What's wrong with Berneuil?"

"Sit down; it's a long story."

Her father listened intently, occasionally interrupting her account about Rausch's death and the subsequent events. She knew she could

153

speak with her father in complete confidence; nothing would force him to betray his daughter or her friends. They had always shared a close, open relationship, even before the death of her mother.

"I know someone who will eventually take the car off your hands but it needs removing as quickly as possible. If they raid your house and discover the vehicle, you'll become their number one suspect." He stood and brought over a bottle of red wine and two glasses. "Beds for everyone may be a problem, but for the time being, perhaps we can make do with a mattress and palliasses for the children." He poured the wine. "When do you anticipate bringing over Eliane and her brood?"

"As soon as we can organise transport."

He reached across and held her hand. "I know you said it may be days, even weeks before they realise the officer has disappeared, but don't delay."

"How will you explain our presence here?"

He smiled. "Under the circumstances, the neighbours will admire the fact that my family…and my extended family…has rallied round me in my hour of need." He sipped his wine. "I'll play on their sympathy."

"I've heard they're talking about providing temporary accommodation for the Oradour survivors."

"The Ministry of Reconstruction has promised wooden barracks followed by new houses. I'll believe that when I see it. In the meantime, I'll look forward to spending time with you and my adopted grandchildren."

Anne-Marie wrapped her arms around her father, hugged him and pecked him on the cheek. "I do love you, papa." She glanced around the room. "We'll help you clean the place up; it looks so neglected. We'll make it seem like home. It could be some time before we know how and when the authorities are going to re-house you."

Members of the Résistance removed Rausch's car that same night; they parked it behind the Mairie in Berneuil. With false number plates, traces of insignia removed, an interior strewn with straw and a broken gazogine conversion fitted, it looked like an abandoned farmer's vehicle. Before they left, they siphoned off the much-needed petrol from its tank. Meanwhile, through his numerous contacts, Monsieur Fauvet acquired two mattresses, two palliasses, bedding and some timber from a local carpenter.

When his daughter returned later that same evening, she helped to prepare a room for their new arrivals, whilst listening to her father explaining how he would make temporary bed frames from the lengths of wood stacked outside the kitchen. Earlier, she had met with Eliane who had organised her father to take them to Blond in his car the next day. Everything seemed to be falling into place to execute their planned disappearance.

*****

Still filled with bitter resentment over Rausch's constant visits and presence in his house when he was absent, Jean-Claude contacted Martial to demand more action against the occupying forces and, especially the *milice*. They arranged to meet on Allée Jean Dintras at the entrance to the municipal cemetery at Bellac. A graveyard seemed appropriate for discussing their mutual desire to destroy the enemy. The encounter prompted a strange conversation; only one of them knew that Rausch was dead, only one had seen the list and the other was only aware of its possible existence. Neither was initially prepared to admit what they knew.

Since Anne-Marie's visit, the gendarme wondered whether Jean-Claude could have been the informer in return for his release, but realised many of the names on the list had died before he had returned from captivity. Now here he was, demanding to wage all-out war against the enemy, hardly the obsession of an informant. Aware of the rumours about Rausch's over-zealous attention to the man's wife, he guessed Jean-Claude had designs on killing the officer personally. Irrespective of the consequences, the angry young man would perceive such an act of revenge to be justified. Believing the occupation would soon be over, he decided Jean-Claude's rage would be best directed towards finding who had provided the SS with the list of resisters.

He showed him the notebook. "We have an informer in our midst. I know I can trust you, because there are names of comrades here who died before you returned home. I want you to smoke him or her out."

Jean-Claude scrolled down the list in astonishment. "Where has this come from?"

"For reasons of confidentiality and to protect my source, I cannot disclose that information; suffice to say that I have good reason to believe it belonged originally to an SS officer."

155

Despite realising the owner of this list could have been Rausch, he refrained from making further accusations, sensing that Martial was not too enamoured by his existing vendetta against the officer. He decided showing surprise would be the sensible reaction. "Good God! This is comprehensive. How long have the Boche had it in their possession?"

"I've concluded that they possibly received it recently because there have been no arrests."

Jean-Claude turned over more pages. "Is this notebook the only copy?"

The gendarme shrugged. "Again, I assume it must be, because of the lack of any specific action against us. I'll lock this copy in a safe."

"What's all this stuff at the back?"

"You tell me; I heard you had some knowledge of the language."

"Only conversational bits; there are words here I've never heard before." Jean-Claude handed the notebook over.

"Well, in the meantime, keep your ears to the ground and watch for any suspicious activity."

"I've decided to spend more time with the Maquis; maybe that might help."

"What about your job with the telephone company?"

He smiled. "They're quite happy to be short of manpower; that way, it takes longer to repair the damage we're causing."

"I've heard Guingouin is amassing several thousand resisters with a view to encircling Limoges. The aim will be to force Gleiniger's Verbingdungsstab to surrender. If you want to be a part of storming the Boche headquarters, I don't mind if you join one of the groups involved."

"Thanks but I'd rather stay here to find our traitor if I can have the authority to kill the bastard."

Martial lit a cigarette before gazing across the vast conglomeration of tombs and headstones. "I wonder what these poor souls would think about two ordinary individuals casually planning to add to their numbers."

"They would perceive us as patriots. Killing the Boche will not only liberate our country but also save lives. The countless skeletons that lie in this hallowed ground are insignificant compared to the thousands annihilated by our occupiers. I have no feelings of guilt when it comes to retribution."

The gendarme gently exhaled smoke. "An eye for an eye…"

"Not even close; we are killing a handful of Nazis whilst they are deporting victims to the death camps *en masse*."

"What about the SS officer who lodges with your in-laws?"

The question caught Jean-Claude by surprise. "What about him?"

"You appear to be unusually tolerant towards him."

"He interceded to secure my release, so I suppose I am indebted to some degree but I wouldn't hesitate to take him down if I considered him a threat."

"You don't think he could be responsible for acquiring that list?"

Jean-Claude shrugged before nervously dragging aside some gravel with his foot. "I don't see how he could get the information; most of the time, he's away on business. My wife reckons he collects data for Vichy. As far as I am aware, his only French contacts locally are Eliane and her parents...and they know very little about the Résistance. As a matter of fact, he's away at the moment."

"Bernard, her father's involved with us...occasionally. He has many clients and contacts in the area but he's totally committed to the cause, so I would rule him out."

"I didn't know that he was working directly with the Résistance." Jean-Claude leaned against the stone wall that surrounded the cemetery. "I didn't spot his name in that notebook." He scratched his head. "Come to think of it, I also didn't see Father Milani's name there."

"Oh, Bernard Dutheil is on the list. There are several names missing but I don't see that as significant." He stubbed out his cigarette on the wall. "What about your wife? I hear that same Boche officer visits her quite often. Could he have pressurised her into producing any names for the list?"

Although the mention of that situation angered him, he remained calm and merely said he doubted Eliane could be responsible. "She wouldn't even know the majority of those names."

"You're right, of course. It must be someone with inside knowledge. Just don't mention the notebook to anyone and keep your eyes and ears open. Our struggle against these bastards is reaching a critical stage. Every Nazi is like a wounded animal, striving to survive. I foresee more atrocities like Oradour before France is finally liberated."

They shook hands but Martial hesitated before leaving. "That friend of your wife...Anne-Marie, code-named Zeta...I hear she's closing down her safe house at Berneuil. Any idea why?"

Jean-Claude shook his head and walked away.

*****

It was almost dark when Jean-Claude arrived home in Saint Sauveur. The children were asleep in bed; Eliane had prepared a meal for the two of them.

"Papa has promised to drive us to Blond in the morning. Are you coming with us?"

"I'll join you at the weekend. There are a few matters requiring my attention. I met with Martial today. He showed me a notebook with a list of names...French names...resisters. Quite a coincidence after you and Anne-Marie suggested the possibility of its existence."

"We found it in Rausch's car."

"You never said."

"I've not seen you all day. Anne-Marie decided to hand it over to Martial. We concluded that someone in the Maquis must have given Rausch the information."

"So that's how he acquired it." Jean-Claude chewed on a mouthful of rabbit casserole before continuing. "I've offered to concentrate my efforts to find the culprit who supplied the Boche with the information. I'm joining the Maquis in the forest tomorrow. I may be gone for a few days or even longer. I'll find this bloody collaborator, even if it kills me...but not before the bastard suffers."

"The Boche will be gone soon. Is it really worth it?"

"You wait and see, Eliane. All those who have collaborated will face retribution after France is liberated. Already, there are rumours that any women who consorted with the enemy will be publicly denounced and paraded through every town."

His wife shuddered. "I hope everyone realises Rausch came here on your behalf. I never invited him into our house." She pushed away her half-empty plate. "What if no one believes me?" Tears welled. "You must make it clear, Jean-Claude, that I never encouraged him."

"Don't worry. When they learn what I've done to the traitor in our midst, they'll understand."

"But, how will you find out who gave the names to Rausch?"

"I intend to start with all those in the Résistance whose names are *not* on the list."

Eliane wiped the moisture from her cheeks. "Father Milani's name isn't on the list. Surely, he's not a suspect."

"I had noticed. However, everyone is a suspect until I eliminate them from my enquiries." He spooned another portion of casserole onto his plate. He was fired up; he needed to feed his anger.

Later that night, Eliane slept fitfully; whenever she dozed, she experienced nightmares. Jean-Claude slept soundly; it was the last time he would sleep in that bed.

Chapter 20

Haute Vienne
1944

Finding the house empty when he arrived home, he guessed his father-in-law, Bernard Dutheil must have already picked up his wife and children to drive them to Blond. He grabbed a small case, stuffed it with a few warm clothes, some of his work tools and, wrapping his revolver in an oily rag, slipped it between two woollen jumpers. Before cycling towards the Maquis camp in the Bois du Roy, he had one more visit to make.

He found Father Milani in the church. After checking the priest was alone, he strode down the nave to accost him. Without greeting him, he wagged a finger in his face. "We have obtained a comprehensive list of local Maquis members that the SS had in their possession," he snapped. "Your name's not on it. Can you explain why?"

The priest gently grasped the outstretched hand of the angry young man. "Calm down, my friend. What are you suggesting?" He indicated they should sit alongside each other in one of the pews. "Now, let us start again...at the beginning. Tell me about this list you have discovered."

Jean-Claude explained at length how his wife and Anne-Marie had found the notebook, which they had passed on to Martial, how he had volunteered to find the informant, and had decided to question all those resisters whose names were missing.

"Ah, I understand your logic and empathise with your anger but fail to grasp your intimidating behaviour towards me. Perhaps I could assist you in your quest." He smiled the benevolent smile of a priest whose empathy and patience knew no bounds. "First, let's discuss the possible reasons why my name could have been omitted."

Feeling embarrassed and slightly deflated, Jean-Claude changed the tone of his voice. "Maybe, the perpetrator was unaware you were a member of the Résistance."

"Good. Now, if we adopt that hypothesis, you can rule out all those who know of my involvement. Does that make sense?"

Jean-Claude nodded.

"So, which names are on this list?"

160

"I've only seen it once, Father. There are too many to remember."

"Where's the list now?"

"Martial has locked it away in a safe at the gendarmerie."

The priest smiled again. "May I suggest that you retrieve the list, bring it to me, and together, we can check each name. You will then be able to compile a shorter list of those who are not acquainted with me, making your investigation so much easier. What d'you say? Would that satisfy your curiosity?"

Jean-Claude left the church confused, unsure whether Father Milani had tricked or helped him. It was too late to contact Martial; he headed towards the Bois du Roy.

*****

The schoolteacher passed the notebook back to the gendarme. They were sitting on a bench, overlooking the river Vincou. Enjoying the warmth of the late afternoon sun, their minds were on darker issues. It was Saturday, June 24th. Two weeks had passed since the carnage that had destroyed the nearby town of Oradour-sur-Glane. The memory of that fateful day still lingered on everyone's mind. Across the region, most people knew someone who had lost a loved one in the atrocity. The hostility towards the occupiers had reached unprecedented heights; consequently, the absence of German troops was noticeable but there remained a constant fear of further reprisals. A meeting in a spot only accessible from the town centre by a bridge across the river afforded a reasonably safe haven away from prying eyes.

"Are you sure all these people named here are in the Résistance?" Jean Baudet asked.

Martial nodded. "All those who are still alive; some have died since that list was compiled. Because it's not in alphabetical order, I originally thought the entries were random, but after a closer study, I realised that some later names were members recruited some months ago. Most were young men, *réfractaires* who had fled into the Maquis to avoid S.T.O. Besides, since the Allied landings, our numbers have swelled so rapidly that I don't even recognise the names of some of the more recent recruits. In addition, those names at the start of the list are amongst the original resisters. I concluded that the culprit must have

161

updated it on a regular basis. However, with more recent arrivals, it is already out of date."

At first, the teacher sounded apologetic. "I was baffled initially, and I'm still unable to ascribe anything to the letters 'EZ' or 'NV'. However, from their names, I concluded that the letter 'F' must stand for Frau and the letter 'M' for Mann, denoting their sex. Using a similar rationale, I thought 'T' could denote 'Terrorist' because that's the term they use for resisters. However, if all these people are resisters, why is 'T' not against every name?"

Martial opened the notebook and flicked through the pages again. "It must represent something else," he replied, seeing some names without the letter. "Could it refer to their occupation, for example?"

Leaning over his shoulder, Baudet pointed towards a name followed by the letter 'T'. "What about him? What does he do?"

The gendarme grimaced. "Nothing...the Boche shot him last year during a skirmish."

"Ah, perhaps that's the answer. The letter could represent '*tot*', the German for dead." The teacher looked pleased with himself.

"Sorry to disappoint you, but there are people here with 'T' who are definitely alive."

Frustrated, the teacher slumped back onto the bench. "Maybe we should concentrate on the other letters, but as I've said, I've tried that option already without success." He scratched his head. "There must be some relevance with regard to the letter 'T'. I still believe it represents 'Terrorist'."

"What about the writing at the back of the notebook?"

The teacher passed him a folded sheet of paper. "I've translated it but it just seems to be random thoughts." He read aloud an assortment of words and phrases. "*Specialist strengths by category...a reward system...determine criteria...cross-check to verify...questions and research...penalties for non-compliance...build networks*. It meant nothing to me; how about you?"

Martial remained mystified.

"Some words were misspelt or the grammar was poor, which leads me to suggest that the writer was not well educated, not a German...or was just careless."

"A Frenchman with a smattering of German?"

Baudet nodded. "Could be."

"If that's the case, it certainly narrows down the list of suspects." He laughed. "Having said that, I'm not aware of anyone in this resistance group who is able to speak an iota of German...apart from maybe '*ja*' or '*nein*'. Some of them cannot even speak French correctly; they rely on the local patois."

For several minutes they said nothing. Apart from birdsong and the gentle lapping of the river, nothing stirred to interrupt their thoughts. The teacher stood and paced the riverbank. Suddenly, he returned to the bench.

"What did you mean earlier when you mentioned their occupation?"

Martial shrugged. "Well, many of them have employment during normal working hours, apart from the *réfractaires*. Why, what are you suggesting?"

"I imagine that the Résistance must have quite a large support network, providing food, equipment, weapons, shelter, et cetera. How many of these resisters are combatants?"

The gendarme went back to peruse the list. After spending a few moments running his finger past each name, he grinned. "You're right. The letter 'T' represents 'Terrorist'. They're the fighters; the rest remain in the background." He selected several names. "He provides false documents, that one's a forger, this one delivers provisions, she collects warm clothes, this one steals petrol, that one carries messages. None have the letter 'T'...only the armed resisters." He leaned back against the wooden bench. "But how does a German officer discover so much damn detail?"

"Precisely...and why differentiate?" Baudet lit a cigarette before handing the packet to Martial. "To possess so much information raises the possibility that you must have a rather intelligent traitor in your group."

The two men sat smoking, both lost in their individual thoughts. An elderly man with a walking stick bid them good day before shuffling across the bridge towards the town.

"It must be frustrating for people like him," the teacher commented. "He probably fought in the Great War, believing he had secured a peaceful future for our generation; we turned a blind eye and have reaped the full force of a vengeful Boche." He drew on his cigarette. "I salute people like you who are standing up for our country's freedom. I wish I could do more."

"Why not join us?"

"I'm a schoolteacher. What can I offer?"

Martial smiled. "The leader of the largest Maquis group in the Limousin is a schoolteacher. In fact, Georges Guingouin was born not far from here in Magnac Laval. He attended the *Ecole primaire supérieure* at Bellac before studying political and social economics at the teacher training college in Limoges. He followed the dogmas and philosophy of Engels, Marx, Lenin, Voltaire and Rousseau."

"I've heard of him...a Frenchman with communist leanings. He taught at Saint-Gilles-les-Fôrets before the war."

"Well, after completing his military service, he also became secretary of the Communist party branch at Eymoutiers, a bastion of communism in Haute Vienne. As a serving soldier, he was hospitalised at Moulins in 1940 but escaped to avoid falling into the hands of the Boche. Now of course, he's Chef du Maquis, producing and distributing clandestine papers like *l'Huma*, false documents and stealing food ration cards.

"He quickly established the Francs-tireurs, the resistance group that blew up the railway viaduct at Bussy-Varache and stole dynamite from the wolfram mines at Saint-Léonard-de-Noblat to destroy the rubber factory at Palais-sur-Vienne. In July last year, his group cut the telephone cables linking Navy headquarters in Berlin with the submarine base at Bordeaux..." He stubbed out his cigarette. "...and he's just a teacher!"

Baudet smiled. "He's not a teacher; he's a one-man fighting machine. I'm surprised the *milice* haven't caught up with him."

Martial shrugged. "He knows every square metre in those hills and forests; their Maquis camps remain hidden in some of the most impenetrable parts of the region. Neither the Boche nor the *milice* will ever apprehend him."

Bardet stood and buttoned his jacket. "You sell the cause well, my friend. I wish I could help more." He handed him the notebook "I've copied all the code letters, and I'll contact you if I can make any more sense of it all. Keep the translation; it may have some relevance."

The two men shook hands before going their separate ways, one feeling deflated by his inability to crack the remaining codes, the other wondering not only who had collated so much information on his Maquis group but also how an SS officer had acquired it.

Chapter 21

Haute Vienne
1944

Martial lit another cigarette before passing the packet to Jean-Claude. "How's life in the 'jungle'?" he asked with the hint of a smile. "No home comforts there...I imagine."

The two resisters were drinking beer in the bar at the Hôtel Central. As lunchtime approached, more customers entered, adding to the noise levels and the distinctive smoky atmosphere.

"Numbers are swelling daily since the Allied landings but we're short of weapons. The new recruits are mostly young men with no experience in the use of firearms, so even finding suitable weapons and ammunition for training purposes is difficult."

The gendarme leaned forwards. "There's a full moon on the sixth. London has promised several R.A.F. drops across the southwest; at least three are destined for this region at Blond, Cieux and Berneuil. I want you to organise reception and storage for the latter." He slid a set of keys across the table. "These are for Zeta's property at Berneuil, which is now empty. The drop zone will be at La Borderic; I suggest we use the barn as a collection point. I doubt there will be much Boche activity in any of those remote areas; they seem to be focussing on town centres at the moment."

Jean-Claude nodded. "Yes, I've noticed there's an increase in military activity around the town. What's going on? Reliable sources reckoned they were pulling out a few weeks ago."

"We're guessing they're expecting a Mediterranean invasion and spare units are heading south to bolster Army Group G, which hasn't the capacity to withstand an assault of that nature."

"So what do we do in the meantime?"

"As I mentioned last time we met, Guingouin is continuing to amass thousands of *maquisards* in the forests east of Limoges. They'll soon be poised to relieve the city of its Kommandantur. Each day the situation changes; liberation is close. Our Maquis, together with F.F.I. groups and possibly the Armée Secrète will most likely be required to assist in the liberation of Poitiers. I suggest you prepare the group for an incursion into the Vienne."

"Any chance of acquiring the notebook again? I have spoken with Danté since our last meeting. We discussed a process of elimination that may help to produce a shortlist of possible suspects."

A group of Wehrmacht soldiers entered the bar and gathered around a nearby table. Some locals finished their drinks and hastily left. Ignoring the interruption, Martial and Jean-Claude continued their conversation but focussed on more mundane topics. Two members of the *milice* stepped through the open doorway, glanced around the room and walked out onto the street.

"What was all that about?" Jean-Claude asked.

Martial shook his head in disgust. "I wouldn't like to be in their shoes when this war is over." He finished his beer. "Fancy another?"

"No thanks, I need to get back." He glanced at the clock on the wall before lowering his voice. "I'm due to accompany Fournier with a delivery for the group. In return for a lift back to camp, I promised to help him load provisions into his van. Apparently, the generosity of the inhabitants of Bellac knows no bounds."

"I'll send a courier with the notebook in a sealed envelope. Make sure no one else sees it...oh, and don't forget to contact me if you and Danté identify a possible suspect. I don't want you diving in until we're absolutely certain."

"That might be difficult."

Martial grinned. "Don't worry, we'll set a trap."

*****

They had travelled only a few kilometres from the town centre when they spotted the checkpoint. Heavily forested on both sides of the road, they turned a corner to confront a barrier manned by German soldiers and the *milice*.

"Bastards!" exclaimed Jean-Claude. "It wasn't there earlier this morning."

"I hope you're not carrying a weapon," Fournier muttered. "Are you?"

His passenger shook his head. "No. Leave it with me. I'll tell them we're delivering food to houses at Blond, houses procured to accommodate some of the survivors of the Oradour massacre. It's true to a degree so let's play on their sympathy."

"I don't think the Boche and *milice* have any concept of sympathy," the old man replied. He drew to a halt.

A soldier walked alongside the van and told him to switch off his engine. He asked to see their papers. Fournier handed over both sets. A young member of the *milice* stood behind him.

"Where are you going?" he shouted.

"To visit some Oradour survivors at Blond," Jean-Claude replied through the open window.

"What's in the back of the van?" the *milicien* asked.

"Provisions for the old folk who have lost their homes. They have to live in rented accommodation with no income. We're helping them in their hour of need."

Not wishing to become embroiled in a topic charged with animosity, the youngster stepped back.

Another soldier approached; he opened the rear door of the vehicle. Loaded with boxes and sacks, it seemed to satisfy him; their story seemed to be authentic. He shouted to a third soldier, who immediately joined him and withdrew a long knife from his belt. He prodded it into various items, spilling out some of the contents onto the floor of the van.

Knowing they would not find any non-food items, Jean-Claude sat nonchalantly in his seat, showing neither interest nor concern. The first soldier handed back their *cartes d'identité*. Fournier muttered a polite 'thank you' and waited expectantly for them to lift the barrier. It was at this point that Jean-Claude noticed a black Citroën saloon slowly emerging from a nearby woodland track.

His heart sank; instinctively, he sensed danger.

The vehicle stopped on the other side of the barrier.

The driver remained seated.

Two men in suits emerged from the car; Sicherheitsdienst men.

They walked casually around the far end of the barrier.

Jean-Claude threw open his door, knocking one of the Wehrmacht soldiers to the ground. In one movement, he wrenched the rifle from the prostrate German and raced towards the nearby line of trees, zigzagging into the thick undergrowth. Shots rang out, splintering the tree-trunks as, suffering the pain in his lame leg, he darted between them. Fournier ducked down in the van as gunfire crackled all around the vehicle.

One of the Gestapo agents opened the door to the van to drag out the unfortunate Fournier. His partner escorted him to the black saloon and bundled him roughly into the rear compartment. Shots continued to ring out from beyond the trees as the soldiers chased their quarry.

The Gestapo stared into the black void of the deep forest, confident the soldiers would return with a prisoner—dead or better still, alive.

Shaking with fear, Fournier realised his time was up; he knew he was too old to withstand torture. He opened the far door and, despite being out of condition, tried to run along the road, waiting for the bullet that would end his life. At first there was no sound apart from his deep wheezing as he stumbled along the tarmac surface. A faint thumping noise grew louder until a strong hand gripped his shoulder. Panting, he stopped and turned.

A young *milicien* faced him. "Sorry old man; they want you alive."

*****

The forest resembled a gloomy cavern, except where random slivers of sunlight pierced the thick canopy of foliage. Apart from the sound of Jean-Claude's own heavy breathing, silence reigned. The fugitive crouched down in the damp bracken. The gunfire had long since ceased; his pursuers must have given up. A heady scent of pine and earthy leaf mould ravaged his olfactory senses; disorientated, he had no idea of the direction in which he had stumbled, such had been his tortuous and painful flight to shake off the soldiers.

Whatever path he were to choose, it was vital to avoid any route towards the Maquis camp. The Boche could bring in dogs; leaving a scent could place many lives in danger. He pushed on through the dense undergrowth, cursing the creepers and brambles that tore at his clothing like an endless sea of tentacles. When it seemed almost impossible to progress further, the trees gradually began to thin out. After ten or fifteen minutes, he encountered a stream. He rested on its bank to determine his next step; most rivers and tributaries in the region flow westwards towards the flat open spaces of the Charente before reaching the coast. He decided to cross the gurgling rivulet to take him in a southerly direction. Sitting there reminded him of young Emile and those precious moments they had spent together after escaping from the camp at Wiebelsheim. He breathed in the woodland flavours; how Emile would have loved this moment.

Determined to put distance between himself and the Boche, he picked up the rifle before crossing the stream and forcing his tired legs onwards. After battling though more virgin scrub, he reached open fields. Once again, he rested; kneeling in the grass he took stock of his surroundings. In the distance a collection of farm buildings gave him hope; at least he would be able to discover his whereabouts. Staying close to hedgerows, he reached the first outbuilding. A dog barked, alerting the occupant.

Leaving his rifle concealed beneath a hedge, he limped towards an elderly woman who had appeared at the doorway of the farmhouse. "*Bonjour*," he shouted. "I appear to be lost following a tramp through the forest. Can you tell me where we are...I'm looking for directions to Blond."

The woman eyed him with suspicion, but seeing the state of his clothes, gave him the benefit of any doubts she may have held. "What were you doing in the forest?"

"My van broke down on the Bellac road. As the road was deserted, I thought there might be a farm on the other side of the forest where I might seek help. I didn't realise the woodland was so dense and deep."

"Why are you going to Blond?"

He decided to stick with the story they gave earlier to the *miliciens*. Any reference to the Résistance could provoke fear or even anger in some parts of the region. "I have a vanload of provisions for some of the Oradour survivors who are lodging there in temporary accommodation."

"You'd better come in. I expect you need a drink after your ordeal."

Jean-Claude followed the woman into a kitchen where the barking dog briefly greeted him with a sniff, and three sleeping cats ignored him by continuing their afternoon nap.

The woman reached for a bottle of wine and two glasses. "I don't get many visitors since my husband died, so I'll join you in a toast. She poured the wine, raised her glass and shouted, "*Vive la France! A la victoire et la libération!*"

Jean-Claude smiled and raised his glass. "Another month, Madame...another month...maybe two, but the end is in sight."

"Have you eaten?"

"Not since this morning."

"You must. A young man like you needs sustenance." Afterwards, we'll fire up the tractor to rescue your van."

Jean-Claude wanted to move on but the offer of a tractor influenced his initial thoughts. At least he would have some transport to reach Blond, a safer haven where he could temporarily disappear alongside Eliane and the children. It would mean telling her the truth but she seemed the kind of person who would empathise with his plight.

The old woman introduced herself as Rose Michelet, a widow who had lost her husband between the wars. Her visitor told her about having been a prisoner-of-war before returning to work as a telephone engineer. She seemed impressed, especially by his commitment to help the victims of the Oradour atrocity; she described the perpetrators as 'cowardly Boche barbarians'.

Jean-Claude felt safe; his choice of sanctuary had been fortuitous. After finishing the impromptu meal, he looked forward to the luxury of the tractor after his earlier ordeal on foot. She escorted him to a barn where the vehicle stood in a veil of dust and cobwebs.

"I've not used it for a while, but it has fuel; I start it every so often to make sure it's in working order. I'll probably sell it after this damn war is over…I don't suppose you'd be interested, would you?"

Jean-Claude grinned. "Not really; not in my kind of work."

"Well, make sure you return it in good condition."

The sound of motor vehicles interrupted their conversation. They stepped outside to see several military vehicles and cars in the distance.

"It looks like one of their sweeps of the area," the woman muttered. She turned to Jean-Claude. "I hope you're not in their sights."

"I'm sorry, so sorry," he replied. "I'll make myself scarce. If they ask, you've never seen me."

"You'll do no such thing. Follow me young man."

He hesitated.

"C'mon…quickly, whilst we have time."

She led him back into the barn. At the far end, she brushed aside some straw and lifted up a wooden cover. "Down you go. Stay there until I come for you."

Jean-Claude looked into a deep square hole before turning to the woman. "I can't put you through this. If they find me, you'll be arrested too…and you know what that means."

"They won't find you." He had no choice. She pushed him into the hole, dropped the lid and swept back the straw to cover the hideaway. Satisfied with her actions, she wandered back to the farmhouse, closed the door and cleared the table of their glasses and plates.

When the German soldiers burst in, they found her seated in an armchair, knitting. The dog growled before skulking into a corner.

"*H'raus!*" shouted the soldiers, waving their guns at her.

She put aside her knitting and walked outside to confront two Gestapo officers. More soldiers entered the house to search the rooms; another group descended on the outbuildings; two inspected the barn.

*****

An hour after his arrest, Fournier stood handcuffed and bruised before August Meier in Villa Tivoli at Limoges. The head of the Gestapo sat imperiously behind a plain wooden table on which he had placed the prisoner's documents and some blank forms. The light from a narrow rectangular window behind the desk glared directly into Fournier's eyes, transforming his interrogator into a menacing silhouette. The walls of the room were of a faded yellow hue, giving the impression of age and neglect. There were no furnishings, no pictures and no hint of the trappings one would associate with Nazi domination. Standing casually by the door, an armed SS soldier seemed either indifferent to the proceedings or routinely aware of what might transpire.

Meier looked up from the desk and, for several moments, stared at his victim before speaking. He relished the power he held over his captives; life or death rested in his hands. However, he perceived the interrogation of an old man like this individual to be a waste of his valuable time. His faith in the security system had waned; he was losing patience with the feeble efforts to arrest the terrorists who were a real threat. During his time with the SS in the Ukraine, he had been responsible for the deaths of more than 45,000 Jews and opponents of Nazism. Here in Limoges, the main target of his murderous zeal was the Résistance.

This old man standing before him offered little but nuisance value. Under torture, he would easily crack but would be unable to provide any information of substance; he was a tiny cog in a machine that dwarfed him. The alternative would be to merely shoot him, but what would that achieve? Locking him up might cause a temporary inconvenience to his Maquis but someone else would quickly fill his role.

He sighed with exasperation. "Name?"

"Adolf Hitler," Fournier muttered.

August Meier repeated the question, and received the same reply. "I want your full name, date of birth and your address," he asked with a look of disdain.

Expecting to be tortured and eventually shot as a terrorist, Fournier had decided to be as obstructive as possible; he had nothing to lose except his dignity, one quality he intended to retain until the end. "You have that information in front of you on my *carte d'identité*, so why bother me?"

His interrogator glared at him. "Who was the other man with you?"

A warm feeling of smug satisfaction crept into Fournier's thoughts as he guessed Claudius must have escaped. He shrugged his shoulders and pursed his lips.

"Do you often drive strangers around with a vanload of food?"

"He asked me to help with a delivery."

"Where were you going with this excessive amount of provisions?"

"Blond. The food was for the homeless victims of your barbarity at Oradour-sur-Glane."

"And from where did you collect the consignment?"

"Hôtel Central at Bellac."

"You expect me to believe this ridiculous story?"^

Fournier shrugged again.

Rising from his chair, Meier sighed again before addressing the soldier. "Take the prisoner downstairs."

The room in the basement was little more than a concrete cupboard, approximately two metres square, no window, no light and completely bare. Fournier sat hunched in a corner as the door slammed behind him. He heard a key turn in the lock before the click-clack of the soldier's boots on the tiled corridor melted into the distance, leaving only silence. In the door, a mesh grill fortified by four vertical iron bars allowed some light from the corridor into the cell but eventually that source faded, leaving him in total darkness.

Resigned to his fate, he had no regrets; France would never recover from this Boche oppression even if she were to emerge as the victor. He saw no point in continuing; he just wanted it to end. Gradually, his thoughts turned to earlier events; he wondered if his friend, Claudius—the name he had intended to give to the Gestapo during any further interrogation—was still at large. *It's strange how I'm more concerned about the Maquis not receiving their provisions*

172

than my current plight. Perhaps, one becomes more charitable as one prepares to meet one's maker.

After a while he became uncomfortable; the concrete floor was cold and damp. In the darkness, his mind began to wander, to imagine other scenarios. *What if they forget about me? What if the occupation ends and no one thinks about entering this building? I could be here for weeks, months; I would die slowly, probably eaten by rats. I hope they return soon and shoot me. I doubt I could stand starving to death.* Eventually he fell asleep, exhausted by fear.

At first light, the following morning, unwilling to waste time on an insignificant captive, Meier ordered the guards to take Fournier to Limoges prison. As head of the Gestapo in the area, he was more interested in apprehending Maquis leaders than geriatric supporters. In any case, a new capture that had arrived seemed a more genuine prospect for his interrogation techniques.

When the guards tried to enter Fournier's cell, something caused an obstruction. With their shoulders, they slowly forced the door open. Once inside they discovered the prisoner hanging from the iron bars at the back of the door, his leather belt around his neck.

The early morning cries and sickening screams of another prisoner undergoing torture had been too much to bear for the old man. Ignorant of August Meier's plans for him, Fournier had resolved to end it after all.

Chapter 22

Haute Vienne
1944

Above his head, Jean-Claude could hear muffled voices. He guessed the soldiers were searching the farm. The old woman had taken a terrible risk on his behalf; his discovery would certainly be her death sentence. Louder noises beyond his hole in the ground signalled they were conducting a thorough search of the barn. Several minutes passed before the shouts and sounds of their pillage receded. With the silence came fear, fear of the possibility they could set fire to the smallholding. He had heard of many such reprisals. Concerned about the possibility of roasting alive, he wondered whether he should chance raising the wooden lid a few centimetres to observe the situation. For the sake of his saviour, he decided to wait until she returned to tell him they had departed.

Having satisfied themselves that there appeared to be no sign of their fugitive, the soldiers gathered in the main yard. The woman stood watching from one of her windows. Relief at seeing them preparing to depart was short-lived; the smug expression suddenly drained from her face. One of the soldiers pointed towards the open door of the barn. He had spotted her dog, busily scratching and whining at a heap of straw. The two who had ransacked the building earlier re-entered to discover the dog had revealed part of a wooden hatch.

The younger of the soldiers raised his rifle to fire through the exposed cover. His colleague stopped him. "Not until we know what's below." He kicked the dog to one side before reaching down to grip the small iron ring for lifting the lid. "Cover me but only shoot if really necessary."

Jean-Claude became aware of the scratching sound before the voices. Uncertain about who might be above ground, he clawed a hole in the earth beneath his feet to bury his *carte d'identité*. If the Boche discovered his identity, his children, Eliane and her family would be in danger. As the hatch opened, a sudden burst of daylight blinded him until his eyes re-adjusted to realise the silhouette above was not the woman but a Boche soldier. Jean-Claude found himself staring down the barrel of an MP 40 submachine gun.

August Meier received the news of Jean-Claude's capture whilst attending a briefing at the Kommandantur. He ordered the SS soldiers to lock up the resister overnight; he would be able to begin his day with renewed appetite and vigour. Having listened to a detailed account of the arrest, experience told him that they had caught a bigger fish than Fournier.

The Gestapo agents whom Jean-Claude had initially eluded had been unforgiving. The *milice* and the soldiers set the farm and its outbuildings ablaze before executing Rose Michelet whilst she watched the inferno. Fournier's van and its contents had also become a smouldering wreck following the detonation of two hand grenades.

SS-Obersturmführer Meier finally considered he had the opportunity to smash a local Maquis that threatened their continued presence. Without these pockets of resistance across France, he firmly believed the Wehrmacht could still overcome the Allied invasion. A bloody battle lay ahead and he remained determined to play a part.

*****

As the first streaks of dawn filtered across the Limousin, Jean-Claude stretched his aching limbs. Deprived of sleep, he had spent the night on a wooden bench in a cold, damp cell behind the grey concrete walls of Limoges prison. No communication, no food, no water, no blankets; nothing but four stone walls, a filthy bucket and a door with an iron grill. An hour passed before soldiers entered the cell. After shackling him, they dragged their captive into a courtyard before marching him to a small gate set in the perimeter wall. A car, parked outside, took him across the city to Villa Tivoli. It seemed ominous that only seven years earlier, Henri Dardillac had stepped through that same gate into the Champ du Foire, where he became the last Limoges victim of the guillotine.

Seated behind his polished desk on a chair upholstered with black leather, August Meier awaited the prisoner's arrival with euphoric expectation. At last, he believed they had captured a terrorist worthy of his title. They had several names on their target list; which one had they caught? He lit a cigarette and checked his watch against the clock on the wall; it showed five minutes before eight. He had chosen to conduct this interview in his personal office; this prisoner deserved to witness the trappings of success.

As the minutes ticked by, he admired the lavish furnishings. This was the grandest room in the building; the focal point of his empire. Framed pictures of the Führer and Nuremberg rallies adorned the

175

walls. Behind his desk, Nazi flags draped the barred windows from ceiling to floor. To this room, he brought the most prized prisoners for their initial interrogation. Other more insignificant captives, like Fournier, would find themselves in less hospitable surroundings for a brief interview before torture and eventual death. In this opulent environment, Meier believed it was possible not only to extract better quality information but also occasionally to turn the captive.

At precisely eight o'clock, the door opened. Two soldiers dragged in Jean-Claude. They placed him on a chair facing the Gestapo chief. One soldier left the room; the other stood by the door. Two men in dark suits entered. Erich Barthels and Franz Eichinger were notorious for conducting operations against the Maquis around Limoges with sadistic ferocity. They sat on chairs to the right of Jean-Claude.

SS-Obersturmführer Meier smiled at his captive. "Welcome to Villa Tivoli. You must agree that this is far more hospitable than Limoges prison. Here, you have several options with regard to your future. It depends on how you intend to co-operate. Do you understand?"

Jean-Claude looked directly at him but remained silent.

His interrogator opened a packet of cigarettes, slowly extracted and lit one before pushing the packet across the desk towards his captive. "Help yourself; we have lots to discuss."

Wary of his motives, Jean-Claude showed no reaction. In any case, the offer was hollow; with both hands cuffed behind him, he stared defiantly at the Gestapo man, hatred in his eyes.

Ignoring his behaviour, Meier opened a file on the desk. "According to the arrest report, you had no identification papers. What is your name?"

Jean-Claude continued to stare at the Gestapo chief, relieved they had no idea of his identity. If Rausch had lived, the colonel may have provided some support, having been responsible for his release and his re-employment, combined with the fact that the SS colonel was lodging with his in-laws. However, could he have risked using the connection? Deep down, he doubted name-dropping would wash with the Gestapo. He said nothing; to protect his family, it was vital to conceal his identity. At the same time, he wondered about Fournier. Had they killed him, tortured him? Had he talked? It was difficult to determine how to play this game without all the facts; at that moment, the Gestapo held the winning hand. Jean-Claude realised there were only two solutions: death or escape. In reality, both options seemed beyond reach at that moment.

Suddenly, he lost his train of thought; his mind went blank but he felt pain, severe pain, as though his head had burst. As his eyes re-focussed, he found himself staring at a pair of leather boots. With his hands already cuffed, it was impossible to move; he sensed he was sprawled on the highly polished wooden floor, the smell of wax permeating his bleeding nostrils. Seconds later, he was again on the chair; two pairs of vice-like hands had lifted him back into a sitting position.

He could see only a blurred image of Meier's blue eyes; the man's lips were moving but the muffled sound entering his pounding ears was incomprehensible. He compared the sensation to when, as a youth, he swam under water in the lake at Saint-Barbant. He found it strange to picture an idyllic moment in his life whilst experiencing such monstrous treatment. His neck muscles seemed incapable of holding his head; it dropped to his chest. Within seconds, an invisible hand yanked his hair, lifting his head into an upright position. Meier's words became audible.

"Once again, what is your name?"

"Claudius," he whispered. As soon as he said it, Jean-Claude regretted he had answered. The notebook sprang to mind. Was the *nom de guerre*, Claudius against his real name? He couldn't remember; he couldn't think. Did they even have a copy? In the midst of his muddled thoughts, he had a vague feeling that one of Meir's henchmen had left the room.

Meir spoke again. "You see, it's far less painful if you answer the questions. Let's start again. Your terrorist name is Claudius. Now, what does your wife call you?" He lit another cigarette. "You are married, aren't you?"

Eliane, I cannot let him find out about Eliane…and the children. I must not mention her name. He doesn't know…he must never know. He watched the bluish smoke from Maier's cigarette curl up towards the ceiling. A chandelier hung above the desk. It seemed to be slowly spinning. *Is it really spinning or is my head spinning?* He sensed the whole room was moving. A need to retch overcame him. He tried but the pain in his head was insufferable. He thought of Eliane again. *Did I say it aloud? I must stop thinking about her…he might hear me.*

He doubled forwards. "Oh, shit!" he screamed silently. This time, the blow powered into his midriff. It felt as though his torso had been bisected. He looked down, expecting to see the contents of his bowels emptying from his body. He wanted to fall to his knees but once again, that invisible hand held him in a sitting position. He convinced himself that any more blows would be painless; the current torture would act like an anaesthetic. Of course, he was wrong.

He heard Maier's strident voice, sounding like a distant radio broadcast. "You're trying my patience." The Gestapo chief spoke again but he lost consciousness.

*****

Anne-Marie slammed the door behind her. "The bastards have arrested Fournier. He and Jean-Claude were taking provisions to the Maquis but were stopped at a road block."

A tearful Eliane leaped from her chair. "What about my husband?"

"Nothing. A contact at Limoges reckons the Gestapo took Fournier to Villa Tivoli, but there's no news of Jean-Claude."

Eliane sent the children upstairs to their bedroom. Wiping the tears from her face, she slumped back into a chair. "What happened? Do you have any other information?"

"According to the local Maquis, there was some altercation with the *milice* when the Gestapo arrived on the scene. Jean-Claude escaped through the forest but old man Fournier surrendered. Something must have happened on the far side of the forest because the bastards set fire to Rose Michelet's farm."

"What about her?"

"Again, no further news. So far, there are no reports from Limoges of any other arrests."

"How could they be so stupid...running into a check-point? Why hadn't the Maquis informed them?"

"They reckon it was one of those impromptu situations."

Eliane snorted. "With the Gestapo present? They must have known about the delivery. Someone must have informed on them." She stood and paced the room. "D'you think it has something to do with that list? I still believe there's a spy, a bloody collaborator in that group."

Anne-Marie shrugged. "Martial's supposed to be investigating."

"What are we going to do? We can't just sit around here waiting. What if they have interrogated Fournier? He's so old; he won't have the strength to resist their brutal torture."

"I'm afraid we must wait; we can't keep on running." Anne-Marie grabbed a jacket. "I'll cycle to Bellac to see what I can find out."

"It'll be dark soon."

"Don't worry; I know all the short cuts and the narrow lanes that the spineless *milice* avoid." Standing in the doorway, she smiled. "Be brave. Jean-Claude will turn up; he's invincible."

*****

He was wet, soaked; *I'm in the lake*. There was no lake. His hands and arms were somewhere above his head when he regained consciousness. It was as though he had awakened from a dream…no, a nightmare. He felt cold, almost numb yet his body was racked with pain. Through swollen eyes, he was able to realise he was in a different room. A strange stench permeated the dank air; the smell of decay, of death. He was alone, suspended upright by…*by what*? With difficulty, he tilted his head backwards to look at his outstretched arms; they were manacled to chains, suspended from a pulley-block fixed to the ceiling. He heard a movement behind him and the sound of metal hitting the concrete floor. It sounded like an empty bucket. *They must have used it to throw water over me.* It was at that moment he realised he was completely naked; strangely, he felt more vulnerable. It's strange how clothes, despite their limited rigidity, seem to assure a degree of protection. *Perhaps, that's why they have removed my clothes. Could there be a more sinister reason?*

The poor lighting, a low wattage fluorescent tube, suspended at one end of the room, prevented any detailed observation of his surroundings. Occasional mutterings behind him suggested that there was more than one person present. He guessed the two men in suits were his torturers. Not knowing what to expect was a torture in itself. A door opened and slammed behind him; was it someone entering or leaving?

In answer to his curiosity, SS-Obersturmführer Meier in his immaculate uniform and black, shiny boots strutted before him, looking extremely incongruous with the environment. "I'm a fair man. You have one final opportunity to give me your name."

179

Jean-Claude wanted to spit at the cowardly monster, but his mouth was too swollen, and sticky with dried blood to offer any saliva. He merely closed his eyes to shut out the image of his adversary. Hearing the man click his heels and depart, he waited for the next test of his endurance.

A rattle of chains was the forerunner to being lifted from the ground to be suspended by his wrists. He fully expected his arms to be wrenched from their sockets as he hung in space. Next, he wondered how long they would keep him in this position. Without warning, the two men, now in their shirtsleeves, approached him from both sides to club the lower regions of his body with solid rubber truncheons. He blacked out.

He drifted in and out of consciousness, thinking that his body no longer existed, yet there was an awareness of existence. His mind wandered into a state of oblivion. *Perhaps I am dead. Why am I still thinking if I'm dead?*

He heard the chains rattling seconds before he felt the concrete floor smashing into his body as they dropped him from the pulley-block. He imagined his body to be a mangled, twisted heap of ruptured flesh, torn skin and broken bones. All localised feeling had disappeared, replaced by intense pain. Once more, he lost consciousness.

He had no sensation of dying.

Part Four

Champ de Juillet, Limoges

Chapter 23

Saint Sauveur, Bellac
1969

Father Milani snipped another decayed head from a stem of one of his rose bushes before massaging his aching back. He straightened his posture and stepped aside to where he could admire his meticulous handiwork. Proud of his garden with its immaculately mown lawns, tailored shrubs and vibrant flowerbeds, he grunted with satisfaction. Removing his wide-brimmed straw hat, he gently dabbed the perspiration from his brow with a clean white handkerchief; intense warmth from the late afternoon sun offered little respite. Butterflies, bees and other darting insects populated the heat haze that hung like shimmering blurred voile from a cloudless sky.

Madame Tricot, now a fussy but endearing woman approaching her fifties, appeared at the kitchen doorway, shading her eyes from the glare of direct sunlight. "Would you like a cold drink, Father?"

He smiled in appreciation. "Just the usual, please; the sun has been quite relentless today."

His housekeeper returned to the cooler ambience of the kitchen where she had already prepared a wooden tray adorned by a fresh paper doily.

Picking up a wicker basket containing the remains of withered rose blossom, the elderly cleric ambled over to a wooden table set beneath the canopy of a wisteria-covered patio. The shaded area offered a welcome antidote to the intense heat from the sun. Pottering about the garden had become his principal means of relaxation, a retreat from the secular world beyond his hedgerows. The fresh air, the proximity to nature, the silence and solitude of the surrounding countryside compensated for the strict routine and demands of officiating as the village priest.

The rural atmosphere throughout the Limousin region of France offered a lifestyle of serenity. He had often considered the peaceful environment a belated reward for the horrors that he and his flock had endured during the Nazi occupation of the Second World War. Almost three decades had passed since the start of those dark years but, despite the current period of peace, he was aware that bitter memories remained. Neighbours, friends and even members of the same family continued to hold grudges against other individuals whose behaviour and reactions towards the occupying forces had, rightly or wrongly, carried the stigma of treachery.

Eliane Tricot returned, carrying a tray now containing a plate of homemade biscuits accompanied by a glass of chilled fruit juice. She set the refreshments down on the table. "You must be parched, Father. It's so hot today; even the garden will need a good watering when the sun starts to fade."

"Sebastien promised to drop by later. Thankfully, he offered to help with that necessary but tiresome chore." He sipped his juice. "This is extremely welcome."

"Well deserved, I would say. You should take up a more leisurely pastime like painting or reading, Father."

"Madame Tricot, do you not think I already spend sufficient time and effort poring over the written word?" He often teased her with her married woman title when she performed her housekeeping role. It also held special meaning for her; after being a widow for many years, she still clung to the memory of Jean-Claude.

"But that's about burying your head in those religious books that fill your bookcases. I mean something lighter, perhaps a novel or even a magazine...anything to take your mind off your work." She pushed the plate of biscuits towards him. "I've just read an interesting article about a man who died on his birthday. Just imagine that!"

The priest looked up and smiled; "A short life indeed, Eliane."

Frowning, she stared at him confused. "No, I didn't mean on the day he was born…"

He touched her hand lightly. "I know. I was joking…though one should not make light of death, especially with regard to the loss of a loved one. Sadly, it's an event that we all must face in time…as you are well aware."

"You must admit it's unusual, though. I suppose for those who knew him it must be like Christmas."

"I don't follow, Eliane."

"You know, Father, I mean, if someone dies say, at Christmas time, the festive season is forever tinged by the memory of that loss."

"Ah, yes…I understand; though for most, bereavement becomes a painful memory whatever time of the year it occurs. As you know, saying goodbye for the last time is never easy. Of all people in this commune, you have experienced tragedy more than others have, culminating with the loss of your husband in such unspeakable circumstances. Even after many years, one must still feel the pain."

The housekeeper stepped away from the table and looked skywards. "Even more so if that special person in your life has died on the moon." With an exaggerated sigh, she shook her head before returning to the kitchen, leaving the priest somewhat bemused.

Father Milani smiled at her parting remark. She must read some strange magazines, he thought, munching another biscuit.

*****

"Do you think dead people can watch us?"

For a brief moment, Sebastien continued reading the newspaper before reacting to his mother's words. Lowering the paper, he stared at her, partly bewildered, partly amused. Though accustomed to his mother's ramblings, he was unaware of anything that might have happened to give rise to this latest utterance. Avoiding her comment was not an option; she seemed determined to discuss the matter. By her nature, she would often make some bold statement to gain his attention.

"Maman, what has prompted that remark?"

Madame Tricot gazed beyond her kitchen window whilst continuing to wash pans in the recently fitted enamel sink. "I have often wondered what happens to the spirit of a dead person. Does it go to heaven and join all the other spirits gathered there, or does it remain

183

behind to watch over its loved ones…or might it even start again in a newborn?"

Not wishing to be drawn into what could only become an inconclusive discussion, her son buried his head in the newspaper again. "I think you should discuss it with Father Milani. He's the expert in those matters."

A short silence followed, interrupted only by the rattling of pans as his mother stacked them to drain. Once more, she peered across the parcels of pastureland that stretched beyond the house into the distance. An air of tranquillity enshrouded the landscape; sturdy Limousin cows grazed contentedly in the warm sunshine, an image common to the region. Wiping her wet hands on a tea towel, she sank into the comfort of a worn armchair by the cast iron wood burner, a vital asset during the winter months but currently redundant at this time of year.

"Do you think your father's watching us now…or perhaps enjoying himself as another person?"

Sebastien folded his newspaper and reached for his cigarettes. "Maman, why this renewed interest in life after death? Papa passed away many years ago during the war…so why ask me…someone who never had the chance to really know him?"

"But you can feel it, can't you? There's a presence; something in the air within these walls…as though…as though the house is alive. Haven't you noticed when you enter a room, it feels like you've disturbed someone…you know…like when you interrupt people and they immediately stop talking." She gripped the arms of her chair. "Listen to the silence, Sebastien."

He lit a cigarette, wafting a cloud of smoke away before leaning back in his chair, a mischievous smile replacing his annoyance. "You've been reading those weird books again from the library, filling your head with silly nonsense."

His mother lifted a pan onto her lap and began peeling potatoes. "I did read an interesting article in a magazine; it made me think about some of the strange things we experience without any logical explanation."

"Such as?" Sebastien had often listened to his mother's speculations about 'the meaning of life' whenever she searched for answers to explain her existence. Smiling, he recalled the questions that seemed to occupy her mind whenever she sank into one of her reflective moods. 'Why are we here at this moment in time?'; 'What is our individual purpose in life?'; 'Have we been here before?'; 'What happens to your soul when you die?'

Unaccountably, they had become topics of conversation with greater frequency. Though he often suggested she should discuss such matters with a priest, he knew she preferred the fascination of scientific proof to the rhetoric of religious dogma—not that she had a leaning towards atheism, but rather an appetite for more factual explanations of life's mysteries. Over twenty-five years had passed since the death of his father, yet, for some strange reason, her morbid interest in the afterlife had recently gathered momentum. Despite his determination not to encourage her obsession, she contrived to indulge him with her beliefs.

"How often have you experienced a brief instance of clarity on realising what will happen next, or a *déjà vu* moment, perhaps encountering a place or somebody seemingly familiar, despite knowing that in reality you have never been there or met that person?"

Sebastien shrugged his shoulders. "Can't say I have...but I'll wager you are about to tell me that you have been moved by some spiritual or mystical event at some point in your life."

His mother continued peeling potatoes without replying. A clock on the dresser shattered the silence with its ticking. Casting her eyes about the room, she seemed captivated by the rhythmic sound. Gazing wistfully at a framed family photo beside the clock, she smiled as pleasant memories flooded her mind.

"When your father and I moved into this house, we were young, very much in love and so thrilled to have the opportunity of keeping the property in his family. Even though it was sad when both his parents died unexpectedly just before the war, I wasn't sorry to leave that cramped apartment in Limoges." She sighed. "It brought us back to Bellac where we had first met and, for me, it meant moving closer to my parents. I have so many pleasant memories of that period...until the war started."

She fell silent, as though deep in thought before turning to face her son. "You know that you and your sister will inherit the property when I'm gone. I hope you'll find some way of keeping it in the family."

"Why are you telling me this? I've heard it all before."

"It'll be comforting to know I'll still be welcome here when I join your father...especially, if I die on my birthday."

Rising from his chair, Sebastien drew on his cigarette. "I'm not listening to this nonsense any longer. I'll see you later. I promised Father Milani I would help with his gardening." He kissed his mother on her forehead. "Please stop reading these stupid books and magazines; they're filling your mind with crazy notions."

He knew she was slowly losing her faculties but the doctor had cheerfully diagnosed her condition as merely a symptom of nostalgia brought on by powerful memories. He had explained how older people seemed capable of remembering past events more vividly than more recent ones. However, having noticed a distinct deterioration over the past months, Sebastien wondered how long she would be able to hold down her housekeeping job at the priest's house. Perhaps it was time to discuss the situation with him but decided it would be prudent to contact his sister first.

His mother called out to him as he opened the kitchen door. "You've not heard my story."

"You can tell me later. I've no time now...in a rush before the sun goes down." He took the opportunity to escape, hoping she would have forgotten by the time he returned.

His mother looked back at the photograph. Her smile quickly disappeared, replaced by an expression of sadness. With a deep sigh, she wiped tears from her eyes before peeling another potato.

*****

Though the priest's house was in walking distance, Sebastien cycled down the lane, having already decided he would meet friends later in the Terminus bar at Bellac. The warm evening air gently brushed his tanned face, weathered by his life outdoors as a postman. The house stood near the church on the Chemin de Geroux on the outskirts of the village. After leaning his bicycle against a corner of the garden shed, he followed the shale path leading to the rear garden.

From the patio, Father Milani looked up from a book he was reading, lowered his spectacles, and called out to him. "*Bonjour* Sebastien...how are you?"

"*Bonjour* Father Milani...another beautiful day."

The elderly priest rose from his cane chair, and they shook hands. "I thought I would take a short break in the shade. Come and join me. I'll fetch a bottle of pastis."

He shuffled off towards the kitchen door whilst Sebastien stood pensively for a few moments, admiring the priest's immaculate garden. With his thoughts drifting towards his mother's obsession with the spirit world, he wondered if he should broach the matter with the priest. The clink of glasses broke the silence. His host appeared, carrying a tray.

"Here we are," he announced, setting down the refreshments. "I've added some ice to the water. I don't know about you but I find warm Ricard most unpalatable."

Sebastien nodded and was about to pull out a chair when the priest grasped his arm, drawing him to one side.

"Before the aperitif, I've something to show you. Neighbours have been complaining about the state of that spare piece of land belonging to the church. I've had an idea about a solution."

He led him to a small section of garden hidden by thick box, its glossy green leaves trimmed to form a rectangular-shaped hedge almost two metres in height. Beyond this screen, an overgrown wilderness met their eyes like an open scar on the otherwise pristine landscape. A hedge of conifer surrounded the remainder of the patch, separating it from neighbouring land.

The priest swept his hand across the vista of undesirable undergrowth. "My neighbours suggested turning this plot into a vegetable garden but I had second thoughts after considering the extra work involved…digging, planting, weeding, and having all that produce maturing at the same time." He sighed. "I fear I haven't the stomach for bottling and preserving; far too messy and time consuming. I'm happier just eating it." He turned to face his visitor. "What d'you think about chickens? Hopefully, their presence will restrict this rampant growth of weeds and nettles."

"You could dig it over and scatter lawn seed."

"No, no," the priest protested. "Too much work for an old man like me. Besides, it would need constant mowing. I have enough lawn already to maintain. No, I believe chickens are the answer."

Sebastien pursed his lips as he pondered the proposal. "You'll need some secure fencing or they'll wander aimlessly and destroy your existing garden." He grinned. "That's provided the foxes don't get them first."

He picked his way to the far side of the patch, avoiding the many thick-stemmed thistles towering above the tangle of weeds like fearsome sentinels guarding their legions. "What d'you intend to do about a hen house where they can roost and lay their eggs?"

"Oh, I've thought of that. We can extend the run as far as the shed. It's large enough to split into two sections; one for the poultry and the other for my gardening tools. I also know someone who can supply posts and netting for the fences but we'll have to leave a space between the hedges and the perimeter fence in order to trim the hedge. It won't take much effort for us to set it up." A mischievous smile spread across his weathered face. "With my brains and your brawn, we'll have it finished in no time." Turning away, he beckoned Sebastien to follow. "Let's have our drinks before the ice melts."

Slowly shaking his head, his reluctant recruit followed him across to the patio, aware the wily old priest had already planned everything, including his involuntary conscription. "You'll only need a few chickens, Father...or you'll be inundated with eggs."

"Perhaps we can sell off any surplus, eh? Of course, I can ask your mother to cook the odd bird that becomes unproductive."

"You'll need a supply of chicken feed."

"Already organised, and there'll be vegetable scraps from the kitchen that your mother can feed to them." He poured the drinks and raised his glass. "*Santé* and trust the good Lord to bless our venture."

Sebastien raised his glass, realising any objection was out of the question. "Speaking of my mother, have you noticed anything odd about her recently?" He seized the moment even though he had not consulted his sister.

"Without being disrespectful, your mother often enlightens me with the strangest topics, so in answer to your question, I have found nothing to suggest that she is veering from her usual, often bizarre chatter. Earlier today for example, she seemed preoccupied by people who die on their birthday." He sipped some pastis and smiled. "Apparently, she had been reading one of those digest magazines she enjoys. It was probably another one of those 'stranger than fiction' stories that seem popular with its readers."

"She asked me if I thought dead people are watching us," Sebastien added with a degree of solemnity.

"Though I've known your mother for many years, she never ceases to amaze me; she has such a vivid imagination, especially when she questions our very existence."

"That's what I mean, Father. At home, death has become her obsession. She's always talking about papa...and she mentioned to me

188

that nonsense about dying on one's birthday. Don't you find her interest slightly creepy?"

"Somewhat morbid, maybe...but perhaps she is still grieving over the loss of your father."

"But he died more than twenty-five years ago...so long ago that I barely remember him. Why is his death suddenly dominating her conversation?"

"It's possible that, as your mother approaches old age, she could be considering her own mortality. Young people like you see themselves as invincible; death is something to face in the distant future. However, as one matures, it becomes a factor in one's perception of one's existence. Maybe your mother has reached that critical stage in her life when she is preparing herself for the inevitable."

"You mean she is about to die?"

"No, not at all, Sebastien. She is merely confronting reality. Perhaps she finds comfort in the memory of your father. Be patient with her; it's just a temporary phase that will pass."

"It depends on what you mean by 'temporary'. She's been like this for some time."

The priest leaned over to touch the young man's arm. "I'll find an excuse to mention it tomorrow whilst she's working. Whatever is causing this morbid preoccupation, it doesn't affect her efforts. I must admit her housekeeping standards are exceptional. Her presence is a great comfort to an elderly priest who can be quite disorganised about the house." He raised his hands and smiled. "Guilty as charged! The garden, however, is a different matter. I admit my true passion lies out here where I prefer to enjoy the predictable phases of earth's natural transformations; a sanctuary where I can meditate and be at peace."

Still confused, Sebastien ignored Father Milani's attempt to change the subject. "But my father died during the war. Surely, she cannot be grieving over his death after all those years." He gazed at his glass of Ricard as though an answer to his rhetoric might lie hidden deep within the cloudy mixture.

"People react differently. As I have mentioned, there could be many reasons for her behaviour, especially as your father died in such tragic circumstances."

Sebastien looked at him quizzically. "What circumstances? I understood he was a soldier, and died fighting the Germans."

189

"When the Nazis invaded France, their superior forces soon overpowered our poorly equipped troops, and still conscious of the dreadful slaughter sustained during the Great War, Maréchal Pétain sought an armistice to prevent another vast human tragedy. You only need to compare the disparity in the numbers of '*morts pour la France*' for each war by studying the many memorials to see the logic in his reasoning. The lists of casualties for the Second World War are miniscule in comparison."

Father Milani poured more pastis into their glasses before sharing the water. "In 1940 our army was overrun as the Nazi hordes swept across northern France. Your father became a prisoner of war for several years before the Germans released him through the *relève*, a scheme to exchange prisoners for additional workers to supplement their labour force."

"I didn't know he was a prisoner."

The priest lit a cigarette before sliding the packet across the table towards his visitor. "Yes, he was captured early in the campaign whilst defending the Maginot line. If I remember rightly, they released him after a couple of years...do you not remember seeing him for the first time at Gare Bénédictins when he came home?"

"I vaguely remember going to the station with maman and Sylvie...but I don't reconcile that with meeting papa."

"Following his release, and after recovering from his ordeal, he joined a local Maquis group. Sadly, he died at the hands of the Nazis...so needless after what he had endured in the prison camp." He drew on his cigarette before gently exhaling a bluish cloud that hung above the table. "Surely, you must have known some of this."

Sebastien shook his head. 'To be honest, having accepted he was a victim of the war, it has never crossed my mind to ask about how he died...in any case, people seem reluctant to discuss the war whenever the subject arises. It's strange that maman never confessed he was in the Résistance. You would think she'd be proud to admit my father was a hero."

"He was another brave soul who gave his life to liberate France from Fascism and the domination of the Nazis. Unfortunately, like many of his compatriots, he is a forgotten hero. Many still blame the Résistance for the terrible atrocities the Germans perpetrated during the occupation. They perceived such actions as retribution for their so-called terrorist activities. It has remained a dichotomy ever since for those who survived."

"She told us about Oradour when we were still at school. Apparently, her friend, Anne-Marie almost lost her father there. She said we visited the town when we were youngsters but I don't remember."

The priest stubbed out his cigarette in a glass ashtray. "A dreadful episode…sadly, one of many. I'm surprised your mother has never spoken about your father's heroic deeds. Has your sister never mentioned it?"

"As I said, few seem willing to discuss the war. Even when Sylvie was at home, we never discussed the war. Whenever it crept into the conversation, maman changed the subject, as though she found the memories too painful. You must think I'm stupid for being so ignorant but thank you for enlightening me."

Concerned about the young man's lack of family history and the current anxiety about his mother, Father Milani thought it wise to close the topic. Wondering what else his mother had omitted to explain, he thought it was not his responsibility to disclose further details. He emptied his glass before rising from the table. "Having quenched our thirsts, shall we administer some needy liquid refreshment to the garden?"

Sebastien nodded, gulped down the remains of his drink and, deep in thought, followed the priest to the well.

Chapter 24

Champ de Juillet, Limoges
1969

The train from Bellac meandered to a gentle halt alongside one of the many platforms extending beyond the main arched canopy at Gare Bénédictins in Limoges. Desperate to overcome the anxiety that had beset him during the journey, Sebastien hurriedly made the long walk towards the main concourse, where he mingled with other commuters heading for the exit.

There she stood, her nurse's uniform barely visible beneath her cape. Craning her neck, Sylvie glimpsed him through the scurrying crowd. On tiptoes, she waved to acknowledge she had spotted him whilst sidestepping the on-coming arrivals in an effort to reach her brother.

She was exactly how he remembered her: slim, petite, auburn hair in a chignon, like an Audrey Hepburn look-alike. Following a protracted embrace, they finally detached themselves from the ant-like mass of humanity. Like two lovers, they strolled hand-in-hand down the slope from the impressive station entrance. Sebastien reckoned it must have been almost three years since they had last seen each other. Sylvie had left home to live in Limoges where she could pursue her career ambitions.

A cloudless sky and warm sunshine prompted Sylvie to suggest a nearby bar, where they could sit *en plein air* with a refreshing glass of kir, before finding a restaurant for lunch and an extended chat to catch up on the latest gossip.

She squeezed her brother's hand and smiled. "You haven't changed...perhaps filled out a bit since we last met. It must be all that exercise delivering letters and parcels that keeps you in good shape."

That's it, he thought, that's the gulf existing between us. Attractive, intelligent and now a qualified medical student looking forward to working in the new University Hospital due to open the following year, Sylvie had become the benchmark that he could never attain. Intellectually inferior to his sister, after leaving school, Sebastien had undertaken a series of part-time jobs before joining the postal service where he earned a living in a job that never challenged him to progress. They lived in different worlds. Still at home with his mother, despite displaying a creative aptitude in practical tasks, he spent his leisure time fishing in the Vincou and aimlessly frequenting local bars. To help him in achieving his potential, he needed a mentor, someone to exploit and develop his talents. Without a father's influence, and plagued by a mother whose life seemed to be imploding, his future looked bleak.

In contrast, his sister, though dedicated to her current nursing career, enjoyed a vibrant lifestyle in the city as a single young woman, renting an apartment she shared with another nurse of similar age and experience. She remained sufficiently ambitious to progress through the ranks to achieve even greater career opportunities.

They strolled into the gardens of the Champ de Juillet. Passing the lake, Sylvie pointed towards Cours Gay-Lussac on the far side of the gardens. "We'll find a bar over there where you can explain why you called me with such urgency."

"I told you on the 'phone that maman is causing me some concern."

"You made it quite clear she isn't ill but you still need my advice on how to deal with her." She grinned. "You made it sound most mysterious...don't tell me she's in some kind of relationship with a new man in her life."

"It's not a joking matter, Sylvie. It's serious. She constantly rambles on about all sorts of nonsense. Her current topic is life after death again and what happens to people who die on their birthday. She seems obsessed by morose thoughts. She's even been spouting the same rubbish to Father Milani. I'm finding it difficult to have a normal conversation with her. She constantly turns it into some rant about dead people...and more disturbingly about papa. In addition, she reads sensational stories in stupid magazines."

"She probably still misses him. We never had that connection, being born when he was fighting the Germans, so it's little wonder you're unable to empathise with her."

"Dammit, Sylvie...it's not like that. She thinks he's in the house, watching us."

His sister tried to suppress a giggle. "Do you hear bumps in the night?"

"Why must you trivialise everything I say? You treat me like a child." He sighed deeply to show his exasperation. "I'm just worried about her. Why can't you share some of the responsibility? I don't feel competent to deal with something like that."

They had reached a nearby bar and, choosing to sit outside in the sunshine, ordered aperitifs. Sebastien lit a cigarette. Sylvie draped her cape over an adjacent chair.

"I don't see why you need me. I'm sure you can handle her. You're far closer to her than I am. She'll listen to you. I was never her favourite. Life revolved around you all the time; constantly protective of poor little Sebastien."

Her brother ignored the comment. "I think she's losing her mind. She's now starting to believe that men are dying on the moon. That's how bizarre it has become."

His sister grinned broadly. "She must have been dreaming about the moon landing. Did you watch it? What an amazing feat; I couldn't take my eyes off it, though it was a bit fuzzy."

The waiter arrived with their drinks.

"I'm not here to talk about men landing on the moon. What about maman?"

Sylvie took a sip before commenting. "So what do you expect from me?"

"I just want your advice. Should I ask the doctor to see her...or would you prefer to come over and talk to her?"

"It sounds as though she needs a psychiatrist...not a doctor. I see no point in my involvement, even in my role as a medical student. I'm not qualified in mental issues; my specialism will be cardiology. We'll only end up rowing. In any case, I hate that house. From my own hazy recollections, our family seemed to fall apart there. There's something evil about it."

"It's strange you say that. Only this week, maman explained to me how much better their life had been there after relocating from Limoges."

"Then the war began, we arrived on the scene, papa became a prisoner and their little bubble of happiness burst. I tell you, Sebastien...it's that damn house."

"If you say so but it doesn't resolve the issue with maman," he said dismissively whilst stubbing out his cigarette. "How did you know papa was a prisoner? I only discovered that the other day."

Sylvie shrugged. "I don't remember. It must have cropped up at some point in conversation."

"Where d'you suggest we have lunch?"

"I know a little restaurant near Les Halles but before we wander over there, I want to show you something."

After paying for their drinks, Sylvie escorted her brother across the road returning to the Champ de Juillet where they wandered through the symmetrically landscaped gardens. Taking a path that led to a gate opposite to where Impasse Tivoli joined Cours Gay-Lussac, Sylvie indicated they should sit on a wooden bench near one of the openings in the metal railings that formed the perimeter.

"Take a long look at the large property on the corner across the road."

Wondering what in particular he should be noticing, Sebastien shrugged his shoulders. "I don't see anything special about it; it's just a house. Who lives there?"

His sister held his hand before wiping a tear from her eye with her free hand. "When maman helped me to move into my apartment, she brought me here before she caught the train back to Bellac. She explained that papa died in that house."

His brow furrowed; Sebastien looked at her in disbelief. "After the Germans released Papa, he died fighting with the Résistance. Father Milani told me that only recently because I had always been under the impression that he died as a soldier during the war. Why would he die here?"

"The fighting in France finished just before we were born. The government signed an armistice with the Nazis. Surely, you must have worked that out."

"But the Germans were still here afterwards. Because no-one speaks about it, I always imagined the war continued until the liberation." He glanced across the road again. "Anyway, why would papa be here in Limoges…in that house? I'm still confused."

"The Germans caught him and brought him here where they interrogated him, tortured him and eventually killed him."

"But why there?"

"That house is called Villa Tivoli…it was the headquarters of the Gestapo in Limoges during the occupation. Arriving there was tantamount to a death sentence."

*****

Lost in their individual thoughts, they walked into the town centre, mostly in silence, apart from the occasional grumble arising from Sebastien's annoyance at being unaware of the circumstances leading to his father's death. After ascending the narrow cobbled street leading to Les Halles, he was more than ready to quaff a substantial amount of wine with his lunch. Arriving at the brasserie, Café 1900, they decided to sit outside again to take advantage of the warm weather.

After the waiter had taken their order, Sebastien leaned forwards across the table. "I've something else to tell you."

"What have you done now?" Sylvie looked at him, almost reprehensively, expecting some confession of guilt.

"No, nothing bad." He hesitated as though struggling to find the right words. "I've met someone."

"Someone? You mean a girl?"

"Yes...she's a teacher at the *lycée*."

"Do I know her?"

"I doubt it. She's not lived in Bellac until recently...she's originally from Poitiers but relocated to take up a teaching position...a bit like you moving here to become a nurse."

"Does she have a name...this teacher?"

"Angelique."

"And how did you meet this erudite individual? Don't tell me you're considering a course of further education." She laughed. "Does she give you homework?" She reached over to touch his hand. "I'm sorry. I shouldn't be so mean...it's just that you hated school...and the thought of you taking up with a schoolteacher...well, it's so ironic."

"I thought you'd be pleased."

"I'm only teasing. Of course, I'm delighted you have a woman in your life...besides maman."

Uncomfortable with his sister's barbed comments, Sebastien wished he had never broached the subject. The arrival of the waiter to serve their meal distracted him from considering a suitable riposte. Sylvie continued the dialogue.

"So, are you going to tell me how you met this Angelique woman?"

"I wrongly delivered someone else's mail to her post-box. She pointed out my mistake the following day, and we ended up chatting for several minutes."

"And that brief interlude developed into a romantic liaison?"

Sebastien chewed on his *charcuterie* before replying. "We bumped into each other in the town centre the following weekend. I was reading a newspaper outside a bar in the Place du Palais, when I suddenly became aware of someone stood by my table. She had seen me and came over to say *bonjour*. I invited her to join me for a drink. One thing led to another and...we began to meet on a regular basis."

"What does maman think of this new intrusion in your life?"

Munching more food, Sebastien muttered, "She doesn't know. I haven't told her yet."

His sister grinned. "You're scared!"

He leaned back, wiping his mouth with a napkin. "You know what she's like...how possessive she can be." He carefully re-folded the linen napkin before placing it neatly on the table. "I've told Angelique I live alone."

Sylvie shook her head in despair. "How long d'you think you'll be able to keep up that pretence?"

Her brother played nervously with the napkin, rolling the corners of the material between his fingers. "I was wondering if you could invite her over to spend a weekend with you."

"Who...Angelique?"

"No, you idiot...maman!"

"D'you really believe she would abandon you to spend a whole weekend with me? From what you've been saying about her, you'd have more chance booking her into a psychiatric clinic." She smiled. "Maybe that's not a bad suggestion. Why not pursue your original suggestion and discuss it with Doctor Jerome? You can always ask Father Milani to confirm your concerns if, as you said earlier, she has been bending his ear with the same flippant stories."

Sebastien smoothed the napkin flat again. "I can't be responsible for committing maman to an asylum."

"I'm not talking about an asylum. According to your account of her deluded mental state, she needs some form of therapeutic treatment." She sighed, more from desperation than empathy. "It's up to you, Sebastien. If you act now, you may be able to resolve maman's issues. On the other hand, if you do nothing in the hope that it will go away, you could spend the rest of your life looking after her."

Sebastien remained silent, realising his sister had no intention of supporting him or becoming involved. She had abandoned any hope of repairing the relationship with her mother many years ago.

Sylvie sipped some wine. "Are you sure there's nothing medically wrong with her? Is it just these strange fantasies that cause concern?"

He nodded, wondering why she had asked such a question. She was the medical expert. How would he know what had caused his mother to ramble constantly about death?

Sylvie continued. "In any case, why can't you take your girlfriend home?" She laughed. "She may find maman rather amusing…a challenge perhaps."

"Now you're being flippant. Can you imagine Angelique's reaction if maman starts talking about dead people in the house? She'll think I'm the product of a raving lunatic."

Sylvie forced a smile. "Aren't you?"

Her brother reacted. "What d'you mean by that?" he snapped.

"Nothing…just joking," she muttered, wondering why she made such a meaningless remark. Deep within the memory bank of her childhood, a vague image of their father in military uniform flickered before quickly disappearing. Concerned by her inability to see any expression on the face of the image, she took an extra large sip of wine. The brief reverie prompted uncomfortable sensations, similar to the revulsion she often experienced at the house in Saint Sauveur. Something in her subconscious disturbed her but it remained a mystery.

They finished the meal in silence. Sylvie paid the bill before offering to accompany her brother to the railway station. She attempted to repair the tiff that seemed to divide them. "Give my regards to Father Milani. I trust he's in good health."

"Oh, he's fine. Last time we met, he conscripted me to assist him in constructing a chicken pen on that spare piece of land beyond his garden. Why he wants the hassle of poultry at his age is beyond me. I guess I'll end up looking after them. I told him to dig it over and plant vegetables but he said it would be too strenuous at his age."

Sylvie laughed. "Remember when we had chickens. Maman used to give them kitchen scraps, and they followed us everywhere when we had corn to feed them."

"I don't remember that. In fact, I don't remember us having any chickens at all."

"Surely you remember when they disappeared. Maman told us that she couldn't afford to feed them. However, when we were older, Father Milani told me the foxes had attacked and killed them but maman didn't want to upset us."

"I'm sorry but I don't remember that at all."

Sylvie nudged him and grinned. "I think you're suffering from maman's mental problems…not really. Seriously though, when I look back, there are lots of weird things that happened when we were youngsters I have never understood."

"Such as?"

"Perhaps it's me, maybe it's because we were only toddlers but why did maman suddenly take us to live in another house with her friend, Anne-Marie? It's all a blur…and do you remember that soldier? Who was he, and why did he spend so much time at the house? He must have been in the army with papa; perhaps they fought alongside each other. They both disappeared about the same time. Do you think he also died fighting the Germans? There are so many unanswered questions. Don't you find it all rather strange? Maman has always refused to talk about the past, and when I once broached it to Father Milani, he just shrugged and said it was the war, a period of turmoil."

"I'd forgotten about the soldier. I used to think he was papa in his uniform until I heard he had died during the war…and only the other day, Father Milani mentioned about going to meet him with maman at the station. I have faint memories of that but only fleeting memories of him. I find it all very confusing."

He drank the rest of his wine. "You're probably right about the two soldiers dying together but why did Father Milani say he was a hero of the Résistance? Perhaps they were both in the Résistance…and died in that house."

Looking at his watch, he pushed his chair back. "I should make a move to catch my train."

Still mulling over their earlier conversation, they crossed Place de la Libération whereupon Sebastien stopped. "Back there in the restaurant, you mentioned Anne-Marie. I remember going to her house; we played in her barn. Do you remember that van with those strange markings? We buried it under a huge mound of straw. I realised when I was older, they were swastikas, so it must have been a German vehicle. After we returned from that other house, it seemed a long time before we saw Anne-Marie again. I wonder if it's still there."

"I thought it was a car…but it could have been a van, I suppose. I don't think I would have known the difference at that age. I vaguely remember, after I found something under a seat, everyone became very excited until you covered your hands with oil, and maman scolded you!" She laughed. "It's the only time I've ever seen her angry with you. Do you remember going to Anne-Marie's wedding when she married that foreign man who talked to us in a different language?"

"Oh, that was much later when we were living at home again."

"Maman used to visit her occasionally but I don't think I've seen her since I finished school."

"I wonder why she rarely comes to Saint Sauveur. She used to visit quite often when we were younger."

"I've never given it much thought...too long ago, I suppose. People lose touch over the years. To be honest, I don't remember much at all about the past...apart from the chickens." She giggled. "Anyway, it's all water under the bridge, as the saying goes, so what's the point?"

"It could be the cause of maman's state of mind."

"I think you're clutching at straws...literally!"

They had reached the forecourt leading to Gare Bénédictins. Sylvie pecked her brother on the cheek. "Ask maman what happened when we were little; it may unlock what's troubling her." She turned to walk away and suddenly stopped. "What are you going to do about Angelique?"

Disappointed with his sister's apparent unwillingness to co-operate, Sebastien shrugged before heading towards the platform. His relationship with Angelique was not the main issue. The problem was his mother, Eliane Tricot.

Chapter 25

Bellac, Haute Vienne
1969

Several days passed before Sebastien returned to the enigma of his mother's ramblings. During the course of his postal duties, he found himself filling in for a colleague who was absent through illness. The round took him to the street where Angelique lived. Aware she would not be at home but teaching at the *lycée*, he slipped her letters, including a short note from him, into her mailbox and continued the round. Deep in thought, a possible solution to his problems began to crystallise. Stepping from the shaded side of the road into the warmth of mid-morning sunlight, he quickened his pace, determined to complete his deliveries in record time.

Before cycling home after his shift, he stopped off at the Tabac near the railway station. Whilst drinking with a few friends, his thoughts turned to his meeting with Sylvie. Something she had said was an irritation at the time but he now thought it could have a positive impact, not only on his mother but also on Angelique. 'You could spend the rest of your life looking after her'. Those were his sister's words. He would use those same sentiments to gain Angelique's respect, sympathy and possibly her professional advice. It would necessitate a few harmless lies but the outcome could be advantageous to all parties.

He set off home in a buoyant mood, fortified by several glasses of pastis. Excited by the prospect of a brighter future, he strolled into the house, and hugged his surprised mother before retiring to his room to determine how to achieve his objective. Everything would depend on his mother's reaction to the news he was about to impart. Somehow, he would have to control the conversation before she began to regale him with her latest spiritual revelations.

His mother was in the kitchen, busy preparing their evening meal when Sebastien came down from his room. Outside, an overcast sky had replaced the earlier sunshine; in the distance, storm clouds had gathered as dusk descended over the region. The air in the kitchen was warm and oppressive.

"How was your day, maman?" He helped himself to a glass of water.

"Oh, I finished early; Father Milani went off to some meeting at Limoges. The house was quite tidy, so I thought I would come home, catch up on my housework here and spend some time in the kitchen. I've already baked some bread...that's why it's so warm in here...and there's *bourguignon* in the oven. It'll be ready quite soon, so don't disappear. How's your day been?"

"Filled in for Germain...he's off sick."

"He's always ill, that man; he drinks too much. I don't think I've ever seen him sober. Pastis and that homemade eau-de-vie will be the death of him. I can never understand why people drink so excessively; invariably it ends in remorse."

Sebastien sat at the table and grinned, knowing that her comments were a veiled reference to his own regular drinking sessions. His mother swore she never touched alcoholic beverages but he knew there was always a bottle of Cognac in the cupboard with ever decreasing contents. Saying nothing was his way of letting her believe her occasional tipple remained secret. She never had visitors; clearly, she was the secret tippler.

"I've some news you might like to hear."

Eliane was vigorously kneading dough; she stopped and looked across at him. He was seldom forthcoming; usually, when she queried his personal life outside the home, his answers revealed little. For her son to offer any kind of information voluntarily suggested he had a problem to resolve or an exceptional moment was at hand.

She brushed flour from her hands. "Good news?" She hoped he wasn't losing his job; his income was vital to supplement the moderate earnings from her part-time housekeeping duties with Father Milani, and the meagre war widow's pension she received from the state.

Sebastien took a deep breath. "I've met a young woman and I'd like you to meet her."

Somewhat relieved, Eliane returned to dough kneading before responding. "Do I know her?"

"She's a schoolteacher at the *lycée* in Bellac. You'll like her, she's nice. She's called Angelique."

"A schoolteacher...how on earth did you meet a schoolteacher?"

"It's a long story. I've told her all about you, and she's looking forward to meeting you. I'd like to bring her home for lunch...say, next Sunday. You can tell her about those amazing stories you read. I'm sure she'd be thrilled to listen." He hoped that final comment would prevent any rejection of his suggestion.

His mother looked across to the faded family photograph by the clock. "I also have some news. The other week, I read an article about that recent landing on the moon."

Sebastien folded his arms, preparing himself for another bizarre revelation.

"The Americans weren't the first men on the moon." Eliane stopped, waiting for some reaction; Sebastien remained impassive. "A Russian cosmonaut landed there several weeks earlier."

Her son still offered no response.

"His spacecraft crashed, and of course, he died instantly. The article said the Americans saw the wreckage as they were orbiting before they landed."

Sebastien laughed. "If that were true maman, surely such dramatic news would have been on the radio, the television or in the newspapers."

Eliane shook her head dismissively. "Well, the Americans would not wish to report it because the world would know they weren't the first men to land there. And certainly, the Russians would not admit it because they wouldn't want the world to know they had failed."

"If that's the case, how did the person who wrote the article know what had happened?"

She shrugged. "How should I know? He must have had access to some secret material." She smiled mischievously. "Perhaps he was a spy. The article said the Russian spaceship was called Luna 15 but western scientists named it 'Scoopy' because they thought they had sent it to scoop up moon dust! Anyway, it must be true because the writer said that the Russian cosmonaut died on his birthday. Why would he say that if it wasn't true? Just think...he could be here...on the earth...living his next life."

"Maman, what are you going on about?"

"I told you the other week about people who die on their birthday. They come back again; they're re-incarnated...a second chance. That spaceman's spirit could be here for all we know." She glanced around the room. "I tell you, there's something here...inside this house."

Sebastien ignored her ramblings, hoping that, for his plan to work, he could induce another similar performance from his mother during Angelique's visit. Time to be brave. "So, can I invite Angelique over here to meet you next weekend?"

Eliane's mind was elsewhere.

Her son leaned across the table to hold both her hands; he squeezed them gently, his expression oozing the charm of his 'little boy lost' ploy.

After several seconds, she responded. "Angelique? Who is Angelique?"

"I told you; she's my teacher friend. Would you like to meet her next weekend?"

His mother smiled. "Oh, that would be nice, Sebastien. Invite her for Sunday lunch. I'll ask Father Milani if he'd like to dine with us after the morning service. Anne-Marie and her husband may fancy joining the party. It's a while since I've seen them. It'll be like old times." She lowered her eyes, sadness replaced the smile. "It's a pity your sister cannot come too...but I expect she will be busy at the hospital."

"Thank you, maman." He hesitated before his next suggestion. "If you like, I could ask Sylvie. She may be free."

"Yes, I suppose it would be nice to have both my children and my friends here to meet your young lady."

He had achieved the first stage of his plan. He had four days to complete the next one.

Eliane's eyes glazed as though she were in a trance. She turned towards the photograph again. "Those dear to us who died on their birthdays could be watching us at this very moment."

In the distance, the first rumble of thunder heralded the approaching storm; a flash of lightning seemed to charge the room with electricity.

She turned to her son and whispered. "He's here. I feel his presence."

"Who's here?"

"I remember; it was his birthday when he died. It's him...he's here."

A second lightning strike that seemed to fill the room with white light extinguished the supply of electricity to the village, plunging the house into contrasting darkness. Sebastien lit a candle on the dresser. It was normal for the electricity to fail during thunderstorms; candlesticks adorned most rooms in readiness for such occasions. The flickering flame cast an eerie glow, exaggerating his mother's anguished expression.

Sebastien opened a drawer in the dresser. "I'll lay the table. With luck, the storm will pass and the electrics will be back on before we sit down to eat. Did you say you've cooked *bourguignon?*"

Without replying, Eliane picked up the candlestick, walked towards the staircase and looked into the shadows. The downward draught from upstairs caused the flame to flicker. Eliane believed other entities were responsible. "Yes, he's here, Sebastien; he's most certainly here."

The candle fell from its holder, hit the floor, extinguished the flame, and plunged the stairwell into darkness. Eliane screamed and hurried back into the living room.

Sebastien continued to lay the table and, ignoring her hysterics, failed to glimpse the terrified expression on his mother's face.

*****

"You've invited your mother?" Angelique voiced surprise but looked slightly amused. She flicked her ponytail to one side, her hazel eyes widening with incredulity. Young and attractive, she could have passed for one of her students. This unexpected aspect of Sebastien caught her unawares. Captivated by the young man's physique, his rugged posture and his enigmatic allure, she had perceived him as a challenge. Meeting his mother had not been on her agenda.

Sebastien leaned back in his chair, brushing his dark wavy hair away from his sallow features. "I thought it would be an opportunity for you to get acquainted. After all, you'll have to meet her sometime." The second stage of his plan began to appear more difficult than winning over his mother.

They were enjoying a Saturday afternoon shopping in Limoges, stopping for lunch on the terrace of a restaurant in the Place de la République. He had arranged the trip, believing the pleasant ambience would provide the perfect setting to announce the family gathering.

Angelique was unprepared; the relationship was moving too fast. She enjoyed his company but had no thoughts of taking their involvement to the next level. Playing 'happy families' with Madame Tricot would create the wrong impression, if not for him, certainly for her. He had placed her in a difficult position. Rather than cause an argument, she decided to use the proposed opportunity to dispel any dreams of a permanent relationship. She would explain to his mother that her career took priority in her immediate plans; surely, she would understand.

"Does she live in Bellac?"

"Les Singuelles; it's a village on the outskirts but, because she lives alone, she often stays over at my house," he lied. "She can be a little incoherent at times. Doctor Jerome says it's her age so I try as often as possible to pass some time with her. I believe it's my duty as her son."

Although his grandfather had died two years previously, his grandmother, Madame Dutheil continued to live in the family home at Les Singuelles with Gérard, her son and his wife, Lydie. To suggest his mother resided there as opposed to the house at Saint Sauveur only served to reinforce the fabrication that he lived alone; he perceived it more attractive than confessing to living with his mother. Somehow he must convince the other guests at the proposed Sunday luncheon to endorse his fantasy.

Angelique paused before sipping more wine. "You mentioned you had a sister. Will she be joining us?" She had the feeling he was setting her up for his family's approval.

"It depends on her shift; she's a nurse."

"Yes, you said previously that she works at the new hospital. It would be nice to meet her."

"Father Milani might join us. He's a family friend. You'll like him; he rears chickens. I helped him to construct his chicken run. He could bring you some eggs."

Angelique had visions of sitting before a casting committee to audition for the role of the future Madame Tricot. "A priest? Are you regular churchgoers?"

Sebastien shrugged. "Not really. I've known him since I was a youngster. Maman's his housekeeper. She looks after his him...well, not him but his house."

Resigned to the unsettling prospect of this 'command performance', Angelique bravely continued with her meal, unaware of Sebastien's own disquiet about the event.

If Anne-Marie and her husband turned up, together with Father Milani, Angelique could be overwhelmed. Perhaps the presence of Sylvie would provide a welcome distraction; the two young women were of a similar age, both at an early stage in their respective careers. He decided Sylvie's presence had become a priority, despite the ongoing mother and daughter feud. As he finished his starter of *terrine forestière*, he was beginning to doubt the wisdom of arranging the luncheon.

The remainder of the meal passed in comparative silence, both lost in thought about the consequences of the forthcoming weekend. They parted company later at Bellac station, one concerned about meeting a group of strangers, the other hoping his family and friends would behave normally. If Angelique could not establish a rapport with his sister, he knew he could rely on his mother to provide sufficient entertainment to realise his original scheme. Wondering how to entice his sister to join the party, he wearily ascended the steep hill leading to Saint Sauveur.

*****

Although Sylvie tried to resist her brother's entreaties to attend the impromptu family reunion, her curiosity to meet the new woman in Sebastien's life overcame her initial reluctance. During his teenage years, her brother had only experienced fleeting crushes on local girls. His interest had always waned, preferring to conduct his social activities in convivial drinking sessions surrounded by male company. The arrival of a mature woman in his life, especially a schoolteacher, presented such unexpected circumstances that meeting her promised to offer a not-to-be-missed occasion.

Sylvie also reckoned that the chance to witness her mother's reaction to the possibility of a female competitor frequenting her house created an extra dimension to the event. Of course, there was the additional prospect of Eliane drifting into one of her fleeting moments of pure fantasy. The more she thought about the reunion, the more enticing it became. It seemed to present an opportunity to witness a unique occasion. How could she refuse?

Naturally, Sebastien believed the mere presence of his sister would bring a welcome diversion from his mother's irrational behaviour, on which he was depending. He anticipated the luncheon could develop on a knife-edge but it was a gamble he was prepared to take. With luck, Angelique would be impressed by his concern for his mother's welfare, provided Eliane used the occasion to entertain her guests by exhibiting her strange obsession with dead people.

The other guests would be able to contribute to the general conversation, offering an antidote to his mother's ramblings if he felt she was becoming too outrageous and unmanageable.

The scene was set for a drama of unpredictable consequences, combining the comedy of fabrication with the tragedy of truth. Revelations about the past were not high on Sebastien's agenda for this momentous luncheon. Nevertheless, all the ingredients would be around the table, ready for the pot. It only required someone to innocently light the fire to bring the mixture to the boil.

Part Five

Cathédrale Saint-Etienne, Limoges

Chapter 26

Bellac
1969

Dawn swept up and over the Massif Central, bringing bright early morning sunshine that enshrouded Haute Vienne with a hazy pink veil. Eliane Tricot stood at her kitchen door, breathing in the fresh warm air that heralded another fine day. The last time she had invited guests to the house for a special meal was to celebrate the twenty-first birthdays of the 'twins'. She tried to recall who attended that auspicious occasion, and sadly realised some had passed on since that last gathering of friends and relatives.

She looked upwards to gaze at the azure blue sky. "I hope you all honour us with your presence today," she whispered, before returning indoors to begin the preparation of food for her guests.

Sebastien spent the morning ensuring the house looked presentable as well as seeking out some decent clothes to wear. His mother had never seen him so fussy about his appearance; his attention to detail convinced her to make a similar effort with her own attire after completing her catering responsibilities.

Sylvie arrived on the late-morning train. The village of Saint Sauveur rose above a narrow valley, separating it from the station on the far side of Bellac. For that reason, she had intended to seek a taxi for the trip across town. The fine weather changed her mind. She decided to take a detour with a short stroll to visit her grandmother, Madame Dutheil at Les Singuelles. She would have the opportunity to meet up with her uncle Gérard, his wife, Lydie and their two teenage daughters, Gabrielle and Brigitte, none of whom she had seen since her twenty-first birthday party.

Grand'maman seemed somewhat irritated to hear that her daughter was hosting a luncheon to welcome Sebastien's young woman without her knowledge. "My invitation must have become lost in the post," she remarked bitterly.

Sylvie smiled. "Well, you know how unreliable these postmen can be!"

Gérard offered her an aperitif whilst they sat updating each other with the latest news. "I hear you're working at the new hospital."

"I start there permanently in a couple of months." She smiled again. "I'm wondering whether to specialise in mental health; maman would be a perfect case-study."

Her grandmother sat alongside her. "Is she still experiencing those dreadful hallucinations?"

"According to Sebastien, it's getting worse. She believes the house is haunted by dead people who died on their birthdays."

"It seems she needs help," added Gérard, concerned about his sister's well-being. "She's never recovered since losing Jean-Claude."

His mother agreed. "She was already in a state when he was a prisoner of war. Mind you, the presence of that Colonel Rausch, the German officer didn't help matters, despite his intervention."

"A German officer?" Sylvie asked, mystified.

Madame Dutheil nodded. "Yes, they billeted him here during the occupation. I think he used to pester her on the pretext of securing Jean-Claude's release. However, I always suspected my daughter secretly enjoyed his flattery."

Her remark caused Gérard to frown in astonishment. "What are you inferring?"

Sylvie looked surprised. "I didn't know about that. In fact, Sebastien and I were talking only the other day about our vague recollection of a soldier. We thought he must have been one of papa's army pals."

"There's a lot you don't know, my child...most of which you don't want to know." Her grandmother rose from the sofa. "Anyway, that's enough about the war; those dark years are behind us and should stay there." She ambled across to her comfortable armchair, helped by Lydie, her daughter-in-law. "So, who else has been invited to Eliane's party?"

"Sebastien said that she had suggested asking Anne-Marie and her husband."

"Oh, her!" Madame Dutheil looked annoyed. "She's the one who married that airman after the liberation whilst her first husband was still warm in his grave. I never liked her...too full of herself, claiming she played an important role in the Résistance. I can still picture the brazen hussy, parading through the streets of Bellac after the town's liberation...holding aloft the tricolour, singing and marching, surrounded by members of the A.S. and the F.T.P. It was as though she had fought alongside them, when all she had done was to provide them with the Berneuil bordello, boasting she ran a safe-house for stranded Allied airmen...more like a brothel than a refuge, if you ask me!"

"Grand'maman! What an awful accusation."

A cynical smile spread across the old woman's face. "Well, at least she wasn't entertaining Boche soldiers like some of the *filles de joie* in the town.

Gérard topped up their glasses with Ricard and water. "I thought we had finished talking about the war, maman."

His mother peered at him over the rim of her glasses, aware of her son's painful experience as a prisoner-of-war. Feeling guilty of trivialising what had happened during those dark years, she turned to Sylvie. "Is that it...one married couple and just you to greet Sebastien's young woman?"

"I think she's invited Father Milani."

"Ah, yes...the devil's own priest!"

"Sylvie gasped again. "Grand'maman, how can you say that about a clergyman?"

"Huh! He's another I wouldn't trust but I suppose we all had to be skilful liars to survive in those days. The only decent one amongst all of them was your father. Sadly, Jean-Claude didn't make it." She wiped a tear from her eyes with a white, lace-trimmed handkerchief. "I had a good life with your grand'papa but have always regretted the loss of my son-in-law, especially as he died only days before the liberation."

Gérard placed a hand on his mother's shoulder. "Enough about the war, maman. I'm sure Sylvie would rather chat about the future."

Her granddaughter looked at her watch. "I suppose I should make a move. Are the girls not around?"

Lydie, who had been a fascinated bystander during the previous exchanges, stepped forward. "Gabrielle is spending the weekend with her boyfriend's family in Le Dorat and Brigitte is in Bellac with some college friends."

"Good gracious...don't they grow up quickly. It seems only yesterday when they were running around the house, playing hide and seek."

"They'll be sorry to have missed you, Sylvie."

"Give them my love."

Gérard glanced at his niece. "If you like, I'll give you a lift in the car to Saint Sauveur. I'd like to say hello to my sister...it's a while since I last saw her." Their comments about the effect of the occupation on his sister concerned him.

Gratefully accepting the offer, Sylvie bid farewell to her grandmother and to Lydie before embarking on the next stage of what would become an even more revealing day.

Chapter 27

Saint Sauveur, Bellac
1969

Father Milani had already arrived when they pulled up outside Eliane's house. Effusing copious compliments, the elderly priest greeted Sylvie like a long-lost friend. Gérard shook hands with him before finally embracing his sister who, in turn, kissed her estranged daughter on both cheeks, showing little affection.

"You've just missed Sebastien. He's walked down towards the town to meet Angelique."

"I drove over from Les Singuelles via the back road," Gérard explained. "Maman sends her regards....likewise Lydie. How are you? I feel awful for not calling in to see you, but work and my daughters commandeer most of my time."

Eliane patted his arm. "I'm fine. Sebastien is always on hand if I need him, and in any case, looking after Father Milani's house keeps me occupied. I imagine the girls are quite grown-up since I last saw them."

Gérard smiled. "Yes, typical teenagers; I've merely become the financial provider for their social lives."

"Would you like an aperitif?" Father Milani seemed to have taken charge of the alcoholic beverages.

"No thanks." He checked his watch. "It's time to pick up Brigitte from Bellac on the way home...perhaps another time." Gérard kissed his niece before hugging his sister, bidding everyone farewell and driving off.

Eliane turned to her daughter. "It's about time you came to see me."

"You never invite me," Sylvie retorted. "In any case, what's to stop you visiting me? You know where I live."

"I never know when you are working. Besides, I have a commitment to my housekeeping duties with Father Milani."

Her daughter turned away. "A part-time role; I'm sure you could arrange a day off," she snapped.

Eliane knew the argument would never be resolved. ""How was grand'maman? I expect she was pleased to see you."

Sylvie forced a smile. "Looking well but very grey since I last saw her, and certainly on form at the moment."

"On form?"

"Oh, she was reminiscing about the war." Sylvie took a glass of Pinot from Father Milani before continuing. "It was quite an eye-opener. I didn't know that a German soldier had lodged with her during the occupation."

The colour seemed to drain from Eliane's face; she glanced towards the priest. "Yes, he was there until the army moved out after the Allies arrived." She crossed to the table where she had arranged *casse-croûte*. "Would you like a snack whilst we await the others? You must be hungry after your trip from Limoges."

"I'm fine maman. I'll wait until our 'guest of honour' arrives." She sat on a chair near a window overlooking the rear garden. "It must be years since Sebastien and I used to play out there, yet it just seems like yesterday." She turned back to face her mother. "Was that the same soldier we saw here…the one who, according to grand'maman, arranged papa's release?"

Eliane looked across at Father Milani before replying. "Yes. He called once or twice to update me on how papa's repatriation was progressing."

Father Milani moved towards Sylvie. "You see, they introduced a scheme to release prisoners in exchange for workers. To show his gratitude for accommodating him, the officer organised your father's release."

Eliane passed her a glass of Pinot. "I took you and Sebastien to the station at Limoges to meet papa."

"Mm, I remember that. It's strange no one has ever mentioned it before. You must have been extremely grateful to the German soldier."

At that moment, a car drew up outside. Anne-Marie had arrived with her husband.

After the usual pleasantries, Eliane withdrew to the kitchen to check on the food, leaving her guests to engage in the polite custom of informal conversation about meaningless topics. Father Milani ensured that everyone enjoyed a steady supply of refreshments to complement the *casse-croûte*.

Whilst the priest was engaged in conversation with Ann-Marie's husband, Sylvie followed her towards the table where she was helping herself to a few slices of *saucisson*. Intrigued by her grandmother's earlier remarks about Anne-Marie, Sylvie decided to delve further. "Grand'maman tells me you hid Allied airmen from the Nazis during the war. That must have been exciting but extremely dangerous."

Anne-Marie nodded. "It was fortunate that I lived in a remote area where we saw very little of the enemy."

"Were you hiding any when Sebastien and I stayed with you?"

Unsure how to reply, she dismissed her query with a lie. "Oh no; you were with me after the liberation of Limoges. At that time, most German troops were desperately heading back to their beloved Fatherland; the war had almost finished by then."

"I remember playing in your barn on one occasion. We discovered a vehicle hidden beneath piles of straw. Sebastien said it was German. Is it still there?"

"No, not any longer."

"Why was it kept under the straw? Sebastien and I often wondered about it." The memory became clearer. "I remember you had a gun. That's right…Maman ran out of the barn with us."

Irritated by Sylvie's questions, she turned away, shrugging her shoulders. "The Germans had left it behind; we just hid it in the barn because it was full of petrol…difficult to acquire at the time. I found the gun in the car." She popped a slice of meat into her mouth, before glaring at Sylvie. "Your mother tells me you're a fully-fledged nurse now."

From her attitude, Sylvie knew instinctively she was hiding something. She needed to speak with her brother; she suspected there was more than a grain of truth in what her grandmother had said. If Anne-Marie had been a member of the Résistance, what part did she really play? More importantly, had their own mother been involved? She sensed a certain amount of tension amongst the guests. At one point earlier, her mother had tried to change the subject before Father Milani had stepped in to offer a plausible explanation. Several times they had exchanged concerned expressions. Perhaps her mother's strange obsession was a result of something that had happened during the occupation; maybe it concerned the death of her father. Immediately, her thoughts turned to that day when her mother showed her the house where her father had died…Villa Tivoli, Gestapo headquarters in Limoges. Was that the catalyst for her strange behaviour?

She crossed to Father Milani. It was time for some answers. At that moment, the door opened. A smiling Sebastien stood there with Angelique. Sylvie had missed her opportunity.

After several minutes of prolonged introductions, Sebastien eventually managed to seat everyone around the dining table in the places he had designated for each guest. Sylvie found herself alongside his girlfriend. Having expected to see a young woman who matched her brother's stunning description, she was mildly surprised to see that Angelique looked quite ordinary but possessed a demeanour that exuded intelligence—the schoolteacher posture. She relaxed, satisfied that Sebastien had obviously been influenced by her personality rather than by her looks.

Quietly spoken and obviously at ease in unfamiliar company, she soon impressed the other guests. His new partner joined in the general conversation as though she was an old friend of the family. It seemed that Sebastien's gamble would pay off, provided all the guests played their part as he had arranged previously. The unknown factor would be how Angelique might react if the question of Eliane's residential situation with her son entered the conversation.

Father Milani had provided two bottles of Bordeaux Supérieur that even tempted Eliane, the self-proclaimed abstinent, to indulge herself. Angelique sat opposite Sebastien between Eliane and Sylvie, a position at the table that placed her firmly in the family's inner circle. Liam, Anne-Marie's husband sat next to Sylvie, facing his wife seated alongside the priest. The conversation continued in a light-hearted vein until Father Milani suggested Cognac to accompany the coffee. By this time, Eliane had consumed a little more alcohol than usual, resulting in a drift towards unreality where her mind began its descent into her more bizarre spirit world.

Content with his mother's behaviour, Sebastien watched her regale Angelique with her theories on life after death. His plan seemed to be on course. He would be able to explain why, as a concerned son, he took every opportunity to care for her at his house here in Saint Sauveur. He could add that, by hiring her as his housekeeper, Father Milani was also assisting with her therapy.

Unfortunately, his mother, though often predictable, could occasionally slip into one of the deeper recesses of her mind, an area that had become a refuge for all her dark memories. Without warning, she reached out to grip Angelique's arm; her eyes became glazed as though nothing existed except some image of the past.

"What do you think about Jews?" she asked.

The room became silent. Anne-Marie turned to stare at Father Milani. Sylvie frowned and looked across towards her brother who also seemed puzzled. Liam quietly sipped his Cognac, unaware of the dramatic effect of his host's question.

Father Milani attempted to diffuse the awkward hiatus in the conversation. "I'm sure our guest supports all faiths as reflected by our secular state, especially in her capacity as a teacher." He looked across at Angelique. "Wouldn't you agree?"

"I have no preferences with regard to religious issues; an individual's character is far more interesting. Apart from Sebastien, I have not met any of you before. However, one only has to look around this table for example, to see there is a mix of backgrounds and cultures, but we still enjoy the company of each other. We must celebrate our differences, even though sometimes we disagree. France is a melting pot of diverse cultures, yet I believe it is that diversity, which creates the building blocks of our society."

Anne-Marie smiled. "You should renounce teaching and enter politics, though I doubt your liberal views would sit well with our current electorate. A quarter of a century has passed since the Second World War, and the enduring experience of the Nazi's occupation still provokes recriminations, jealousy and bitterness."

Liam nodded as though in agreement but remained silent.

Eliane seemed oblivious to the conversation at the table. Her face presented a bland, distant expression; she remained locked inside her memories. "David was a Jew," she uttered, placing her hand on Sebastien's arm.

Anne-Marie glanced swiftly at the priest.

Turning towards Angelique again, Eliane suddenly appeared to regain some composure. "Do you know the Nazis sent thousands of Jews to concentration camps in cattle wagons? At Nexon near Limoges, we had a transit camp...and we just watched and said nothing, showing no compassion or voicing any objection whatsoever to the authorities. The only help that some of us offered was to hide them to prevent the Boche from arresting them...isn't that right, Father?"

"That's true, Eliane." He looked specifically at Angelique. "It's worth pointing out that Eliane's aunt, her mother's sister Thérèse, married an Austrian Jew. They were deported and sadly, never returned. The memory of those dark years still lingers but as time passes it will become less painful." He reached for the bottle of Cognac. "May I suggest we move on from the war years and look towards a brighter future...starting with a little more of this excellent *digestif*."

217

Anne-Marie sighed with relief; Father Milani had diverted what could have been an embarrassing situation if Eliane had continued her reminiscences. Of the seven guests seated around the table, only three were aware of the events that had shaped their lives. However, their secret hung by a thread, which, if broken, could reveal the web of deceit they had fabricated to protect their families, friends and themselves during those final months of the occupation.

The meal ended with Father Milani assisting Eliane to serve *digestifs* of eau-de-vie to everyone. Carrying a glass, he joined Liam in the garden where they enjoyed the warm afternoon sun. They sat on a wooden bench smoking cigarettes like two pals who knew each other intimately. Nothing could have been further from the truth. Anne-Marie and Sebastien helped his mother to clear the table.

Sylvie sat alongside Angelique on the sofa. "What's your impression of our dysfunctional family?" she asked, light-heartedly.

"Everyone's made me extremely welcome." Angelique lowered her voice. "Your mother's a little strange at times...but Sebastien did warn me."

"He only told me about her worsening behaviour a short time ago. I suggested he should seek advice...professionally, of course."

"You're a nurse, aren't you?"

"Yes, but not qualified in that area. I told him to speak first with Doctor Jerome, our local doctor. It's probably just an ageing issue."

"Why did she ask me if I liked Jews? I wasn't sure how to answer."

Sylvie shrugged. "I don't know from where that originated except that, as Father Milani mentioned, her aunt was married to a Jew. I've not had much contact with maman since I left home, so I'm no expert on what goes on in her head. Sebastien reckons she spends a lot of time talking about dead people and especially those who die on their birthday. What's that all about? Perhaps you should ask him about her confused thoughts; he's far closer to her than I am. She always favoured Sebastien...as though she had to protect him for some reason. She never had time for me."

"How strange. I would have imagined that, as twins, you would have shared her affections."

Sylvie laughed. "Twins! Just look at us; we have nothing whatsoever in common, neither in our personality, our intellect nor even our appearance." She lowered her voice. "During the occupation when we were just toddlers, there was often a soldier in our house. As

218

we grew older, I always thought he must have been papa. However, today at grand'maman's house, I discovered he was probably the German soldier who arranged papa's repatriation…he was a prisoner of war." She sipped some eau-de-vie. "I shouldn't say this, but afterwards, I stupidly wondered if he might have been Sebastien's father… until I realised we were both born before the Nazis invaded France." She sighed. "It's all a little mysterious."

"What happened to your father? Did he come home as promised?"

"Apparently, but the Gestapo murdered him."

"Why?"

Sylvie shrugged. "Like all the other stuff, I really don't know. I'm sure Anne-Marie and Father Milani know something. Did you see the expressions on their faces when maman began rambling on about the Jews?"

"What about Anne-Marie's husband? How does he fit into all this? He's English, isn't he?" She grinned. "He's rather handsome, despite his age."

"He's her second husband. Apparently, her first one died fighting the Germans during the first month of the war, so I never met him. I've not seen her or this new one for some time. I believe he's Irish or half-Irish; his father was British but his mother was Irish or something like that. I don't really understand. I think it's something to do with religion; one is a catholic, the other's a protestant."

Angelique smiled. "Ireland is split into two. Ulster in the north is part of the United Kingdom but the southern part is an independent country…Ireland. Apparently, there's lots of trouble at the moment between the Irish Republican Army and British soldiers." She smiled again. "I know a little about it through my studies but we're not experts on foreign affairs, are we? So, how did she meet him?"

"I heard he was part of a bomber crew that the Germans shot down over the submarine bases at Lorient. He baled out, survived and, after making his way south, ended up at Anne-Marie's safe house."

"What's a 'safe house'?"

"She used to hide escapees and evaders from the Germans until they could travel on to Spain and Gibraltar before making their way back to England."

"So, he stayed with her until the war was over?"

"No, I believe he came back to see her after the war, married her and has been here ever since. I remember maman saying his mother's father fought against British soldiers in Ireland about the time of the Great War and they shot him. He probably perceived Anne-Marie as a patriotic resister like his grandfather."

"She was involved with the Résistance?"

"Grand'maman reckons she was…amongst other things. I think they all were. Presumably, that's the reason the Germans killed papa but I'm only guessing. I'm sure that's why they never talk about the occupation, and why those years are such a mystery to Sebastien and me."

"How d'you know the Gestapo killed your father?"

"Maman told me some years ago. She showed me the house in Limoges where it happened…opposite the Champs de Juillet. She called it Villa Tivoli."

Angelique gasped. "I've heard of that place. It was Gestapo headquarters in Limoges during the occupation. It had a dreadful reputation for torturing captives. Does Sebastien know about it?"

"I pointed it out to him when we met a while ago on the day he told me about you. Like me, he originally thought papa died fighting during the war. Looking back, it made no sense because we went to meet him at Gare Bénédictins after his release from the prison camp. However, we were too young to understand." She smiled. "It's embarrassing to admit that I only discovered some of the truth earlier today. I just wish I knew more."

"I teach history at the *lycée*. Sometimes, to research historical events, one must become a detective. History is like a huge jigsaw puzzle. When one finds pieces that connect, a more accurate picture begins to emerge. You seem to have found some of those pieces but, obviously you need more."

"You make it sound so simple but, when everyone seems averse to discussing the war, it seems impossible to find the truth."

"I'll do a bit of research if you like but, from what you have told me so far, one individual here probably has most, if not all of the answers."

Sylvie looked across at the other guests; she frowned, inviting further enlightenment.

Angelique leaned closer to whisper. "There is one person whose life still seems dominated by past events. You must ask your mother."

*****

Father Milani crossed the room towards the sofa where Sylvie and Angelique were still engaged in deep conversation. "Would you young ladies like another *digestif* or more wine?"

Angelique laughed. "I hope you're offering a larger measure than those you serve up at communion."

"Ah, a precious commodity, consecrated wine." He refilled their glasses. "You seem to be enjoying each other's company."

"We've been discussing maman," Sylvie replied. "I'm concerned about her state of mind…as is Sebastien."

"I believe she's your housekeeper," Angelique added. "You must have noticed how confused she seems to be."

"I find her extremely entertaining, though I must admit some of the magazines she reads contain the most bizarre articles. I like to think she uses me as her 'sounding board' but I refuse to endorse her mystical world. My beliefs are founded on the scriptures not on scandalous journalistic fabrications. However, despite my scepticism, we often have some very interesting discussions."

Sylvie seemed unimpressed. "Do you not worry about her, Father, especially when she talks constantly about the resurrection of dead people because they died on their birthday?"

"Oh, it's just another phase she's going through after reading one of those absurd stories." He smiled. "Next week it'll be a different obsession about a different claim; just wait and see."

Angelique remained determined to pursue the topic. Her natural instinct as a history teacher took over. Her intellect and determination for accuracy demanded logical answers before accepting any perceived facts or subjective comments as authentic.

"Sylvie believes her mother's state of mind could derive from the tragic events she experienced during the occupation. It must have been devastating to welcome home one's husband from a prisoner of war camp, only to discover he died soon afterwards at the hands of the Gestapo. As a young woman myself, I cannot imagine the traumatic effect of such a loss."

Father Milani nodded. "It was a sad period for many, particularly for Eliane to lose her husband so close to the liberation of Limoges. There is possibly some substance to your logic. I can only say that time is a great healer but of course, nothing will compensate the enormous burdens we endured."

Angelique's curiosity had played a major part in achieving her current position as a history teacher. Since early childhood she had exhibited a thirst for knowledge; she soaked up data with ease. This day had granted an opportunity to step into unfamiliar territory. Here, she had encountered a group of individuals who had taken part in one of the most dramatic global events since records began. She could delve into the past by talking to those who had witnessed history as it unfolded. Additionally, her conversation with Sylvie had alluded to the possibility of uncovering a family secret.

She leaned across to face the priest. "You know I'm a teacher of history at the *lycée*. I enjoy researching my subject just as much as I enjoy passing on my knowledge. I would welcome an opportunity to interview you about how the occupation of France affected ordinary people in a small village…like here in Saint Sauveur. I'm sure my pupils would be engrossed to learn more about their local patrimony, especially if I could support the information with stories from someone who lived through it. Unfortunately, I wasn't born until after it had ended; consequently, I have no recollections at all. Do you think we could have a chat sometime? Of course, I would ensure my source remained anonymous."

Slightly surprised, Father Milani realised he had no option other than to agree. Perhaps, if he spoke with Angelique privately and on home territory, he would be able to control the dialogue. "I'd be delighted. How about next weekend? We could meet in the church, and I could acquaint you with the historical significance of the building and its role in the community."

They arranged to meet on the following Saturday, each focussing on a personal agenda that neither would anticipate.

Carrying a tray of coffee, Eliane and Sebastien rejoined the party. Anne-Marie and Liam strolled in from the garden.

Radiating a broad smile, Angelique turned to the others. "Father Milani has kindly offered to show me round his church and to help me with my research on the Nazi's occupation of the Limousin."

Sylvie remained silent, content to study the reactions to the announcement. Anne-Marie almost dropped her coffee cup before looking anxiously across at Eliane, whilst Sebastien's expression registered some bewilderment as he stared inquiringly at his sister.

Liam interrupted the sudden but brief mood of consternation. "I suppose it's more exciting and real to learn about it from a participant than from a text book."

"Sadly, there are few books that cover such recent history," Angelique replied. "One has to rely on copies of newspaper reports

222

and articles that lack detail. I'm really looking forward to have the opportunity of delving into an area of social history that remains shrouded in mystery."

Father Milani patted her arm whilst addressing Liam. "I'm hardly what one might call a participant…more an observer."

Angelique glanced at Liam. "Perhaps you also could add to my research with details of your 'safe house' experience."

Wondering who had told Sebastien's girlfriend about her role in the Résistance, Anne-Marie looked angry and perplexed as she struggled to prevent her coffee from spilling.

With an expression of smug satisfaction, Sylvie looked across at her brother. It was obvious they had scratched the surface, a small but decisive step in penetrating the wall of secrecy that surrounded their family's involvement. She stared at her mother.

Eliane stood in silence, seemingly transfixed by the door to the staircase.

*****

Angelique walked alongside Father Milani towards the altar. He indicated they should share a pew to have their initial chat.

"I've noticed so many churches in this style around the Bellac area and, of those I've visited, their interiors are all spectacular in their own individual way," she remarked as she sat on the hard white oak pew.

"I'll give you a short tour later."

"How long have you been the priest in this commune?"

"I arrived here from Grenoble before the war."

"You must have found it very quiet in a small commune like this after Grenoble?"

"It may be small but a rural population has similar needs to those of city dwellers, and of course, my duties as a priest are the same but perhaps not as numerous with smaller congregations.

"Your name has an Italian ring to it. Is that where you're from originally?"

"My father was Italian, my mother Austrian. We lived close to the border between the two countries at a beautiful little town called San Candido in the south Tyrol. Of course, when the Great War began, the whole of Europe became embroiled in the dispute between Serbia and Austria. In 1915, my father became a conscript in the Royal Italian

Army. My mother took my younger brother, my sister and me to her hometown of Saalfelden in Austria. Sadly, my father was killed at Caporetto in 1917.

"A few months after the end of hostilities, we moved back to San Candido for a short time but my mother had little income to provide for three teenage children, and we returned to Saalfelden to be close to her family. The town nestles in a lowland area between the Grossglockner glacier and Berchtesgaden, about ten kilometres from the border with Germany."

"She must have found it difficult."

"She received a small amount from a military pension but had to rely on part-time work, which was not easy to find during that post-war period. By this time I was looking forward to studying philosophy at the University of Innsbruck. After qualifying, I began my priesthood training at Milan to gain my licence and my ordination took place at the Basilica Cathedral di San Vigiglio in Trento. Prior to arriving here, I held the position of assistant priest at the Cathédrale Notre Dame in Grenoble, as I mentioned earlier."

"You appear to have had an extremely exciting upbringing and career progression during a most dramatic period of unrest. You speak French well; what about your native tongue?"

The priest smiled coyly. "Yes, I speak Italian and a modicum of the Austrian version of German, though I prefer to converse in French whenever possible."

"Do you find time to see your family?"

"My mother continues to live in Saalfelden; she's in her late eighties but is still in remarkably good health. I try to see her as often as possible, apart from the war years when it became awkward to make that journey."

"What about your brother and sister. What do they do?"

"Regrettably, they both died in service during the war. My sister was in communications; she was killed in a bombing raid near Berlin."

"And your brother?"

"He joined the military, the *Bundesheer*, the Austrian Army. However, after Germany had annexed Austria in March 1938, he was forced to join the *Wehrmacht*. He too died during the war."

Angelique was intrigued. On the surface, Father Milani gave the impression of an ordinary, devout pastor, yet she was discovering a far more complex individual with an extraordinary background. She wanted to delve deeper but sensed he might suspect her to be too intrusive. It was important not to reveal the real motive for her interview; she decided to focus on less controversial matters.

"Having experienced the Great War in central Europe, how different was it living here in the Limousin under an enemy occupier?"

Her generalized question gave the priest an opportunity to choose the content of his response. She listened intently, occasionally commenting and asking for clarification. Having already gathered the information she required about his background, she allowed him to cover aspects of life in the commune, subjects of no interest to her but necessary to authenticate her original request for this meeting. To add further credibility, she made a few notes as he described various aspects of village life under German occupation.

There followed a tour of the church, where alongside a running commentary, Father Milani showed her some of the artefacts of historical interest, several memorial plaques and the gallery that overlooked the central nave.

At the end of this mini-tour, she thanked him for his time, whilst promising she would add the information to her research material on the subject matter.

"Recent events like the Second World War may not seem like history to many, but I believe my students should be aware of how it has impacted on our lives today, especially from a local perspective."

"A refreshing viewpoint," he remarked as he watched her mount her 125cc Vespa scooter.

She disappeared down the hill towards Bellac, leaving him satisfied but a little curious about the underlying reason for her visit. Was it a pretext for a possibly different agenda? With her hair blowing in the wind, she roared through the town, impatient to tell Sylvie about her encounter with the priest.

Chapter 28

Limoges, Haute Vienne
1969

The café-bar Pont Saint-Etienne in Limoges overlooked the river. Strong currents carried the Vienne on its tortuous journey westwards and northwards to join the river Loire near Candes-Saint-Martin. Dominating the far bank, the magnificent cathedral of Saint-Etienne rose like an edifice, as though hewn from the granite mass below. Famous for its porcelain and enamelling, the city had gradually regained its identity following the oppression it suffered during the occupation.

Sylvie sat at a table on the terrace of the bar, watching and waiting for her visitor. The late autumn sun painted the sky red as it sank towards the western fringes of the city, casting amber and pink reflections on the rapidly flowing river.

In the distance she caught sight of Angelique, crossing the bridge that linked the busy centre with the serenity of the south bank. She carried a small leather document case. Smiling yet breathless, she joined her new friend and investigative partner.

"I ordered a *chopine* of red wine as soon as I spotted you." Sylvie leaned across the table to greet her. "No scooter?"

"Too cold at this time of year; I use it mostly for pottering about locally. I thought I'd be more comfortable on the train."

The waiter arrived with their wine and two glasses. Sylvie poured. "So, what's the great news you have discovered?"

Angelique tasted the wine. "I needed that! It's quite a walk from the station."

"It's all downhill to the river; wait until you return."

"Hopefully, I'll be fortified by this." She raised her glass. "Good health."

"Never mind all that…I'm getting impatient."

"Well, you remember I said several weeks ago that, after my chat with your priest, I would contact my pen-friend in Milan." She withdrew some papers from the document case. "These arrived in the post two days ago." She spread several documents on the table. "My friend, Giulia works in some government department in Milan, and offered to research the priest's family background, based on the information I sent her."

226

"She couldn't have had much to go on."

"His name, the town where he originally lived and some family details were enough for her to trawl through the records. Well, she has unearthed some very interesting material." She sipped some more wine before continuing.

"It seems that Father Milani's family had a musical connection. His father, Claudio...an Italian...was a music teacher; his mother, Martha...an Austrian...was a violinist with the Vienna Court Opera until they married. I presume they met through their love of music. They had four children: the eldest was your priest, Sebastian, presumably named after Bach, Antonio came next...possibly named after Vivaldi...but the infant died from diphtheria, aged two. They had another child soon afterwards...a girl, called Anna Maria. My friend reckoned she was named after the famous Italian opera singer, Anna Maria Strada. Finally, they produced another son, Franz...perhaps named after the Austrian composer, Schubert or the Hungarian, Liszt...who knows?"

"Father Milani's name is Sebastian. I wonder if my parents named my brother after the priest."

Angelique smiled. "The same thought had crossed my mind; it all seems to fit with Father Milani's family history. When I spoke with him, he said his mother, Martha is still alive. However, because she now lives in Austria, my friend has no access to her records. Perhaps we could investigate that further ourselves. Her maiden name was..." She searched through the papers on the table. "Yes, here it is...a copy of their marriage certificate. She was Martha Rausch, born in Vienna in 1879, married Claudio Milani in 1900."

Sylvie picked up the relevant document. "Rausch? I've heard that name before...but where?" She drank some wine before placing the document back on the table. "Rausch, Rausch...dammit. It was only recently...I'm sure." She slumped back in her chair and stared into the glare of the setting sun.

"Where have you been, to whom have you spoken? Could it have been at work or at home?" Angelique tried to stimulate a train of thought.

Suddenly, Sylvie sat upright. "I know...it was the name of that German soldier who stayed with grand'maman during the occupation. I'm sure she mentioned it when I called to see her on the day I first met you."

Angelique sat open-mouthed. "Oh, my God!" she uttered. "Surely, that can't be a coincidence. Perhaps he was Martha's brother or cousin. That could be the priest's connection. Do you think that's what this mystery is about?"

"I don't know. He must have been young because grand'maman hinted that my mother fancied him! Could he have been her brother's son? I can't think straight!" Sylvie drank more wine. "I wonder if maman knows. Do you think this is the cause of her mental problem?"

"I suppose it's possible. If that's the case, surely Father Milani must have known his nephew was in Saint Sauveur but why would it cause problems for your mother...unless there was something going on between them. When I interviewed him, he did say his brother was in the Wehrmacht, the German army. Could it have been him?"

"His surname would have been Milani, not Rausch."

"Of course; how stupid of me." Angelique emptied the *chopine*. "Let's order another one of these." She laughed. "Obviously, I can't think logically when I'm sober!"

Sylvie leaned back in her chair. "So, what are we going to do about it?"

"Like I suggested last time, I believe your mother's the key. If she was entertaining this soldier, she must have known about his relationship with your priest...if there was one. To discover why your mother's behaviour is strange, you need to ask her if this Rausch fellow was indeed related to Father Milani and what happened to upset her."

"What if Father Milani didn't know this distant relative and Rausch didn't know the priest?"

"Surely, he would have asked when he heard his name. There can't be many Wehrmacht soldiers with the surname Rausch. What was the soldier's first name?"

Sylvie shrugged. "I don't think grand'maman mentioned it."

"That might be a start. Ask her."

"Do you think we should tell Sebastien what we have discovered?"

"Let's wait until we have more facts. It's still a confused picture. For example, why did the Gestapo kill your father after an SS officer had made an effort to arrange his release? It doesn't make sense. If there was no intrigue, no cover-up, why such furtive glances between everyone at the family gathering? Furthermore, I wasn't convinced about the Jewish issue. Who is David?"

"Yes, I remember maman making the remark. No one queried that; it was as though she was talking about someone they knew."

"Well, that's another question you can ask…although they did make some reference to your grandmother's sister. Wasn't she married to an Austrian Jew? What was his name?"

Sylvie shook her heard. "That's another question to ask. I'll need a list at this rate."

They chatted some more before crossing the bridge over the river. Since that first meeting, the two young women had become good friends, mostly due to their curiosity about the Tricot family history. What had seemed to Sylvie as an unlikely relationship between her brother and Angelique was developing into a bond cemented by her intrusion. Sebastien's concerns regarding his mother had brought his new girlfriend closer instead of driving her away. Additionally, Sylvie could not wait to see her mother again, a sentiment that had remained dormant since she had left Saint Sauveur to live in Limoges.

They climbed the steep, narrow alley-ways towards the cathedral. "I'll walk over to the station with you before I stagger back to my apartment," Sylvie gasped as they reached the less strenuous area of Place Jourdan.

"I must admit red wine is not conducive towards coping with an energy-sapping hill climb. I think a coffee on the station concourse would go down well."

They reached the Champ de Juillet, where they stopped to admire the immaculate gardens. Surrounded by railway lines on one side and a skyline dominated by three-storey buildings, the miniature park provided a tranquil oasis in the heart of the city. The two young women looked at each other; immediately, their eyes expressed similar thoughts.

"C'mon," Sylvie shouted as she ran across the road. "I'll race you there!"

Angelique laughed and chased after her. They raced through the gardens before stopping by the bench where Sylvie had sat with her brother several weeks previously. Minutes later, they clung to each other breathless before staring in silence at VillaTivoli.

Sylvie wiped a tear from her eye. "If only I knew why. What had happened to bring my father to such a dreadful place?"

"And so soon after his release from a prisoner-of-war camp. It doesn't make sense. What terrible thing had he done to warrant being arrested by the same people who had arranged his repatriation?"

Sylvie grasped her companion's arm. "Together, we are going to unearth the truth."

Angelique sat on the bench, her eyes still glued to the building across the road. "It's so hard to believe that the Gestapo tortured and killed people over there. Imagine arriving there, aware of its cruel reputation; the victims must have been terrified, knowing what lay in store for them. Your father must have been a very brave man. You should be proud of him."

Sylvie turned to face the building. "Papa, whatever you did, whatever reason they had to arrest you, I promise I will vindicate you."

Angelique squeezed her hand. "I think it's confession time, and for that, we need the services of a priest. Anyone spring to mind?"

Part Six

Chapelle de Notre-Dame de Lorette, Saint Sauveur

Chapter 29

Bellac, Haute Vienne
1970

Jean Baudet sauntered into the staff room. The colleague he wished to see was pouring herself a coffee. "Good morning, Angelique. How are you today?"

She turned to see the fifty-year old language teacher standing close behind her. They had spoken in passing since she had started teaching at the *lycée*, but this was the first time he had attempted to engage with her.

"Fine, thank you. Can I pour you one?"

He nodded. "Join me at the table in the corner. I may have something that may interest you."

Intrigued, she followed him, bringing a tray with two cups of coffee and a small plate of biscuits. She sat facing him, wondering which pupil's behaviour or new academic procedures might be the subject of their conversation.

"I hear you are researching local history with particular focus on the occupation."

Immediately, Baudet had her attention.

"You can help?"

"I encountered the elderly priest in Saint Sauveur last weekend at one of his fund raising events for veterans of the French Indochina war. When he discovered I taught languages here, he asked if I knew the history teacher. We had a chat during which, he told me about your project…very commendable, I must add."

"Thank you." Angelique sipped her coffee. "You said you may have something of interest."

"Later that same day, I was at home searching for a book I had purchased during my younger days when I was studying at teacher training college: *Ein Tausend idiomatische Redensarten* by Langenscheidtsche Verlagsbuchhandlung. I wanted to introduce it to my pupils. It's a book of equivalent common words and phrases we might use, translated into German." He smiled. "It's not only educational but also quite a handy travel aid for visitors to Germany." He reached across for a biscuit. "I'm sorry; I digress."

He withdrew a notebook from his pocket. "Amongst my collection of books and magazines, I came across this. I wondered if you might find it useful." He passed what looked like a rather worn notebook across the table. "It's been lying there since the war. Someone asked me to translate the writing at the back; it's in German. I thought you might find it interesting with regard to your research of the Bellac area."

*****

A receptionist at the hospital stopped Sylvie as she walked past on her way to the pharmacy. "Sylvie, there's been a phone call for you." She passed her a slip of paper. "There was no message…just that number to call. It sounded urgent."

Her heart thumping from an expectation of bad news, Sylvie glanced at the telephone number on the paper. Immediately, she recognised it and, feeling a little calmer, smiled; Angelique must have unearthed something.

*****

Angelique was waiting at Bellac station as Sylvie stepped from the train. They hugged each other before walking up the slope towards the main road. Unable to contain their excitement, they hurried into a nearby *tabac*, where they ordered two glasses of wine before sitting at a spare table. Without saying a word, Angelique opened her shoulder bag, withdrew a well-thumbed notebook and passed it to her friend.

With trembling hands, Sylvie scrolled through page after page of names. Suddenly, she stopped to touch the yellowed paper. Tears rolled down her cheeks. "Papa...it's him...his name is there...Jean-Claude Tricot."

*****

Sharing a platter of *charcuterie* and salad, the two young women sat in Angelique's living room discussing how best to utilise the information they had gathered.

"Jean Baudet, the teacher who gave it to me had tried to explain the letters after the names on the list. For example, he reckons 'T' stands for terrorist, the name attributed by the Germans to resisters. He said that, although all the names were members of the Maquis, only those who were combatants had probably been classed as terrorists."

"Like papa."

"Mm, like your father. It's obvious that 'M' and 'F' are for male and female. I think the German words are '*Mann*' and '*Frau*'. Your mother's friend...the one I met at her party...is there but without the 'T', probably because she ran a 'safe house' instead of running amok with a machine gun. Although he had tried to decipher the significance of the other letters, he admitted that the only ones he considered a possibility were 'NV'." She reached into the pocket of her jacket and pulled out a scrap of paper. "He said it could be '*nützliche verbindung*', which means 'useful contact'." She shrugged. "I suppose that's a possibility."

"Where did your colleague find it...the notebook?"

Angelique broke off a small chunk of baguette. "I asked the same question. He didn't want to tell at first but I explained that if I knew, I might find other leads that I could follow."

"So?"

"He said a gendarme who had been in the Résistance had given it to him after the liberation. However, he added that he had seen it in the summer of the previous year when the Germans were still here. The gendarme had asked him to translate the writing in the back of the notebook." She leaned over to show Sylvie the page. "At the time, because the notebook contained so much detail, they thought it had been produced by a spy, an infiltrator...possibly someone

233

collaborating with the Germans. Also, it had been discovered in the car of an SS officer."

"SS soldiers were said to be extremely cruel, weren't they?"

"They were responsible for that dreadful atrocity at Oradour-sur-Glane."

"Oh, my God! So who found the notebook originally?"

"The gendarme wouldn't say except that it was given to him by a young woman who was in the same Maquis. Apparently, it was discovered in a German soldier's car."

Sylvie put down her knife and fork before leaning back in her chair, an expression of resignation on her face. "So what can we do with it? How can it help us if we cannot trace it back to anyone?"

Angelique waved her fork at her. "A woman in the same Maquis! Think about it. We have all their names here...'F' for Frau!"

"You're a genius! How many are there?" Sylvie's excitement returned.

"I've already checked...eleven. One of them of course is your mother's friend, Anne-Marie."

Sylvie grinned. "Let's start with her."

*****

Hearing the whirring noise of a high-pitched motor, Anne-Marie looked out of her living room window to see two young women skidding to a halt on a scooter outside the barn. Immediately, she recognised them. Too late to hide, one was already waving to her.

She opened the door. "Good afternoon, Sylvie...oh, it's you, Angelique. What brings you both here?"

Sylvie walked to the door and waved the notebook in her face. "What d'you know about this?"

Anne-Marie stepped back, startled by her forthright attitude. "Nothing," she exclaimed, feigning innocence. "What is it?"

"It's a notebook you gave to a gendarme years ago."

"I know nothing about it," she protested.

"Your name's in it."

"My name?" she uttered, trying to appear surprised.

"You found it in a German soldier's car..." Another instinctive thought struck her. "...you had a German car hidden in your barn when I was just a youngster! Is that where you found it?"

Anne Marie wanted to slam the door shut but Angelique was leaning against it. "I never found it. I swear to God I never found it."

"Yes, you did…you found it in the car in that barn." She turned to point her finger towards the outbuildings. Suddenly, her face lost its colour; she staggered against the doorframe, her features ashen. "Oh, shit…you're right…you didn't find it. Sebastien found it! It's all coming back to me."

She seemed to become limp; her eyes rolled.

"Quickly, get her a glass of water," Angelique screamed. "I think she's going to faint."

She helped her friend through the doorway onto the nearest chair. Anne-Marie returned with the water.

"Don't fuss. I'll be fine." She stared at Anne-Marie. "It was the day maman ran into the house with us. You had a gun. I remember now. We were frightened; we heard gunshots."

At last, Anne-Marie seemed to show some concern; she knelt beside the chair. "I'm sorry; I didn't mean to upset you. It's all in the past…best forgotten. It was a difficult time for everyone." She glanced at the notebook, still in Sylvie's hand. "It wasn't important. I had found an old suitcase in the car. It was locked; I used the gun to smash it open so we could see what was inside."

As Angelique listened in disbelief, tears welled in Sylvie's eyes. "I can remember finding a black leather case before Sebastien found the notebook." She wiped the moisture from her cheeks. "We covered the car with straw…why? At the time, we thought it was just a game…we were having fun, but why was it there and what happened to it? More importantly, whose car was it? Did you steal it?"

"I told you last time we met that the Germans left it behind when they fled France. A neighbour took it away. It was merely one of many abandoned vehicles."

Sylvie looked up at her puzzled. "You're lying again!"

"No, I'm not."

"Well, explain to me how, after finding the notebook, you gave it to a gendarme, who in turn, showed it to a language teacher at the *lycée*…the same teacher who, two days ago, told Angelique that your gendarme asked him to translate the writing at the back of the notebook…whilst the Germans still occupied France."

"He must have got his dates wrong."

Sylvie ignored her. "He also explained the meaning of some of the letters after each name…like this one here…" she opened the notebook and pointed at the letters 'NV' alongside one of the names. They represent…" She turned to Angelique. "Can you remember what he said?"

"I think it was '*nützliche verbindung*'. It means useful contact."

"There you see," remarked Sylvie, triumphantly. "This one here is a 'useful contact'…" Her voice fell to a whisper. "Oh, my God, it's grand-papa." She looked appealingly at them both. "Why would he be considered useful…and more importantly, why was his name amongst a list of resisters?"

"Your grandfather was a notary," Anne-Marie replied. "He would know a lot of important people in the town, an extremely useful contact, I would imagine."

For several moments, the three women seemed lost in their individual thoughts. Sylvie sipped more water; her mouth felt dry with emotion.

Angelique broke the embarrassing silence by addressing Anne-Marie. "It's obviously a list of all those involved in the Maquis, so who d'you think compiled this list?"

She shrugged. "I've no idea."

"If it was in the hands of an SS officer, what action was taken against these people? Were there no consequences?"

"No, nothing."

Sylvie looked up. "That's not true; they killed my papa." She glared at Anne-Marie. "Why are you being so bloody secretive? What are you hiding? Why were you all looking apprehensive on the day we welcomed Angelique? You're a liar, Anne-Marie. Even grand'maman saw through you…entertaining young airmen in your Berneuil bordello, and calling it a safe house, she said."

"You should hold your tongue, young lady. You have no idea what went on at that time."

"So, why do you keep lying to me?"

"You should talk with your mother."

"It was noticeable that Father Milani was also rather evasive on that day. What's his involvement in all this?" Angelique asked, trying to divert the attention from Anne-Marie, whilst cooling the situation.

"You should ask him."

Sylvie stood up. "Maybe, that's a good idea." She glared at Anne-Marie. "Priests cannot tell lies…can they?" She turned to Angelique. "C'mon, let's go. We're wasting our time here." She shouted at Anne-Marie. "You can't bury the truth forever."

Despite the warmth of the afternoon sun, Anne-Marie shuddered. With mixed emotions, she watched them cross the gravel path to mount the scooter. Seconds later they were heading down the lane towards Berneuil and the road to Bellac.

Feeling her world was about to fall apart, Anne-Marie gazed into the distance, fearful not for herself but for Eliane. How would her friend deal with this, if the truth were to be revealed? Perhaps it was time to confess.

Normality returned as Liam appeared from the nearby woodland with a shaggy black Briard. The dog bounded affectionately towards Anne-Marie.

"Was that Eliane's daughter just leaving?" he asked.

Anne-Marie nodded before turning inside the house to hide her tears and inner anger.

"C'mon, Hector," cried Liam to the dog. "I don't think she wants to play today."

Chapter 30

Saint Sauveur
1970

At the junction with the main road connecting Bellac with Limoges, Angelique slowed and halted between the church and the grocery shop. Concerned they were making little progress with their enquiries, an air of frustration and disappointment had replaced their usual outgoing personas. Even the warm, sunny weather had no effect on their mood. Beneath a clear blue sky, a more localised depression was forming.

Still angry with Anne-Marie, Sylvie leaned forward to whisper in her friend's ear. "Stop off at the church in Saint Sauveur. I think it's time to hear Father Milani's version of events."

The scooter roared off northwards on an almost traffic-free road where the odd farm vehicles seemed to outnumber the occasional passing cars. Ten minutes later, they stopped outside their destination. The Madonna topping the stone spire of the church sparkled in the sunshine, as though she was offering some light at the end of a long, dark tunnel.

"I doubt he'll be here," Angelique said, pulling the scooter onto its stand. "He'll be taking his siesta."

"If that's the case, we'll go to his house and wake him up if necessary."

"Won't your mother be there, carrying out her housekeeping duties?"

"I think she usually goes home after lunch."

Angelique was correct; the church was empty; the priest would probably be at his house. They stood for a few moments, deciding how to approach him and what questions they should ask before wandering up the road. They found him seated on his patio, reading a book and enjoying the pleasant weather. On seeing his visitors, he rose to greet them before extending a cordial invitation to join him at the alfresco table.

"How pleasing it is to see you both together again. Do I perceive a budding friendship?" He smiled at Sylvie. "Your brother will be jealous." He faced Angelique. "He's always talking about you whenever he pops over to help me in the garden."

"He still helps out, then?" Sylvie asked.

"It depends on his work schedule. Sometimes, he stays in town to drink with his friends. He helps me now and again with my chickens. Did he tell you I've converted that spare land into a chicken run?"

"He did mention it when your ideas were in the planning stage."

"You must take some eggs back...I always have more than I need." He returned to his chair, whilst waving an arm, reiterating his invitation to join him at the table. "I imagine you're not here to discuss poultry rearing." He looked specifically at Angelique. "How is your research coming along?"

"Extremely well, thank you. In fact, a colleague at the *lycée* has given me a most unusual book about the local Résistance."

The benign expression on the priest's face immediately changed. "A book...how interesting...and what is the title of this publication?"

"Oh, it's not a publication. It's a just someone's personal notebook."

Father Milani shifted uneasily on his wicker chair. "A recollection written since the war ended? The only one I've encountered about the Maquis in this area was a version recounting the exploits of the Vienne Maquis, written by Eugène Desgranges and published in October 1950. He was a captain in the F.F.I....the Forces Françaises de l'Intérieur."

"No, we...that is my colleague and I...believe this booklet was written by a semi-illiterate German or possibly by a Frenchman with limited knowledge of that language...or a combination of the two."

His visitors studied his reaction closely.

"That is an extremely profound assessment," the priest replied. "How did you arrive at that conclusion?"

"The grammar and spelling had a lot to be desired but the information seemed very detailed; it used codes consisting of letters and numbers. However, my colleague...he's a foreign language teacher...managed to decode most of it, and what looked to be a complex conundrum is now almost complete."

"Obviously, you are inferring that something is missing." He lit a cigarette, rose from his chair and walked to the edge of the patio. He stood with his back to his visitors, whilst contemplating his immaculate garden. "Sometimes in a certain light, one can imagine a different aspect to that beautiful vista out there...at different times of the day...in different seasons of the year. It doesn't always appear to be what it is in reality."

239

He turned to face them. "Life's like that; one often sees what one wants to see, and by so doing, one misses what is in front of one. The antithesis however, is that there are things out there one should not see…things best left alone. That way, there are no unexpected surprises; no one gets hurt."

Only birdsong interrupted the ensuing silence. The young women looked at each other, realising that the priest would not associate himself with the notebook, despite giving the impression that he was fully aware of its existence and its contents.

Sylvie broke the silence. "We each have one question we would like to ask. Would you allow us that?"

Father Milani smiled; he assumed he had averted a situation that could upset many individuals whose lives were already difficult to bear. "If I can answer your questions honestly, I will do so."

"Thank you," Sylvie said. "My question is about Sebastien. Did my parents…probably just maman because papa was a prisoner at the time…did she name him after you?"

"Almost right…I suggested it to her."

"Can I qualify that with another question about the same subject?"

The priest nodded.

"Why is his name spelled with the letter 'e' and yours is with the letter 'a'?"

"Simple…his name is the French version as opposed to my Italian version." He turned to face Angelique. "I hope your question is not too difficult."

She glanced at Sylvie before speaking to him. "When did you find out that SS-Standartenführer Rausch was related to you?"

He remained silent for a few seconds, puffed on his cigarette and smiled again. "When I was seven years old; Franz was born; he was my youngest brother."

Two faces stared at him with wide eyes and dropped jaws. "But his surname was Rausch…like your mother's maiden name," Angelique protested.

"Ah, it appears you have been busy conducting a thorough research." He returned to the table to extinguish his cigarette. "He changed his name when he joined the Wehrmacht. He thought an Italian surname would prevent him from joining the SS. At that time, he was probably correct. Later in the war, the Nazis were content to recruit anyone into the SS, provided they had two legs and two arms…that's how desperate they became."

He stood up and looked at his watch. "Can I offer you an *aperitif*; it's almost time to think about an evening meal. Would you care to join me? My housekeeper…your dutiful mother, has left me a sumptuous chicken casserole…more than enough to feed us all."

The young women looked at each other; how could they refuse after all he had said? Perhaps his invitation implied there could be more than food on offer.

Twenty minutes later, they sat outside enjoying not only the meal prepared by Eliane earlier but also further revelations washed down by several glasses of wine. They learned that Rausch had been using his position to assemble a group of French patriots who would rise up at a given moment…hence the list of those whom he had identified as possible allies.

The priest also informed them that SS-Standartenführer Rausch had been involved with a group of German conspirators headed by Claus von Stauffenberg who were plotting to assassinate Adolf Hitler. Known as Operation Valkyrie, the attempted coup on July 20th 1944 had failed badly. Subsequently, many of the high-ranking officials who were involved were sentenced to death. If it had been a success, Rausch and his partisan group would have had the responsibility to purge southwest France of remaining Nazi sympathisers.

"Is that what happened to your brother?" Angelique asked. "Was he a victim of Hitler's revenge?"

"I want you to understand that my brother was a good man. He joined the SS believing in the concept of a New Europe. When he realised the Führer's dream was based on perfidy and power, an ideology that used racial extermination, domination, exploitation and terror to achieve its aims, he vowed to fight for truth and justice. Sadly, he became an angry young man who, seeing his dream of future peace and prosperity being destroyed by those he had trusted, fought back. Consequently, he would cast aside anyone at any level who betrayed that trust."

In his exposition of the truth, Father Milani avoided any reference to the accidental death of his brother and the death of Sylvie's father. He suggested that any account regarding Jean-Claude's tragic demise was her mother's responsibility.

"Are the obscure circumstances of papa's death the reason why maman seems possessed by strange demons?"

241

"Your mother endured five years of desperation and heartache. I believe we should allow her to grieve in her own way, and if her fascination with death comforts her, why should I or any other person interfere. Like my brother whose intentions were for the most part honourable, so too is your mother a good woman and caring mother. She loved your father deeply but the occupation drove wedges through every relationship...some are perpetuated even to this day. There are many unsavoury secrets still untold; they served a purpose during such a brutal conflict but now, it is time to let go."

"I'd still like to know how papa died."

"Perhaps one day Eliane will find the strength to talk about it. My advice, for what it's worth, is to accept that, like many other patriots, he died for France."

His remark seemed to resonate with some inner emotion. He quickly emptied his glass and rose from the table. "If you can spare the time, I would like to show you something in the church." He turned to Angelique. "I suppose I should have shown it to you on your previous visit. This time however, I imagine you will not need a lengthy explanation."

They helped to clear the table before walking down to the church, Father Milani leading the way, Sylvie and Angelique curious to discover what he had in mind.

On arrival, he pushed open the huge oak doors; a cold but musty chill from the church's stone interior wafted past them as they entered. Their footsteps on the flagstone floor echoed in the vast arched structure, as though they were announcing their presence to any ghosts that cared to listen. Stone Romanesque archivolts supporting the vast arch-braced roof formed several apexes over an interior lit by vaulted stained-glass windows. Above the entrance, an ornate gallery facing the chancel overlooked the nave. On both sides of the nave, an eye-catching array of marble plaques dedicated to departed souls adorned the walls.

Father Milani led them to a simple rectangular plaque, so insignificant that one could easily ignore; no ornate edges, no special script, just plain gold lettering that read:

IN MEMORY OF FRANZ MILANI
1908 - 1944
PATRIOT OF ITALY
DIED FOR FRANCE

The two young women stared at the inscription in silence. Sylvie glanced briefly at Angelique before addressing the priest.

"Has maman seen this?"

Father Milani shook his head. "I don't think so...and even if she had noticed it, I doubt she would connect it with colonel Rausch." He stroked his chin. "I imagine she would have asked me if Franz Milani was a relative, if she had seen it."

"Would you have told her the truth?" Angelique asked, smiling.

"I would probably have told her that Franz Milani was my brother."

"Nothing more?"

"Only if she had asked."

Sylvie butted in. "Doesn't she have a right to know?"

"Why do you ask that?"

"I believe he visited often...and grand'maman thought she was rather fond of him."

The priest sat on a nearby chair; he looked exhausted. His face was drawn and almost as grey as his hair. "I feared how she might react on learning she was responsible for the death not of a Nazi officer but of my brother."

Sylvie looked astonished. "You're saying that maman killed him?"

Angelique frowned. "When we met at the church to discuss my research, you said your brother was killed in action."

"In a way, that was true." The priest turned to face Sylvie. "He often visited your house in his capacity as an SS soldier. On the night he died...according to your mother and Anne-Marie...he arrived rather intoxicated after celebrating his birthday. There was an argument, he slipped and tumbled down the staircase after your mother pushed him away. It was an accident but sadly, Eliane shouldered the blame. In some ways, her response towards him was perhaps justified under the circumstances but it could have been avoided." He stared at the plaque. "On reflection, perhaps I should have explained to her that Rausch was my brother."

"So, why didn't you?" Sylvie demanded.

"Franz said it was vital to maintain total secrecy about his identity and his secret mission until the assassination of Hitler was validated." He sighed. "If the plot misfired, he had no wish to be implicated; similarly, he wanted to protect all those whom he had

243

involved. Also, as I said previously, I had to consider your mother's reaction."

He rose from the chair and walked towards the chancel. "After his death, I saw no point in divulging his identity, and of course, because the plot to kill Hitler had failed, I swore never to divulge my brother's involvement...certainly not until the war was over. Later, it seemed pointless to pass further comment. The time had come to look forward until of course, you came along and began researching the past."

"How sad," Sylvie whispered, still staring at the plaque.

Suddenly, a new voice reverberated around the empty church. "I knew they were brothers."

Sylvie turned towards the entrance. "Maman?" she gasped.

The shadowy figure of her mother stood in the doorway against a backdrop of bright sunlight. She stepped inside before walking down the nave towards Father Milani.

"I fell in love with Franz the first time I set eyes on him. I was young, impressionable and lonely. Despite his arrogance, I recognised a good man; there was an aura about him. He kept his promise to rescue Jean-Claude; how could I not be grateful?"

Eliane Tricot sat on a pew facing the altar. "He discovered I was concealing a secret that could have cost the lives of my entire family. We made a pact; he would keep my secret safe if I could help him with his mission."

Sylvie was astounded to hear her mother speaking sensibly, openly and so lucidly.

"He told me he had joined the SS believing in the dream of a New Europe but had lost faith when he witnessed the Nazi's brutal methods. Having met like-minded people who vowed to overthrow Hitler's regime, his posting to France had offered the opportunity to prepare for the post-Hitler period. To achieve his aims, he needed contacts in the Résistance but the only one I knew at the time was you, Father. You had brought David's papers, which people in the Résistance had produced. When I mentioned your name, his eyes lit up."

She shrugged. "We know what happened next. You met your brother, though I was unaware then that you were related, and you agreed to provide him with the information he sought. Much later, he made me promise never to acknowledge that you were brothers. Everything he told me had to stay with me...in case the plot to assassinate the Führer failed. I'm sorry I had to lie to Anne-Marie by inventing the blackmail story. I was unable to think of any other reason I could give her for his frequent visits. However, I do admit there was a grain of truth...our relationship was close. I adored him as a person and admired him for his endeavours. I don't think I'll ever recover from the terrible accident that resulted in his death."

Sylvie crossed to the pew and sat alongside her mother. "Why have you kept it a secret for so long?"

"I was hurting already over the unfortunate accident that killed Franz when your father died. I loved Jean-Claude; his death was a tragedy. I not only loved him but I respected him. How could I tarnish his memory by being open about what had transpired. Like Father Milani, I thought it was time to move on. Sadly, the memories tormented me; the past still haunts me."

Eliane hung her head to hide her tears.

Her daughter placed an arm around her mother's shoulder. "I just wish you could have explained all this when we were younger. I'm sure we could have helped."

"I don't think anyone who didn't experience the occupation can understand how difficult life had become during those dark years."

Father Milani nodded in agreement. "So many good people died needlessly, and those who survived still suffer from the brutal treatment they had to endure."

Sylvie turned back to her mother. "I have just one question that still bothers me. Who is this David person you keep mentioning?"

Eliane gently held her daughter's hands. "Sylvie, you must promise here before God that you will never repeat what I am about to tell you, especially to your brother." She turned to Angelique. "And the same applies to you, my dear."

Father Milani stepped forwards. "Are you absolutely sure about this Eliane?"

"It's time, Father." Tears seeped from her eyes again, as she turned to face her daughter.

Sylvie shuddered, fearing more dreadful revelations. In her own mind, she began to regret asking the question.

"I had an aunt...you have probably heard mention of her...Aunt Thérèse. She was married to Johann Steinburg, an Austrian Jew. They became victims of Hitler's 'final solution'. Sadly, after arrest and transportation, they died in one of the Nazi concentration camps. However, they had the foresight to send their only child via

Switzerland to France, where your grandparents looked after him. When the SS billeted colonel Rausch at their house, they panicked, fearing they could no longer conceal David, especially as he would have been classed as a Jew...hiding a Jew resulted in certain death."

She wiped the tears from her cheeks. "I offered to care for him but we needed false papers for his survival...those procured by Father Milani that I mentioned earlier." She hesitated; her mouth was dry. "The new documents indicated he was my son, Sebastien."

The church fell silent.

Chapter 31

Saint Sauveur, Bellac
1972

A light breeze drifted down the lane, wafting the hemlines of the female guests' summer dresses. The christening ceremony over, Sebastien Tricot and his wife, Angelique posed for photographs with their baby daughter, Claudette. Friends and relatives crowded in the shade of the 13th century church as the main participants took centre stage in the warm sunshine.

At one point in this spontaneous capturing of photographic memories, Sylvie, alongside her mother, Eliane and her grandmother, Jeanne Dutheil held the infant, posing for a photo opportunity to record the moment when four female generations of the same family came together for the first time.

Anne-Marie watched from afar, probably the only guest outside the immediate participants who realised that not one male descendant of that family existed; even the child's father was the offspring of an Austrian Jew. She found it ironic that Eliane revelled in a grandchild whose genes had only a slender relevance to her own dynasty. On the other hand, Angelique's parents, watching the proceedings were blissfully unaware of their granddaughter's heritage.

To have received the invitation to the christening had been a surprise for Anne-Marie. Since the war, and especially since the day that Sylvie had accused her of lying, she felt ostracised by the Tricot family. For almost a year, her hurt had festered; she reflected constantly on how she had covered for her best friend throughout that traumatic period, yet now, twenty-five years later, her daughter had the affront to call her a liar. She had vowed revenge; today would be her day of reckoning.

Gradually, the guests began to peel away, heading for the *salle des fêtes*. Eliane had booked the village hall for a small celebration in honour of her new grandchild; not a lavish affair, just a token event with a buffet and drinks to mark the occasion.

"I hope you will join us, Father," she said to the priest as he bade farewell to each individual of the small congregation.

"I will be honoured, Eliane. Allow me a few moments to change into something less formal, and I'll be more than happy to toast the arrival of your beautiful granddaughter into the domain of our Lord."

Eliane swiftly joined the other guests heading for the party venue, looking forward to playing host to friends and relatives. Once again, Angelique became the centre of attention; several guests from further afield were meeting Sebastien's wife for the first time. Their marriage ten months earlier at the Mairie in Bellac had been a hastily arranged affair, forced upon them principally by her parents, despite their misgivings about the relationship.

Anne-Marie circulated amongst the guests before choosing her moment. Spotting Angelique holding her baby whilst enjoying the attention of doting grandparents, she managed to manoeuvre herself alongside the family trio.

Addressing Angelique's parents, she grasped what seemed to be a perfect opportunity to repay Sylvie for her insults. "Hello, allow me to introduce myself...Anne-Marie...a close friend of Eliane. Your daughter and I have met on a couple of occasions. You must be very proud of such a delightful granddaughter. I was wondering how you must feel having an Austrian Jew as a son-in-law."

Anne-Marie felt exhilarated by her own audacity; it was short-lived.

Angelique's mother smiled. "It was quite a surprise to learn of Sebastien's past but, being refugees ourselves, we fully understood how remarkable his flight from the Nazis must have been. You see, my husband and I originate from Catalonia; we were fortunate to escape the civil war and Franco's Fascist purges by fleeing to France. Consequently, our two families have a lot in common."

Angelique watched the colour drain from Anne-Marie's face as the woman realised her revelation had not prompted the reaction she had expected. Dismayed and somewhat embarrassed, Anne-Marie raised her glass to baby Claudette, muttered a few congratulatory words and quickly moved away. In a state of petulance, she crossed to her husband before ushering a reluctant Liam towards the exit.

Sylvie watched the couple arguing as they left the *salle des fêtes*. She approached Angelique and her family. "What was that about?"

Sebastien's wife smiled. "Anne-Marie came over to cause trouble. I'm afraid she met her match with my mother. It looks as though she's venting her frustration on her poor husband. I'll explain later."

Anne-Marie and Liam drove home in silence to Berneuil. Her anger was such that her confused mind failed to realise she had missed an alternative approach to upset the Tricot family. She was unaware that Sylvie and Angelique had kept their promise to Eliane to withhold from Sebastien details of his natural parents. Throughout his life, he would always believe Sylvie to be his twin sister.

As other guests began leaving the *salle des fêtes*, Father Milani circulated amongst those still present to thank them for their attendance and to bid them farewell. He encountered Sylvie by the door. "It's a while since I've seen your mother looking so relaxed."

"Do you think the arrival of this baby will take her mind off her weird fantasies?"

"Since that day in church when, with your mother present, we spoke openly about my brother, I've noticed remarkable changes in your mother's attitude to life in general. She no longer mentions life after death or people dying on their birthday. It's as though she has finally accepted what happened, and has now buried it somewhere in the recesses of her memory. She arrives each morning, performs her duties, occasionally chats about day-to-day issues and leaves. She is once more my housekeeper."

"Talking about burying things, Angelique and I have a question for you. We've known for some time now what happened to your brother but, neither you, nor maman explained in detail what transpired on that dreadful night."

Father Milani hesitated before looking across the room towards Eliane. "Let me say goodbye to your mother and the others and, if you can spare a few minutes, I would like to show you something."

Once again, intrigued by this fascinating priest, Sylvie nodded her head. "I'll wait here by the door."

After several handshakes and kisses on cheeks, he returned to accompany her through the exit doors. Together they walked up the lane in silence. The sun still shone, though it was later in the day, and consequently slightly cooler. On reaching his house, he took her hand and led her into his garden. There was a gap in the conifer hedge surrounding the adjacent spare land; on the far side the chicken enclosure was visible. He guided her through the opening before walking her past the mesh fencing towards the far end of the chicken run. Anticipating food scraps, the hens scurried after them on the other side of the wire mesh barrier.

On a patch between the fencing and the conifer hedge, a small brass sundial topped a carved stone pillar. Standing alongside the priest, Sylvie looked at the ornamental timepiece before turning to face him. "Is that what I think it is?"

"It was the early hours of the morning; there was a new moon. To bury my brother in the cemetery was not practicable. We brought him here. After the liberation, I did consider moving him to the cemetery but I couldn't imagine anywhere more peaceful than here, and of course, this patch of land still belongs to the church."

Sylvie felt shivers down the back of her neck.

Father Milani sighed, almost apologetically. "The plaque in the church is a visible memorial. This plot is his resting place. I visit Franz each morning. Here in the solitude of my extended garden, we pass the time of day together. I am his housekeeper."

Sylvie wiped tears from her face and gently held his hand.

THE END

To my children, Simon, Jay and Stéphanie
In memory of my parents, Mona and James

Bibliography

Desgranges, Eugène : *Martial-Maquis de la Vienne* (L'Union Poitiers)

Farmer, Sarah: *Martyred Village* (University of California Press, 1999)

Gildea, Robert: *Marianne in Chains* (Macmillan, 2002)

Hastings, Max: *Das Reich* (Pan Books, 2000)

Kedward, H.R.: *In Search of the Maquis* (Oxford Uni. Press, 1993)

Le Populaire du Centre: *Haute-Vienne, La Guerre Secrète* (2006)

Louty, Pierre: *C'était le Maquis* (La Veytizou N.P.L.-éditeur, 2007)

Parent, Marcel: *Georges Guingouin* (les éditions de la Veytizou, 2006)

Vinen, Richard: *The Unfree French* (Penguin Books, 2007)

Special thanks to:

Trisha FitzGerald-Jung for her patience in selecting and producing an appropriate book cover.

Members of La Souterraine Writers' Group for their occasional advice.

Robert & Elizabeth Blackburn, Jeannette Cassidy, Derek & Moira Lawson, Stéphanie Martin, Jayne Milne, Vivienne Morgan, Jay Norbury and Lynne Rees for their support and feedback.

Printed in September 2021
by Rotomail Italia S.p.A., Vignate (MI) - Italy